Praise for the

Merry W

Noyes possesses a unique talent f᠁   ᠁ing original romances that resonate deeply with readers. The connection between Evie and Annika feels genuine and quickly pulls readers into their world. As the story unfolds, they are treated to beautifully written scenes filled with warmth, humor, and heartfelt emotion. Wrapped in the tradition and spirit of Christmas, *Merry Weihnachten* invites readers to reflect on the true meaning of love and family. While Christmas romances are timeless, there is something truly special about this one. I can't recommend this lovely tale enough.

-Women Using Words

Merry Weihnachten is a heartwarming holiday tale featuring an irresistibly charming meet-cute that blossoms into a profoundly emotional and cozy romance. The blend of German and American Christmas traditions adds a delightful touch of cheer, balancing the story's more serious themes.

-The Lesbian Review

Loyalty

Loyalty, the latest installment in the Halcyon Division Series, is just another shining example of Noyes' storytelling prowess. Her exhilarating narrative simply solidifies her place as a master writer and queen of sapphic romantic thrillers.

-Women Using Words

Loyalty is equal parts exciting, thrilling, suspenseful, angsty, romantic, and funny–it's perfect and exceeded my expectations, and believe me, my expectations were high.

-The Lesbian Review

Leverage

It's pure Noyes storytelling, and fans won't want it to end!

-Women Using Words

Integrity

Noyes' writing is beautiful and real, I loved getting lost in the main character's head and re-read several paragraphs because they were so poignant. Noyes always writes witty, funny heartfelt dialogue and this book has all of that in bucket loads.

-*The Lesbian Review*

Noyes never fails to impress me with her talent. She is fearless in her storytelling, never hesitating to flesh it out and let the story take her where it will. ...Book one of the Halcyon Division Series is a fantastic beginning. This is heart-pumping, non-stop, page-flipping fun, and one heck of a ride! My recommendation: don't miss out!

-*Women Using Words*

Schuss

This is an absolutely charming first-love, new-adult romance between characters that I had already bonded with [in *Gold*]. Seeing how they have grown and matured in the four years is a treat and watching the two struggle with their feelings for each other just melted my heart...

-Betty H., *NetGalley*

If I Don't Ask

If I Don't Ask adds a profound depth to Sabine and Rebecca's story, and slots in perfectly with what we already knew about the characters and their motivations.

-Kaylee K., *NetGalley*

Overall, another winner by E. J. Noyes. An absolute pleasure to read. 5 stars.

-*Lez Review Books*

Go Around

In *Go Around*, E. J. Noyes has dipped her toes in the second-chance romance pool and was masterful in blending angst, enduring love and suspense in it. The chemistry and dynamics between the pair were thick and palpable but what stood out for me throughout the book was the type of love everyone wished they had; fierce and protective, grounded in loyalty, passionate yet to be able to just be when you are with the other. Noyes also made Bennet, Avery's dog, another highlight for me. He was the tension breaker and a giant darling.

-Nutmeg, *NetGalley*

Pas de deux

This story is not the traditional enemies-to-lovers romance, and I love that. Noyes really puts emphasis on how skewed memories can become as you get older, and how an experience may appear different to another person who had the exact same one. Even if you are unfamiliar with dressage, Noyes' writing is still spot-on and delivers the same compelling, fun, and intriguing story with loveable characters of both the two-legged and four-legged kind. This love letter to a sport she obviously has a passion for is so evident, and I felt honored to have her share her passion with me and every reader who picks it up. If you love horses, enemies-to-lovers, or even just Noyes' stories in general, this one will definitely be a favorite on your list.

-*The Lesbian Review*

Reaping the Benefits

The story is quite eccentric with its paranormal context but in fact is a pure romance at heart with a nice dose of humor. The book is written in third person, from the point of view of both protagonists, which is not common for Noyes, but it is executed perfectly. With all main elements done well, this makes an awesome read which I could easily recommend to all romance fans.

-Pin's Reviews, *goodreads*

It's fresh and original. It's everything you crave when you want to dig into a great romance. I highly recommend it.

-Deb M., *NetGalley*

If the Shoe Fits

… a beautiful slow-burn romance with a couple of steamy interludes that will leave you hungry for another sequel with these delightful women. I adore the way this author has portrayed the realistic aspects of relationships and what makes them work because differences and flaws weren't shown as stumbling blocks.

-The Lesbian Review

Alone

E. J. Noyes is easily one of the most gifted writers pulling us into whatever world she creates making us live and feel every emotion with her characters. Definitely, loudly, vehemently recommended.

-Reviewer@Large, *NetGalley*

Alone is an absolutely stunning book. This book is not a 5-star, it is well above that. You don't see books like this one very often. Truly a treasure and one that will stay with you long after the final page.

-Tiff's Reviews, goodreads

There are only a few books out there so compelling they seem to take control of you and force you to read them as quickly as possible. You can't put them down. You just want the world to go away and leave you alone until you can finish this story. *Alone* by E. J. Noyes is that book for me. This novel is absolutely wonderful.

-Betty H., *NetGalley*

Ask Me Again

Not every story needs a sequel. *Ask, Tell* demanded it, and Noyes delivers in spectacular fashion. Sabine and Rebecca show us their fortitude and their strength in their love for each other…Thank you, Noyes, for giving us a great story, a great series, and amazing women that teach us the best things in life are worth fighting for.

-The Lesbian Review

Gold

This book is exactly the way I wish romance authors would get back to writing romance. This is what I want to read. If you are a Noyes fan, get this book. If you are a romance fan, get this book. I didn't even talk about the skiing... if you are a skiing fan, get this book.

-Lex Kent's Reviews, *goodreads*

Turbulence

The entire story just flowed from the first page! E. J. Noyes did a superb job of bringing out Isabelle's and Audrey's personalities, faults, erratic emotions, and the burning passion they shared. The chemistry between both women was so palpable! I felt as though the writer drizzled every word she wrote with love, combustible desire, and intense longing.

-*The Lesbian Review*

Ask, Tell

This is a book with everything I love about top-quality lesbian fiction: a fantastic romance between two wonderful women I can relate to, a location that really made me think again about something I thought I knew well, and brilliant pacing and scene-setting. I cannot recommend this novel highly enough.

-*Rainbow Book Reviews*

Noyes totally blew my mind from the first sentence. I went in timidly, and I came away awaiting her next release with bated breath. I really love how Noyes is able to get below the surface of the DADT legislation. She really captures the longing, the heartbreak, and especially the isolation that LGBTQ soldiers had to endure because the alternative was being deemed unfit to serve by their own government. I applaud Noyes for getting to the heart of the matter and giving a very important representation of what living and serving under this legislation truly meant for LGBTQ men and women of service.

-*The Lesbian Review*

MAKE OR BREAK

E. J. NOYES

Other Bella Books by E. J. Noyes

Ask, Tell
Turbulence
Gold
Ask Me Again
Alone
If the Shoe Fits
Reaping the Benefits
Pas de deux
Go Around
If I Don't Ask
Schuss
Integrity
Leverage
Loyalty
Merry Weihnachten

MAKE OR BREAK

E. J. NOYES

BELLA
BOOKS

Bella Books, Inc.
P.O. Box 10543
Tallahassee, FL 32302

First Edition - 2025

Editor: Cath Walker
Cover Designer: Kayla Mancuso

ISBN: 978-1-64247-683-5

PUBLISHER'S NOTE

About the Author

E. J. Noyes is an Australian transplanted to New Zealand, which may be the awesomest thing to happen to her. She lives in the South Island with her wife and the world's best and neediest cat, and is enjoying the change of temperature from her hot, humid homeland.

An avid but mediocre gamer, E. J. lives for skiing (which she is also mediocre at), enjoys arguing with her hair, pretending to be good at things, and working the fact she's a best-selling and award-winning author into casual conversation.

Acknowledgments

I feel like it wouldn't be an E. J. Noyes novel if I didn't write about something I have very little knowledge about, but thankfully I had a bunch of knowledgeable people helping me with the ins and outs of making a television show. I've still taken a few creative liberties with Steph and Harper's workplace, but that's the joy of fiction, isn't it? Mea culpa.

Anna, thank you for helping my characters sound like Angelenos! Your navigational and directional insights and lil LA tidbits were immensely helpful.

Thanks to Danielle Jones, who shared the inner workings of a makeup artist's work life to help me make Harper sound like she knows what she's doing, even when her author doesn't…

Thank you, my lil television show production experts crew Heather Mazur and Susan Duerden, who made sure my industry lingo was the proper lingo.

Thank you to Shane Nagle for answering my blathering questions about what goes on behind the scenes with production. I'm now mentally using "Martini Shot" late in my workday. Unfortunately only mentally.

I'm eternally grateful to Regina Taufen for helping me make my fictional life on set feel authentic, and for being so fun and kind with your knowledge. I hope you get to do a cop show!

Abby, thanks for gathering industry pros for me and for doing it so quickly when I procrastinated so much. 10/10 friending.

Jade, welcome to the alpha-reading team, and thank you for your thoughtful, insightful feedback. I really do wonder if, now that you've seen how the sausage is made, you don't want to eat any more sausages. That sounds a little wrong for a sapphic book, but it really is the right analogy.

Kate, my pal in all things fun. Twice a year you dutifully read my terrible first drafts in record time, and twice a year I feel so thankful for you. Full marathon together next? Lawl, please, no.

Thank you to all the legends at Bella Books. Teamwork makes the dream work, and I'm so glad you're on my team.

Cath – after sixteen books together, for once I taught you something during our editing process, even if it's only the wonders of Mazzy Star. Personally, I think that's far more interesting than nouns and verbs and split infinitives.

Pheebs, you still haven't read any of the acknowledgements I've written in my published novels so I'm going to confess something here because you'll never see it, and I actually feel a little bit guilty. When you go away, I just toss the soft plastics in the bin instead of making the trip to the recycling station. I know, I'm a terrible recycler. But, baby, I'm *your* terrible recycler.

CHAPTER ONE

Steph

Laura settled carefully on top of me, holding herself up on her forearm. The fingers of her free hand worked at the buttons of my shirt, deftly undoing them one-handed. "I missed you today."

I'd already pulled her tee off before we'd tumbled onto the bed, and her bra-encased breasts hovered above me. I ignored them to look into her eyes. Grinning lazily, I said, "It's not like you couldn't have found me to say hi."

"That's true," she mused. Laura planted a quick kiss on each of my cheeks before finding my mouth for a slightly longer kiss before she pulled away again. Her eyebrows scrunched together, her nose wrinkled. She pouted. "But Halloran's been riding my ass."

"The only person who gets to do anything to your ass is me," I said, a hint of seriousness in the teasing tone.

Laura smirked, and after kissing the tip of my nose, declared, "You know it, baby." She lowered her weight fully onto me and we rolled and writhed, kissing and touching in perfect synchronicity. I shucked out of my shirt, and after maneuvering us so she was on top again, Laura helped me out of my bra, her hands covering my breasts as we kissed. I'd just slid my hands up her back when the silken strands of her perfectly coiffed hair brushed against my cheek and nose as she kissed my neck.

Oh no. No no, please no. Anything but tha—

I tried desperately to hold it back, to stay present, but my nasal passages had grabbed the tickling sensation and were running merrily toward a sneeze. For a brief, stupid second I considered hiding the sneeze in Laura's neck so I wouldn't ruin the moment. Another touch of her hair on my face meant game over. I only *just* managed to bring my hand up to block snot from spraying all over her before I sneezed a sneeze that would have been heard in Antarctica.

"Cut!" Monty yelled, packing both amusement and exasperation into that single, short word.

Laura burst out laughing. She wriggled up, still keeping her hands on my breasts, then quickly pulled the duvet free to shield me from the crew who, over the course of creating five and a bit seasons, had probably seen all there was to see.

I grabbed the duvet with my snot-free hand. "I'm so sorry," I said. My sneeze had just cost us time, and when you already spent ten to twelve hours on set, added time was a problem.

Laura twisted to face me, artfully helping keep me covered. "I knew it was coming when you tensed," she teased, playfully waving the ends of her long, dark hair at me, threatening my nose again. Smiling when I recoiled, she said, "I almost started laughing before you sneezed."

"Oh great, so you let it be *me* who ruined the scene," I said dryly.

Laura shrugged, smiling smugly. Luckily I was immune to her charm, otherwise work would be incredibly awkward. We both sat up. The set had come to life at the 1st Assistant Director's call of, "Reset. Back to one, everybody. Touch-ups please." We waited for Wardrobe to collect our discarded clothing, so we could wait some more for Hair and Makeup to come over and fix whatever we might have smudged or mussed, and then wait for everything to be reset for the next take. I felt like shit for basically wasting everyone's time, even though it was an involuntary sneeze.

Our intimacy coordinator, Meghan, came over to check we were both good and ask if we thought anything needed be done differently, confirm the placements of hands during the scene for our levels of comfort with the nudity and to ensure no accidental nipple exposure that would upset the censors. Our network was strictly no nips allowed. Side boob, and a little side butt was fine though.

Laura and I both confirmed all was fine.

My PA, Kayla, appeared by the bed. "Steph, do you need a tissue?"

"Yes please."

She offered me the box and I took a couple, delicately wiping my nose and my hand before dropping the dirty tissues into the trash bag she held. I patted the hand Laura had put back on the duvet to keep it over my breasts while I dealt with sneeze aftermath. "I know your hair won hottest hair of the summer last year, and it really is gorgeous hair. But if we could try to keep it out of my nose, that would be *amazing*."

Laura held up her free hand, three fingers extended like Scout's honor. "I'm doing my best."

"I know you are." There was something in her expression—unusually contemplative for Laura—that made me add, "You okay?" Normally I wouldn't interrupt shooting to talk about something unrelated to the scene, even if we were technically just waiting for reset. But she looked *so* weird, and it was an intimate scene, that I was suddenly worried.

Her eyebrows bounced upward. "Huh? Oh. Yeah. Totally. This"— she gestured vaguely around the bed—"just made me think."

"About what?"

"I broke up with Chad."

"Whaaat?" I'd really thought this was the one relationship of hers that might last at least four months. "When? Why?"

Harper, our Key Makeup, had been making a beeline for us, unzipping her red fanny pack holding Laura's products. But at Laura's declaration she'd paused a few steps away. I caught Harper's eye and shrugged. Laura wasn't shy about discussing her rotating collection of boyfriends, so I was sure she wouldn't mind Harper being there. And if she did, she wouldn't be shy about asking for privacy. Laura wasn't shy about anything.

"Last night," Laura said. "And I broke up with him because he's a whiny moron who doesn't like my job. Specifically, *this* part of my job." She adopted a low dude-bro voice as she put her shirt back on. "It makes me feel weird seeing you so into it with her, babe, like…you know, that you want her more than you want me. I mean it's hot but also she's nowhere near as hot as me." She sighed and went back to her regular voice. "It's called *acting*, Chad. I explained, as I always do, how choreographed and mechanical intimate scenes are. No offense, Meghan!"

"None taken," Meghan said.

Laura carefully pulled her best-of-list hair through the neck hole of her tee. "But he just couldn't get past it. So, it had to be goodbye."

I only just held my laugh on the able-to-speak side of hysterical. "Oh my *godddd*." A snort fell out. "Did his penis shrivel and fall off because you kiss me at work?" I held out a hand for my bra—well, not *my* bra, but the black, lace-edged bra I was wearing for the scene—and mouthed my thanks to Susan from Wardrobe. "Also, I've never met this guy, but I'm pretty sure I'm hotter than him."

Laura honked out a laugh (it always amazed me that *that* laugh came out of *that* body) while Harper's was more of a chuckle. I grinned at her. As soon as she realized I was about to get dressed, Harper turned away. Nobody on set ever looked on purpose, but I kind of wished Harper would. Actually no, I wished I could show her, consensually of course, and have her show me in return.

I put the bra back on, hidden by the duvet Laura kept up as a screen. Warm fingers—thanks again, Susan—untwisted the bra straps before my shirt was returned. Now that I was suitably covered, Laura and I climbed off the bed so it could be remade. Everyone buzzed around us as the set, props, and equipment were reset for another take.

Laura blew a raspberry. "I mean, I don't know what I expected. His name is *Chad* for fuck's sake. Steph, why can't I find men who aren't jealous idiots?"

"Maybe you should think about dating other actors…" I almost choked, because hadn't that worked out so well for me.

"There's no room for another actor ego because my ego fills my house already, thankyouverymuch." She forced a dry cough. "Anyways, Mami is thrilled about this breakup because she *still* thinks I'm going to marry Esteban. She forgets I was sixteen when I dated him. We are *not* going back there."

"Shame. He's cute." Early in our friendship, we'd swapped yearbooks during a day-drinking session, bonding over braces and bad hair.

"He *was* cute," she corrected me. "Fifteen years ago. Now he resembles a sleazy used car salesman, complete with chest rug."

I laughed. "Okay, I see your point." Gently, I touched her shoulder. "Are you okay about the breakup?"

"Oh yeah, sure." Laura didn't let having her lipstick touched up divert her, and Harper pulled her hand back as Laura ranted, "I mean, yeah, I'll miss him in bed. And on the couch, the kitchen table, bathroom counter, car—"

"Yeah, yeah, we get it," I interrupted good-naturedly as I put my button-down back on.

Harper shot me a grateful look before resuming Laura's touch-up. I winked at her, and the grateful look turned to a smile that made my stomach do flip-flops.

While Laura's face was redone, I was checked by an adult to make sure I hadn't buttoned my shirt wrongly. Once I was deemed dressed, I turned to Harper, smiled, then bent my knees to bring my face down so she didn't have to reach up as much. She pulled lipstick and a brush from my fanny pack—green—for a quick reapplication, her top teeth pressed into her lower lip the way she always did while she concentrated. I made sure to keep my gaze away from her face, not wanting her to feel weird about being stared at, even though I really wanted to stare.

Harper's delicate heart-shaped face, kind, warm brown eyes under arching eyebrows, and sensual mouth with full lower lip was surrounded by rich, thick reddish-brunette hair she usually wore loose, which meant I often smelled her hair product. The soft apple scent always made me want to close my eyes, bury my nose in her hair, and inhale deeply.

When Harper was done with my lips and touching up my cheeks, Laura and I sat and waited for Monty. She nudged me gently. "Sorry. TL;DR on Chad. I'll miss the sex. Maybe the way he made coffee. But that's it."

"So, situation normal then?"

Laura laughed. "Yeah. Situation normal." She shrugged nonchalantly. "Hopefully his crap is out of my place by the time I get home tonight. Otherwise I'm dumping it on the curb." She blew out a loud breath. "Sorry to just go all out on my shit in the middle of shooting."

"It's fine. I asked."

"Do you need some time to focus? I'll tell Monty it's my fault you need a few minutes."

"Nah, I'm good, but thanks." This was my sixth season playing this role, and by now I found it easy to slip into.

Monty rushed over. He was one of my favorite regulars on *North Precinct*, and we had him on board for a three-episode arc. "That was looking good, you guys. Steph, are you okay?"

I nodded. "Yep, sorry sorry. I'm fine. It was just a sneeze."

He gave me an attagirl smile. "Great. Let's go again, don't change a thing." He glanced at Meghan, who nodded that she'd checked in with us. "And, Steph, just…maybe less sneezing this time?"

I should have won a fucking award for the self-control I exerted over my eyeballs, which were begging to do a full spin-on-all-axles roll. It was a sneeze! An involuntary sneeze! I hadn't flubbed a line or dropped a prop or missed a mark.

"Do you want us to change positions so my hair isn't on Steph's face?" Laura asked. She shot a look at me and I caught the ghost of a smirk.

Monty shook his head emphatically and answered the way everyone knew he would. "No, we've already blocked it. And Steph finished without sneezing the first take," he said diplomatically, with the quickest glance in my direction.

Yeah yeah, I got it. No sneezing. It wasn't like I'd done it on purpose. But instead of saying that, I smiled and nodded.

That earned me a double thumbs-up.

It took another ten minutes or so before everything was ready for another take, and Laura and I went back to our first marks.

Our 1st AD, Zoe, called for, "Last looks!"

Our Key Hairstylist, Chrissy, moved Laura's hair to where she wanted it—hopefully where it wouldn't attach itself to my nose—then finger-combed my short hair back into place. Susan twitched bits of Laura's and my clothing into place. Harper studied both our faces, nodding to herself. I winked when she caught my eye, eliciting a smile that came with a dimple peeking through on Harper's left cheek.

I made it through the next take without hair tickles, and Monty's relieved, "Cut" echoed through the set. We did another few takes for coverage, but even if it'd needed fifty takes, I would never complain. The relationship between Amy Spicer (me) and Valentina Lazaro (Laura) was given the same screen and sexy time as the heterosexual relationships, which was nice for a mainstream network show.

It was totally possible I'd been cast as Detective Amy Spicer to tick a diversity box—an out lesbian actor in a queer role—but I honestly didn't care. I had bills to pay, a niece and nephew to buy gifts for, and my cat, Asimov, had allergies that required a special, ridiculously expensive diet and semiregular veterinary attention.

When I was cast, they told me my soft butch look paired well with Laura's femme exterior which, in code, meant if I looked butch-butch, I probably wouldn't be on the show. "Aggressive masculinity" in a same-sex relationship on television made some viewers uncomfortable. Apparently. According to some think-tank. Some possibly homophobic think-tank. Mmph.

By the time Monty was satisfied, we were due for our meal break. And not a moment too soon. As I was putting my bra back on for the zillionth, and thankfully final, time, my stomach growled loudly.

Dave, our boom operator, laughed. "I don't need a mic to hear that."

"It's all for you, Dave. I know how much you love hearing things with your actual ears instead of through headphones."

"You're so thoughtful."

"I know."

"Except for that sneeze," he added, "which nearly blew my eardrums out."

"Sorry." I patted him on the back.

Kayla silently handed me my phone, my script, and a bottle of water.

Harper, Chrissy, and Susan were deep in discussion as I slipped past. I smiled and murmured my thanks to the group. Susan's and Chrissy's return smiles were warm, but Harper's was both warm and inviting. Her light-brown eyes crinkled at the edges with her smile. But she didn't say anything. A pity. Harper's voice gave me some serious ASMR vibes. I didn't know if it was the tone—soft and calm—or the accent—a hint of Southern—but whenever she spoke, a pleasant tingle built at the base of my spine. If I had to allocate a voice to personify sweetness, it would be Harper's—it was honey trickling from a spoon.

I rushed through the maze of sets toward the Catering tables, knowing everyone would be hungry and waiting for Laura and me to get our food first. Laura was already settled at the far end of the dining area, so I nabbed another bottle of water, a chicken and salad wrap, and a fruit salad and went to sit with her. If we were at work together, we always ate together. In the almost six years we'd been coworkers, we'd grown fond of each other and I counted her among my closest friends. Probably my only close friend if I were honest.

Being close made things at work easier, because kissing someone you didn't like or trust was pretty unfun. Of course, our friendship meant we had excellent chemistry on-screen, which led to the constant less-cool speculation about us secretly fucking.

Laura squashed the rumors by dating every hot guy she could get her hands on, and doing it very publicly. I'd squashed the rumors by being in a relationship with another actor, Jordan Leclerc. Until about six months ago, that is.

My breakup had unfortunately been very public, thanks to Jordan's drunk make-out session with the lead singer of the Grammy-winning band Squad Queens, and then her abuse of the paparazzi who filmed it. My favorite bit of irony about the whole thing was how she cheated on me with the woman I'd introduced her to after I'd been in the music video for Squad Queens's multiplatinum single, "Purr."

It was a pretty good "I want to break up" message, but I wished she'd just come to me quietly and told me it wasn't working for her. I wouldn't have been upset, honestly—even after eight months I hadn't reached the I Love You stage, and clearly neither had she. I'd spent a lot of time and money in therapy processing the breakup and had settled comfortably into some sort of acceptance and realization that there was nothing I could have done; Jordan and I just weren't compatible. The problem was I'd then spent even more time and money to realize I'd never been compatible with anyone I'd dated.

As if she'd also been thinking about my failed relationships, Laura dove right in as soon as I sat down across from her. "So, now that I'm single again, when are you going to get back out there? I think I need a break from dating. I need to pass the baton to you for a bit, please."

Frowning, I asked, "What baton?"

"The baton of being out in public with a romantic partner to stop people speculating about you and me." The words dripped with "duh, you know this."

I did know that, I just didn't know that's what we were calling it now, but whatever. I used my foot to nudge her under the table. "You mean you don't like people making assumptions about your personal life?" I gasped dramatically. "No way."

Laura pointed her salad-laden fork at me. "Regular speculation is fine. Creepy speculation that requires my attention and takes my focus away from my nice little life is fucked up."

I knew what she meant, and she was right—since my breakup I'd let all the attention fall on Laura, and that wasn't fair. We were friends, and friends shared. Even if that meant sharing public attention and scrutiny. I suppressed a sigh at the thought of having to Do Something about this bullshit. "Okay. Could you call Mia for me, please? She's always happy to pretend to fawn all over me for a free dinner or two and a couple drinks 'dates.'" Laura's cousin had been my decoy a few times during single spells, to do exactly what Laura was suggesting.

Laura nodded slowly. "I could," she mused. She glanced at something over my shoulder. "Or you could look...closer to home."

Wrinkling my nose, I tried to decipher what she meant. I couldn't, so I just asked, "What do you mean?"

She leaned in, and lowered her voice to a whisper I had to strain to hear. "This thing you have with Harper. You should see if you can turn years of flirting into years of...*fucking*." She all but mouthed the last word, it was so quiet.

Laura had barely finished speaking before my skin erupted into goose bumps. If I hadn't had years of practice mastering emotions, I would have embarrassed myself with a reaction akin to a cartoon dog panting.

Harper Bell.

Flirting with Harper Bell.

Fucking Harper Bell.

The thought was undeniably attractive. And undeniably terrifying. Because at the moment, there was no expectation, no seriousness—just flirtatious fun. And if I tried to take things further, then I risked ruining what had become an important part of my workday. And I risked ruining the relationship with one of the people who made me look good for my job.

Not ideal.

But...if I took things further and it worked out, then I'd have both work and home fun.

Nope. Nope-ity nope. The chances I'd fuck it up and lose the fun flirty work vibes and trusted work relationship were too high. I hadn't been able to be the partner Jordan wanted. I hadn't been able to be the partner any of the women I'd dated before Jordan wanted. So what made me think I'd be a good enough partner for Harper, who was ten times the woman all my exes were?

I fought down the urge to utter a disgusted-in-myself, "Ugh," and instead picked up some red cabbage that had jettisoned itself from the wrap, and popped it into my mouth.

Laura wrinkled her nose. "Is that onion?" She was smart enough to know when to drop a topic.

"No. But we're done kissing for today." She couldn't stand onion. I hated tuna with every fiber in my body. We thoughtfully abstained if there was kissing.

"Oh yeah. I swear the days are just one great big blur at the moment. I don't know if I'm old, or tired. Or both." She shook her head theatrically, like either thought was horrible. "You know, speaking of kissing, I wish I was a lesbian. It'd be so much easier if we *were* just dating."

"Yeah," I agreed, licking mayo from the corner of my mouth. "Except we'd probably kill each other in the first month."

"That's true."

"Also, I'm probably the only person on the planet who doesn't want to fuck Laura Allende. Sorry. I love you, but..." She was gorgeous, but thankfully there was not an ounce of sexual spark there for me, because that would have made our work life weird.

She batted her mascara-laden eyelashes. "I love you too, but I don't want to fuck you either."

"Also again, can you imagine dating a colleague? Like...they're there at home and then they're there at work. And let's not get into what happens when you break up." Okay, so maybe I was projecting a little after Laura had sprung the Harper Idea on me, and desperately looking for reasons to not go for it so I wouldn't screw it up.

"*If* you break up," Laura corrected me.

Thankfully I didn't have a mouthful of food, because I probably would have choked on it. "You, saying *if* not *when* for a breakup? You're killing me."

"Hey, just because I can't stay in a relationship doesn't mean I don't believe in love. I'm an idealist. Do I need to list people in our industry who work together and are married or dating?"

I'd just put a forkful of fruit salad into my mouth and couldn't answer, which seemed to give Laura permission to start giving her examples.

"Anna Paquin and Stephen Moyer, Greta Gerwig and Noah Baumbach, Samira Wiley and Lauren Morelli." She took a deep breath and opened her mouth to continue listing.

I chewed and swallowed just so I could cut her off. "I get it, Entertainment Industry Trivia Machine."

She spread her hands in an "I rest my case" gesture. "All I'm saying is that people who are married or dating are working together all over the world, right now. It's a thing. Why is our job any different?"

"I know it's a thing, but this point is moot. I'm not even sure how we got to this point. Listen, I'm going to take a nap and meditate before I'm due back on set." We still had a couple scenes to shoot together and it would take the rest of the workday. A solid nap would give me the energy I needed to power through. And…I freely admit that I was running the hell away from this conversation.

"I hate you and your napping ability."

"You too could master the art of the micro-nap if you really wanted to." I stood. "See you in a bit."

Laura, mouth full, nodded.

I dumped my dirty plate and fruit salad bowl in the dish bin and beelined for the sweet-stuff section. The line had dwindled, and I slipped in beside Harper who was adding a brownie to her plate.

I plucked one from the pile and put it in a napkin to eat on my way back to my trailer. Leaning down to speak close to Harper's ear, I murmured, "Great minds…"

She startled, then immediately apologized. "Sorry. In my own little world there." Her nose wrinkled adorably. "What was that you said?"

"I said *great minds*." Pointing at her brownie, I elaborated, "Great minds who both want a brownie."

She laughed. "Oh. Yes, ma'am." I'd only ever heard her direct a *yes, ma'am* or *no, ma'am* at me, no one else, and I fucking loved it. There was never a hint of subservience in it; it was more like a light, almost teasing response. Harper stared longingly at the pile of desserts. "Sometimes sugar is the only thing that gets me through the afternoon."

"Not the caffeine in those twenty-four ounce iced coffees you devour most afternoons?" As soon as I'd said it, I wished I hadn't. I spent a lot of time sitting around waiting, and my phone was only so good at holding my attention. I did a lot of people-watching, and noticing her beverage choice wasn't as weird as it sounded. It was amazing how good I was at rationalizing things, like an attraction I'd been ignoring for years.

Harper's eyebrows shot up, which made me think she'd noticed my noticing. "It's decaf. No caffeine after two p.m. or I don't sleep." Her eyebrows settled back down over her eyes, which had creased with her smile. "And I *really* like sleep."

I grinned. "Me too. And that's exactly where I'm headed now. See you soon."

Harper nodded seriously. "Nap well."

I saluted and skulked off before someone nabbed me and stole precious minutes from my nap. I was exhausted and still had to make it through the rest of today and then another three days of work before I had two days off over the weekend.

Aside from a few smiles or "heys" as I slunk away, nobody bothered me. A gift from the universe. I let myself into my trailer, took off my shoes, and fell back onto the twin bed. After checking my messages and emails—nothing important—I set an alarm and closed my eyes. As I drifted to sleep, all I could think of was how nice it would be if I could hold the baton with someone I liked, someone I wanted to spend time with, someone I wanted to kiss, someone I wanted to sleep with.

Laura was right.

I wanted that someone to be Harper.

CHAPTER TWO

Harper

I dropped my keys in the bowl on the table in the narrow entryway of my apartment. "Per? You home?" If my roommate left his keys in the key bowl like a normal person, I wouldn't have to call out every time I got home. I hung my vintage military-style jacket, dropped my handbag on the kitchen table and my distressed-leather messenger bag on a kitchen chair, and began my hunt.

I already knew he wasn't in the living room or kitchen. On my way through the house I added bathroom to the list. But his bedroom door was closed. I hastily backed away. Per only closed his door when he was sleeping, which was very unlikely now, or when his boyfriend, Ben, was around.

Though it was Per's night to cook, there was no evidence of dinner having been made or even planned, so I grabbed a packet of spicy dill pickle chips to cover me until a meal arrived. After settling myself on the couch, I opened up my language app and moved to my next Polish lesson. I'd been at it for ten minutes, and finished the chips, when I heard a door open.

A quick, "Hey, Harpies!" preceded two pairs of footsteps going into the bathroom. I raised a hand in greeting and made sure to not turn around. I'd finished another ten minutes of lessons before Per and Ben emerged pink-skinned, damp-haired, and thankfully dressed. I turned my head as Per leaned over the back of the couch and kissed my temple before greeting me with a warm, "Hello, gorgeous."

"Heya."

He rested his arms on the back of the couch, pointing to my phone. "How do you say 'I need to get laid' in Polish?"

Ben snickered, patting my shoulder reassuringly. "Give her a break, Per."

I shot my roommate as withering a stare as I could manage. "I don't think it's in these language courses." Frowning, I thought back over my previous course. "But in Italian, it's probably something like…Ho bisogno di fare…sesso?"

Per burst into laughter. "*Ho?*" he exclaimed around his mirth. "Oh my god, I *know* you just made that up. You wanna traipse through Europe, huh, just living your best ho life?"

I raised a middle finger to him.

He sniffed. "Fine. Whatever. You do you, babe. It still sounded hot. How many languages do you plan on learning exactly?"

"No plans. I'll stop when I'm bored or run out of languages. And it's not like I'm learning each one to fluency, just to basic touristy conversational stuff for when I go to Europe." When. Not if. I was determined to spend at least a month, preferably two, during a hiatus, traveling. A hiatus, as yet undetermined which one in which year. When I'd started saving for a house, I'd started a travel fund, and if I was careful and went cheaply, my Europe trip dream was totally doable. "And learning languages is good brain food."

"Mhmm." Per turned to Ben. "Yeah, so she definitely needs to learn to say 'I need to get laid, can you help me?' in every European language if she's using phrases like 'brain food.'"

Ben nodded decisively. "Agreed."

"Are y'all trying to set me up with hypothetical European women?"

"We're trying to set you up with *any* women," Per said emphatically.

Frowning, I muttered, "I don't know if I should be offended or thankful." Sure, my five-year plan included buying a house and being in a steady relationship, but being thrown at someone *just because* wasn't my idea of a good time.

"You can be both," my roommate assured me. "Oh! I booked that men's health magazine photoshoot. I might need to swap some of our dinner roster around."

"If it fits with my schedule, sure. Otherwise it's Pop-Tarts for dinner."

He raised his tee and patted his enviable eight-pack. "No thanks."

Ben piped up with, "Speak for yourself." Though he took care of himself, he wasn't *quite* at the level of Per's vanity, which made Per's vanity easier to tolerate.

I worked with actors. I got it. And it was probably the only reason I didn't devolve into eating as much as I wanted whenever I wanted and never exercising. I already felt plain next to these professionally attractive people and loved myself too much to poke more holes in my self-esteem. I liked the way I looked. I just didn't like the way my job forced me to think about it.

"Thank you, Ben," I said graciously. "So Per booked a magazine job. You sell any multimillion-dollar celebrity mansions today?" Ironically, real estate was how he and Per had met—he was the real estate agent who'd shown us this apartment. I'd joked to Per that his flirting game was pretty bad if we didn't even get a rental discount. But he got Ben's number and almost four years later they were blissfully happy, yet showing no sign of cohabitation.

The fact Ben and Per weren't cohabiting left me to cohabit with Per, not that I really minded cohabiting with him. It worked out for both of us—him because his work was sporadic and he didn't want to stress about being solely responsible for rent, and me because I was saving for a house and a roommate made that easier. We'd lived together for six years now, after meeting at a makeup workshop I'd run for models and actors wanting to maximize their look for auditions. Per liked anything that made him look better. In the almost-seven years I'd known him, Per had had a number of girlfriends and boyfriends, but Ben was the only one who'd stuck.

We didn't talk about how many girlfriends I've had since I'd known Per.

Ben puffed up his chest. "I sold exactly one multimillion-dollar mansion today, no celebrity included."

Per gave him a tight squeeze. "Get yourself that sweet, sweet commission, baby."

"I have to," Ben laughed. "My boyfriend has really expensive taste."

Per faked a pout. "Don't you think I'm worth it?"

Ben, master of domestic harmony, just smiled.

"Thought so." Per checked his watch. "Okay, dinner. Shit, I'm late. Sorry." He waved dismissively. "Whatever, we can eat on the couch."

Tuesday nights were *North Precinct/Make the Cut* nights, and Per and Ben were devoted fans of both shows. I enjoyed watching, but it also felt a little like work to me, and I found it hard to switch from the production I'd just finished that day to watching the production from months ago.

I tried hard to not focus on my work—did that wound look good, should I have given Jared a little more eyeliner, was that blood trickle perhaps a little too artistic instead of realistic—and just enjoy the entertainment value of the show. And for me, that entertainment value rested on one person's shoulders, and those capable shoulders belonged to Stephanie D'Arripe.

She really did have capable shoulders, broad and muscular without being bulky. She also had capable arms…legs…abs. Could a face be capable? Because if it could, Steph's was. And I'd know, because it was my job to pay very close attention to that face. It was also my hobby.

There were worse hobbies to have than thinking about Steph's fine, angular jaw and chin, her full, almost pouty mouth, the bright blue of her eyes under expressive eyebrows, the sharpness of her cheekbones, her thick blond hair with waves tamed into a short cut that leaned more masculine but wasn't *manly*.

Everything about her features was balanced, proportionate, like she'd been created by a sculptor. And she had a personality to match her face. Fun, kind, attentive, generous. I'd spent the past six years harboring an attraction to her and enjoying the ease of our professional relationship, while simultaneously wishing I also had a personal relationship with her.

While the boys prepared dinner, I took a shower and washed my hair. I was just finishing up my post-shower skincare when Per's obnoxiously loud, "Dinner and a show!" permeated the house. I had no idea how we'd never had any neighbor complaints, but apparently the soundproofing was as good as Ben had promised when he'd shown us this place.

I quickly pulled on sweatpants that should really be tossed out and an old hoodie, and rushed into the living room with five minutes to spare before *North Precinct* started. Between them, Per and Ben carried a bottle of white wine which was mostly for Ben and me, wineglasses, and dinner for all of us—grilled tilapia with steamed veggies in a buttery glaze and the seasoned rice for which I'd been trying to get the recipe for as long as I'd known Per. He had twice the amount of fish as me and Ben, a heaping mound of plain steamed veggies, and a noticeably smaller portion of rice. God I was glad I worked off camera.

Per eyed my "relaxing comfortably at home with friends" outfit, and sighed dramatically. Apparently, he thought the fact I wasn't totally done up while in my home was the reason I didn't have a girlfriend. I stared back, popped the hood up over my head to spite him, then looked away before I was the recipient of an eye roll. Per and Ben claimed the couch, and though it was large enough, I sat with my back against Per's shins and my plate on the coffee table.

"Ladies and gentlemen and everything in between," Per intoned as he turned on the television. "It's time."

I knew this episode began with Spicer and her partner, Johnson, responding to a crime scene. I forked up some rice to stop myself from reacting audibly when it was time for Steph to appear. If I was recalling the episode correctly, Amy had been called in off-duty and Steph looked smoking-hot in a torso-hugging tank top and running tights that showcased the sublime length of her legs. Yes. I was recalling it correctly, and was grateful I was facing away from the guys so they couldn't see my expression or my intense focus on her.

On-screen, Steph changed from Amy's gym gear into a borrowed crime-scene tech jumpsuit, stripping down to a running bra and boyleg underwear to get into the garment. They'd only shown her pulling up the jumpsuit over her underwear, but the flash of her abs and the swell of her small, tight breasts left absolutely nothing to my already overactive imagination. I still didn't know why the character didn't just put the jumpsuit on over the running tights and tank top, though if I had to guess—it was titillation and nothing more.

We watched in silence until the first ad break, except for Per's mutterings to himself which were thankfully, and unusually for him in any other circumstance, infrequent and quiet. Not that I didn't love Per and all his extravagance, but sometimes I ached for some quiet in my house, and these hours of television provided a little.

He muted the volume on an ad with a guy trying to sell us erectile dysfunction medication. Definitely only targeting two of three, though judging by the bedroom antics that occasionally woke me up, I'd say zero for three. "I'm sorry, babe," Per said earnestly, "but Laura Allende is so fucking hot. *And* she's straight."

I turned back to look at him, raising an eyebrow. Straight, and now single, but that was beside the point and not a point anyone would hear from me.

Ben said what my eyebrow raise was conveying. "And *you're* taken," he pointed out dryly.

Per patted his boyfriend's thigh. "I know, I know. I'm just indulging in a little fantasy, which never hurt anybody. I love *you*," he said seriously.

Ben smiled. "I know you do. And objectively, I agree that she's fucking hot. But"—he raised a forefinger—"I think I have to give Stephanie D'Arripe the edge."

Me too, friend. I drank a large mouthful of wine to keep my mouth closed on my thought.

"Meh. I think she's too tall for me." Per nudged me in the back. "How tall is she, Harpies?"

The perfect height for a solid, comforting hug. The perfect height for me to pull her face down a little for a kiss. The perfect height for her to pick me up, put me on a table or countertop, and— "About three inches taller than me."

"Right. So five-nine-ish. Too tall for me." Per leaned over to kiss five-foot-eight Ben.

I stared incredulously. "You're six-two and think *that's* too tall?"

Per shrugged. "I like what I like."

Ben flashed him a cheesy grin. "Thankfully that's me. And Laura Allende…" He grabbed his phone and held it up. "But what about Stephanie's episode watch-alongs on social media. Look at this selfie, she's gorgeous, and so is her cat. And she's hilarious, listen." He read, "'Fun ep fact. This is the first time we see that photo in Amy and Val's apartment. I'm convinced Laura made them take it on my worst hair day of the year to make herself look better. Hashtag Valmy.'"

I studied the post Ben was shoving in our faces—a picture of Steph on her couch with her cat, Asimov, a slightly fluffy, not-slightly tubby tuxedo curled up against her chest. I loved Steph's watch-alongs too, but I deliberately didn't look at them during the episode because I'd absolutely give myself away with a flurry of reactions to her posts. I left looking at the posts and reading her reactions to fans for when I was lying in bed that night.

Ben continued, "Also, sorry, but not only does she look hot but she sounds hot. And I say all of this as a man who has never considered himself anything other than one hundred percent gay."

He was right again about Steph. Her voice held a huskiness so sexy that it frequently permeated my dreams. When Amy Spicer was angry, the huskiness turned to roughness, and when she was soft with victims and kids her voice softened too. And when Steph talked to me, I got the softness, and something else that I could never pinpoint, but that I liked to believe was pleasure.

Per squeezed his boyfriend's arm. "Okay, sweetheart. We get it. Is there something you want to tell me?"

"No! But I can appreciate gorgeous women for being gorgeous," Ben insisted. "I just don't want to kiss them or anything like that." Then Ben did the thing that he or Per always did, which for some reason sent a shiver of annoyance down my back. He asked, "Come on, Harper, who's the hottest out of Stephanie D'Arripe and Laura Allende? In their pure, unfiltered, fresh-out-of-bed form, I mean."

I didn't know if the annoyance was because I wasn't sure if they were fishing for information, which I had to admit that they didn't really do, or if it was that it felt like they were trying to make me incriminate myself by sharing that I thought a certain someone was hot. So I answered the way I always did. "They're both attractive. So is everyone on *Precinct*. And on *Make the Cut*."

If I admitted that I thought Steph D'Arripe was one of the hottest women I'd ever seen, let alone worked with, there would be no end to the teasing. I had no idea how someone could look so damned hot first thing in the morning, but she did.

"You're no fun," Per grumbled.

Laughing, I disagreed, "I'm all kinds of fun."

They both shot me looks that made it clear they thought my fun quotient could be dialed up a notch. I was beyond grateful that neither of them ever crossed the line into gross territory and asked me if I'd ever seen Steph's or Laura's tits, or Jared's ass while shooting intimate scenes. For the record, I hadn't. I would never look uninvited, especially not when I harbored a secret attraction to Steph.

Thankfully the ad break was over and the boys ceased their chatter in favor of watching. Until the next break, when Per started up on another one of his favorite topics of conversation surrounding my workplace. Socializing with the people I worked with. "I still don't know why you don't just invite them around for drinks or something."

For two guys who lived in a city full of celebrities, it astounded me that they were so interested in the ones on my show. When I'd mentioned this to them during a Tuesday viewing session, Ben had gaped, then said matter-of-factly, "Yeah, but they're on a show we watch and love."

I held back a sigh. "I don't invite them around because we're colleagues. Not friends." At Per's expected pout, I said, "Maybe you should audition for *Precinct*, and then you can meet Laura. I think you'd make a great Suspect Number Two or Creepy Peeping Tom Guy."

Ben snorted. "He's too pretty to be a creepy peeping tom."

Ben was right. There was a reason Per's primary source of income was from modeling, and acting was the side gig he was trying to break into.

"I can look creepy," Per muttered grumpily. "I grow a great beard, you know."

I shook my head. "Beard doesn't equal instant creep." After refilling Ben's and my wineglasses, I gathered the plates and took them into the kitchen.

When I came back, Per had twisted around, his forearms hanging over the back of the couch as he adopted his best puppy-dog expression. "I don't see what the big deal is about introducing us. You're not shy."

"It's not about being shy or not shy." I held in my exasperation, not wanting to have an argument or ruin my mood for the rest of the episode. "It's about being weird and making my work relationships strained. What do y'all want me to say? 'My roommate and his boyfriend are huge fans and want to meet you'? That's like…the height of poor form."

"No," he said petulantly. "But you could still ask them around for drinks or something."

"Again, we aren't friends." Friendly, sure, in the way colleagues who got along were, but not friends. "And after working a ten- or twelve-hour day, I'm quite sure the last thing anyone feels like doing is spending time with people from work."

Of course, I was just imagining what the others might think, because I would spend any amount of time with Steph after work.

"Fine," he muttered.

Ben redirected. "Okay, so you won't dish on Stephanie D'Arripe or Laura Allende, but what about Jared Kimber? Liz Spencer?" His eyebrows bounced up as he added names to his hopeful list. He was going to run into actual show time if I didn't cut him off.

"There's nothing to dish," I insisted.

"I don't believe you. One day you'll tell us something fun."

Again, I insisted, "There's nothing fun to tell."

"Come on, Harper," Per whined. "Can't you find something? Or just make it up. Like are they secretly mean? Do they eat nothing but garbage?"

"I'm not going to make up some silly thing so you feel better about your midnight cheese binges."

Ben snorted out a laugh.

Per looked mortally wounded. "All I'm saying is that it would be nice to know big stars are human and flawed. That they're just like the rest of us little stars or nonstars."

If Steph had flaws—physical or emotional—I didn't know of them. "None of the people I work with are terrible people or secretly or not-so-secretly mean." Some were a little diva-ish, but nowhere near problematic levels, which I'd absolutely encountered on set for other shows and movies I'd worked on. "And why would eating…'garbage,' did you say, make them fun?"

"Not *fun*. Fuck. I don't know. You know what I mean."

"Actually, I really don't."

"I don't want gross gossipy shit," he whined. "I just want to know they're as human as I am."

Ben snorted. "I love you, but you're not human, Per. You're a peacock. It's part of your job."

"A peacock with a cheese addiction," Per reminded him. He leaned over and planted a smacking kiss on Ben's mouth. "I'm human."

Human. What had Steph said to me at our meal break today? Something about a brownie. *Great minds.* I smiled when I remembered. She'd been teasing, yet soft, especially when she'd realized I'd been so caught up in getting food that I hadn't known she was there.

Per narrowed his eyes. "What are you smirking about?"

I scrambled for an answer. "You. And your weird obsession with the people I work with."

"It's not an *obsession*," he insisted. He was right. Per's adoration was nowhere near the "you're going on a security watchlist" level. He was just a fan, and because of my proximity to the thing he was a fan of, it felt to me a little over the top sometimes.

Ben came to my rescue, kind of. "Ad break is over."

I managed to stay reasonably focused for the rest of the episode, and thankfully the boys had gotten their fanboying out of their systems and didn't hassle me further about work. After I'd seen my name in the credits, which was part superstition, part pride, I stood up and stretched. Per looked up. "Not staying for *Make the Cut?*"

I shook my head. "I have had a huge day and a huge rest of the week awaits me. Y'all can catch me up on what I missed before next week."

Ben nodded, and as if the mere hint of me going to bed had swayed him, smothered a yawn. "Night, Harper. Sweet dreams."

I gave them each a hug good night, and left them to watch *Make the Cut*, where they'd fawn over those actors the way they did for *North Precinct*. I rushed through my nightly prebed routine, then dove under the covers.

God I loved being in bed.

But I really, *really* hated being in bed alone.

CHAPTER THREE

Steph

Jared glanced off to his left, his expression thoughtful. "She was damned lucky. Could have been a homicide." He turned his gaze back to me, then paused for a beat before growling, "Or something worse."

"Yeah, well. It *wasn't* a homicide or something worse," I said, injecting a little gruffness into my voice to convey the emotion Amy—and I for that matter—felt about kids being hurt. My character had once put a pedophile in hospital, and had proudly proclaimed the broken hand and suspension were worth it.

Jared crossed his arms over his chest, widening his stance. "How'd the little girl get away?"

I shook my head, letting out a laugh of disbelief before delivering my line. "Her mother saw some social media video about a help signal for kids in danger and taught her children how to use it."

He raised his eyebrows. "And the woman who called it in *really* recognized the symbol for what it was and not just a kid being a kid?" Skepticism dripped from the question.

Shrugging, I said, "Apparently so. Her husband grabbed the guy and held him until patrol got here."

Jared paused long enough that I knew he'd gone blank, so I remained still and waited for him to remember his line. He didn't.

After a few more seconds, Zoe called, "Still rolling!"

Jared looked over my shoulder and nodded. "Line, please."

From behind me, Jeannie calmly said, "Well, I never thought I'd thank social media trends, but here we are."

Jared schooled his face, and repeated the prompted line, dryly deadpan with a hint of an eyebrow lift.

I let the edges of my mouth quirk up. "I'll take anything, even social media. And we're sure it's our suspect?"

"Description matches. MO matches."

"Okay then. Let's have a chat with him." I slapped my notebook closed, turned around and walked off. My costar followed.

"Cut," Monty called. "Jared, do you need a moment?"

"No, I'm good." He flashed me an apologetic smile.

I winked to assure him it was all good. I'd been in the flubbed or forgotten-lines glass house and there was no way I'd throw stones.

Monty popped up over the monitors. "Great. And, Steph?"

"Yeah?"

"We had some Steph's Eyebrows that take."

Laughter broke out around the set. Both Amy and I had expressive eyebrows, me far more than my character, and sometimes I had to be reminded to rein them in.

"Gotcha. Thanks."

Zoe said, "Okay, let's reset. We'll go again."

We did another take, and another, and then another until Monty was finally happy. I had a break while a set was prepared. Then it was time to shoot a scene with Amy and Val interacting at a crime scene—a.k.a. "Alleyway C," one of the many sets that had been built on the lot—before we broke for a meal. I loved "Amy and Val interacting at work" scenes. Trying to balance their love with the professionalism of a crime investigation and also Amy's unconscious "I'm a detective so I'm better than this beat cop" attitude was always fun. And Laura somehow managed to balance Val's professionalism with an underlying "I want to jump Amy's bones" vibe.

Laura showed no ill effects of her breakup, though I'd never actually seen her get truly upset about any of her relationships ending. Unlike when Jordan had cheated on me and I'd been basically nonfunctional outside of actually shooting scenes. The closest Laura had come to despair was when an ex had dumped her instead of her usual dumping of the guy, and she'd expressed a modicum of disbelief that he could do that. But then she'd brushed it off like shaking out an umbrella. So I felt no need to check in with her mental state when we sat down for our meal break.

"What are you doing this weekend?" she asked as she stabbed her fork into a mound of salad.

"Sleeping in. Laundry and housework. A trail run, even if I have to go out in the dark and fend off coyotes and mountain lions." My body did not like stillness.

"Love that for you."

I asked, "How about you?" even though I was sure of the answer.

"Abso-fucking-lutely nothing. Except maybe reading a book." She stretched luxuriously. "I don't even know if I'll get out of bed, except to use the bathroom and gather food and then vodka in the afternoon. You should run by my place for a drink."

It was a genuine invitation, but we both knew I wouldn't accept. It was an unspoken agreement between us that during production season we didn't socialize outside of work unless absolutely unavoidable. We already saw each other five long days a week, and though we were good friends, neither of us wanted to make the friendship stale. Hiatus was a different ballgame and we often caught up for hikes, walks, drinks, and meals. So I smiled, and gently brushed her offer aside with a, "I'll see how things go."

"Good. Also, housework on your days off? You need a cleaner, friend."

I'd thought about it. Mostly when I was doing housework. But given how little I was actually awake and doing things at home, it didn't take long to do my weekly cleaning. "I like housework," I said. "So does Asimov, because I retrieve all his toys from under the couch and fridge every time I clean the house."

Laura's subdued eye roll conveyed just how much she thought I should get a life.

I became aware of the vibe of the room changing and looked up from my plate of pesto chicken with quinoa and roast veggies. Thankfully I was chewing so I didn't verbalize my internal groan. Gabby, the show's lead publicist and someone we only saw when she wanted something, was here. And she was beelining for Laura and me. This couldn't be good.

Gabby pulled the chair next to me a polite distance away and sat down, setting her iPad on the table. "Sorry to interrupt your meal, ladies."

"No problem," I said. She wasn't the first, and she wouldn't be the last to do so. Laura and I kept eating, waiting for her to spill what she wanted from us.

It was a messy spill. "Liz Spencer fractured her foot over the weekend which means she's had to pull out of the tennis match at the end of the month." As soon as Gabby said "fractured her foot," I knew exactly what she wanted.

The network had organized a charity doubles tennis match between *North Precinct* and *Make the Cut*, with proceeds going to Purple Refuge, a charity helping women and children who'd been displaced due to domestic violence. Gabby's smile was so bright, so unwavering, so "please *please* help me" that I almost laughed.

Gabby continued, "Participation is completely voluntary of course, and no remuneration is offered for your time, except for the publicity which you know is priceless. We need to do some spin and fast because people are expecting Jared and Liz, but I know you two are a bigger drawcard." Yeah, we were and we'd been asked, but Jared and Liz had jumped in first.

I finished chewing and set down my fork. "Can I just get this straight. Are we…doing you a favor, Gabby?" I asked slyly.

She flashed me a cheeky "you almost got me" grin, then wagged a finger. "Not me personally, no, but you're doing the network a favor."

Laura and I exchanged a look, and I knew from her expression that she was in. There were worse things than helping out the network in a tight spot. "Sure," I said. "We'll do it."

Gabby's entire body deflated. "Thank you." She straightened like she hadn't just shown her relief, because if she was relieved, then that meant we'd helped her and now she owed us a favor. "A few logistical things. Of course, any practice you can get in before the game would be a bonus. We want to give the people donating to the charity a good show. Basically, people will buy tickets to attend in person and you do a meet and greet, autographs and photographs. Others will pay to watch the live stream. There will also be a donations page up and running. Anyone attending that aren't friends and family will be thoroughly vetted, of course. Now you've confirmed you're in, I'll send the details to your managers and publicists, and check in on how comfortable you are with fan interactions at the game, so you'll each have a tailored level of comfort."

I was fine with fan interactions. Photos, autographs, chats, hugs for those who didn't seem like they'd grab my ass. And if anyone got inappropriate, I was good at getting myself out of the situation—I'd perfected my "that's not cool" demeanor without coming off as nasty, which would get me nowhere except plastered on the Internet as a "bitch who didn't appreciate her fans." That had happened before when someone had gotten aggressive with me, and the resulting backlash had made me press every people-pleasing button I had. It was a fine line. But if the fans didn't behave, there would be security there.

I hadn't been part of the event until now, which meant I hadn't been privy to the nitty-gritty details, like when the match was being held. There were only two obvious days of the week when we'd all be available around shooting, and I was sure I wasn't going to like either of them. "What day is the match?" I asked.

Gabby grimaced. Mhmm, yup, here it comes. "The last Saturday of the month."

So…three and a bit weeks' time. Laura's audible groan would have been funny if I hadn't felt like uttering the same sound. Saturday was the day I used to wind down from a week of long days, because we had table reads on Sunday afternoons, which cut into my two days off.

Gabby hastened to do damage control. "Yes, I know. And I'm sorry. But it was the only logical and available time for everyone, and it's been set for a while now and can't be changed because people are expecting it that day. Of course the donation of your time for a worthy cause is incredibly appreciated. And again, I'd like to stress—participation *is* voluntary, I *can* ask someone else."

Right, the kind of "mandatory volunteering" where you don't *have* to do it but refusing makes you look like an asshole and makes you feel bad. What kind of bitch would I look like if I didn't participate in an event that benefited women and kids who were victims of domestic violence?

Gabby leaned closer to us. "But, like I said, you two are huge drawcards, bigger than Jared and Liz."

I held back my "So why did you accept them instead of asking for us originally?" because I was worried I didn't want to know the answer (cough-cough homophobes), and simply nodded benevolently. Damned right we were huge drawcards. My name was billed above Jared's, for fuck's sake.

Laura chimed in with, "I know we are. Who are we playing against from *MTC*?"

"Jenna and Yusef."

Good. I was friendly with both due to crossovers between our shows—cops got hurt and went to the hospital a lot, and for some reason the employees of Mercy East Hospital had a lot of crime going on in their lives. The network often tried to smoosh our two shows together, even when it didn't feel logical to do so.

Then Gabby dropped a bombshell. "And Harper Bell from our makeup department is umpiring the match."

What? Actually no—what the fuck? Before I could ask the question, in a slightly less expletive-y way, Gabby rapped her knuckles lightly on the table. "Right, I'll leave you two alone. Thanks again, look out for those emails."

As I watched Gabby leave, I spotted Harper standing in line for food. I'd complimented her on her top this morning—a clingy, long-sleeved burgundy wrap. What I hadn't said was how the color complemented her features, made her seem even more beautiful. A faint flush had appeared on Harper's neck as she'd thanked me, lightly running her palms down her stomach to her hips as if smoothing down the fabric. Of course, that gesture had dragged my eyes to the places her hands touched, and I'd been lost for a few seconds.

Harper leaned over to say something to Nina, her assistant MUA, and they both laughed. Still smiling, Harper shook her head, then looked up. Looked right at me, and her expression turned from pleased to surprised.

Yep, I'd been caught staring. I decided to just own up to it, and flashed her the happiest, cheesiest grin, gratified when she smiled back before returning to her conversation. And I tried to return to mine with Laura, but my chest was buzzing from Harper's smile. I cleared my throat, flailing for something, *anything*, to say.

My brain decided on the most basic thing. "So. Tennis."

"Yeah." Laura picked the few grapes from her fruit salad and dropped them onto my plate. "Probably a good thing they didn't choose softball or something for this charity game."

I ate her grapes. "Why's that? I think more people are interested in watching softball or baseball than tennis. I don't think I've ever heard of a charity tennis thing?" My first guess when I'd heard about it was they just didn't think they'd be able to wrangle enough participants from each show to make two full teams.

Laura indicated her face with a few sweeping circles. "Can you imagine taking a hard ball to the face?"

"Oh yeah. Not ideal. Harper would fix it right up. Or they'd write in us getting punched by a perp or something." And Harper would probably be responsible for that too. The makeup to look like we'd been hit, not an actual punch. I couldn't help it, I glanced over at Harper again, and was childishly disappointed to see she was engrossed in her conversation, not looking at me.

Laura didn't say anything about my tone, which had leaned slightly toward hero-worshippy. Since my breakup, I'd been trying very hard not to notice the way I felt around Harper. But after six months of singledom,

I was starting to feel hornier than a sex addict who'd been celibate for a year. And Harper just looked so fucking good. Smelled so fucking good. Sounded so fucking good. I bit the inside of my cheek, hoping the sharp pain would reset my thoughts.

It didn't, and thankfully Laura cut into my runaway obsession by addressing the elephant in the room. "Can I just say, I'm all for worthy causes."

"I know," I agreed. Both of us were all in on worthy causes, which had funnily enough been one of the (many) reasons Jordan had given me as to why she'd cheated. *You're like the poster child for every needy person or animal, Steph. I feel like you care more about people you've never met than about me.*

"But, giving up a free day for this game blows."

"I know," I said again.

She sighed. "Good cause, good cause, good cause."

"Exactly." I tried for a glass-half-full approach. "And you might meet some cute guy there."

Laura blew a raspberry at me. "Shut the fuck up. I'm taking a break from the baton, remember?" She glanced at something I couldn't see, then back to me. "And speaking of that…Harper's umpiring this game? What the hell is that about?"

"No clue."

"Well you need to get a clue, because we're going to need all the help we can get if we don't want to embarrass ourselves." She leaned across the table, lowering her voice. "And if you have to flirt your way to our success, I'm not going to stop you…"

Once I'd brushed my teeth after our meal break, I settled into my quiet corner on set to go over my lines and read until I was needed. Laura and I were shooting a scene of Amy and Val at home directly after work. They'd talk about their day, then have a little argument over differing approaches to working a crime scene, and what had happened at the scene with the young girl earlier.

Sensing someone approach, I looked up and found Harper standing a few feet away. She patted the green fanny pack on her hip. "Can I borrow you for a minute?"

I checked the time. I used to be amazed that I could sit down at work to wait for things to be made ready, and suddenly an hour had passed. But now it was just one of those things. "Of course." She could borrow me for as many minutes as she wanted, for anything she wanted. "Sitting or standing?" I asked.

"Either way's just fine by me. Anything on your face bothering you?"

"Nope." I remained sitting and tucked the script behind my back as Harper adjusted the stand light set up by our chairs. "So I heard you're umpiring this charity tennis match," I said as she looked over my face. It was the first thing that came to my head, because the intense way she studied my features was short-circuiting my synapses.

I knew she was just doing her job, but sometimes I wished her job didn't involve her being so close to me. Obviously it wasn't that I didn't *want* her close to me, but having her in such intimate proximity when I was attracted to her was borderline torturous. And since Laura had mentioned me asking Harper out, my synapses were short-circuiting even more.

"Absolutely! Sports are basically a religion in my neck of the woods." She grinned. "My original neck of the woods that is."

"Isn't it a like a religion everywhere?" I teased. Except in my life. Sports were fine, I watched games, but usually accidentally. Despite appearances, I was not a jock.

"We take it extra serious." She began touching up my face. "And in my family?" Harper exhaled loudly. "You love sports and that's that. My dad was drafted to play football right out of college, but he blew out his knee in the preseason and that was it. NFL dream over."

I had a sudden urge to ask her how long she'd been in LA from… wherever she was from in the South. I wanted to dive into knowing her more deeply. But I didn't want to ask her here, where we'd have our conversation overheard or cut short by work. So I feigned thoughtfulness, nodding slowly. "I see. What about you? Secret NFL career?"

Her laugh was so rich and bright it was like a burst of sunshine. "No, ma'am. No football for me. But…I played tennis from when I was about six or seven. I played division two in college."

Ah. That explained the umpiring of our charity thing then. "That's seriously impressive, Harper."

"Thanks." She shrugged, but it seemed less like nonchalance and more like embarrassment. "I was told I should try to push into division one and then go pro, but I didn't want to spend my life traveling, doing nothing but playing tennis or training in the gym."

"Sounds fair. So was this match your idea?"

Harper pretended to recoil. "Oh, lord no. I think they just needed something that was easy to organize. Trying to get y'all sorted for a team would be a nightmare, especially if there were more injuries like Liz." Harper hesitated for a couple seconds before tentatively asking, "Are you playing instead of her?" Clearly she'd seen Gabby chatting with me and Laura earlier.

"Playing is…a generous term for what I'll be doing. I've been asked to participate, yes. With Laura," I said hastily.

"Great," she enthused. Then she seemed to register the enthusiasm, and offered another, more casual, "Great. I mean…you're the drawcard. One of the drawcards," she hastily amended. Harper indicated that I should tilt my face up and I complied.

I couldn't help myself. "What do you mean *one of*?"

She didn't hesitate, didn't stop working as she reeled off, "You're the drawcard. The only person fans will be coming to see. Everyone will be supporting the *North Precinct* team solely because of you. I know I will."

"You're very good for my ego."

Harper laughed. She met my gaze, and her eye contact felt almost too sustained, too unwavering. "I feel like your ego is healthy enough without my encouragement."

I grinned, bringing my thumb and forefinger close together. "Maybe a little."

Harper matched my grin. "So, if *playing* is a generous term for what you'll be doing, can I assume you're not a tennis player?"

"I am the furthest thing from a tennis player you can get," I said cheerfully.

"Oh." She paused. "I, uh…If you need any pointers, or if you just want a hitting partner to practice with, let me know."

"That sounds amazing, thanks. I'll definitely take you up on that."

"You absolutely should," she said emphatically, and I wasn't sure if she was worried our show would lose, or if she really wanted to help me not be terrible at tennis because she liked me. "The sooner we start practicing, the better."

"Is Saturday too soon?" We had three and a half weeks to get match-ready. Maybe I should have pushed Gabby harder on that whole doing her a favor thing, considering how little time we had to prepare.

"Not at all. I'll get us a court."

"Great. One question though. Is there any way I could like, bribe you to look the other way whenever I hit a ball outside the line during the actual official match?"

Harper's eyebrows rose slowly. "What kind of bribe are we talking about?" she asked, and I was certain I wasn't mistaking the teasing flirtation in her tone.

I was in danger of saying something inappropriate, and held my breath until the urge passed. Thankfully, I was called to get my ass on camera. I smiled, covering up my frustration at being called back to work when I was enjoying a conversation with Harper. Though it was probably for the best given the direction my brain had run off in. "That's me."

"So it is. I'll talk to you later about tennis?"

"You bet."

There were a lot of moving parts to the scene with Laura: getting plates from cupboards, dishing up food, and all those little actions people did while making dinner that they never thought about. Once Monty was satisfied, we moved on to sitting down to eat.

I put a forkful of cold pasta in my mouth, chewing slowly, trying not to look like I wanted to spit out the unappealing mouthful—which I would get to as soon as I'd said my line...with the food still in my mouth, tucked into my cheek so I could articulate.

Early in the first season, it was decided that Amy often ate and spoke at the same time, being a busy detective who liked to have her opinions heard and all that. And for some unknown reason, a lot of fans really liked it. There was even a website and a hashtag dedicated to scenes of me talking while eating in character. #AmySpicerEats. People were so fucking weird.

As soon as we'd cut, a bucket was held out for me and I leaned forward and spat out the chewed food. I loved my job. After I'd had a mouthful of water, Harper checked my lipstick, made a small touch-up, and left me to touch up Laura. Hair checked. Wardrobe checked. Set, cameras, lighting reset. Food I'd eaten rearranged for continuity. Redo scene. And again. And again...

When we were finally done for the day, Laura and I thanked everyone, said goodbyes, and left set together. I needed to grab Harper to talk about tennis practice, but she was huddled in a corner with Chrissy as well as Brian, one of our producers, and I didn't want to get roped into a conversation with a producer if I could avoid it. Laura raised an eyebrow, then pointedly followed my gaze.

That look made me feel like I needed to explain. Overexplain. "Harper offered to hit a few tennis balls with me so I'd know what I'm doing for this thing. She said she almost went pro, so it seems like she knows what she's doing. Probably why she's umpiring, you know? I'm sure she'd help you out too."

Laura smirked. "Thanks, but I'll pass. I've decided that part of my charm will lie in my ineptitude. I'm going to play up the useless tennis damsel act."

"Solid plan. But, you know me..."

"I sure do, Ms. Won't Do Anything In Public Unless She's An Expert Already."

"Guilty. I think I'm going to go full tennis pro look. Shorts, not a skirt of course," I added hastily. Of course I'd need to buy an outfit. And other things. Like a tennis racquet.

She whistled. "The world is not ready for your legs, my friend."

"That's my plan. Distract the opposition with my legs instead of my terrible tennis game."

Laura hiked an eyebrow skyward. "Well, if Harper's as good as you say she is then you're not going to have a terrible tennis game for much longer."

"I guess we'll see…"

The email about the match was in my inbox when I checked before leaving work. Pretty straightforward. It was being described as a "gently competitive" game for charity. They'd rented out an entire college campus tennis center, though only one court would be used, and with makeshift seating the venue would hold up to about a thousand spectators. I skimmed the rest of the email which had some attendee and donation metrics etcetera, which was information my team would be more interested in than me. They'd been CC'd.

There was nothing about practice sessions, so I was sure that was just Gabby wanting *North Precinct* to win. Hell, I wanted us to win even though I was terrible at tennis.

Lucky for me, I now had just the person to help me.

CHAPTER FOUR

Harper

Why the hell had I offered to coach Steph? Aside from the fact I'd had a raging crush on her for years and wanted to spend more time with her away from work. But it felt like a bad idea, even if it was going to help her. Help the *North Precinct* team. Of course I would umpire fairly and without bias, but I *did* want the show I worked on to win the charity match. I could just keep pretending that was the reason I was helping Steph.

When I dragged myself into the kitchen at five a.m., Per was up and about, dressed in his gym gear. "It's almost the weekend!" he exclaimed. As soon as he saw me, his expression transformed into something between pity and concern. "And you look like you really need it."

I would have said something snide, but I was still precoffee. We danced around each other—he prepped a preworkout shake, I dropped a bagel into the toaster and popped a pod in the Keurig.

Per broke a banana into the blender. "What are you doing tomorrow? Got time for a hike?"

"Sorry, I can't. I'm playing tennis." Or I assumed I was playing tennis. I hadn't had a chance to talk with Steph about it yesterday after I'd said I'd help her out, and had made a mental note to pin her down about it today.

He frowned. "Ben didn't mention anything." His boyfriend was my usual tennis partner, though I'd play with anyone who'd return a ball, and often grabbed random people who'd used the court before me, or sweet-talked my way into doubles games with strangers. "*Excuse* me? Are we doing some country club ladies tennis and champagne event and you forgot to tell me?" He scooped protein powder out of his Goliath-sized tub.

"Unfortunately not. It's a work thing." I didn't want to tell him I'd be playing tennis with one of his favorite television people, because that would lead to gushing and then probably grumbling that I wouldn't let him be a fake ball boy, so I left it there.

"Please explain."

I did, briefly, while spreading cream cheese on my bagel and adding sliced strawberries and a tiny splash of balsamic to one half, and tomato and capers with a healthy shake of everything seasoning and an unhealthy shake of salt. Breakfast was available at work, and I took advantage on days I didn't wake up hungry like I had this morning. An ex had once told me she'd never seen anyone do hangry like me, and she was right.

He started the blender, ruling out any conversation until he was done, though the noise had barely stopped when he exclaimed, "They're making you do what? Why didn't you tell me about this?"

Because it'd totally slipped my mind around all the other tiny thoughts I had filling up space in there. While he gulped down the shake, I explained, "They're not *making* us do anything. It's totally voluntary." Though it felt like the cast members might have been voluntold. "And it's a tennis match for charity. You know, a good cause?" I took a big bite of my strawberry bagel.

"I support many good causes," he said dryly. "I *know* what a good cause is."

"Oh good. Then you can support this one too."

"Harper," he sighed.

"Per."

"I support a lot of causes," he repeated. He added almond milk to my coffee so I could keep eating before I had to leave the house. For all his annoyances—which were honestly few and inoffensive—he was a great and thoughtful friend.

"I know you do," I soothed him. "But this one is really worthy. If you buy tickets for the game, not only will you be helping a charity for women and kids affected by domestic violence, which is reason enough to do it, but you'll get to meet the cast of *North Precinct* and *Make the Cut* after the match is done."

"I could meet the cast of *North Precinct* for free if you'd introduce me."

"Your broken record is getting scratchy, you should probably switch to digital."

He chuckled. "Okay, that was funny. But I'm serious."

"So am I. Come on." I nudged him. "Are you really gonna be the dick who doesn't donate to charity? And a good charity at that."

Per shrugged expansively. "Maybe, yeah. Those tickets are going to be so fucking expensive, if they aren't already sold out."

"Good. Cause."

"Struggling. Actor."

I knew he wasn't *that* struggling. Between his part-time waiter job, his modeling, and a little help from the Bank of Mom and Dad Akselsen, he was fine. Still, he had a point. Kind of. I finished the last of my strawberry bagel and picked up the tomato half. "Okay, look. I'll talk to the organizers. Maybe we can get you a ticket cheaper or something. You'll still have to donate something though. Something as in cash."

He grabbed me and swept me up into a hug until my feet dangled. "Oh I love you!" Per kissed the top of my head and swung me around. "Have I ever told you you're the best friend ever?"

"No promises. And tell Ben, get him on board with donating," I said when he'd set me back down again. I checked to make sure none of my bagel toppings had fallen off. Luckily for Per they were intact. "And no, you haven't told me that."

"Well you *are* the best friend ever." He hugged me again, planting rapid-fire kisses on my temple before releasing me. "And not just for this."

"I know," I said airily. "But this is just a *maybe* on the cheaper ticket thing, so don't go getting those sweet little hopes of yours up because I don't want you to be disappointed." I knew the actors got two free seats each for family or friends, but I was just the umpire and they hadn't said anything about free seats for me. I got it, watching someone umpiring a charity match wasn't as exciting as watching your spouse, partner, mom, or dad play.

Per grinned as he gave me a condescending pat on the top of my head. "I have complete faith in you."

"Well, that's just dumb," I drawled.

As she always did on Fridays, Steph brought in a box of pastries. I knew there'd also be boxes for the other departments and crew too, and every one of the treats would be gone by the time we wrapped. I snuck an apple fritter and set it aside.

Steph clocked what I'd done, the same thing I always did with her pastry delivery, and laughed. "Savesies again, Harper?"

"Yes, ma'am." I raised my chin. "There's only ever one apple fritter in the box that comes to us, and they're my favorite. No criticism of your generosity, of course."

"Of course not." Her eyes creased at the edges just before she smiled. "But I know. I should ask them to put more in the box." Steph's eyes tracked me as I adjusted the lights toward her face. "Or maybe I should bring you an apple fritter each day…"

"Oof. That could be dangerous."

I knew I wasn't imagining the way she looked me up and down. Nor was I imagining the teasing, flirtatious glint in her eyes. She leaned slightly forward, her knee bumping against my leg as she murmured, "I can think of plenty of things that are more dangerous than that."

Her proximity, that look, and the teasing tone sent a shudder down my spine. I fought down the sensation. All I could offer in response to that was an "Mmm." Did she mean actual dangerous things like leaping from moving cars, or dangerous things like…flirting? "You ready for me?" I asked. As soon as I'd spoken, I mentally cursed myself for my wording and hoped she didn't take it any other way than what I'd meant: Was she ready for makeup?

Steph nodded, all business now. "I am."

Laura rushed in, and after exuberant good mornings, practically threw herself in front of Nina and Chrissy. I'd never admit it aloud, but I loved that Steph's hair required less styling than most of her costars, which meant I often worked on her alone instead of tag-teaming.

As I sanitized my hands, Steph asked, "Are we still on for tennis practice tomorrow? Sorry, I meant to find you after work yesterday to confirm times but you looked busy and I needed to get home."

Out of the corner of my eye, I caught a little movement from Nina's chair. Laura had clearly overheard and I wondered if I should have offered to coach her too. But Steph and Laura were friends; surely they'd talked about it and Laura would ask me if she needed help. "Absolutely. And you read my mind. I was going to talk to you today. I'll book a court?" It was last minute, but if I couldn't get a spot at my usual club, I'd just find somewhere with an opening. Somewhere that wasn't a public court where she'd probably be observed. "We might have to play at a weird time to get a booking. Is early or late better for you?" I assumed she'd want to catch up on sleep, but I also knew some people liked getting all their stuff out of the way early in the day.

"I can fit in whenever. But…sometime after late morning would be best if you can swing it. Also, I have to reiterate that I'm not going to be great. Or even good. You won't get a proper tennis game out of me."

I got to work, thankful for muscle memory so I could talk while I made Steph camera-ready. "That's unfortunate. I kicked my usual tennis partner out so you could play instead," I joked. A small lie, but the grin she gave me was worth it.

"Oh. I'll have to send them an apology for taking their spot."

Though I knew she was only joking, I had to hold in a laugh at what would happen if Steph contacted Ben. "He might die if you did that."

"Shit, okay, I won't apologize then. But I will feel bad. But only for taking your friend's place, not for being the one who gets to spend time with you."

Our eyes met and held. She smiled first, and warmth suffused me. I managed to set aside my reaction to finish and get everyone out the door on time. After gathering my fanny packs, I took my apple fritter and went to set to wait until I was needed.

After blocking their scene, Steph and Laura came off the set, Steph tapping her script against her thigh as she walked. When she spotted me, she detoured slightly and came over, leaning down to speak near my ear. "You eaten that donut yet?"

The question was warm, teasing, a little conspiratorial, and made tingles trickle down my spine. "Long gone," I said, hoping my voice didn't give away my body's reaction.

She winked. "Good."

Laura mock-pouted. "Where's my pastry?"

"Still at the bakery because you've never wanted one before," Steph shot back.

"But I want one now."

Steph shrugged. "Then you can try to grab something from one of the crew boxes."

Laura's overexaggerated shudder was comical. "I wouldn't dare."

Steph opened her mouth, presumably to respond, but something behind me made her shut it again. She nodded, then tapped Laura on the shoulder with her script. "We've been summoned." She turned back to me, a warm smile curving her mouth and softening the corners of her eyes. "Catch you later, Harper."

"You sure will." I deliberately kept my eyes on the ground as she walked away. I'd be looking at her face again soon enough.

Our morning of shooting went without a hitch, and we broke for our meal on time. Once the cast had their food, I got into line and tried not to look like I wanted to eat the world as I loaded my plate with quinoa, salad, and a turkey burger patty. Nina had already found us a spot, and I made my way through the tables toward her. As I walked past Steph, she leaned back in her chair, reaching out to snag my hand. "Hey. I forgot to ask if I need to bring any tennis balls or stuff like that."

"Nope. I've got everything we'll need. You just need a racquet." A brief flicker of panic passed over her face as soon as I said *racquet*, and I hastily added, "But I do have a few spares."

"It's all good, not needed, thanks." Steph squeezed my hand, then seemed to realize she was still holding it. She dropped it like a hot potato.

I had to take a breath before answering to make sure my response wasn't breathy and hoarse. "Great." I curled my fingers against my palm, like I could hold Steph's touch against my skin. Laura was looking at us like we were speaking an alien language, and I smiled at both of them, then walked away before I could do or say something stupid.

I sat a little too heavily, jostling my plate to the table. The sound of my food hitting the surface made a few people look up from where they were inhaling food like they hadn't eaten in days. The thought of drawing attention to myself made my body tighten uncomfortably. Nina stopped sifting her fork through her food long enough to look up and study me. "Are you okay?"

My eyebrows shot up in surprise and I tried my hardest to sound light and breezy. "Of course. Why?"

"Because you look like someone just handed you a bomb and ran away." She looked to where Steph and Laura sat then back to me, and in that moment her entire demeanor had changed. "Did they say something to you?"

"No! Absolutely not. I'm fine, I swear."

Nina eyed me somewhat dubiously. "Okay then, if you say so. But I *will* kick their asses if I need to. I don't care who they are…"

Before we went back to set after our meal break, I went online to find a tennis court. Someone at my usual place had canceled their booking at three p.m. tomorrow and I snapped it up like someone grabbing Taylor Swift concert tickets. I'd assumed I'd catch up with Steph to confirm details for our coaching session, like where and when we were actually playing, before finishing for the day. But when we'd wrapped at five p.m. and she'd disappeared into her trailer without stopping to talk to me, I resigned myself to waiting for her to reemerge.

I just needed to figure out how to do that without seeming creepy. I *could* go knock on her trailer door, but couldn't shake the feeling that

I shouldn't. I knew all I wanted was to wind down when work was done, and butting into her transition from work to home felt intrusive.

I finished cleaning my brushes and readying my station and fanny packs for Monday, then went out to chill by the garden between the parking lot and the ginormous concrete slab where the trailers for cast, crew, and our production office stood.

Luckily I only had to wait a few minutes, which was great for me getting home to unwind after the work week, but not so great for me checking my Instagram feed for the day.

Steph jogged over to me, hitching her bags up on her shoulder. "Hey." She quickly looked me up and down. "Hope you haven't been waiting long. And…I assume you're waiting for me?" The question rose hopefully at the end.

"Nope, just a few minutes. And yes," I added, smiling at her relief, "I am waiting for you."

Steph wilted a little. "Sorry to make you wait. You should have come by my trailer or called me." Her forehead wrinkled. "Actually, do you even *have* my number?"

I laughed. "Why would I have your number?"

"I don't know. I just assumed, I don't even know why."

I pulled out my phone, unlocked it, and went to the contacts so she could put her number in. "Here. Add your phone number and then I'll have it."

She finished adding herself then passed me her phone so I could reciprocate. Once I'd handed it back, she asked, "Do you have WhatsApp?"

"Yes, ma'am, I do," I said, surprised by the question. Not the query about my communication preferences, but that she obviously wanted to communicate with me, and with what sounded like reasonable frequency.

"Do you mind if we use that for messaging? I'm a little paranoid about unencrypted messages. Just, they're frighteningly easy to get into and I like my privacy. Not that I think we're going to talk about anything interesting, but…" She grinned the slightly crooked grin that I'd noticed always snuck out when she was feeling shy or embarrassed about something.

It appeared rarely, but often enough that I noticed. I held in a groan at the realization that I spent way too much time looking at her in a nonwork capacity.

"Absolutely, no problem." Actually, it was huge problem—not the communication method we'd use but that she had to worry about crap like that. It wasn't a new thing for celebrities, but it really was one of the things I hated about the industry. Thinking about Steph dealing with this made a swirl of anger rush through my body.

"Thanks."

"So, I've booked a court for three tomorrow afternoon." As soon as I spoke, I realized I probably should have checked where she lived before booking. But she hadn't said anything about location. Hopefully she didn't have to trek across the city to get to the courts. I fished my notebook and a pen from my bag and scribbled down the address as I told her, "It's the place where I usually play. It's a small facility, and normally there's hardly any people there. I mean, there's people, playing, but we're not going to have a crowd of spectators."

"Sounds great. And that's a perfect time. Late enough that I can sleep in, but not so late that the day feels wasted."

"Lucky us, sleeping in." I wasn't sure how much sleeping I'd be doing tonight, knowing I'd be spending time with her tomorrow in a setting outside of work. It was stupid to think tomorrow was something out of the ordinary when we worked together, but it was.

"It's one of my most favorite things to do in bed," she said cheerfully. The moment she'd finished speaking, all her cheer fell away, replaced by mortification. Steph hastened to correct herself, and failed. "I mean… it's, I…Never mind. I'm going to go crawl into a hole."

I'd seen her roll with so many dialogue missteps while working, and the fact she was fumbling her words here with me made something warm spark in my chest. I loved her confidence but I also loved watching it unravel a little. The fact Steph let me see this part of herself was exhilarating. She wasn't pretending to be awkward, she was really fumbling with me, and I could only guess, and hope at the reason.

"Shit," she added. "I've embarrassed you."

"No you haven't," I reassured her. People had sex in beds, it was a fact of life. I knew she'd been in a relationship with Jordan Leclerc until about six months ago, and assumed she was in a new relationship that she was yet to go public with. And if I were Steph D'Arripe's girlfriend, I'd want to spend as much time as I could in bed with her too. I took a moment to rein in my runaway thoughts and forced a smile. "Don't die of embarrassment. That would be seriously problematic for the show." And also for me.

"True." Steph gestured toward the parking lot. "Walk and talk? I'm ready to go home, inhale some food, and get into bed." She laughed, and all the endearing fumbliness from before had disappeared when she clarified, "Go to bed innocently, despite my previous blathering that might imply something to the contrary."

I fell into step beside her. "I like your blathering."

"That makes one person."

There was teasing in her words, but when I glanced at her, she looked tense. Obviously there was an underlying nuance there, but it wasn't the time or place for us to discuss it. It wasn't something for me to discuss with her. I decided to move to a safe topic. "Anything you need to know about tennis tomorrow?"

"Nope." Steph hitched her tote a little higher on her shoulder. She gripped the strap hard, knuckles whitening as she asked, "Did you want me to pick you up and we go together, or…?"

It made sense to go together, *if* we lived close to each other. But I was sure we didn't. I also didn't want her to feel obligated to pick me up then drop me off, forcing more interaction than she may want outside of me helping her with her tennis game. So I told a little white lie. "I have a few errands to run beforehand, so it's probably easier if we meet there. But thanks."

"No problem," she said, seemingly unbothered. Though, she'd seemed bothered by what I might say when she'd asked me. Or maybe the white-knuckle grip was because she was just being polite and feared I might say, "Yeah, let's go together."

Whatever the reason, it was too late for me to be pondering such pointless things. I stopped by my Kia. "This is me."

"Great. See you tomorrow." Steph recited the details of our plan for tomorrow like she was trying to make sure she remembered them. Or maybe it was an anxiety thing. My sister, Brittany, did the same. Once I'd confirmed she had it right, she added, "Drive safely and uh…sleep tight."

"I will and I will. And you too." In your bed, where you clearly enjoy doing many things. I shut down that thought.

"Like a baby," she assured me. A quick wink followed and I fought the urge to melt into a puddle of goo. Steph's winks were legendary. I had no idea how she could make one tiny movement convey so much—sexiness, teasing, and a sense that she was agreeing with you and would go along with whatever you wanted. "The sleeping, not the driving."

I unlocked my car. "Thanks for that clarification. I did wonder…"

Steph grinned as if me playing along with the joke was the best thing that'd happened to her today. And for just one second, I let my internal guard down and allowed myself to think of what that would be like—to be the best thing in Steph's life, and vice versa.

Steph waited until I was safely inside my car, then waved and walked away. I watched her as long as I dared, until the thought of her going home to someone else became so overwhelming that I had to look away.

CHAPTER FIVE

Steph

I woke up with plenty of time to fit in a workout, housework, a few episodes of *Antiques Roadshow*, and to stop by a sporting store on my way to the tennis courts. I needed to buy myself a tennis racquet, and hoped I could get in and out of the store without too much drama or attention.

But first I had to get dressed. I mean, I knew what to wear for a workout, but what did I wear to spend time with Harper? Should I put on makeup? Laura never went out in public without an outfit and makeup, no matter what she was doing. But makeup plus exercise equaled my face feeling gross. Of course, it was guaranteed that any time I left my house sans makeup, I'd be photographed and splattered across the Internet. I made a mental note to talk to Harper about what makeup I'd wear for the charity match that wouldn't sweat off or make me feel facially constricted.

Focus. Clothing.

You're being dumb, I admonished myself. Harper wouldn't care what I looked like. She saw me in the mornings when I was barefaced and my hair was crazy, and was there during the day when I fucked things up at work. So who cared if she saw me red-faced and sweating and being awful at something?

It was perhaps the first time I'd ever felt this acceptance of someone witnessing me not being perfect, or at least semicompetent at something. It was probably good practice for the match, I supposed. I pulled on clothes suitable for exercising in public—shorts, a tank top, and a long-sleeved sun shirt—grabbed a hat and my essentials and went to go get tennis-ready.

Even with my shopping pit stop, I arrived ten minutes early and parked near Harper. She popped out of her car, carrying a racquet bag and a small gym bag. But what *really* caught my attention was her outfit. I'd seen her in skirts and dresses before at work, but nothing like this, nothing like the short tennis skirt that exposed a delightful amount of Harper's legs.

Her light windbreaker was unzipped over a tight athletic top, tight enough to make a knot of excitement form in my stomach. Unlike me, Harper wore makeup, but it was less "day on set" and more "playing tennis for an hour." I'd never seen her without makeup, and that realization made me wonder what she might look like first thing in the morning. Barefaced. In my bed.

She'd pulled her dark hair up into a ponytail that she'd threaded through the back of her ball cap. The large and medium hoop earrings from the four holes in her earlobes, and the cute jewelry she usually had in her helix piercings had been swapped out for plain studs and small hoops. As soon as I realized that, I realized just how much attention I paid to her.

After that initial sneaky peek…those sneaky *peeks*…I made sure to keep my gaze firmly above her shoulders. A heroic effort on my part. I deserved a fucking medal or something.

"Hey," I said. Ten out of ten for sounding normally excited to see her, and not like a hormonal teen.

"Hey yourself." I didn't miss the quick up-and-down inspection she gave me before she asked, "You ready to go? We're over on court six."

The fact I wasn't the only one sneaking peeks, that Harper was checking me out, made the knot of excitement grow. "Absolutely. I *think* I have everything I need?"

Harper gestured to my racquet. "Well, you've got the most important thing." At my nod, she grinned. "So you *do* play tennis. You're full of surprises."

"I know. And you know the biggest surprise?" When she shook her head, I confessed, "I bought it on my way here…"

"No!" She started laughing before the word had left her mouth, and she almost choked the back end of it out. "Stephanie D'Arripe, I cannot believe you let me think you were just being modest and were actually a secret tennis player."

"I'm sorry." Her laughter was so delightful, I decided to give her another surprise. Lowering my voice, I confessed, "Did you know my name isn't actually Stephanie D'Arripe?"

That stopped the laughter. Shame. "No, I did not know that." She eyed me, a look of concern and then interest crossing her face. "So...are you gonna tell me what your name is, or did you just drop that as a weird little snippet?"

I snorted a laugh. "It's Stephanie Salter. I borrowed my mom's maiden name. Sounds a little more upmarket and unique. And, I admit, it was calculated. My aunt is Patricia D'Arripe."

"The producer? Of course. I've seen that on IMDb or something."

I squished down the little frisson of excitement that she'd looked me up. "Yup. Little nepo baby right here."

"Mmm. But still, I dunno," Harper drawled. "The alliteration of Stephanie Salter rolls off the tongue. Not that Stephanie D'Arripe isn't a great name, especially for an actor," she added quickly.

I smirked. "Thanks. I think."

Harper flicked the backs of her fingers against my arm. "You know what I mean."

"I do." Grinning wickedly, I said, "Did you know my first name isn't actually Stephanie..."

Harper groaned. "Oh my god. Okay, hit me."

I raised an eyebrow. "The way you just hit me?" She rolled her eyes, and I laughed at the expression. "And I'm kidding. My name *is* Stephanie. Sorry, but the look on your face right now is *totally* worth it."

The return of Harper's laugh was also worth it. Once she'd stopped, she asked, "So, do you want me to call you Steph Salter, or D'Arripe?"

Nobody had ever asked me that. Of course Harper would want to do what made me feel the best. "D'Arripe is my legal name now. Has been for a while. I don't think I'd even respond if someone called out 'Yo, Stephanie Salter!'"

"D'Arripe it is." She bumped me with her shoulder. "Come on." I'd thought she might share something personal in return, maybe something about her family, but she didn't.

I feigned innocence at her trying to get me to move. "Come on what?" At her exaggerated sigh, I just smiled wider. "And no, to answer the question that started this silliness, I don't play tennis. Or, I mean, I can play, I *have* played when I was younger, but not seriously at all. But I have a chronic problem where I can't stand doing anything unless I have all the right gear." I held up the racquet. "It'd be a very expensive problem if I had the time for a new hobby every week."

"That's an interesting problem to have."

"Yeah…and I—" I almost didn't admit it, but Harper's look of interest loosened my tongue. "I don't like doing anything unless I know what I'm doing and I'm good at it. Especially not if people are going to watch me. So this tennis match is problematic. A nightmare scenario for me really."

"It won't be a nightmare once I'm done with you," Harper promised. She raised her eyebrows. "Also, how do you become good at something without doing it?"

"Exactly. Like I said, it's problematic."

She crossed her arms over her chest. "You really are full of surprises and interesting little quirks."

I shrugged, affecting a nonchalant expression. "Quirks sounds about right."

"That was a compliment." She pulled out a couple cans of balls from her gym bag, and started walking. "Come on, our court time is about to start."

We were on the court farthest from the clubhouse and once we'd closed the chain-link door nestled in the tall fence, Harper beelined for the umpire chair and dumped her things underneath it. She unzipped her jacket and draped it over the chair. I swallowed hard. The athletic top was actually a tank top. A tight one. A tight one that hugged all her assets, and she had some incredible assets. I crouched down and busied myself pulling out my brand-new racquet and my water bottle, and trying not to stare too obviously at her.

When I straightened up, Harper tapped the brim of my hat. "Glad to see this." She touched the long sleeve of my sun shirt. "And this. Are you wearing sunscreen? You need to protect your skin," she said, her voice a singsongy lecture.

"I am. Never leave home without some sort of sunscreen, and I've got my sports lotion on today to combat all the sweating I'll be doing."

Harper paused just a beat too long. "Good. You have beautiful skin."

I made sure to sound appropriately thankful, but also I had to inject a little silliness into my, "Aw, thanks" in an attempt to avoid sounding too egotistical. Harper looked at my skin for a living, of course she knew what it looked like and what products kept it looking "beautiful."

I knew I fit within the bracket of actor beauty standards, and I was vain enough to enjoy what I looked like. But at the same time, people commenting on my appearance often made me feel strange. Not uncomfortable, but more like I felt compelled to remind them I wasn't just a face and body whose job was to emote and parrot words someone else had written. But for some reason, having Harper comment on it didn't make me feel like cringing.

Harper smirked. "As if you didn't know."

"Of course I know." I shrugged. "I'm paid to make sure my exterior looks as good as it can."

"Well, it shows."

Was that? Yes, it was. Another flirty compliment. Harper somehow looked like she didn't know she'd just set my skin on fire by telling me she thought I was attractive. This move from teasing banter with a flirtatious edge at work to outright flirtation outside of work was thrilling.

"Good to know," I murmured. Okay, time to move or this was going to turn into a compliment-Steph session. Compliments were great, but not when they were one-sided, and I wasn't sure how to compliment Harper without sounding either lecherous or a little lovesick. I cleared my throat. "And are you wearing sunscreen? You...have a lot of arm on display there." Very nice arms on display.

"Of course I am," she said incredulously. "So, how much do you know about tennis?"

Her question snapped me out of my jaw-dropping study of her arms, and gave me a kick in the ass. She was talking about tennis. Maybe she didn't actually think I was attractive and I'd just taken her comment out of context. "I've seen some Grand Slam tennis. I know the basics. I can hit tennis balls. Not always where I want to hit them, and not always at all, but I can hit them."

"Good. That's part of my job done if you can already hit the ball. I'm not sure of the rules of this charity match around serves and whatnot, but I'm assuming you don't need to do an overarm serve."

"I *can* do a proper tennis serve," I said, surprised by the defensiveness in my voice. Her amused eyebrows raise made me tone it down. "Or, I mean, I could the last time I played. Which was...I don't even remember how long ago. It was a long time long ago."

Harper looked like she was barely restraining a smile. "Good to know. Okay, let's just have a hit back and forth. Nothing fancy, just connecting with the ball and sending it over the net. Show me how you hold your racquet."

I gripped it and held it up, and Harper came right into my personal space. It wasn't the first time we'd been close—it was normal when she was doing my makeup for work—but now it felt deliberate, more intimate. Before I could let myself think about that, she adjusted my grip slightly, twisting my hand around.

"Imagine a handshake." Harper used her forefinger to stroke the space between my thumb and forefinger. "Keep this close to the edge of the handle, the 'corner.'" She air-quoted, then turned my hand over again. "And your forefinger knuckle over this corner. That'll help stop the ball from dropping down into the net when you hit it."

"Got it. What if it goes up too much? Like over the net and out of the court."

"You're going to have to hit it pretty hard for it to be out."

"Are you saying I'm not strong enough to hit it that far?"

"I'm not saying that at all," she said innocently. "But statistically, it'll go into the net." Her eyes went to my arms, lingering long enough to make it clear she was checking them out. I guess it was an arm-checking-out kind of day. "I'm quite sure you're strong enough to hit it over the baseline or out of this court entirely if you wanted to."

"Okay," I said, embarrassed at the high pitch that'd attached itself to that word.

Harper checked my double-handed backhand grip and declared I was good to go. Though maybe *good* wasn't the right word. I was just… ready to go. She jogged around to the other side of the net and after tucking a couple balls up under the Lycra shorts beneath her skirt, she bounced one on the court with her racquet. "Ready?" she called.

I gave her a thumbs-up, and Harper hit the ball over to me. It landed to my right, in a perfect spot for me to hit it back with a forehand. I connected, and congratulated myself when it went straight toward the net. I uncongratulated myself when it hit the net. Yup, I was a statistic. But there was no time for self-flagellation because Harper had another ball in her hand. "Ready for another?"

"Yeah."

This time I managed to get the ball back to Harper and she ran to it, then returned it easily to my forehand side again. We got into a rhythm, and I hit some reasonable backhands as well as forehands until I buried it in the net again. We played a couple more easy rallies—easy because Harper hit the ball exactly to me every time—and when we met at the net to collect balls, she was exuberant. "You're doing great."

"You're incredibly sweet."

"I'm incredibly right."

"It's easy when the ball basically puts itself on my racquet. How do you make it go *exactly* where you want like that?"

"Decades of practice." Harper managed to sound both humble and smug all at once.

"Think you could condense those decades into a few hours for me?"

She nodded seriously. "I can certainly try."

"Thank you."

"Do you want to try a little more movement around the court?"

"Sure. Not everyone is going to be as kind to me as you are and I need to train for that."

"That's right. But I'll still be a little kind to you."

"I appreciate that." I ran to the back of the court and waited for Harper to hit the ball to me.

We played some more rallies, with Harper gently moving the ball back and forth along the baseline so I had to chase it down and position myself to hit it. I managed to return it about sixty percent of the time, which was about thirty percent more than I'd expected.

When we met for another ball collection, Harper asked, "You want to try some returns of serve and maybe a little more movement?" She checked her watch. "We've got about twenty minutes left."

"Sounds good. I need to learn, so…maybe don't go easy on me with your serving."

Her eyebrows rose above her sunglasses. "Are you sure?"

"Yes. No. Yes. Yes, I'm sure. Jenna and Yusef are probably going to be walloping tennis balls across the net for serves." I might as well get used to being afraid.

"Or they'll be trying to," she joked. Harper used her racquet to bounce the ball as she walked back around and to her service line. "Ready?" she called.

I gave her another thumbs-up and got into position to receive her serve. I tried to keep my eye on the ball like she'd told me to, but my eyes strayed to her arm…then her shoulder, down her torso, her legs. The way her body arced as she wound up to serve was mesmerizing, and a tightness in my stomach took my focus away from the ball.

The ball rocketed by me so fast I couldn't even react, and it hit the fence behind me with a loud clang. I held up my racquet to stop her launching another missile and jogged up to the net. "Okay," I said. "I changed my mind. Go easy on me."

Her smile radiated satisfaction. "Sure thing," she called back.

Harper's second serve came flat over the net, then popped up high, confusing the shit out of me. I managed to connect with it, just, but it landed squarely in the net.

I walked up to the net and this time, Harper jogged over to meet me. As soon as she was close I threw my hands up and demanded, "Why? That was baffling as shit."

Harper laughed, her nose crinkling. "Topspin."

"Okay. Cool. That's cool. But. Can you…not?"

She laughed again, and was still laughing as she agreed, "Sure, if that's what you want." She backed up. "Just to be clear, no spin at all?"

"There's more than one kind?" I sounded more defeated than I cared to.

She nodded, biting her lip on a smirk. A smirk that was far sexier than it deserved to be.

"Okay, yeah, no spin of any kind until I've figured out how to just hit a normal serve ball."

"Yes, ma'am. You got it." She grinned. "But to be clear, *technically* all balls have spin on them."

"Am I about to get a physics lesson?"

"Do you want a physics lesson?"

"I could not want one less."

I heard her laughing all the way back to her baseline.

By the time our hour was up, I felt like I had a reasonable grasp of the basics and would at least not embarrass myself too much for the match. Not that being embarrassed would matter—it was an event for charity and nobody was a tennis professional. But I didn't like feeling incapable, especially not in public.

And the best part was that nobody had been obvious about watching my practice. I'd noticed some looks, but nobody approached the fence to stare at my ineptitude, and nobody was waiting for me to come off the court.

Harper dropped the balls into cans. "Next time, we'll do more serves, moving around the court and maybe some volleys. The match isn't going to be pro level, but I think you should be prepared for anything that might come at you. And I think we could try two hours if you think you'll be okay with that much tennis instruction in one chunk."

"I'm sure I will be. So, are you available next Saturday, or Sunday morning for another coaching session?" I bit my lower lip, suddenly worried she'd say no.

Harper laughed. "I'm *only* available Saturday or Sunday. Or after work if we finish early enough and we're not exhausted. Which…you know, is not likely."

"Well that is a wonderful coincidence. We could do both days? Or tomorrow morning too? If you're free, and want to," I added quickly. "The more practice, the better, right?"

She studied me intently, as if she'd realized something and was trying to put pieces together. After a few seconds, Harper shook her head. "No. I don't think you need more than one session a week. You work hard enough, Steph. Injuring yourself through overtraining for a charity match is silly. And you don't need it. I can already tell you'll be fine."

Her reassurance that I'd be fine only *just* outweighed my fear of being terrible. I sighed heavily. "Okay. But I'll be swinging my racquet around my living room and probably my trailer too."

"As long as you're not doing it every day…" Harper squeezed my wrist. "It's for *charity*. They're coming to see *you*. They're expecting fun, not perfection."

"Why can't I give them both?"

She rolled her eyes. "Lord help me."

"I'm sorry. I'll try to behave. Or at least not be neurotic about this match."

"You don't have to behave," she said, the words trickling slowly out of her mouth.

Jesus. I cleared my throat. "We, uh, haven't talked about it, but I feel like I should be giving you something for helping me."

"I'm part of the match too, and I'm supporting our team, so technically I'm helping myself. But if you're worried, buy me a drink sometime." There was an almost desperate edge to the casualness of her offer that felt exhilarating.

"Do you want to grab a cold beer now? Maybe something to eat?" I'd spoken without thinking, but I wasn't concerned with what I blurted—I was glad my subconscious was so smart and in tune with what I wanted.

Harper paused for just a second. "That sounds great. I know a good place nearby. Follow me?"

CHAPTER SIX

Harper

I didn't want to admit that I came to this Tex-Mex place after almost every game of tennis because it was delicious and close. But when Steph jumped out of her car and exclaimed, "Hell yeah," my embarrassment abated.

She'd changed out of her workout shirt into a plain black T-shirt that snugged nicely around her torso. Her sports sunglasses had been swapped for a pair of aviators, and she'd pulled on another ball cap to replace the sweaty one. Hat and sunglasses were an adequate and standard LA disguise, but Steph was so striking I didn't think anyone would be fooled. Especially not when she removed her sunglasses inside, tucking them into the neckline of her tee.

The hostess clearly wasn't, but she didn't say anything. I actually didn't know how Steph felt about being recognized or approached, and I decided I'd wait until I had a better idea of what she preferred before I said anything. We were seated inside next to the window, and Steph paused, her hand on the back of the chair. "Looking in or out?" she asked.

"Either. I don't mind," I said honestly.

She sat facing the window, with her back to the restaurant. And then I knew for sure that she didn't want to be noticed if she could avoid it. I made a mental note for the next time we were out together, then promptly laughed at myself. I was assuming there would be a next time. The other thought that struck me was that she'd asked which I'd preferred instead of just taking a seat. Would she have sat facing the entire restaurant if I'd said I wanted to look out the window?

Steph glanced at the drink menu for a few seconds, then handed it to me.

"Made a decision already?" I asked. What a completely foreign concept. Studying menus was like a hobby to me, and anytime I went to a new place I either checked the menu beforehand, or spent ages poring over it before making my choice.

"I think so, yeah." Steph reached for the food menu. "Share chips with guac and salsa?" she asked hopefully.

Her expression was so cute, almost like an excited kid, that I didn't hesitate. "I insist on it."

She grinned. "Good."

A server appeared promptly with waters and we ordered drinks. Steph went with an Estrella Damm, while I ordered a Space Dust Hazy IPA. I hadn't thought of it while we'd been playing, but now we were sitting close, about to eat, I realized I felt a little awkward. It *was* strange to be with her outside of work, to be given insight into her likes and dislikes. Like…what beer she'd pick from a menu.

Steph downed half her water and once she'd set the glass down again, gently admonished me. "You should rehydrate."

"I hydrated plenty during our game," I rebutted, but dutifully picked up my water.

She arched an eyebrow. "Game? That's a generous term for what we were doing."

"You think so?"

Steph nodded. "I do. And again, I'm sorry if you were expecting a competent tennis partner."

"I wasn't expecting anything except a fun time, and that's exactly what I got."

"Me too," she murmured. Her pointed look at the glass in my hand was somehow sexy and demanding, and made me desperate to do what she wanted.

So I drank some water. Once I'd set my glass down, I rested my arms on the table, leaning toward her. "I have a question."

"Quest away."

"What would you have done if I'd said I wanted to sit where you're sitting?"

She confirmed my suspicion without hesitation. "I would have sat where you are."

I caught sight of a different server beelining toward our table with two beers balanced on a tray, and made what I hoped was a subtle gesture to let Steph know someone was approaching. I thought she'd like to know when we weren't alone, though realistically anyone with good hearing and a bit of motivation could eavesdrop.

The new server gave Steph more than a cursory glance, which told me she'd recognized her, but she said nothing. Steph flashed a bright smile and offered a cheerful "Thank you" that made the server blush. Blushing was fine, dropping drinks was less so. I'd been to this place enough times to have a sense of the service, and I'd put money on the fact it was speedier than usual.

I wonder why…

As soon as the server left, I asked, "How do you deal with the attention? Not just the celebrity attention but the…" I wrinkled my nose, aware of the implication of what I was about to say. But I said it anyway. "The attractive-person attention?"

I'd seen it firsthand with Per, the way people watched him, gravitated to just be near him, how many people hit on him when all he did was exist. Ben was attractive too, and thankfully secure enough in their relationship that he never seemed bothered. And I wondered idly, totally not projecting my desires onto any one person, if *I* could handle that in a relationship, or if my insecurity would make it an issue.

She stared down at the table for so long that I was about to apologize for such a stupid, thoughtless question when she answered me. "You learn to ignore it after a while. It's hard, because the easiest way to discourage it would be to look unapproachable, but I've never been able to cultivate that." Steph shrugged. "It is what it is. I'm not going to lie. There are some benefits, and I try to focus on those rather than the constant attention."

"I honestly don't know how you deal with it."

She smiled slyly. "Don't tell me people don't look at you, Harper, because I don't believe it." Her eyes made a quick sweep up and down. Then, as if she hadn't just blatantly flirted with me and checked me out, Steph picked up her beer and raised it toward me. "Cheers. To both of us surviving my first tennis training session."

I fumbled out a "Cheers" and clinked the bottom of my glass against hers.

Steph drank a healthy mouthful. She sighed deeply, contentedly. "God I love beer." After another smaller sip, she set the glass down and pushed it a little ways away.

"I'm more of a wine drinker, but there's something about a cold beer after a workout that just hits right." I laughed. "Though, it does seem counterproductive to down a pint after working out."

"I don't think so," Steph said, her eyebrows bouncing upward. "A beer is great for rehydrating. Or so I've heard."

"A beer," I said, emphasizing the *a*.

Steph nodded seriously. "Exactly. And *a beer* is what I have right now."

I picked up the thread of probing I'd started before our drinks had been delivered, gesturing to my seat. "So if you would have just sat here where I am, then why not sit here first up?"

The smile playing about her mouth made me sure she knew where I was headed. "Because I prefer to sit where it's harder to recognize me. It's hit and miss, but if I want a modicum of privacy then I need to do as much as I can to avoid being seen."

"I figured, but I wanted to be sure. And I'm not sure you can *not* be seen, Steph." I bit my lip before I said more. Before I said that she was so attractive there was no way she could ever blend in or hide.

"I know, but it's worth a shot." She turned her beer glass around in circles. "I know it's part of the job but sometimes I feel like I'm constantly on guard, especially around people I don't know, or know well. And I hate that. Because I just want to be casual and make jokes, but in the back of my head I'm worried they might not get the joke or maybe they might go tell someone that I don't shower or that I eat mice or something and then suddenly everyone thinks that's a real thing." Her eyes widened. "Just examples of something silly. I do shower, and I do not eat mice."

"I know. Well, I know you shower." She always smelled incredible, a light cologne that made me think of citrus in a cool forest. "But I'm not sure about the eating mice part. I don't know you that well." Despite my teasing, I realized a truth. I didn't know her well, and I didn't like that.

There was always a degree of intimacy between the talent and Hair and Makeup—we kept people's secrets, heard about their lives, talked about ours, every day. But I only knew what Steph let me know, saw what she let me see. And maybe it was all carefully crafted. I dismissed the thought—nobody was that good an actor to pretend 24/7 to be a kind, funny, talented human instead of a pile of garbage. Realizing I maybe didn't know her as much as I wanted to made me suddenly desperate to cross that barrier.

Steph nudged me under the table, bursting my bubble of introspection. "You're funny." The easy expression turned to a frown. "You think you don't know me?"

It felt like we were approaching dangerous territory, but I wasn't afraid. Or maybe I was just dumb. "Not closely. Not...personally." I took a deep breath then took a plunge. "Not the way I'd like to."

Her eyebrows, always so expressive, crinkled inward. "I'm sorry. It's not intentional. I didn't realize and now I feel like shit."

"That's not what I wanted you to feel like at all. I didn't mean it like that."

"No, no, it's not you," she quickly assured me. "It's...it's reinforcing something that's always bothered me."

"And what's that?" I prompted gently.

"I—I don't like feeling apart from people. It's not everyone, but some people make me feel like they don't know how to talk to me and it's hard. Feeling apart." Steph shrugged. "Like at work, how they let the actors go first for meals. I actually hate it." She wrinkled her nose. "Well, actually, I like it because it's the only time I get a full meal break around everything I have to fit into a day and I'm hungry and want to eat. But everyone standing around waiting for us when they're hungry too makes me feel bad. And having to walk through everyone is so...conspicuous. It makes me self-conscious."

"You? Self-conscious?" I barely held in a laugh. "I don't believe you." Steph was the epitome of self-contained confidence.

"It's true!" she insisted, though she kept her voice low enough that we shouldn't be overheard.

I lowered my voice too. "Does having fans bother you?"

"No, of course not," she said instantly. "I think confusion is probably the best description. Intellectually I understand the attraction, but also, I don't think I'm any more special than another actor. I'm just doing my job."

She was so wrong. She was beyond special. "I get it. It's what people see on their screens and they connect with that."

"I know," Steph insisted. "But we all know it's not just the on-screens creating the product. It's the whole cast and crew." Her nose wrinkled. "Ugh, let's not talk about work. Unless you want to."

"I don't need to talk about work, but if it's something that's a problem for you and you need to unpack it, then let's talk about it."

She laughed, but it lacked her usual warmth. "It's fine. I'll bombard my therapist with my mental gymnastics, but thanks."

The original server came back, unobtrusively setting the chips, salsa, and guac between us and refilling our water glasses. She looked from Steph to me, tapping something on a small tablet. "You both ready to order?"

Steph raised an eyebrow at me, and I nodded for her to go first. Steph went with shrimp, achiote chicken, and potato tacos, reading from the menu and pointing at each item as she ordered. This pointing while ordering was another detail about her that was surprisingly thrilling. After tossing up between my favorites I decided on al pastor, baja fish, and carne asada. Steph set the menu in the holder, squaring it up.

"Food'll be out soon," the server assured us before leaving again.

Steph twinkled her fingers over the basket of tortilla chips before selecting one to scoop up a healthy amount of guac. "So, you want to know me better?"

"Yes." I dipped a chip in the salsa and ate it, enjoying the crunch and spicy heat.

"Then we agree on something." She pointed at the salsa. "That good? Your face looks like it's good."

"It's good," I confirmed, trying to parse what she'd said. Did she mean she wanted me to know her better, or that she wanted to get to know me better? Did the nuance really matter?

Steph went for the salsa and after eating a laden chip agreed, "Yeah, it's good." She wiped her fingertips on the paper napkin. "What do you want to know about me?" she asked. The tone was forced casual, and while she'd moderated her voice she forgot to moderate her face. It seemed as if she *wanted* me to ask questions, to dive into things that were important to her, things that made her tick. Maybe not a deep dive, not yet, but I felt sure she wanted to share herself.

I ate a naked chip. "Why acting?" I asked, deeming it an easy slide into getting to know her outside of work.

Steph grinned an easy, charming grin. "My parents tossed me and my younger sister, Kelsey, into acting classes because they were some of the cheapest extracurricular activities close to us. And they thought it might help me with my shyness and awkwardness, which it did." She laughed, and added, "Mostly. And I liked being out of my head for a while, pretending to be someone confident until I really was confident. I think being out of my head and in someone else's is the big thing I love about my job."

Her answer surprised me. "You don't like being in your head?"

Steph blew out a noisy breath. "It can get pretty hectic in here. It's nice to have some time where it's not like a hundred sugar-hyped puppies sprinting around."

"Do dogs actually get sugar highs?" I asked, smiling.

"I actually don't know. But now I want to know." She tapped her temple. "Remind me to Google that."

"Yes, ma'am."

She bit her lower lip, but the edges of her mouth twisted into a smile. "I'm going to hold you to that."

"If you've forgotten to Google and need my reminder, how will you remember to hold me to reminding you?"

Laughing, she rolled her eyes. "I just will." Steph drank a small mouthful of beer and again pushed the glass slightly away from herself. "So, if we're asking about career choices, how'd you end up here, doing this?"

"Promise you won't laugh?"

"No, I can't promise that at all," she said facetiously.

I narrowed my eyes at her, but was foiled by her exaggeratedly cheerful expression, which made me smile. "I was really good with my own makeup in high school, and I liked doing it. I did all my friends' faces for parties, cotillion and debutante balls, weddings, anything like that. Then I started asking for money. And then I started doing it for people I didn't know. It just branched out from there. Got a cosmetology license, did some SFX makeup courses, apprenticed with some amazing artists, got some small jobs, got some bigger jobs. And here I am."

"Oh, I was expecting a funny or weird story. Not just like…a normal story." Steph smirked. "Also, are debutante balls still a thing?"

"They are in Georgia."

Steph nodded. "Noted. I wondered exactly where you'd grown up."

My hometown was a sticky subject, and I hoped she wouldn't ask about it, or try to dig too deeply into my family. I didn't want to ruin a nice day by talking about that. "I've been here long enough that some of my Southernness has fallen away."

"Not all of it. Thankfully there are still little traces," she added.

"Thankfully?"

"Mhmm. I like those little traces. A lot. But if you're worried, which you really shouldn't be, you could always hire a dialect coach," she joked.

Our server politely interrupted to deliver our tacos, saving me from having to think too deeply about the fact Steph clearly thought about me.

Steph immediately picked up her achiote chicken, and her expression of anticipation was strangely arousing. "So hungry," she declared. But instead of digging in, she looked at me. Then looked down at her hand. The hand holding her taco. The hand holding her taco, that she held in front of her breasts. "You're staring at this taco. Want a bite?" She took a big one, a quiet sound of pleasure rumbling from her throat as she chewed.

If only she knew it wasn't the taco I was actually looking at. "Sure. Any of mine look good for you?"

She hmmed. "Maybe the baja?"

I could have cut it, but it was just as easy for her to take a bite. We swapped tacos, and I debated for a millisecond about whether to take a bite from the other end or against where she'd bitten. The other end would ruin the structural integrity, so I just bit the same side as she had.

Steph covered her mouth as she chewed. "Fuck, that's really good." She passed the baja fish back over to me. "Honestly, I'm having a little choice regret and FOMO right now."

"We can come back after our next tennis session and you can try more," I promised. "Or, now you know this place is here, you can come alone."

"Deal." She wiped her hands on a paper napkin and for a moment I thought she might try to shake on it. "But I don't want to come alone."

We finished our first tacos and as Steph picked up her potato one, she asked, "So how long have you been doing this? Working in the industry, not doing makeup for your friends' debutante balls." Her forehead wrinkled, and I knew she was trying to do the math to work out how old I was.

"Almost twelve years." I threw her a bone on my age. "I'm thirty-six."

"Thanks for telling me. I'd already run out of questions to try and figure it out without asking you outright. I'm happy to reciprocate with the telling-our-age thing."

"I know how old you are." Thirty-four. And her thirty-fifth birthday would be in August, which I knew from celebrating it at work.

"Thanks, IMDb," she deadpanned.

"It is a wellspring of important information," I agreed.

"And nonimportant information. Speaking of information…I'm curious why you moved here. Not that I'm not glad. But GA has a serious film industry. You could have stayed and worked there easily."

I fought the urge to fidget. "Wanted a change, I guess. Wanted something different."

"Did you get it?"

I shook my head. "Not really." I used the respite of us swapping bites of potato taco for carne asada to debate if I wanted to elaborate. When I had my steak taco back, I did. "I've never really felt like I fit anywhere. Too much of a lesbian for my hometown. Not really queer enough for the community here." I held back a frown. I was out at work, as in I wasn't in the closet, but I wasn't sure if I'd ever explicitly mentioned my sexuality.

Steph didn't react to my revelation. Or maybe it wasn't actually a revelation. "What do you mean?"

"I think the South is pretty self-explanatory." Steph nodded as she worked on her taco, and I continued, "But I don't know. I don't do big Pride things. I'm not out and about in the LGBTQ-plus scene. Maybe it's just remnants from where I grew up, but yeah…" I shrugged helplessly. It made it hard to feel comfortable in some relationships, almost like I didn't quite deserve it if I wasn't out proudly shouting my sexuality from rooftops.

"You don't need to go to Pride to be a lesbian, or any shade of queer."

"No, of course, I know that. But, you know…"

Her eyes softened. "I know. You're a quiet queer and that's totally valid and okay." She opened her mouth then closed it again when a man, probably in his very-early twenties, came over from a few tables away and paused by us.

He walked a few steps past the table then backtracked. Though he was behind Steph, her body language and expression made it clear she knew he was there. He stopped to her right, and it was obvious he wanted to approach her but was nervous as heck about it. I kept my eyes on Steph and she met my gaze. She looked like she wanted to evaporate.

The stranger cleared his throat. "Hey…sorry to bug you," he said quietly. When Steph turned to face him, his voice gained a little volume and courage. "I feel kinda weird asking. But…Are you…Stephanie D'Arripe?"

She nodded, smiling warmly, kindly. "I am."

Her confirmation seemed to give him even more courage. "I love you on *North Precinct*." The red on his cheeks was joined by red on his ears.

"Aw, thank you." Steph's smile remained in place, but her body had taken on some tension. "What's your name?"

"Nick."

"Thanks so much, Nick, that's really sweet. I'm so glad you enjoy the show."

He held up his phone. "Could I like…get a selfie with you? And maybe an autograph?"

Her smile transformed. It was still warm and kind, and I could tell that now she was absolutely forcing it. "Nick, I'd love to oblige, but I'm just having a private conversation with my friend here, so I'd ask people to please respect my personal time."

She somehow managed to make it sound apologetic without actually saying sorry, and yet it somehow came across as unapologetic too. I could see how the tone would make the fan realize that now wasn't the time. They'd probably feel contrite without feeling like she'd been rude or made them feel awful for approaching. And by saying "people" not "you," Steph made it seem like she wasn't just saying no to them personally— she'd say no to everyone. It was masterful. Clearly this wasn't the first time this had happened.

The fan could not apologize fast enough. "Sure, of course! Sorry, I didn't mean to interrupt. Sorry," he said again, wilting just a little.

"No worries. Thanks for watching. And enjoy your tacos!" Steph said cheerfully. She turned slightly away without turning her back completely on the stranger, and the guy smiled, nodded, and then left us. As soon as we were alone again, Steph caught my eye. The edges of her mouth lifted with the ghost of a smile. "Now it's time for me to say sorry," she said quietly.

"No problem." I wanted to nudge her out of the strange mood she was in, but wasn't quite sure how. "Honestly I'm surprised it took this long."

"Mmm." She turned her beer glass in a circle, her fingers tapping against it. Steph surreptitiously looked around before she finally picked it up and drank some of her beer. She wiped her mouth slowly, folded the napkin on the table, then finally met my eyes again. "Every time someone asks me if I'm Stephanie D'Arripe, some ridiculous part of me just wants to say 'No, who's that?' and hope they just accept it."

The image made me laugh. "Yeah, I don't think anyone would. Steph, you're…" I fumbled for the right descriptor. "Distinctive. Your face and voice are pretty recognizable."

Recognizable *was* right, but it wasn't the only descriptor I'd apply to those attributes. Unfortunately I didn't know if I should verbalize the descriptors I wanted to use, like gorgeous and sexy and memorable, right now.

Her mouth twitched. "Thanks."

"You're welcome." I picked up the taco I'd set down during the fan thing. "Do you always decline?" I'd been surprised that it'd taken this long into our time together for her to be approached. I'd noticed a few people looking briefly at her while we played tennis, but that was it.

She shrugged. After another glance around, she leaned in, lowering her voice. "I have rules. If I'm outside, like walking around in public then yeah, fine, that's fair game. If I'm walking around a store, grocery shopping or something, it's fifty-fifty, mostly depending on how they approach me. But if I'm sitting down with a drink or food and I have a friend with me then that's a one hundred percent no. This is my personal time, with you, and I want you to have all my attention." Steph grinned. "As much attention as I can give you around those interruptions."

I was both grateful and pleased that she made me a priority. No, she didn't make *me* a priority, she made time with people she knew a priority and I was just a person she knew. "I appreciate that. But I don't want you to feel like you have to turn people away because you think I'll get annoyed. I won't get annoyed."

"I don't think that," Steph assured me. "Plus, you know, being interrupted when I've got a mouthful of tacos is kind of problematic."

Laughing, I agreed, "I could see that. It's just that people want to connect with you." *I* wanted to connect with her, but not as a fan.

Her eyebrow bounce conveyed how she felt about that. "Believe me, I know. And I *love* connecting with fans. But...I want it to be comfortable for all parties involved, and that doesn't make me comfortable. Feeling like a commodity isn't nice. I get enough of that in my professional life. And some of them get weird about me eating and talking, like they're trying to force me into being Amy in real life for some weird kink thing." She grimaced. "Sorry, this conversation has become about work after all. And it's turned into a bit of a bummer."

"No it hasn't," I assured her. I carefully chose a chip to scoop up some salsa and used the time chewing to think of how to word what I wanted to say. "I'm...grateful that you're sharing this with me."

"Sharing?"

"Yeah. You know." I suddenly regretted starting this line of conversation, but Steph's expression made it clear she wasn't going to let me let it go. So I plunged ahead. "Like friends share things."

"Friends..." she said slyly. "Harper, are you saying you want to be my friend?"

My heart thumped hard and fast at her words, and the teasing grin that accompanied her words. "Yes. I am."

"Good." Steph winked. God. That wink. I swear she could get me to do anything she wanted just by winking at me. "I'm saying that too."

Before we could dive into the new potential dynamic of our friendship, a woman, maybe late twenties, came charging over like she'd just seen her best friend. "Excuse me?"

Steph hastily swallowed the bite of taco she'd just taken, wiped her mouth, and turned around. "Yes?"

"You're Stephanie D'Arripe, right?"

"I am, yep," Steph confirmed, smiling.

"*Huge* fan," the woman gushed. "Amy Spicer is a badass. Can you sign something for me? Can I get a pic with you?" She held out her phone toward me, like she expected me to take the picture for her.

I held back a laugh at the fan's audacity. Until I saw Steph's expression.

Steph's response was the same one she'd given to the previous fan, though she seemed far less accommodating than she had been for the guy. I wondered why the slight change in approach between the two. But as soon as she'd finished the spiel, she looked expectantly at the woman, whose expression had been going through every shade from excitement right through to anger. And then I knew why—Steph had clearly seen something I hadn't.

"But thanks so much for watching," Steph added calmly.

The woman sneered. "Well...fuck you too. You know you're only famous because of fans," she spat out. Before Steph could respond, she'd stalked away, muttering to herself. Some of the other patrons stared at her, then glanced at Steph. And thank god, all of them decided it was none of their business or not worth their time and went back to their food.

Bright-red spots blossomed on each of Steph's cheeks. She looked like she was simultaneously trying to calm herself and work out what to say. After ten seconds or so, she looked up. Steph smiled tightly. "Well. *That* reaction is always a possibility too."

"Does it happen a lot?"

"Maybe...two or three in every ten. Today was just the unlucky day it happened in front of someone I really didn't want it to happen in front of." She took a deep, steadying breath. When she met my gaze again, her eyes burned with sincerity. "I'm so sorry, Harper."

"You don't need to be sorry. Unless those people were plants to impress me with your fame."

She laughed, some of the tension in her shoulders dissipating. "No."

"Good." I reached over and lightly touched her hand. "Because I already know how great you are."

CHAPTER SEVEN

Steph

After the second fan encounter at the restaurant, the mood had dimmed a little. It was mostly my fault, because as much as I tried not to let the woman's attitude affect me, it did. Harper had been sweetly understanding, asking if I was all right but not pushing when I said I was. Because I *was* all right, in the scheme of things. But I'd never quite gotten used to people saying shit about me, especially to my face.

When I'd sat down for makeup on Monday morning, it was almost as if we hadn't spent any time together outside of work. And that bothered me. I'd expected there to be a little more familiarity at work between Harper and me after our time together on Saturday. Sure, she'd been as friendly as ever when I came in, but now, friendly somehow didn't feel like enough. I didn't know if I should ask if I'd done something wrong—though what, I had no idea—or just accept that she was making a clear distinction between these aspects of her life.

Maybe I should do the same. But I'd never been great at doing that, which was hilarious given how much I compartmentalized in my professional life. In the fifteen years since I'd moved to LA from Iowa, I'd had too much fucking around, people dancing around the truth, or flat-out lying to me. I didn't want any of that shit in my personal life if I could avoid it.

So if I didn't want to dance around the truth, why hadn't I just told her how I really felt? That I enjoyed being with her. That I felt safe with her. That the flirting wasn't just me being gregarious or trying to get on her good side (every side was her good side, she was magnificent from all angles). It was me clumsily trying to tell her I found her attractive, that I was interested in her, romantically.

The flipside of that romantic attraction was that I still felt like I was figuring out where I fit in the dating world. *If* I could fit in it, after Jordan had yanked out my heart, stomped all over it with her Martine Rose stilettos, then punted it down Mulholland Drive.

Wow, did you take a little hyperbole with your morning coffee this morning, Steph?

I sat quietly as Harper went about getting me ready, silently working myself up into a fizz. I'd gone too far on Saturday with my flirting. And what kind of idiot asks if someone wants to be their friend? Let's go on a playdate, Harper. Wanna see my toys, Harper? You wanna sleep over, Harper? God. *Idiot.*

I should have just asked her if I could kiss her—that probably would have been less mortifying. At least I'd know where I stood. Eventually I came to the conclusion that I'd read way too much into the whole afternoon. She was just helping me with the tennis thing because that's the kind of person Harper Bell was.

A light hand touched my shoulder. "Close your eyes," Harper said quietly. I complied as she sprayed my face with makeup-setting spray. She touched me again, my hand this time. "You're all set."

I opened my eyes, surprised by how close she still was—usually she'd moved away by the time I opened my eyes. I rushed out a "Thanks," embarrassed that my voice betrayed how affected I was by Harper's proximity. She was the only person who managed to sneak underneath the calm, confident exterior I kept up at work. "See you soon."

I popped up out of her chair and left before I made an even bigger fool of myself.

Shooting was rushing by and we were making great time. The extra, Jill I think it was (don't judge me, my brain is a very busy place and I knew her character's name, which was the important thing) sobbed. "I didn't mean to do it. I didn't want him to think I was a rude bitch but he just wouldn't listen to me saying no. So I bit him...you know...on his junk. He fell backward and hit his head and he just—" Her sobbing reached a crescendo as she wrapped the gray blanket more tightly around herself.

I made my voice as gentle as I could while still keeping a little steel in it. "Hey, hey…listen to me, Sara. You did the right thing. Would you rather be called a rude bitch and still be alive, or be dead because you didn't want to offend him?"

She nodded slowly. The corners of her mouth lifted ever so slightly. "Right," she said tremulously. "I'd rather be alive."

Smiling, I agreed, "I'd rather that too." I patted her shoulder, withdrawing instantly when she flinched. "Come on, let's get you checked out. Then, if you're up for it, you can talk me through what happened."

She bit her lower lip. "Can you come with me?"

"Of course." I smiled, making sure my eyes joined in. "I'll be there with you the whole time."

Could Be Jill wiped underneath her eyes. She nodded, loudly whispering, "Thank you."

"Cut."

I exhaled noisily. The emotion and energy in the scene had felt good, which was great, but also left me as tightly wound as Amy.

The extra smiled up at me. "Thanks," she murmured.

I made sure my smile was friendly and open and didn't reflect my jangling emotions. "Backatcha."

Monty came over, beaming so brightly he could have lit the set. "Loved it, loved you guys, love that we're going to keep the same high for our next takes. Jill"—yes! I was right!—"that emotion, oof. You got me. And, Steph, fabulous balance there. Let's go again." After a paternal shoulder pat for both of us, Monty went back to sit in video village.

We did another few takes before it was time for a break while the crew set up the "squad room" for the next scene. I settled myself in the quiet, out-of-the-way corner everyone unofficially called Steph's Sanctuary, with a bottle of water and my script. I reread the notes I'd made on the pages and mentally rehearsed the scene until they needed me.

After about ten minutes, a shadow came over me and I looked up, expecting Kayla making sure I was hydrated and checking if I needed anything, or maybe Jared wanting to shoot the shit or rant about something meaningless to blow off steam.

But it was Harper. And that made me more pleased than I'd thought seeing one person could. "Hey."

"Hey yourself."

Though I'd talked with her only a few hours ago—if our quick public small talk while she worked on me could be called talking—her proximity made my chest feel warm. "Touch-ups already?" A big part of me hoped she was just here because she wanted to be here, not because she'd been sent to make sure I'd be ready for the next scene.

"No, not yet."

"Ah. Then what's up?" Now I was sure she was here because she wanted to hang out with me. Hell yes.

"Nothin'." She was just a little too casual, too forced, but I couldn't figure out what would elicit that sort of demeanor. And despite my certainty that she wanted to just spend time with me, her response felt kind of flat and made me rethink that certainty.

So I went with a standard fallback—joking or teasing. Anything to try to find the Harper I knew. The Harper I really enjoyed spending time with, in any context, working or not. "Ah. So you just *happened* to find yourself here, in my special quiet place, that's not near any thoroughfare? The place that's pretty out of the way of almost everything, actually."

A faint blush covered her cheeks. Harper raised her chin, affecting an imperious air, though the edges of her mouth quirked as she told me, "It is purely coincidental that I happen to find myself here with you."

"Mmm." I leaned closer. "Careful, Harper. I might start thinking you like me or something."

The blush deepened. After an eternal pause, she murmured, "I think that's a fairly safe bet. As I'm sure you know."

Having her confirm it sent a rush of excitement through me. "I do know. But it's always nice to hear it." I rested an elbow on the arm of the chair and twisted toward her. "So, you came over just to tell me that?"

"Not intentionally."

"Ah, but you did come over to tell me *something*?" Like how you've noticed the chemistry between us that seemed to have taken steroids the last week or so? Because I really want to talk about that, Harper. The problem with wanting to talk about it was I just didn't know when I was going to find time outside of work, because it was not something to talk about in a place full of ears.

"Yeah," she finally admitted. Then in the next breath, she added, "I just…don't want to bother you."

"Do I seem bothered?"

That pulled a small grin from her. "No. You rarely seem bothered. *But* you're working right now."

Smiling, I made a vague gesture. "Right now, I'm waiting to be working." And it wasn't like we'd never chatted before or between takes while she was doing touch-ups. I pulled a chair closer, patting it to entice her. "Have a seat. What did you want to talk about?"

Harper took her time getting herself settled next to me, fussing with the fanny packs around her waist so they weren't in her way. I waited patiently, aware that she was stalling. The potential reason for her stalling made me nervous, though I doubted she'd do or say anything troublesome, especially not between shooting.

When she finally spoke, her words surprised me. "I just wanted to check that you're okay. After Saturday."

"Of course I am." I rolled my right shoulder, testing for stiffness. There was none. "Should I be sore from tennis?"

"No. I mean, maybe? If you don't work out at all ever, which I know you do." She leaned closer, lowering her voice, not that anyone was nearby. "I mean, what happened at the restaurant. You said it was fine, but…it didn't feel very fine."

"Ohhhh, that." I'd employed my usual brain trick and set it out of my mind the moment I stepped out of the building. Years ago, I'd have let it fester, poisoning my mood for a few days. My whole body melted at her compassionate expression. She looked like she wanted to gather up all my upsets and carry them herself so I wouldn't have to deal with them. "I am, yeah." Unable to resist, I reached over and squeezed her hand. "Thanks for checking."

Harper glanced down at our hands. "No problem. I just wanted to be sure. I don't want to keep bringing it up, but it was really shitty. And I felt bad for you."

I shrugged and let her hand go, not wanting to force her to hold mine, or have anyone see us and start a rumor. "Like I said Saturday, it happens. I have strategies to deal with it in the moment and for my mental health afterward. And honestly? It was a tiny blip of unpleasantness in an otherwise spectacularly great day."

She took a few moments to absorb what I'd said. "Okay, if you're sure…"

"I am sure, but yeah, thank you for checking up on me. Not that I needed the confirmation that you're the sweetest, but you really are."

I was called to set, which cut off Harper's response. Maybe that was for the best. But her pleased expression was enough.

I raised my script. "Guess that's me."

"And me."

I stood first and offered my hand, though she didn't actually need it, and relief flooded me when she took it and stood. Something passed between us, but it was gone so quickly I didn't have time to dissect what it meant. All I knew was that it felt good, felt safe. And it'd been a while since I'd felt safe like this with another person.

Her expectant look made me blurt, "But we can chat more about this later?"

Harper exhaled loudly. "I'd like that."

We didn't chat about it later. Not that I really wanted to have a conversation that could turn super personal at work, but I *did* want to have the conversation. Unfortunately, work kept getting in the way and there was no quiet time for the rest of the day. When I wrapped, I thought I might grab Harper and suggest maybe we go for a coffee—decaf for her—or something and finish that talk, but I couldn't find her.

After checking all logical spots, I headed toward the parking lot. I hadn't given up on talking, but running around the lot for an hour looking for her when she'd probably left already was pointless when I could just text her. Maybe we could meet somewhere now for a chat and a drink or something. Five thirty-ish was still plenty early enough for civilized meetups.

As I walked, I opened up WhatsApp. I'd tapped out a few words when I realized the object of my thoughts was waiting for me. Kind of. Maybe. Okay, on closer inspection—not at all. A few spaces over from my car, Harper sat in the driver's seat of her Kia. She threw her hands up, then leaned forward to rest her forehead on the steering wheel. I diverted toward her and tapped lightly on the rear window so I wouldn't startle her. I still startled her, but she flashed me a tired smile then opened her door.

I asked a stupid question. "What's up?"

"My goddamned car won't start."

"Oh no. Does it usually throw tantrums about working?" I asked, trying for a little levity to cut through her frustration. Clearly now wasn't the time for Our Talk, and I wasn't sure if I was relieved or upset about it. It wasn't that I really wanted to rehash the whole "how Steph feels about rude fans and interruptions," but I *did* want to have a conversation with her that went beyond superficial. Something that might open the door for more serious conversations.

"No," she groaned. Harper turned it over again, and the car made a sickly attempt at a rev before spluttering to a stop. "But today, it *is* throwing a huge tantrum."

I set my bags down. "Pop the hood."

After flashing me a dubious look, she did, then stood and leaned her forearms on the top of the driver's side door. I fumbled for a few moments until I figured out how to open and prop the hood up, then peered into the engine bay, resting my hands on the edge. Nodding, I confirmed to myself that yup, it looked like a car engine.

Harper came to stand beside me, her hip brushing mine. "You know about cars?"

"A little." I was trying to impress her, and didn't want to admit that the *little* I knew was how to put fuel in mine and then drive it to the dealership for regular maintenance. My lack of automotive knowledge made my father cringe, and despite his best efforts to teach me the basics of car maintenance, my brain was staunchly resistant. "But not enough to diagnose whatever the heck is wrong with this one." I straightened up, dusting my hands off. "Sorry."

"Oh. Damn."

I bit back a grin. "I was hoping staring at the engine would magically impart car knowledge into my brain and make me look cool, but no such luck."

She closed the hood. "For the record, you did look cool." Her next breath came out as a sigh. "I guess I need to call Triple-A." Harper covered her face with both hands, muttering something under her breath. The only thing I could make out was a frustrated, "Perfect."

"I can take you home," I said without thinking.

Harper dropped her hands away from her face. "Oh...it's fine, but thanks." She waved dismissively. "I can just wait for Triple-A."

"Here? In the dark? Alone?"

She raised an eyebrow. "It's not dark yet. And with all the security and other shows' crew around and nobody without a lot badge or vetted pass allowed here? Yes."

I tried a different tactic. "Triple-A will take forever to get here, maybe hours. Plural. That means more than just one."

Harper's mouth twitched, but she held back the smile. "Yes, I know what plural means."

"Good, I knew you weren't just a pretty face." Christ. Why the fuck did I just say that? I rushed to cover my slip-up, blurting, "Hours is ages, especially after work. So, come on, I'll drive you home."

Harper rubbed the side of her neck with her fingertips. "But then I'll still have to get Triple-A to come check my car tomorrow..."

"Oh for sure. But you can organize it so it's during the day and your car will be ready to drive home after work. And if it needs towing, I can give you a ride again."

Harper laughed. "You're not good with being told 'no, thanks,' are you?" Thankfully her tone made it clear she wasn't bothered by my insistence.

"I'm an actor. I'm *excellent* at being told no," I deadpanned.

"I find it hard to believe people say no to you," she said, and the teasing drawl had goose bumps popping up over my skin.

I only just held back an incredulous laugh. I'd heard "no" so many times in my life I could sense a *no* coming a mile away. "You're kind of doing it right now, and I'm not sure why, but you don't have to."

Harper hesitated, but I could see common sense winning. Thankfully, because while I was great at persuasion, I also wanted to go home and spending ten minutes arguing back and forth wasn't my idea of a great end to my day. Driving Harper home was. Her expression softened, gratitude and relief mixing with pleasure. "Okay, thanks. That would be great. Gimme a minute to grab my stuff?"

I pointed to my Land Rover Defender. "I'll be over there, when you're ready."

She nodded and I grabbed my bags and rushed to my car to make sure I hadn't left anything I didn't want Harper to see on the seat or in the footwell. I wasn't prone to leaving old smoothie cups or dirty dry-cleaning in my car. Much. But it'd been a full-on few weeks of work and my brain function was not allocated to things like everyday living.

Harper climbed up into the passenger seat and set her bags on the floor.

"Right. Where to?"

She gave me an address in the NoHo Arts District then added a quiet, "Thanks again."

"You're welcome."

We made a quick stop by Security to tell them Harper's car would be there overnight so they didn't go looking for her, thinking she'd passed out somewhere. As I pulled out of the lot, she said, "This is a great car."

"Thanks." I didn't know whether to say more, or to just leave it. But I hated silences, and this one felt like it could easily move into awkwardness. "My dad's British, so old Land Rovers were a staple of my childhood." Laughing, I admitted, "He *hates* this one though. Hates all the newer models. Says they got too soft-looking, all smooth lines and curves instead of hard edges able to tackle anything. Whatever that means."

"So why'd you get this one then?"

"Tradition. And for when I find time to go camping. And sometimes I get the urge to go off-roading." I paused, wondering if I should elaborate. "Camping, off-roading, hiking, fishing...all that outdoorsy stuff is kind of a big deal in my family."

"And you go do all that stuff alone now? Or does your family visit?"

"They don't visit, no. It's too hard to coordinate with work. I spend some time with them during hiatus and we pack *so much* outdoors into that time. But when I'm home it's go outdoors alone or not at all." I cleared my throat, uncomfortable with how it felt. I'd tried to get ex-girlfriends interested in outdoors adventures, or even just basic outdoors activities, but every attempt had failed.

"Outdoorsy stuff is great," Harper enthused.

"It sure is." I made a mental note to invite her on some hikes. Maybe camping later, once we knew each other better. "Plus I'm prepared, you know, for when The Big One hits and all the roads are ruined from the earthquake and undrivable unless you have a four-wheel drive." I glanced at her and winked, gratified to see she was watching me, smiling indulgently.

I had a sudden, probably irrational, fear that I was talking too much. About pointless things. Maybe she'd just agreed that we could have our talk later to be polite, and she didn't really want to and that's why she was fleeing work without coming to find me when we'd wrapped.

Nervous sweat cooled my armpits. "We don't have to chat. We can be quiet if you need time after work to decompress. Or you know, you can look at your phone."

"I know I can. But it'd be awfully rude of me to sit here silently while you drive me home. Like me treating you like a chauffeur or something."

I waved dismissively. "Just pretend I'm an Uber driver and you've chosen the 'prefers quiet' option when booking the ride."

"Wait, what? No, but I always say 'conversation please' when I order an Uber."

"Oh my god, seriously?"

"Seriously."

I blew out a loud breath, pushing myself back into the seat. "I'm so talked out day to day that I take every opportunity I can to be silent."

"Ah. So is this your polite way of telling me that it's *you* who doesn't want conversation with *me*?" she asked, but underneath her dry tone was an edge of worry.

I reached over and patted her thigh. "No. I promise. I just don't want you to be uncomfortable."

Harper looked down at my hand, then turned to face me. "I'm never uncomfortable with you, Steph," she said quietly. After a few seconds, she added, "But I *am* curious. How did a British man end up in Iowa?"

After removing my hand, which had stayed there of its own volition, I raised an eyebrow at her. "How'd you know I'm from Iowa?"

Her smile was so charming I wasn't even bothered that she'd obviously done research beyond a glance at IMDb. "Same way I know Laura's grandparents came to California from Mexico. You're my coworkers, so I read articles and interviews."

The thought made me feel warm, until I remembered she'd just said *coworkers*. She paid attention to everyone's press. I wasn't special. And that thought was actually upsetting. I shoved it into a deep, dark part of my consciousness. "He was a visiting lecturer at an agricultural college, talking about their farming practices. My mom was a receptionist at the college. Love at first sight, apparently."

"That might be the sweetest thing I've heard in a good while."

"Yeah, they're kind of adorable together. So you know about my parents." I snuck a look at her. "How about yours?"

A faint hint of unease crossed Harper's face before she answered. "My mama was a dentist. And after his grand pro-sportsperson ambitions imploded, my dad worked for the local government."

"Was? Worked? Did your parents retire early, or…" Though Harper was about my age, it was obviously possible her parents were older than mine, and I felt silly for mentioning retirement. I decided not to run a yellow and coasted to a stop at the lights so I could face her.

She shook her head. "My dad died about ten years ago. And my mother was in an accident that damaged some nerves in her hand, so she can't work anymore."

"Ah, damn. I'm so sorry about your dad. Are you close with your mom? Do you have siblings?"

"One. An older sister." Harper cleared her throat. "I'm, uh…no, I'm not really close with my family."

My heart sank. "I'm really sorry."

Her mouth turned up slightly in one of those smiles designed to appease people rather than convey any sort of happiness. "Thanks."

Things weren't exactly stilted for the rest of the drive, but I couldn't shake the feeling that I'd somehow unintentionally stuck my foot in things. I pulled up outside a light-salmon colored Spanish-style apartment building and Harper directed me into her parking space. I turned on the interior light and Harper began gathering up her things.

"Do you need a ride in the morning?" Stupid question. Of course she did. It wasn't like she could teleport to work.

She twisted on the seat toward me. "No, it's fine, thanks. I'll grab an Uber or beg my roommate to take me." There was something that sounded like a grimace in the second option.

"I can come by and get you."

"Oh no," she said quickly, almost tripping over those two words in her haste to decline. "It's fine."

"Seriously, I don't mind."

Harper narrowed her eyes at me. "Why are you being so insistent?" It was like she couldn't compute that anyone would do something just because it was right. Or maybe it was just me she couldn't believe would do that, which was a whole other problem.

"Because I haven't hit my acts of charity quota for the month," I said facetiously.

She coughed out a dry laugh. "I see. So…I'm a charity case?"

I flashed my best smile, and chose to ignore the minefield she was leading me to, the minefield where I might blow up this tentative friendship by trying to be too charming and funny. "We're both going to the same place. We have to be there around the same time. Isn't it logical that you ride with me?"

The best part about early call times was that traffic was only mildly fucked instead of completely fucked. So going slightly out of my way to pick Harper up wasn't *too* diabolical. And even if it was, I didn't mind because it was her.

"It is logical, but I have to be on set earlier than you and you're going to have to wake up even earlier and then even earlier again to detour to my place from…wherever you live."

"Glendale," I said.

"Okay, so a *complete* pain in the ass, going the opposite way detour." She fretted. "Why didn't you tell me where you lived before you drove me home?"

Her attempt to put me off with LA's horrendous traffic wasn't really working. "Because I wasn't bothered. Look. Harper. I'm nice, but I'm not that nice." Laughing, I explained, "If I didn't have an early call time, I wouldn't be offering to take you in tomorrow morning. I love working out at the gym on set, but I love sleep even more."

She countered instantly. "Yeah. The only reason I didn't tell you 'absolutely not' is because I know you have an early call time. There's no way I'd let you pick me up if you didn't have to be in 'til way later."

"Exactly. Listen, if you can organize your own ride then that's fine, but I'm offering because I genuinely want to help out if I can." I wasn't exactly sure why. I mean, yeah, I was a nice fucking person. And yeah, I believed in karmic give-and-take. But there was something deeper than just that. Something I didn't want to admit to myself because that meant I might have to do something about my emotional well-being.

She finally gave in. "Sure, okay. A ride in the morning would be great. Thanks. And thanks again for this ride. I appreciate it all."

"You're welcome." I smirked. "That wasn't that hard, was it?"

"Excruciating, actually." She pushed open the car door. "Thanks again. I appreciate it."

"Anytime. Sleep well. See you at…about 4:40 tomorrow morning?"

She smiled wearily. "I'll be here. With bells on."

CHAPTER EIGHT

Harper

Per wasn't home, and neither was his gym bag. Good for him. I wished I had a fraction of his dedication to bodily perfection, though I supposed if I got paid to look like a Greek god I'd view working out with more excitement instead of resignation. I opened the fridge ready to get dinner started, and realized we were low on almond milk. Per could pick some up on the way home, if he wasn't already onto it.

To be safe, I'd text him. No almond milk was a big issue at our place. There was just one problem with texting him… I couldn't find my phone.

I'd patted down all my pockets, checked my bags, and done a walkthrough of the house when I finally accepted that I really didn't have my phone. "Perfect," I muttered. "This is just perfect." Dead car. No phone. I was done with annoyance for the day.

I closed my eyes, trying to picture leaving work. I knew I had it when I'd said bye to everyone, because Nina had sent me a reel on Instagram as I was walking out. And I had it when I'd realized my car wouldn't start, because I'd picked it up ready to call Triple-A. So I'd either left it in my car, lost it between Steph dropping me off and walking to my door, or left it in Steph's car.

I pictured the drive home. When Steph made the comment about me looking at my phone, I'd set it in the storage compartment on the passenger door, totally intending to grab it as I got out of the car. I couldn't remember grabbing it, but I also couldn't remember *not* grabbing it.

I retraced my steps back to the curb, and from the curb to my door and inside. No phone. Someone could have picked it up in the few minutes since I'd arrived home but before I started panicking, I opened up my MacBook and brought up Find My. My phone wasn't at work or around my building.

But it *was* moving. Away from my house, toward the 134...toward Glendale. It was too much of a coincidence and I chose to believe Steph had it instead of some stranger that'd nabbed it from the sidewalk then booked it out of here in the same direction Steph would be driving. I didn't expect her to bring it back but wanted to ask her to take it into her house to keep it safe overnight before she picked me up tomorrow morning.

The big problem with that, of course, was I couldn't call her because she had my phone. I didn't have a landline, and even if I did, I was embarrassed that I was such a millennial that I didn't actually know Steph's number. It was on my phone. Which seemed to be in Steph's car. Ah, but I did have WhatsApp on my Mac.

I brought up the app. Which had to update, because I never used it on my laptop. And then I had to sign in, see above with the never using it. And then it had to sync or something. After way too long, it was finally ready for me to make the call.

Steph answered almost immediately with a "Hello?" that was both excited and cautious.

"Steph, hi, it's Harper."

She laughed. "I know, thanks to the big *Harper Bell* that flashed on my screen and was also announced by my handsfree dealio."

"Funny. Hey listen, I'm pretty sure I left my phone in your car."

"What? How? Where?" Each question rose in intensity, like my lost phone was the worst thing she'd been part of all day.

"Probably because I was distracted, and probably somewhere near where I was sitting? I really don't know but I feel like I remember putting it in the door storage compartment?"

"What exactly were you distracted by?"

You. All you. How hot you are. How sweet you were about Mama and Dad. Did I mention how hot you are? "Uh. Just...worrying about my car not starting. You know. Things. Boring stuff."

"I see. Gimme a moment." The sound of an indicator came through the call, then loud scuffling. "Yup, it's in the door. I'll turn around now and bring it back."

I hurried to stop her. "No. It's fine, as long as I know where it is. You can just bring it to me in the morning. But if you could just take it inside overnight, I'd be grateful."

"I can't leave you without a car *and* a phone," she teased.

I'd already seen where arguing with her about her helping or going out of her way got me—nowhere. So I acquiesced. "Thank you. You're a goddess."

Steph laughed loudly. "I've been called many things, but never that."

"I find that very hard to believe."

"Mmm." There was a pause, a quiet throat clearing. "See you soon."

We said goodbye, and I ducked into the bathroom to check I looked okay. Even as I fluffed my hair and inspected my face I realized how ridiculous it was. She'd literally just seen me and I hadn't been at all worried about how I looked. And all I was doing was meeting her in my parking space, and grabbing my phone.

Or so I thought. When I reached the arched wrought iron gate to my apartment complex, Steph stood on the other side. She held up my phone and with an eyebrows-raised, Amy Spicer expression said, "I believe you abandoned this device in my vehicle?"

Laughing at her silliness, I unlocked the gate. She handed me my phone.

"Thank you," I said emphatically, clutching it against my chest. "You really didn't have to bring it back, but I'm really grateful you did."

"You're very welcome. How did you call me without a phone?"

"Laptop."

"Ohhh. Right. Smart. Of course." Steph stifled a yawn. "Fuck. Sorry." She rubbed her face. "I'm tired and hungry, which makes me really dumb."

"What have you eaten today?"

Her expression blanked for a moment before her entire face scrunched up adorably. "Um."

"If you have to think about it, it's not enough." My concern peaked. Maybe that's why I spoke without thinking. "Why don't you come inside? I'll cook you dinner, you can relax for a while before you go home." I leaned against the edge of the gate and quickly gave her an easy out. "But if you just want to go home and crash then obviously that's totally fine." I knew the moment I'd said it that the idea of being fed appealed to her. I could also tell her innate politeness was pushing into her decision-making process, and she was about to decline.

"I—"

"Don't be polite," I said firmly. Then I smiled to soften my words. "I'm offering because I want to help you."

"Then yes. That would be great." She exhaled loudly. "Thanks. I was going to get a drive-thru something on the way home just so I'd survive the drive, but I so did not feel like seeing 'Stephanie D'Arripe loves In-N-Out' on TMZ or something tomorrow, along with a picture of me drooling as they pass me the bag through the window, or me stuffing my face as I peel out of there after spending half an hour of my life in a line."

Laughing, I assured her, "I'm sure you'd even look great in a picture of you drooling or shoving things in your mouth."

Steph opened her mouth, then closed it just as fast. I was desperate to know what she'd been about to say, but quickly realized I'd added more innuendo than I'd meant to, which was no innuendo.

"Come on, let's get you fed." Once inside, I kicked off my shoes. "I'll get started on dinner. Tofu okay with you?" Neither Per or I were vegetarian, but tofu was quick and easy, and had enough protein to keep Per quiet.

Oh shit. Per.

I'd totally forgotten about him. Maybe he'd be late home from the gym and Steph would be gone. Of course not—the universe was totally going to mess with me. I would have texted him and told him not to rush home, maybe lied a little that my day had run long, so keep building his muscles for a while. A long while. But he had a rigid workout and rest schedule and wouldn't stay back at the gym even if there was a year's free protein on offer.

Steph nodded. "Absolutely. Can I help?"

"I'm sure you can. But you don't need to." This meal was easy, and she'd just be hanging around watching me cook, and being bored. The thought of us in the kitchen together, playing at being domestic, was appealing though. "Chill out on the couch. TV remote will be there somewhere. Make yourself at home."

She smiled the smile I rarely saw. And now that I thought about it, had only ever seen used around me. Maybe she smiled at other people, other...*friends* the same way, but I'd never seen this smile at work. I *had* seen it during our tennis practice session and while we ate tacos after. When directed at me, that smile made me feel like I was the only person who mattered. "I'll catch up on some social media chores then. But let me know if you need help."

"I won't, but thanks." I paused. "Just checking, any dietary restrictions? Hard no-goes?" I'd worked in the business for long enough to know how diligent most actors were with their diets. Steph ate plenty, but it was always heavy on the leafy greens and lean proteins and light on the sugary and delicious. When we'd been out for food after tennis, she'd left some of each taco. Yeah, okay, clearly I paid far too much attention to her.

"Nope. I eat whatever I want. Just"—she wrinkled her nose comically—"not as much as I want. It's tedious. But..." Steph shrugged, forcing a smile. "Part of the job."

"Then you can serve yourself whatever you want to eat. And I can do a batch of cauliflower rice as well as rice-rice."

"Thanks," she said quietly. "Appreciate it."

"What would you gorge yourself on if it was consequence-free?"

Steph didn't hesitate for a second. "String cheese. It's disgusting, but I fucking love it. Kayla rations it for me otherwise I'd eat the whole pack. And probably get myself into a weird crazed string cheese state and force her to go empty out the stores of all string cheese. Pizza. Also soft-serve ice cream, I'd eat it all day. And fries. Who doesn't love fries?"

"I don't think anyone doesn't love fries." I made a mental note to get some string cheese, in case she ever came around to just hang out. Hang out... I couldn't *quite* picture us being here watching a movie or something, but it also didn't feel completely out of the realm of possibility. "Is it the taste of the cheese you love, or do you like playing with it?"

She grinned. "Both."

"So noted." I opened the fridge. "And how do you feel about garlic?"

"I love it." Now her forehead wrinkled. "And I'm free to love it tonight. No kissing at work tomorrow."

I smiled, and hoped she couldn't tell how forced it was. Kissing. I thought of a few answers to that, mostly just teasing like "Lucky you" or "Unlucky you" but I honestly didn't know how she felt about intimate scenes, and didn't want to make a verbal misstep.

Steph gestured around herself. "This is a really cute apartment."

"Thanks. We've been here about four years now." I'd have thought having her in my space would make me anxious, worried if she'd like it or think it was basic. But I felt nothing but comfortable.

Her eyebrows rocketed up, but quickly settled. Her expression was completely neutral, as was her "We?"

"Me and my roommate. I'm saving to buy my own place and for a trip to Europe but, you know, LA." I flushed. I was sure she knew the outrageous cost of this city, but of course our salaries weren't comparable. "So, roommate."

"Ah. Gotcha."

"You want something to drink?"

"Just water is fine."

I gave her one of Per's bottles of FIJI Water from the fridge—I was sure he'd be okay with sharing his stash with Steph—and pointed through the open doorway. "Seriously. Go relax. You've had a huge day."

"So have you."

"It's not a competition."

She stifled another yawn, then rolled her eyes. I wasn't sure if the eye roll was at me for suggesting she should be tired, or herself for giving it away. "Fine. But consider this my objection to not helping."

"Consider it considered." Suggesting she go back to the living room to chill was both selfish and unselfish. She needed to relax, but I also wanted her out of the kitchen while I made dinner. I'd cope with her being in the same room, and knowing Steph, in close proximity, while I cooked, but I'd be a lot faster and probably a lot less on edge if she wasn't in the kitchen. Comfortable with her in my house wasn't the same as being relaxed about having her close to me.

Dinner was going to be about half an hour, so she'd have a little time to wind down before we ate. And I'd have a little time to talk myself out of a small anxiety attack at having Steph in my house eating food I'd cooked. It wasn't that I was a shitty cook. The opposite, actually. But I wanted her to like what I'd made because I wanted her to like me.

The tofu was simmering in a simple garlic-ginger-soy sauce-chilies mix with an abundance of veggies, the rice was in the rice cooker, and the cauliflower "rice" was ready for a quick spin in the microwave when the front door opened. Per didn't put his keys in the bowl. I heard him walking down the hall, pausing, then quietly creeping through the living room until he was in the kitchen. I pressed my lips together to hold back a laugh at the thought of him seeing Steph, waving hi, then fleeing right away.

I turned and smiled as he set his gym bag down by the table then put a couple of almond milks in the fridge. Good Per. He stepped right into my space and I had to nudge him with my elbow so he'd back up and give me room to chop the greens I still needed to add. He didn't move so I elbowed him even harder. When he finally shifted, I asked, "Good heave-and-grunt session?"

Per didn't answer. Instead, he said, his voice a strained whisper, "Harper. Why is Stephanie D'Arripe asleep on our couch?"

I smiled sweetly. "Probably because she's tired." I took a few steps backward, peered into the living room, and had to stifle my laugh. It was like she'd just slid sideways on the couch without moving her legs. Her feet brushed the floor but her upper body leaned against the couch arm, one of her arms stretched out, the other hand tucked up near her chin.

Per lightly slapped my shoulder. Then slapped it again. And it was only me moving away that stopped him from continuing to do it in a frenzy of mania. "Smart-ass. You know what I mean." He was barely containing his excitement, and I was sure it was only the fear he'd wake Steph and she'd discover him not being cool that was keeping his voice somewhat down. "*Why* is she in our house?"

"Because I'm making her dinner."

He inhaled deeply, and I recognized it as his give-me-strength inhalation. If Steph weren't here, he'd probably be getting pretty bitchy right about now. "Fine. That's just fine. I'm going to fill in the blanks myself."

"Good. Can you add red curry paste to the grocery list, please. I was going to make tofu curry but we didn't have enough."

His eyes widened incredulously, like talking about groceries when one of his celeb idols was in his house, on his couch, was the most ludicrous thing he'd ever had to be part of. "Sure." He made a show of walking over to the whiteboard stuck to the wall and writing on it. The lid he'd been keeping on his excitement burst off as if a bomb had torn it open. "Harper Bell, you'd better spill what the actual fuck is happening right now or I am going to *lose* my shit."

I brought my forefinger to my lips. "Shh. Can you maybe not yell, please? You're going to wake her up." I raised an eyebrow. "And you've already lost your shit. You're being weird, and you're doing it loudly."

A throat clearing prevented a retort. Thank god. "Am I…interrupting something?"

Per spun around so fast an ice dancer would have been jealous of his rotation speed.

Steph waved. "Hey. I'm Steph." She ran her hands through her hair, managing to tame it and sexily muss it all in one movement.

Per managed to moderate his voice enough to enunciate, "Hi. I'm Per, Harper's roommate. Great to meet you. Big fan. Actually, not like a *big* fan, just a regular non-weird fan."

I sniggered. "Yeah, you're really sounding non-weird right now…" I decided to hold my tongue on the fact he was an even bigger fan of Laura's, and not just her acting, even though making him feel awkward was one of my favorite things because it was so rare.

He shot me a fuck-you look before turning a dazzling smile to Steph. It seemed my joking admonishment of his weirdness had held his tongue for now.

Steph was laughing, and I let myself think it was my funny "non-weird" quip. She smothered the laugh to ask, "Pear like the fruit?" She stuffed her hands into the pockets of her pants, her shoulders hunching slightly. The movement made her seem super chill and easygoing, someone you wanted to hang out with. It was probably a calculated decision to put Per at ease, make him realize she was just a person.

I chimed in before Per could answer, probably for the best because he seemed utterly delighted that she was taking an interest in him. "It's short for Periwinkle. He's such a dainty little flower, can't you tell?"

He spared me a withering look before smiling apologetically at Steph. "It's Per like the Norwegian parents…Per Akselsen."

Steph bit back her grin to be serious about my roommate's name. "Ahhh. Well, that's more logical." She pulled a hand out of her pocket for him to shake and he grabbed it immediately. "It's great to meet you. Harper's told me absolutely nothing about you"—this with a quick smirk at me—"I only knew about your existence like…half an hour ago." Her mouth twitched again. "Sorry for monopolizing your couch for a nap but my watch has been bitching at me all day about resting, so I did."

Per waved her off quickly. I got the feeling he would have excused her absolutely anything. "Totally fine. And, Harper, you haven't mentioned me? I'm wounded," he teased.

"Sorry, but you just don't come up at work," I said airily as I scraped the greens into the pan and set the lid back on to let them wilt.

Thankfully Steph redirected the conversation. "Harper, that smells amazing."

"Thank you. Per, can you grab some bowls please?" I looked at Steph. "And no, you don't need to help."

She nodded. "Wouldn't dream of asking, the way you kept shutting me down before." She turned her attention to my roommate. "So, let's get the boring stuff out of the way. I guess you know what I do. How about you, Per?"

Per laughed. "Same as everyone in this town. I'm a waiter…with modeling and a *tiny* bit of acting on the side."

She nodded slowly. "Modeling. I can see it."

He nearly exploded. "Uh, thanks." I couldn't wait for when Steph left and Per pounced on me to crow that she thought he was good-looking.

"You're welcome."

He rubbed his jaw. "I uh…I mean, the acting isn't anything serious. I just felt like I probably should, living here."

Steph grinned, and I almost melted. "I hear you."

I gently broke up Per's ego-boosting session. "No Ben tonight?"

Per looked panicked. "Shit, sorry, no. I forgot to text. He's at last-minute work drinks, so not here for dinner. He'll be around later." He flashed a look at Steph that was both wistful and smug. Clearly Per meeting her and Ben not meeting her was going to be a thing.

"Guess you'll be eating this for lunch tomorrow then."

He smiled. "Not a hardship."

Steph gently inserted herself back into the conversation, and I mentally slapped my forehead for excluding her. "Because it's an easy lunch, or because Harper is a great cook?"

"Little from each of those columns. But mostly column B." He gently bumped my hip with his, though our height difference meant it was more of a hip-waist bump. "It's why I agreed to move in with her."

I rolled my eyes. "Mhmm."

"Oh?" Steph mused. "I thought it was just because she's cute."

Per's expression matched the "What the actual heck?" that rattled around my brain, but he quickly recovered. I did not recover, and after Per shot me a quick look, he gave Steph a charming smile. "Well, yeah, she is, but my affections are otherwise allocated."

"Ahhh. I see. The elusive Ben at the work drinks?"

"Exactly." Per finally collected some bowls as the rice cooker clicked off. "Are we eating civilized or chill?"

"We have company, so let's at least pretend to be civilized."

Per wrinkled his nose. "Fine."

"Thank you for at least pretending on my behalf," Steph said, feigning seriousness. She lightly touched my back. "Where's your bathroom?"

"Down the hall, second door on the left. This will be ready when you're done."

"Great." She paused, then deadpanned, "I'll make sure to wash my hands."

I grinned and Per chuckled, thankfully getting that it was a joke. I loved that she felt comfortable enough to make a joke like that. By the time she was done, everything was set out ready to be dished up. By unspoken agreement, Per and I stood back while Steph served herself. While I scooped food into my bowl, Per poured water, allocating Steph's with the same care I imagined a sommelier would pour a $10,000 bottle of wine.

Though she'd been sitting down with a bowl of food in front of her for a few minutes, she hadn't touched it. And she didn't until both Per and I had sat down. Per shoveled food into his mouth, swallowing quickly to tell me, "Amazing dinner as usual, Harpies."

Steph ate a forkful and almost swooned. "It tastes so good." And then she asked an out-of-the-blue question that made my stomach drop. "Do you play tennis, Per?"

He almost gasped. "Me? God no. Why do you ask?"

As she dipped her fork back into the bowl, she clarified to Per, "Harper mentioned her regular tennis partner and I wondered if that was you."

Shit. It wasn't Steph's fault—it wasn't like I'd told her about my roommate and his boyfriend and their love of *North Precinct*. But the expression Per directed at me made it absolutely clear he now knew it was Steph I'd been playing tennis with on Saturday.

Thankfully, he didn't do what I'd thought he would—tease me about it. Instead, he laughed. "Oh, no. Ben plays with her mostly." But the side glance I got told me I was in for a grilling the moment we were alone. I had no idea how my personal and private lives had collided so spectacularly, especially when I'd spent so long trying to keep them apart.

"I feel like I should apologize to him."

Per coughed, pressing his hand hard to his mouth.

I took the unspoken cue that Per agreed with my earlier thought that Ben would probably combust, and repeated what I'd told Steph when she'd suggested it the first time. "You're sweet, but there's no need. Ben'll be fine with not playing a few games of tennis."

The rest of the meal was so easy, I almost felt like thanking the universe. Not that I'd expected Steph to be any different, but meshing my worlds could have gone very badly. Around eight, when we'd finished eating and were yet to move from the table because we'd been enjoying our conversation, Steph snuck a glance at her watch.

I took the cue immediately, and rather than risking Steph feeling awkward, I said, "Your carriage is about to turn into a pumpkin, Cinderella?"

"Exactly. I hate to eat and run, but I need to get home and pay attention to my cat before he shits in one of my shoes or something."

Laughing, I said, "We wouldn't want that."

"Harper, dinner was so good. Thanks for the food, and the company." She turned to smile at Per and he almost levitated when she added, "Both of your company."

"Of course." I stood and leaned over to collect her empty bowl.

Steph touched my hand as I picked it up. "Thanks," she murmured, getting to her feet.

I was eternally grateful Per didn't suggest they catch up again or something. Instead, he stood up and offered a very restrained, "Great to meet you, Steph."

She lightly patted his shoulder. "You too. Hope to see you again." There was something in the way she said it that made me think she was angling at coming over again. I was all for it.

"I'll deal with these dishes, Harpies." His slightly widened eyes said what his unspoken words didn't: Get your ass to the door and see her out. Not that I'd ever just wave bye and point her to the door.

We walked to the gate and before she opened it, Steph said, "Thanks so much for dinner. Way better than In-N-Out."

"It was small thanks for bringing me my phone."

"Anytime. Though I hope I don't have to do it anytime soon." Steph quickly clarified, "Not that I didn't want to help, but being without your phone sucks."

"It does," I agreed. Shit, I could have stood out there, just talking with her for ages, but it was getting late and we both had early starts the next day. So I heroically closed the conversation with, "Drive carefully."

"Will do. And I'll be back, as promised, in the morning."

"Can't wait," I said.

"Me too." She hesitated for a few seconds then moved in and gave me a hug. I returned it, and then Steph was releasing me far too quickly.

I waited until she'd started her car before I locked the gate and went back to my apartment, dragging my feet a little. A hug. What did a hug mean? At the very least, it meant she liked me, she was comfortable with me. I tried not to dwell on how tightly she'd held me, the way her body felt—firm yet soft—and how my body had felt against hers.

The moment I stepped into the kitchen, Per stopped spooning leftovers into a container for his lunch. I'd thought he would start gushing about meeting Steph and how great she was and normal and sweet and funny. Instead, he put his hands on his hips and leveled a stare at me. His voice was anything but level when he said, "Girl. She wants to fuck you so bad."

The idea wasn't as absurd as I'd have thought a week ago. But still... The thought of it was too much right now, and I reacted with spluttering incredulity. "Oh grow up. She does not."

"She absolutely does. She was shooting you fuck-me eyes the whole time. And she called you cute! And, *and*, she was sussing out whether or not you and I were involved." He stuck out his tongue, like us being in a relationship was the grossest thing he could think of.

Luckily for my ego, I knew he didn't think I was gross. He'd actually hit on me pretty seriously when we'd first met, before I'd told him that him being a guy was a huge stumbling block for me.

"She was not. To any of those things except the cute thing and that was just her being Steph." Despite my protests, I let myself believe it was true. Yeah, there had been times tonight when I'd felt like there was something beyond the "we're friends" vibe we'd just begun cultivating. But she could have anyone she wanted for sex or whatever it was that floated her boat.

"She absolutely *was*. Because she wants to fuck you." He sighed dreamily. "You lucky fucking bitch."

"What does Ben think about the fact you drool over pretty much every other human on this planet?"

"He knows I'm a slut for platonic attraction and that he's my true love. That is not the point. The point is, Stephanie D'Arripe is *attracted to you*."

I gave in and stopped arguing. Partly because I didn't feel like a debate, but mostly because I wanted it to be true and I wanted Per to tell me everything he'd noticed, all the ways he thought Steph was into me.

She wants to fuck you so bad.

A rush of heat sped down my spine, settling low in my belly.

I wasn't a *completely* oblivious lesbian—I was generally aware when women were into me. But I was so smitten with Steph, and had been for what felt like ages, and knowing some of the background with her ex and the added problem of our working relationship, I'd just put our interactions into my "probably just wishful thinking" basket.

Maybe it was time to move them tentatively into the "you should make a move" basket…

CHAPTER NINE

Steph

When I pulled up at 4:40 a.m., Harper was locking the gate behind her. Even in the dim light cast by bulbs along the wall of her building, she looked so beautiful that I gave in and just stared at her. How was it possible for one person to be so fucking gorgeous? And how was it possible that I'd been able to (mostly) suppress my attraction to her for all these years?

Jordan had something to do with it, I thought wryly. She probably would have cut my uterus out if I'd even looked at another woman with anything more than a friendly glance. Probably even with just a friendly glance.

But Jordan was gone and I was single and still attracted to Harper—if anything, I was more so. And now, after last night, I was certain it was at least a little reciprocal. The way she'd looked at me while I'd driven her home, while I'd been in her house, and during dinner was unmistakable. Then the way she'd hugged me, how her face had pressed into my shoulder before she'd inhaled deeply and reluctantly let go. It was more than just friendly.

There'd absolutely been a moment when we were saying bye when I'd considered kissing her. But I couldn't just spontaneously kiss her, as much as I wanted to, as much as I thought it would be welcomed.

Because if I'd misread the cue and kissed her when she wasn't fully on board yet, I could be setting myself up for some serious issues at work.

I wasn't a relationship guru, but I also wasn't stupid. Not much. For years, I'd taken our at-work flirtation and banter as something fun and easy, when it seemed it could be real to Harper. It could be a precursor to something more, something deeper, something better. A sudden mental image of *this*—me picking her up to go to work, or her picking me up, or us living together and going to set at the same time—nestled itself snugly in my brain. But that would mean that Harper and I were…

The thought was so frightening that I had the sudden desire to do something silly to counter it, something ridiculous to push the thoughts from my head. Because if I let it stay there then I might act on it and if I acted on it then I might get hurt. Or worse, Harper might get hurt.

I resisted the urge to facetiously beep my horn hello at her, not wanting to unendear myself to her neighbors. Harper juggled her handbag, messenger bag, keys, and a large insulated coffee mug, and looked so surprisingly un-put together that I almost leapt out to help. But she was at the car before I could unbuckle my seatbelt.

I leaned over to open the door for her, and instead of saying "Hi," or "Good morning," or "Hey you look great," like a normal person would, I blurted, "Oh good, you have coffee. I thought about bringing you one, but I didn't know your morning routine. Your before-work morning routine that is. I know what you do at work." Why the hell was I blathering like a nervous teen picking a girl up for a date? Probably because you *want* there to be a date, Steph.

Thankfully Harper ignored my idiocy. "It varies, depending on the morning." As soon as she'd belted herself in, she turned to me. "Thanks again for coming to get me."

"My pleasure. Least I could do, especially after you made me dinner last night." I pulled out and started driving.

"Well, that was *my* pleasure."

My neck was suddenly very hot. I felt her eyes on me, and chanced a quick glance, confirming my suspicion. "What is it?"

She shrugged. "Nothing important. Just…it was nice."

Nice was at the very lowest end of what I'd use to describe last night, but I couldn't very well wax lyrical about how much I'd enjoyed the simple act of having dinner in her home. So I smiled, and agreed, "It was."

We talked easily for the rest of drive to the studio, around Harper drinking her coffee like each sip was filling her with life, that is. I reversed into a spot close to Harper's car. Once I'd cut the engine, I leaned over to the back seat to grab my bags, aware that I was almost kissing her shoulder as I fumbled for them.

Harper didn't move, even when I squirmed back into my seat, carefully pulling my bags over. She caught my eye and for a moment I thought she might lean into me, brush a soft kiss onto my cheek as thanks for the ride. I noted a faint blush streaking over her cheeks. But she didn't move. In fact, she held herself almost rigidly, but it didn't feel like discomfort. Restraint, maybe? The thought buoyed me a little.

"Well, my car's still here," she said.

I laughed, aware of how tight it sounded. "Were you hoping it'd be stolen overnight?"

"It probably would have been less annoying than trying to coordinate Triple-A today."

"True." I touched her forearm. "If there's anything I can do, let me know." It was a genuine offer, but also pointless because we both knew I would have no time to hang around while the mechanic did whatever. I had plenty of downtime, but I also had to be easy to find and ready to go with a moment's notice.

She smiled knowingly. "I will."

I desperately wanted to prolong the moment, to sit in my car and just…talk. But holding up production because I wanted to be with Harper would earn me a disapproving mom sigh from Zoe. I pushed my door open and Harper did the same. When I met her by the passenger door, she smiled up at me. "Thanks again, Steph."

"Anytime," I said. "See you in a bit."

"You sure will." The sensation of our brief hug from last night lingered, and I almost moved in for another one. Thankfully I remembered where I was and kept my hugging arms to myself.

As if by unspoken agreement, Harper and I split away from each other after a few steps, acting as if my driving her hadn't happened. It wasn't like it was forbidden, or even problematic, but gossip was like oxygen around here and the last thing I felt like was either of us being the subject of it. So when I walked away from her to drop my bags in my trailer, drink my coffee now that it'd cooled to lukewarm, and then brush my teeth, it was just like any other morning. Or so it seemed on the outside.

On the inside, everything felt different.

I'd been invited into Harper's home last night. She'd cooked dinner for me. I'd met her roommate, who was obviously someone important to her and not romantically—which had made me far happier than I wanted to admit. I was very good at not lying to myself, and I wasn't trying to deny my attraction to her. But I was trying to avoid it becoming a huge thing, because I didn't want to rock the boat at work.

I locked my trailer and set off to the gym. I could fit in a quick workout, then shower in my trailer, get to Wardrobe, and be in Harper's chair right on time. There were a few crew in the gym finishing up their workouts, and after quick greetings, I started my music and jumped on a treadmill.

I was done with my cardio, showered, and dressed in Amy's clothes with time to spare. Time to spare meant a few extra minutes with Harper, and I'd take all the minutes with her I could get. I'd barely taken three steps toward Hair and Makeup when one of the other Wardrobe dressing room doors flung open with a loud bang.

Laura called "Steph!" from behind me.

I waited until she caught up. "Morning."

She waved her phone at me. "Guess what I just got sent."

"The new iPhone?"

"Funny," she said dryly.

"I know. What is it that you got sent?"

"An article from *TV Cops*. About the show. About…us. Remember we got that heads-up?"

"Oh, right." I didn't look at her phone. I was allergic to people being less than complimentary about my professional life, and did everything I could to avoid reviews.

As if she sensed my worry, Laura leaned her shoulder into mine. She was well aware of my aversion to poor press and, like my team, humored me by keeping as much of it from me as possible.

She made a show of flourishing her phone again. After dramatically clearing her throat, Laura read, "'*North Precinct* brings a fresh take to the oft-stale police procedural drama.' Blah blah, Jared is fine, Anna is fine, Harry is fine, Liz is fine, Liam is fine." She grinned as she looked up. "Get this. 'Stephanie D'Arripe has been a standout since *North Precinct*'s pilot, bringing joyful nuance to her character, Detective Amy Spicer. Sometimes gruff, sometimes soft, sometimes vulnerable, always captivating, it's a pleasure to watch a character presented with so many layers and such depth.'"

Okay, that felt nice. "Go me."

The volume of Laura's voice rose. "'Alongside D'Arripe, costar and on-screen love interest, Laura Allende, brings fieriness, wit, and a subtle sexiness to the character of Valentina Lazaro, and—'" Her voice rose with excitement as she continued, "'The normality with which this same-sex relationship is portrayed is a breath of fresh air.'"

"Wow. Wait, I don't bring sexiness?" I deadpanned.

She laughed, flicking the back of her fingers against my shoulder. "I get paid for sexy, you get paid for gruff. We knew what we were signing on for."

"Mmm." It seemed like a great article, but I was still tense waiting for the inevitable homophobic backlash. I reminded myself that it was not my problem. I stayed away from that as much as I possibly could. I had a team to keep an eye on that sort of stuff.

Laura fanned herself. "Damn. Good reviews never get old. There's more, but you probably already have it, and you know how to read."

"Sounds like I should really ask for more money next year." I checked my emails, noting that my manager, Ingrid, had sent me the same article a few minutes ago—she was not as much of a morning person as Laura's manager. The only text in the email was *$$$!* And I smirked to myself. If my manager had sent me the article, it was confirmation that it was Steph-friendly. I'd read the rest of it later.

Laura laughed. "We both should. *Precinct*'s power couple, baby."

Smiling, I agreed, "You know it." I opened the door to Hair and Makeup and let Laura go ahead of me.

Harper looked up as I closed the door. Her gaze went straight to me, her eyes softening as we made eye contact. "Good morning."

I'd spoken to her an hour ago, but the warm pleasure I always felt near her hadn't dissipated at all. "Hi."

"Morning!" Laura said cheerfully, clearly hyped up by the article. She went right to Nina's chair and dropped down heavily. She held up her phone. "Everyone loves us, Nina!"

Nina popped one hand on her hip, the other running over her short Afro. "Tell me something I didn't know."

Harper caught my eye in the mirror and we shared a smile.

Chrissy hovered, waiting for Laura to settle so she could tag team with Nina. They always started on Laura's longer hair first, which meant I had more time alone with Harper.

Harper rested her hands on my shoulders, fingertips gently digging in to massage. "How is my favorite canvas this morning?"

I pulled a face. "Your favorite canvas had a zit last night. I put a patch on it." My voice came out completely normal instead of breathy from her touch, and I gave myself a mental pat on the back.

Harper's eyebrows rocketed up. "I didn't notice anything last night." She shot a glance at Nina, who was absorbed in Laura's face, then cleared her throat. "Before you left set." If anyone else in the room picked up on the pointedness of her clarification, they didn't let on. Harper sanitized her hands then carefully cupped my chin in her palm to turn my face side to side. Her eyes narrowed as she scrutinized my complexion. The pimple patch had done its job and anything left would easily be covered by Harper's expert hand.

Laura piped up, laughing. "Thanks for reminding me that you're human too."

I turned to her. "Do you want me to go rub my face in some dirt to try for more zits?"

"Please don't," Harper said.

Laura cut in before I could respond, with a singsongy, "Teacher's pet." She was in high spirits, and I didn't stifle it with an indignant response, because I wanted that energy for our scenes this morning—an interaction at work where Amy and Val would chat about a case and engage in some teasing, flirtatious banter.

I raised my eyebrows, then turned back to face the mirror so Harper could get started. The look she gave me made it clear she agreed with Laura's teasing sentiment of "teacher's pet." Hey, I agreed too. It was no secret I preferred Harper, and it had nothing to do with my raging attraction.

Laura twisted around to look Nina in the face. "Don't worry, Nina. I still love you, even if Steph doesn't."

Nina affected a heavy sigh, but she was smiling. "It's okay, I know where I stand."

Thankfully Harper stepped in. Though it was all teasing good fun, the last thing I wanted was to upset someone. Especially someone who was part of the team responsible for making me look my best. A little sugar came out as Harper drawled, "Nina, honey, it's all about the eyebrows, and I'm not sorry to say that I'm just better than you."

Nina guffawed, and with a firm "Mhmm" of agreement, went back to working with Laura. They were a pair of gossips, and spent the whole time together chatting like a couple old ladies in a nursing home with nothing better to do. Add Chrissy to the equation and it was like a gossip magazine in Hair and Makeup, another reason I preferred Harper. I liked gossipy news well enough, but it didn't fuel me the way it seemed to for some people around here.

Harper frowned as she went through the kit she used for me, apparently double-checking things, murmuring fretfully to herself. I had sensitive skin, and certain products made me break out, but I trusted her completely to use clean tools and tried and tested products on my skin. But Harper seemed so concerned, almost borderline panicked, that I decided to intervene.

I touched her arm to grab her attention. "Everything okay?"

"Seems to be." Despite the assurance, her face radiated worry.

I reached for her wrist, unintentionally grabbing her hand instead. Harper stopped dead. I decided to roll with it, though the heat passing between us made thought and action feel impossible. I squeezed Harper's hand, gratified when she squeezed back. "It's fine. I'm sure it was just a random pimple, probably just one of those occasional hormonal ones or something, or just a 'why the fuck not get a pimple today?' pimple. No harm, no foul." Reluctantly, I released my grip, lowering my voice as she leaned in to start on my eyes. "I trust you."

She caught my eye, and the tightness around hers eased. "Thank you." She exhaled loudly. "Now...close your eyes, please."

I did, grateful for the small respite from looking into hers and feeling so utterly seen.

Something lingered between us while she finished my makeup. Not tension exactly, but a slight discomfort that had never really been there before. And I didn't like it.

I was done before Laura and patted her shoulder on my way out. "See you on set."

She glanced up from her phone and nodded.

As I opened the trailer door, I looked back and found Harper watching me.

By the final scene of the day, I was beginning to flag. I was tired, and trying desperately to not let it affect the mood on set. If I let my energy drop, it would become a slow-leaking balloon that could sap the energy from everyone. Though I was the lead actor, the dynamic of the entire cast working together was why our ratings remained high and we won awards. I walked back to my first mark for the third time, rolling my head around to keep my body loose.

For some reason, after last looks, I was hyper aware of Harper off to the side, and it annoyed the shit out of me. I was *working*. I should be focused. But in the back of my mind I was replaying the conversation from this morning, replaying our time together yesterday evening.

I gave myself a gentle mental ass-kicking. Get your shit together, or you're going to fuck up and keep everyone back. And I hated doing that. Both fucking up, and making everyone stay later because of said fuck-up.

Zoe's voice shook me back into here and now. "Quiet on the set!" After a few seconds, she said, "Roll sound."

"Sound speed," came the response.

There was a rapid-fire back-and-forth between Zoe and crew members while I hyped myself up into a rushing, late-for-something-important mental space. "Roll camera."

"Rolling."

"Mark it."

"Scene four, take three, mark."

Monty called, "Action!"

I waited a few seconds for background to start moving, then pushed my way into the room, weaving through bodies toward Amy's desk, pulling myself up hard on my mark.

Jared, at the desk that bordered Amy's on the long side, looked up from the keyboard he'd been pretending to type on—he always typed out song lyrics. I usually typed out random words and expletives. He frowned. "Aren't you due in court in fifteen minutes? Did he crack, or do I need to go in there?"

"Yeah, yeah. I'm going. And yeah, he did. Full confession and flipped on his buddies. He's back in holding. I'll let you do the paperwork, seeing as you're playing desk jockey already." I pulled my suit jacket from the back of the desk chair and started putting it on. In my "Amy Spicer's perpetual hurry" combined with turning and walking away, I totally biffed it. I got one arm in, but my other arm kept missing the hole. I kept trying, but the more I tried, the more stuck I became.

Monty, the sadist, hadn't called cut, so I kept trying to get the jacket on and eventually succeeded in getting my hand just inside the armpit. It refused to go further. I gave up and threw my arms up. Kind of. The stuck arm made the jacket flap around, and the sleeve hit me in the face.

I knew there was *no way* this take would be used, so I sighed, affected my best deadpan "are you fucking kidding me?" look, and stared right into the camera.

Jared had given up and was snorting with laughter. When I caught his eye, I lost it too. Finally Monty called, "Cut," barely getting the word out around his chortles. That gave everyone else permission to laugh and the set erupted.

I bent over, almost crying with laughter at the image of the stupid flapping sleeve whacking me in the face. It'd been a long day and I would have found a carrot funny at this point. When I straightened again, Harper had moved closer, looking like she was going to charge in to help. She paused, apparently changing her mind when Susan, whose job it was to deal with wardrobe things, came over and extracted my arm from the jacket then helped me get my other arm out.

"Thanks," I said. "Sorry, everyone. Clearly I need more sleep."

Of course I couldn't mention the reason I needed sleep was because I'd lain awake thinking about Harper before leaving home extra early to pick her up.

Monty wandered over. "Steph, do you need another rehearsal so you can practice getting dressed?" he asked dryly. "Should we call in a jacket expert for you?"

I laughed. "Nope, all good. But I want to look at that when we're done, see if it looked as hilarious as it felt." I usually had a vague idea of the things I wanted to put out on socials, and made lists of interesting facts from shooting, when I could remember them. If something really funny happened—like me getting stuck in clothing—I made a note so I'd be able to remember it months after the fact when I was watching the episode as it aired. The jacket incident would be watch-along material for sure.

He nodded, then spun on his heel.

Zoe's call of "Reset!" had everyone hustling.

I waited until last looks were called again. My wardrobe was checked before Susan moved on to Jared. Chrissy quickly twitched some hair back into place, finger-combing the strands into the spot she wanted. She was replaced by Harper. When we were alone—relatively speaking—Harper moved right into my bubble.

She used two light fingers against my chin to move my face side to side, then, murmuring about a hot spot, quickly fixed up a shiny patch on my chin. I wished she'd touch me like this outside of work. I redirected my brain away from hopes and wishes. "Is your car fixed?"

"It is."

"Good." I lowered my voice. "Though I was hoping to be a knight in shining armor again."

Harper smiled, though her focus was on touching me up. "Well, the next time my car craps out, you can do just that."

Once she was done, I indicated with a smile and tilt of my head that I had to get back to my first mark. I loved my job, but right now it was getting in the way of me and Harper. I held back a snort. There was no me and Harper.

Not yet anyway.

CHAPTER TEN

Harper

"Ahoy, ahoy," Steph said cheerfully as she came into the trailer. With the hand not holding her box of Friday pastries, she held the door open for Jared, who shuffled in behind her.

He offered a wave, and a tired, "Morning, ladies."

I pushed down the nervous excitement that had bubbled up as soon as I'd seen Steph and responded to both of them. "Good morning."

As usual, Steph came right over to my chair, leaving Jared for Nina. "Hey," she murmured quietly as she sat down. She leaned forward to place her phone and water on the wide shelf in front of her, then pushed herself back in the chair. "There's an apple fritter already in a bag for you, inside that box."

She was too darned sweet. "Thank you." I rested my hands lightly on her shoulders then stepped in front of her to adjust the lighting. "How's my favorite face feeling this morning?" Maybe I asked her a little more softly than I asked others, but that didn't *mean* anything, except that I was a nice person.

Her eyes creased at the edges. "It's feeling…wonderful."

I matched her smile. "Glad to hear it. You good?"

"Mhmm." Steph caught my eye, winking before she directed her focus to Nina, the biggest gossip on set. "Any news for us this morning?"

Nina jumped right in. "Nothing here yet, but I saw Yusef as I was leaving yesterday and he is *panicking* about the tennis match."

"Might be an easy win for us then." Steph turned her head to catch Nina's eye. "You're supporting the *Precinct* team, right?"

"Damned right I am," Nina said emphatically. "Never any doubt."

"Good," Steph said. "Especially now that it's me and Laura stepping in."

Jared mumbled something I didn't catch, but that made Nina laugh.

I got to work on Steph. My job was to show off features that needed little help. The little bump at the end of her otherwise perfectly straight nose. The almost electric blue of her eyes. The fullness of her lips, and the ease with which they'd twist into a cocky smirk. She and Laura were my favorites to work on, even with Laura's tendency to talk when I was trying to do her lips. Both of them were punctual, polite, and never had stale morning or coffee breath.

Because Jared's hair was short and only required a little styling, once Chrissy was done with him, she came over to coax Steph's short waves into a style that was soft, with a hint of masculinity. The perfect look for Amy Spicer.

Steph's body was relaxed, her breathing deep and slow as Chrissy and I worked in unison. She muttered a "See you soon" to Jared when he left, then picked up conversations with Nina, Chrissy, and me.

Chrissy was talking about a running race she was training for, which sent Steph into a frenzy of genuine excitement. "I've been thinking about a half-marathon or maybe a fifty-k ultramarathon or trail-run race or something. But…trying to find time to train will be a *nightmare.*"

"You should totally do it," Chrissy enthused.

"I'll think about it." Steph's expression brightened. "The weather looks amazing this weekend, so I think I'll go run trail laps at Runyon tomorrow afternoon. Maybe I'll get inspired to go fast and it'll give me the kick in the butt I need to sign up for a race."

"Totally." Chrissy nodded vigorously, then moved away to get her kit organized.

And I nudged Steph gently. "That sounds really great. But did you forget about tennis?"

"Of course I didn't," she said emphatically. "I can do both." She paused. "Did you…want to come along? For the run, not for tennis. Of course you'll be at tennis."

I had no idea why, but I didn't even think before agreeing, "Sure. That sounds fun."

"Great. We could move tennis to Sunday morning if you don't want to do both the same day?"

"I have a thing, sorry." As much as I'd like to spend time with Steph, trying to get a Sunday appointment with my esthetician could be a nightmare, and I didn't want to cancel. Smiling, I pointed out, "You could move the run to tomorrow morning."

She pretended to recoil. "Oh no. Harper. You know I like to have my Saturday mornings free as do-nothing hours."

"Okay, okay," I conceded, laughing. "We'll make it work."

"I'll text you the details for Runyon?"

"Sounds good." Now was possibly the worst time to catch a whiff of her distinctive scent as she leaned closer, the clean citrus-coconut soapy smell layered underneath a hint of cologne. It made my stomach muscles tighten, my breath hitch. I'd worked with her for years, so why was it affecting me so much now? I had no idea, but I knew I wanted to run my nose over her skin, kiss the spots I'd just smelled.

Steph caught my eye, raising her eyebrows. Her lips parted like she was about to say something, and I knew then she'd heard my breath catch. I hastened to stop her from mentioning my embarrassing audible reaction to how amazing she smelled. "Close your eyes."

Steph did as I'd asked and I sprayed her face with makeup-setting agent. I carefully tilted her face up, and she opened her eyes again, catching mine. My throat felt tight when I said, "Hold still a moment." I snapped a quick picture for the folder of Steph's looks. "You're all done."

She winked at me, a quick grin following that made my stomach flutter. "Thank you. See you soon." Steph practically launched herself out of the chair, raising her voice to address everyone in the small space. "Thanks, team! See you out there."

Nina startled and offered an automatic smile, wave, say goodbye. I let myself watch Steph exit for a few seconds, then turned back to tidy my things and go through the fanny packs I'd take onto set. Chrissy slipped out too, leaving me alone with Nina. I could sense her watching me, and deliberately didn't look up. I didn't need to.

Nina pounced. "What the hell was that about?"

"What was what about?"

"You and Steph hanging out on your days off."

"Oh, yeah." I resumed checking Steph's bag had everything I needed. Everything she needed was probably more accurate. Each of the main talent had preferences for products, which we all stuck to like they were the Ten Commandments, but I always double-checked Steph's bag. She had sensitive skin, and broke out with certain products. Her pimple the other day had sent me into a spiral. "What about it?" Except for the fact it was pretty much unheard of for cast and crew to mingle outside of work, and the casual invite to something outside our established tennis coaching had me more excited for an activity than I'd been in a while. "I'm just helping her with her tennis game for the fundraiser. She got roped in at the last moment and needs a hand."

"Yeah, no, I got that. Good for you. I mean the trip to Runyon beforehand? What's that about?"

I tried for light and breezy. "Just a good warmup for tennis." I was going to be utterly beat by the end of the day, but it was worth it. "Nothing wrong with a little extra movement."

"Mhmm." Her eyebrows came down from where they'd shot up to I-don't-believe-you level. "Well, better you than me. If it doesn't involve bed, alcohol, a screen, or food on the weekend, I don't want to know about it."

I laughed, grateful Nina had moved on from pestering me about Steph. "I have plenty of days like that, trust me."

"Right." Then she moved the conversation in a direction I never expected, and wasn't sure I was ready to discuss. "Seriously, is something going on between you and Steph? You guys have always been close and kind of...flirty, but now it seems like there's more."

I fumbled for a response. "No, nothing. She's newly single, or... newly-ish, and I think she just wants a nonjudgmental, noninvolved person to talk to. You know what it's like to hold on to secrets. I think I'm just a...safe place to flirt."

There, that sounded like a plausible explanation for the zingy chemistry that'd been between us for almost as long as we'd worked together. The chemistry that had grown zingier recently. I didn't want to admit that my feelings ran deeper than just superficial flirtations.

"A safe place to flirt..." Nina mused. "Right. If that's true, then what's all the rest of it?"

"What do you mean? What 'rest of it'?" It felt like I'd swallowed a huge stone that now sat immovably in my gut. "I'm not...I mean there's not—" The stone rose up into my chest. I had no idea why the thought of someone thinking Steph and I were somehow doing something we shouldn't made me feel like I was going to vomit. But it did, and at that moment I couldn't allocate mental or emotional energy to unpack that feeling.

Nina's expression turned motherly. "Look, I don't give a shit what's going on between you two, as long as it's consensual and exactly what you want. *And* after watching you two engage in verbal foreplay over the past few years, mentally undress each other for the past few months, and then eye-fuck each other for the last week or so, I'm all for it. I just don't want to see you get hurt. Personally, or professionally."

"Thank you." I took a deep breath, grateful when it settled some of the anxiety swirling around my body. Only some of. The thought of people noticing that Steph and I were friendly and flirting was at the forefront of the anxiety. I felt far too exposed, too vulnerable. "And…I don't know what's going on between us, honestly."

"Do you want something to be going on between you?"

I nodded. "Of course I do. Who wouldn't want something with Steph?" That thought gave way to a horrible one—who wouldn't want to be with Steph? Steph, who could be with any woman she wanted. Women far more attractive than me. Women far wealthier than me. Women far less ordinary than me. Women far better than me.

"Who wouldn't want something with you?" Nina said gently. She reached over and squeezed my shoulder. "You're fabulous. And from where I'm sitting, she thinks you're the bee's knees."

"Thanks." The thought of what I wanted, and what would probably never happen made me feel like I might cry. Because how could I make a move, put myself out there and risk rejection? And then come into work every day and look at the face of a woman who didn't think I was enough. "Could we talk about something else?"

With another shoulder squeeze, Nina said, "Of course." She glanced at the door, then back to me. "I heard a rumor about a cast member, and I haven't even told anyone yet."

I turned to the mirror and carefully dabbed under my eyes, checking I didn't need to do a touch-up on myself. "Wow. That's a first."

Nina rolled her eyes playfully. "Funny. Don't even pretend you don't love all my newsy tidbits."

"I'm not pretending. So, what's this rumor?"

"Anna's splitting from her husband, and it's getting *messy*."

"That's terrible." Anna was one of the regulars on *Precinct*, and not one of my favorite people to work with. She could be abrupt and rude, acting like a lead when she was far from it. Nothing like Steph.

But breakups were still horrible, even if I didn't particularly like the person. The walkie-talkie on my belt crackled to life, making further conversation impossible. Time to get to set. Once we'd both gathered our fanny packs, Nina grabbed my wrist. "Hey. You know what we've talked about won't leave this room."

That made me laugh. "Then it'd be the *only* thing that didn't make it out of this room." We all knew that anything discussed in her presence was fair game for distribution.

"I swear." She pressed a hand to her heart. "Gossip's honor. We can talk about this more later. Or…never talk about it again."

I swallowed the hard lump in my throat, but I still couldn't respond with anything other than a tight, "Okay." Drawing my shoulders back, I forced a smile. There was nothing I could do about it right now, and I had work to do. I picked up the apple fritter Steph had already set aside for me. "Let's go."

Thankfully the busyness of the day made it nearly impossible to dwell on the fact people were watching me and Steph "eye-fucking," and what it meant that I'd be spending time with Steph outside of work and tennis coaching. I decided to set the first issue aside. I couldn't control what people thought and I sure as hell didn't want to stop flirting and having fun with Steph at work.

Which left me to think about the Runyon date. Was it actually a date? No, of course not. We weren't even close to dating. Friends did things like this together all the time. And we *were* certified friends. I was okay with friends, truly I was, though I would have preferred more than just friends with Steph. Of course, if I wanted that, I'd need to stop messing around with subtlety and just tell her.

Oh god. What a scary thought. What if she said no? What if she said yes?

Maybe I could ease into it, mention what Nina had said about noticing the ramped-up flirtation between us, ask her if she was okay with people at work being aware of it. Steph would either laugh it off and confirm it was nothing, just a bit of fun, maybe say something like "Oh shit, I don't want people at work to think that about us." Or she'd tell me she meant it and, if I was looking at the best-case scenarios for my personal life, she'd then go on to ask me out.

I didn't know what I'd do if she told me the flirtations weren't intentional and that she didn't realize people had been paying such close attention. But surely Steph wouldn't have asked me at work to come with her for a run if she didn't want people to hear, if she didn't want two of the biggest gossips around to hear it and likely spread that bit of news. And she wasn't unintelligent; Steph would know people noticed everything on set, which meant she likely knew exactly how she was behaving and how it might be received by me, and anyone else who saw it.

Realizing this made me feel slightly less anxious. Slightly.

When I checked my phone at our meal break, I found a message from Per. I could almost hear the desperate whine through the text.

Ben's dumping me to go see his parents tomorrow. How does a movie, mani/pedi, and day drinking sound? I need a blowout before I start cutting for this magazine shoot.

Per's definition of "a blowout" differed wildly from mine, but the plus side was he would always be a designated driver for day drinking.

Sounds amazing but I can't. Heading to Runyon for some exercise. And then I'm playing tennis.

Practicing for the work thing again?

Yes.

The work thing where you're tennis coaching the woman who wants to fuck you senseless. He added a tongue-poking emoji to get his point across.

I didn't respond. Mostly because the thought of being fucked senseless by Steph, or fucking her senseless made my insides feel twisted with desire. Unfortunately, then my insides immediately felt twisted with anxiety.

Per responded into my void. *Interesting. Your lack of an answer just confirms it. If you get done early, let me know. But I feel like you won't be done early.*

I sent back a thumbs-up emoji, hoping it would suffice. Ordinarily a movie, getting my nails done and then spending the rest of the day holed up with my best friend at one of our favorite cozy bars sounded like exactly the way I wanted to spend my day off. But this time, I had something even better to look forward to.

The emoji didn't suffice. Almost as quickly as I'd hit send, Per had sent another text. *We're going to talk about this.*

Sighing inwardly, I typed out my response.

I can't wait.

CHAPTER ELEVEN

Steph

I was a little early for our trail-run date. Oh god, was it *actually* a date or had I just kind of assumed because of all the weird attraction tension zinging between me and Harper? After texting her to confirm I'd parked on North Fuller Avenue, I settled in to wait. I reclined the driver's seat and went back over the conversation we'd had yesterday morning.

I really, honestly hadn't considered it a date when I'd asked Harper to join me for a run—I'd just wanted to spend more time with her. But now I was wondering if maybe she thought it was a date. I hadn't been overtly flirtatious, but I'd definitely been more than just friendly, and I hadn't missed the way Nina had caught Harper's eye in the mirror when I'd asked her to join me.

I wasn't bothered by people at work knowing Harper and I were spending time together, but I didn't want her to be uncomfortable about it. Not that she'd ever indicated she was. I was totally overthinking it. But I'd learned how not normal my life was for some things, like a simple attraction or dating. And the last thing I wanted was to ruin the friendship I'd cultivated with Harper. Nor did I want to ruin a possible more-than-friendship.

The problem wasn't me—I was always an utter delight. The problem was all the external stuff. Like people cashing in with photographs of me doing boring shit like grocery shopping. I generally tried to go places where the paparazzi weren't known to frequent, but I'd been caught out before. Then there might be fans speculating about who Harper was and why I was always seen with her.

I'd known it was a possibility since I'd become more "famous," but Harper didn't sign on for that. Sighing, I mentally added having to talk to her about boundaries and comfort levels for our friendship to my to-do list. God I wished these weren't things that I had to think about during the day to day.

Tapping on the window startled the ever-living fuck out of me but seeing Harper and her cute "what the heck are you doing?" smile instantly settled the rush of adrenaline. I brought the seat back upright and opened the door. And nearly fell over when I realized she was wearing running tights, and what looked like a fitted tank top underneath a long-sleeved zip-up sun shirt. The tank was apparently standard for her exercising and I was here for it.

"Hey," I said, hoping she attributed my breathiness to how quickly I'd exited the car and not because I was dumbstruck by the body clearly outlined under her workout clothing. I mean, I'd had an idea of Harper's shape from her work clothing and the tennis outfit she'd worn last week, but this was something else. Now I knew those perfect curves and swells and dips were there, and it was going to be very hard to not think of that image when I looked at her at work.

Harper's smile was easy, warm, and I didn't miss the way her eyes roamed over me before she answered, "Hey yourself." She took a small step backward to make space for me, but not backward enough that she couldn't easily touch me. "You looked totally zoned out. What were you thinking about?"

"I was thinking about hiding from people who might spy on me through my window." Her quick laugh made me forget to censor myself. "Kidding. I was thinking about you, actually."

Apparently that was the right answer. Her eyes softened a moment before she smiled. She couldn't have looked more pleased if she tried. "What about me?"

Telling her exactly what I'd been thinking about would probably lead to an uncomfortable conversation that I didn't want to have right now. I didn't know if it was a conversation we'd ever need to have. So I went with the truth, but not the *truth* truth. "Just that I was looking forward to spending time with you."

Harper gave me a look that made me think she suspected I wasn't being entirely honest, but she didn't push. Instead, she quietly agreed, "Me too."

"Where'd you park?"

She pointed down the street.

"Nice." I put my sunglasses on, then leaned back into my car to grab my running vest. I fastened it and asked, "Ready to go?"

"Yeah." She didn't sound particularly convinced, but didn't elaborate.

I crouched down to tighten my shoelaces ready for the run and casually looked at Harper's legs, encased in those black running tights. Strong thighs and firm, shapely calves that I was desperate to run my hands over, desperate to kiss and lick. An enjoyable rush of pleasure made my stomach tingle. I popped back up before my staring got conspicuous.

After checking she had water and snacks—I was an overprepared trail runner and hiker—we set off along the city streets toward the gate. The short walk to the park entrance passed in easy companiable chatter. Until we reached the stone-and-iron-gated entrance. Harper's nervous "So…" made me look over at her. She was fidgeting with the straps on her hydration pack. When I raised an eyebrow, she continued, "Maybe now isn't the best time to admit this, but…I've never been on a trail run before."

"No? Then why'd you agree to come today?" I couldn't help myself, I checked her out again. "I gotta say, you look perfectly capable of trail running."

"Like I said, I wanted to spend time with you. And, the weather is amazing for being outdoors and enjoying the view."

I grinned. "Those are both excellent reasons." After a pause, I decided to just say what I was thinking. "I think I like the first reason best though."

"Me too," she said quietly. "It's probably the main reason." A light blush filled her cheeks and Harper cleared her throat. "I mean, I've walked all through these trails. But I'm not a runner."

"At all?"

She shook her head. "I used to run a little for training when I was playing tennis competitively. But I've always preferred lower impact stuff like cycling. My knees are grateful for my care."

I gestured for her to go first through the gate and we moved off to the side, out of the way of people funneling past us in both directions. "You don't really run, and yet you agreed to a *trail run* in a place where there's ups and downs and uneven ground." I held back a laugh—not a mean laugh, a disbelieving laugh—because I didn't want her to take it the wrong way. "Like…this is *not* the place to go for your first trail run, Harper."

"Believe me, I know this."

Nodding, I mused, "I see. So, reading between the lines here, what I'm picking up on is that you really like me. You like me so much that you lied about running, *trail* running, just to spend time with me."

"I didn't *lie*," she said indignantly. "I just…omitted some facts."

"Right. Also known as lying by omission." I only just got it out without laughing and was glad my response came out jokingly, as I'd intended.

Harper nudged me in the ribs. "You're a pain in the ass, you know that?"

"Actually I didn't know that. Probably because people ignore the things they don't like or can't do, like running, just so they can spend time with me…So I never learned that I'm not fun to be around."

She rolled her eyes. "You're impossible." It would have been a more convincing assertion if she hadn't moved forward into my personal space as she'd said it.

"Now that, I *did* know. But only because you just told me."

Harper shook her head, clamping her lips together. I raised an eyebrow, silently daring her to say something, but she didn't take my bait.

I glanced down, my eyes automatically straying to her mouth. So tempting. I forced my gaze back up to meet hers. "We can just walk if you want. I don't need to run. I just need to move. Walking is moving."

Harper looked like she was going to argue that she was fine, let's go for a solid trail run, but then common sense seemed to butt in. She deflated. "That would be really great, if you don't mind."

"I don't mind," I said immediately. I would have crawled the trails if it meant I could spend time with her. "Easier to talk if we're walking."

"That's true," Harper agreed. "I *can* run, obviously. I just don't. And if we run then I might die and you'll probably get annoyed."

"I wouldn't get annoyed," I assured her. "Very sad, yes, but not annoyed."

"I can jog," she said suddenly. "If you want to jog."

"Harper," I said, smiling at her all over the place-ness. "Let's just walk. But if you feel like a jog, then just jog along and I'll follow. But there's no pressure." When I took her hand, she didn't put up an ounce of resistance. "Come on, let's go." I pulled her along with me, reluctantly releasing her after a few steps. "The sooner we go, the sooner we're done, the sooner we can play tennis, and then the sooner we can go out for tacos and a beer."

"Tacos? I didn't know tacos and beer were on today's agenda."

"Oh, I didn't mention that? It's the law for us now after we've gotten sweaty together." My face heated as I realized what I'd just said and what it might imply, and I hoped I wasn't blushing as much as I suspected. *Why would you want to blush, Steph? Oh, I don't know, Self, maybe because all I can think about now is being naked and sweaty with Harper.*

"I don't know who wrote that into legislation, but I'm all for it."

"Good."

"Does it have to be tacos? Or can we grab a burger, or gyros, or… something else equally tasty?"

"It can be anything you want as long as I get a beer." Once we'd stepped off the paved trail onto the dirt and passed through a gate denoting the dog off-leash area, I asked her to "Tell me about Europe."

"It's a group of countries all sharing borders. About an eleven- or twelve-hour flight from here."

"Now who's being a smart-ass," I said.

"That would be me," Harper said cheerfully. She sighed, biting down on the end of it. "Europe is just…it's a dream. A dream that's going to happen for sure when I have the money to spare," she added quickly. "But there's so much to plan that I'm actually kind of paralyzed by it. And then there's the whole traveling as a single woman thing."

I hooked my thumbs in the sides of my running vest. "Yeah? It's pretty subpar unless you enjoy men being gross. But if you can set that aside, it's an amazing experience meeting so many different people, having all those new experiences."

Her voice seemed a little tight when she asked, "Have you ever been to Europe?"

"I have, yeah. For work and vacation. I think you're going to have an absolute blast. It's amazing." I snuck a quick look at her.

"Which countries did you visit?"

My work trips for promotional obligations were boring, so instead of talking about that, I filled her in on the European countries where I'd been when I was twenty, when I'd saved every spare dollar I could to travel. I'd worked for cash under the table to extend my stay before I had to face the inevitable truth that I'd run out of money and had to come home.

"I feel like there's still so many more countries I need to visit. Typical." I laughed dryly. "Before, I had all the time but not enough money. Now, I have the money but no time or energy." I glanced at Harper and found her gentle, understanding gaze on me.

"What jobs did you do before acting? Or, before acting was fulltime?"

"Waitress and barista, of course. Then I was a nanny, and I kind of stuck with that."

"A nanny? Really?"

"Mhmm." She looked dubious, so I nudged her with my shoulder. "What about that are you having problems with?"

"I'm not. I've seen you with kids on set. You're so sweet with them and I can tell it's not just an act. It just wasn't what I'd expected, that's all."

"No? What did you expect? Aside from the obligatory actor second job of waitress and/or barista."

"You know, I honestly don't know. I just know it wasn't that."

We walked on quietly for a minute or so. I caught the occasional sideways look from people, but thankfully nobody approached. It was on the tip of my tongue to tell Harper maybe we could find time for Europe together, but I managed to restrain myself. But it did make me think about how much I enjoyed doing things with her.

"Thanks for coming out here with me today. Even if you totally misrepresented yourself," I added teasingly.

"Of course. I mean, this is what friends do, right? They do stuff together?" There was a hint of shyness in the questions, though the second one didn't really seem like it needed to be a question. "And you're never going to let me forget that I agreed to a run when I don't run, are you?"

"Nope," I confirmed cheerfully.

We kept moving up the trail, past the abandoned basketball courts, still talking about Europe, and other trips we'd been on or wanted to do. Ten minutes in, the Downtown viewpoint was in sight when a sharp shriek echoed from up the trail. A woman. My stomach dropped. I looked to Harper, her face contorted in confusion. The woman shrieked again.

I looked around. The trail was nowhere near packed but it was clear other people had heard it. But they weren't moving. Unlike the character I played, I was no fucking hero, but I couldn't just stand by while someone was being attacked. And, most importantly, I knew how to dial 911.

I pulled my phone from the thigh pocket of my running tights and started running. "I think, maybe, we should go see what that's about."

"Yeah," Harper agreed breathlessly, keeping pace beside me.

If we stayed together, we'd lessen the chance of a disaster of the being-attacked variety. I fully expected to come across an assault, though the dude would have to be pretty fucking bold in daylight and on a populated trail. As fast as I could, I ran up the hill, and after twenty seconds of lung and leg agony, reached an older couple huddled around a large dog lying off the trail next to the scrubby undergrowth.

Thankfully, no assault seemed to be taking place. But something was. The woman had stopped shrieking, but she was babbling, panicking about something to do with her dog, which was struggling desperately to get up.

It seemed like once other people realized that someone else was there and willing to assist, they didn't need to and so, melted away. "Do you need help?" I asked around gulping in air.

Both of them seemed startled by our arrival, though surely they'd have to expect that someone would come see what was going on after that shrieking. The man knelt next to his dog, and as he tried to pull him up, he grunted, "I think he's been bitten by a snake."

Ew. I recoiled instantly, looking frantically around for the offender. I wasn't really scared of snakes, but I also didn't want to have anything to do with them if I could avoid it. I had always ignored the "Beware of Rattlesnakes" signs, rationalizing that if I ignored the signs, the snakes would ignore me.

I didn't know if it was actually a rattlesnake…attack, but *something* had clearly happened to the dog, a black Labrador mix by the look of it. The dog was sprawled about three feet off the dusty track in some sparse vegetation, pushed into a scrubby bush. The Lab panted loudly, drooling copiously as he tried to get up. He let out a high-pitched whine as his owner tried to get him on his feet.

This was not fun to watch. "Okay. Uh, where is the snake?"

"I don't know," the woman wailed. She was three seconds from literally wringing her hands.

Harper, bless her, took charge. "Are you sure it's a snakebite?"

"I don't know," she sobbed. "He just went off the trail and then started yelping. He came back and just…he just collapsed."

Harper looked to me. "Do you know anything about first aid for dog snakebites?"

"Nope. Do you?"

"No. But I'm pretty sure 'get the dog to a vet ASAP' is top of the treatment plan."

"Yeah." I turned my attention to the couple still trying—unsuccessfully—to get the dog to stand. They couldn't even get it off the ground. I realized a few things simultaneously. This dog looked pretty fucking sick. And there was no way either of its frantic owners would be able to carry it, especially not back down the hill.

I closed the distance between me and the dog, warily watching the ground for snakes. "I think your dog needs to go to a vet. Right now." The issue was the dog obviously couldn't walk, and clearly neither of the owners seemed capable of carrying it, even back down where the trail was less steep. "I'll carry him."

Harper looked at me like I'd just told her I was going to fly. She opened her mouth, then closed it just as quickly. After a quick nod, she agreed, "Good idea."

I gently inserted myself between the owners. "I'll carry the dog. Are you okay with that?"

The woman looked up, blinking slowly. "What?"

I bit back my annoyance. Sure, I wasn't perfect in a crisis, but I could at least make decisions when shit went sideways. "I'll carry the dog. It needs to get to the vet." How they did that once the dog was at their car wasn't really my problem, and I had to assume they were local enough that their vet was reasonably close by. "Do you live near here? Is your vet close?"

The couple looked at each other. The guy answered, "No, we're visiting from Washington."

Fuck. "Where are you parked?"

He pointed vaguely in the direction we'd come from.

Well that was a start.

And that's all it was. They didn't really do anything else except look utterly helpless. Okay, time to do something or this dog was going to die and I really wasn't cool with that. Permission or not, I had to carry him. God I wished someone else would carry him, but no gym bros were stepping up to help out.

I crouched down. "Just…I need you to hold him up so I can get underneath him." There was no way I could carry him in my arms like a small child, so it had to be a fireman's carry on my shoulders. Luckily, I knew how to do that, thanks to Amy carrying a sixty-pound "homeless child" out of a warehouse fire. That was a fun afternoon of muscle-trembling repetition, even for the takes where I had a dummy, because it needed weight so it'd look realistic.

Now I was close, I could see how swollen the dog's nose was. Fuck. It didn't look at me, just lay there panting rapidly. It took a few tries to coordinate the owners lifting the dog enough for me to get my body under it, but eventually I managed to get him up onto my shoulders and stand without falling over. The trembling canine made it hard to balance but aside from that, the dog was surprisingly cooperative.

I started walking back down the trail, assuming everyone would just come along. I was going to need all my breath to get back to their car, carrying what felt like seventy pounds of dog on my shoulders. Asking them to follow me was wasted breath and time. People moved out of the way as I carefully made my way down. Harper rushed to my side, turning around to tell the owners, "I'll Google emergency vets while we get this guy down to your car."

The dog's rapid panting was beyond alarming, as was his occasional whining. I put my head down and went as fast as I could. The problem was that the loose surface could be slippery and I didn't want to fall. Especially not with a dying dog on my shoulders.

I could hear Harper talking with the couple, but couldn't make out what they were saying. Even if I had been able to, all my concentration was on the dog and not skidding over. It took an eternity for the gate to come into view, and I slowed enough for Harper and Co. to catch up. I sucked in a deep lungful of air, and turned my head to ask where they were parked, but after a quick look at my face, Harper blurted to the couple, "Where's your car?"

They pointed down North Fuller and I sent silent thanks that these tourists had somehow found a coveted, close parking space. I ignored a fresh round of disbelieving looks from those just arriving at the park. The lights flashed on a Lexus SUV. It took no time to get the dog in the back seat, and the woman slid in beside him. They thanked us, then sped off.

I leaned my back against an electrical pole and dipped my head to suck in some water from the soft flask in my right chest pocket, gulping down fluids around trying to get in some air. I'd always considered myself to be in pretty good shape, but clearly I wasn't in "carry a 70lb dog for half a mile downhill on an unstable surface" good shape.

Harper touched my bicep. "You good?"

"Yeah." I shook my arms out, trying to ignore the trembling burn. How could muscles do both? "Just...wasn't expecting to do that today."

"I'll bet. I talked with them on the way down. Hopefully talked some sense into them about getting the dog to the vet right away. I gave them directions and rang ahead to alert the vet." She shook her head. "They were pretty out of it, but it seems they've at least got that part down."

"Understandable. And thanks for taking care of that."

"Of course. Do you want to go back up and try again, or...?"

Looking up the street toward the park, I groaned. "Yes. No." I checked my watch, annoyed to realize that in the hilarity of chatting to Harper about her run-lie, I hadn't started my activity tracking. Though, Garmin didn't actually have a dog-rescue activity setting. "We're too early for tennis." She'd booked us a court at three p.m. and I'd expected to be running for at least another hour. So now we had an hour to kill. But the thought of going back into the park was spectacularly unappealing right now.

Harper ran her hand down the outside of my upper arm. "I'm going to make an executive decision and say let's go get a coffee or something to pass the time before we have to play."

"Sounds good."

As we walked back down to our cars, I plucked my sun shirt away from my body, wrinkling my nose at the gigantic wet patch over my shoulder and down my front. It wasn't sweat. It was dog drool. Hopefully. I disliked feeling sweaty and thankfully had clean shirts in my car for tennis and afterward.

I shrugged out of my vest and extracted my keys. "I'm just going to get out of this wet shirt before we grab coffee. I think it's drool. God, I *hope* it's drool and not pee." For the life of me, I couldn't quite remember which end of the dog was over which shoulder.

Her eyebrows shot up. "And you'll wear…what?"

I unlocked my car. "A clean shirt?"

She laughed, the sound unusually nervous. "Right. I should have known you'd have ten clean, dry shirts with you. I'm surprised you didn't run off to change into one every fifteen minutes the last time we played tennis. I noted the clean one for tacos…" The teasing, joking tone was obvious, but there was also a lingering nervousness in her words.

"You know me too well." It was no secret at work that I didn't love feeling sweaty, and Wardrobe always had multiple shirts for me on hot days. I slipped around to the back of the car where I'd have a little privacy. Sure, I was wearing a running bra, but I still didn't want to strip down to it standing on the sidewalk, even if people regularly saw more than just that of me on television. The rear door of the Defender would block me from view of the sidewalk, but not any cars driving past.

Keeping my back to the street, I pulled the sun shirt and tank top underneath it off and examined the wet patches. "Yeah, I think it's just sweat and drool, not pee." I tossed them in the cargo space and grabbed the shirt I'd allocated for tennis. I'd either have to put the drooled-on sun shirt back on or slather my arms with sunscreen for our session.

She cleared her throat. "For your sake, I hope so too. Though what you did warrants some sweat."

I turned around, trying to find the right end of the shirt so I could put it on. The expression on Harper's face was fritzing my brain for this most simple task. She looked like she wanted to devour me. Coupled with the fact my shoulders and biceps were still on fire, my coordination felt shot. I fumbled for something to say to break the tension—good tension, but tension nonetheless. "Speaking of sweating. You ran."

She shifted her gaze away from my abs, back to my eyes. "Pardon me?"

"You ran with me up to that dog."

"It was unintentional," she said, laughing. "I got caught up in the drama." Her eyes swept back down my torso, lingering long enough at my sports-bra-encased breasts to make it clear she was enjoying what she was seeing, before coming back up to my face.

The way she looked at me made me want to stay in just my bra a little longer, but we *were* on a public street. I slipped into the shirt. "It was pretty dramatic."

"It was pretty heroic," Harper said, and it sounded like a correction to what I'd said.

"Heroism was *not* what I had in mind. I just wanted the dog to survive. I hope he does." I regretted not getting their contact details, but checking in after the fact had been the last thing on my mind.

"Hopefully he will if they do their part. You did yours. You did more than yours." Harper took a step forward until she was well into my personal space. I didn't move. "Steph, I'm gonna be honest here."

"Oh?" Honesty was great, but I also wasn't sure if I wanted honesty if it was going to be something like "I don't want to hang out with you anymore."

"That was really cool. And also, you looked really hot."

The moment she said *hot*, my heart started thudding as much as it had while I'd been running up the hill. "Can I just clarify you meant like…attractive hot and not sweaty hot? Because it just felt sweaty hot."

"Yes, I meant sexy hot. All intense and athletic carrying that dog." Harper pulled her lower lip between her teeth. "Really. Sexy."

Her expression, the tone of her voice, the way her eyes searched mine, sent a thrill of excitement through me. I thought through a dozen things to say, trying to come up with a response that sounded suave. I failed. I also failed to moderate my voice, and my response came out a little rough. "I'm glad you liked it."

"I more than liked it," Harper clarified. She leaned in, then paused.

My heart felt like it stumbled over a few beats when I realized what she was doing. Then it stumbled some more when she didn't kiss me.

Harper inhaled deeply, then muttered, barely audibly, "Oh, screw it." She gripped a fistful of my shirt and tugged me until I closed the gap between us. With her other hand, Harper held the back of my neck and pulled.

I needed no further encouragement. We made eye contact for a second, and I saw everything I needed in the warm brown of hers. Harper made a small sound that was so fucking sexy that I wrapped my arms around her waist, pulling her closer until our bodies pressed along their lengths. The hand on the back of my neck shifted up until it was in the short hair at the back of my head, her fingers gently massaging my scalp.

Our lips met softly at first, but the kiss took barely any time to build. It was almost greedy, the way Harper's mouth moved against mine, and I let myself fall into the kiss. The hand on the back of my head gently gripped a fistful of my hair as Harper's lips parted, her tongue softly brushing my lower lip. A brief vision of stepping backward into the Defender, pulling her on top of me, and making out like horny teens in the cargo space rushed into my head. Unfortunately, the reality of our location intruded.

I stifled a groan of frustration and pulled back until Harper released me. "Fuck," I whispered. "That was, uh…"

"Yeah, it was," Harper agreed breathlessly. The hand that'd been in my hair slid down the back of my neck until it rested on my shoulder. Her thumb stroked the side of my neck and I suppressed a shudder.

"So, um…" I jerked my thumb behind myself. "I have a cat to rescue from a tree. Wanna come watch? And…congratulate me. Or reward me. Or…whatever that was."

"That?" Harper laughed. "What did you want *that* to be, Steph?"

I decided to be brave. "I want it to be something that happens again. More than just once again."

"I want that too," she said, all traces of laughter gone now.

"Good." Inhaling deeply, I asked, "Was this a date?"

"Did you want it to be a date?" She sounded almost too innocent, but I detected a touch of vulnerable hope in her question.

"I'm not sure. I thought it might be, then I thought it wasn't, but I think it qualified as a date, except for the dog thing, but it also *could* have just been two friends hanging out because neither of us said anything about a date and I mean, we haven't talked about dating *at all* even though I feel like maybe we've both been thinking it recently?" Oh I just loved how much I rambled around her, especially when trying to talk about something that was technically so fucking simple.

"Do you want us to be just two friends hanging out?" Harper asked. She exuded calmness, and everything from her body language to her expression to her tone made me feel like no matter how I answered, it'd be okay.

So I answered with more honesty. "No. I want the date. And I want more than a date. I…" I shook my head. Verbalizing what I really wanted was dangerous right now. "What about you?"

"I think me kissing you is probably all the answer you need to that question."

"Okay. Thank you for clarifying."

"You're welcome." She glanced at her watch. "So, coffee before tennis?"

"Do we really need to play tennis?" I whined. "My arms are so tired. I don't even think I could hit the ball."

Harper's expression softened. "No. We don't have to do anything we don't want to. But, if you want to do justice to the people supporting this charity match, then maybe we should take a little time to play tennis today."

I sighed. "Fine. But when we're done, I want to talk more about that kiss."

"Just talk?" she asked innocently.

"If you kissed me again, I wouldn't object."

Harper's smirk was so sexy I almost told her to forget tennis and come back to my place. "Neither would I…"

CHAPTER TWELVE

Harper

I decided to go a little easier on Steph, reasoning that she'd carried a big dog on her shoulders for ten minutes and she wasn't a bad tennis player so she didn't need a lot of help. We spent the hour mostly just working on her directional ability with the ball, trying to get it where she wanted it to go, and nailing down her serve percentages. I was very careful not to send her all over the court, though I did enjoy watching her run around.

Instead of just replaying the kiss over and over again, I'd surprised myself by managing to focus enough on tennis to teach Steph some useful skills. I wasn't sure exactly when I'd decided "screw it, I'm going to kiss her," but I was incredibly grateful I'd made the leap. At least now she knew exactly where I stood. And I knew where she stood too.

The session went by so fast that I was disappointed when we had to finish. We'd be able to fit in another one before the charity match, which should give her enough practice to get through the planned three sets. She wasn't going to qualify for any real matches anytime soon, but neither was she going to embarrass herself on the court, which I knew was her major concern.

The next players were waiting outside the gate as we finished up, and I waved the young women over. They stood out of our way to get ready as Steph and I began packing up our gear and getting all the balls back in cans.

After a polite smile to acknowledge them, Steph somehow managed to ignore the strangers standing nearby, even when one of them clearly asked the other, "Is that Stephanie D'Arripe?" to the slightly awed response of "I think so!"

Steph grinned at me, leaning in close to whisper so they wouldn't hear. "Maybe I should say 'Who's Stephanie D'Arripe?'"

I laughed. "If you talk, you'll give yourself away instantly."

She winked, and when she spoke again, she'd put on an English accent and raised the pitch of her voice. "Not if I talk like this."

Geez. I fanned myself. When I went to respond, my words stuck, and only came out after I swallowed and cleared my throat. "As hot as that sounded, I like your real voice."

"Do you now?" she asked coyly. Thankfully she didn't prod me to elaborate. Steph pushed open the gate and waited until I'd gone through. She closed it behind us, then waved cheerily at the women. One of them completely missed her shot and the laughter from her playing partner followed us as we walked away.

The path along the back of the courts was narrow, forcing us to walk with our hands brushing. Sure, one of us could have moved slightly ahead or behind but it was almost like an unspoken agreement between us that we were both happy right as we were. We reached Steph's car first and she went around to the rear.

The dog-drool tank top lay crumpled in the cargo space where she'd dumped it. The shirt she'd taken off right in front of me, as if she didn't care at all that I was seeing her in nothing more than a sports bra. It was a treat to be able to stare with undisguised interest, then linger as much as I wanted instead of averting my eyes as I did at work.

The way Steph had watched me as she'd changed her shirt made me certain she knew exactly what I'd been thinking, exactly how much I'd enjoyed looking at her. The tight swell of her breasts in the running bra, the firm definition of her abs—not ripped six-pack firm but nicely visible—and the obvious muscle over her shoulders and arms had made my whole body hum.

I hadn't been able to help myself. I just had to kiss her. There had been the tiniest moment of fear, of hesitation, but as soon as I'd seen the willingness on her face, my fear melted away. Kissing her had been everything I'd thought it would be; she was delicious, responsive, enthusiastic, passionate. And now all I wanted was to kiss her again.

As if Steph read my mind now, she pulled off the long-sleeved sun shirt and fished out another clean shirt, this one a plain black tee.

"Changing your shirt in front of me again? Hoping for another kiss?"

The edge of her mouth quirked. "Always." But there was no kiss. Instead, she asked, "Do you still want to grab something to eat? Maybe talk about that kiss?"

With the dog and aborted run-walk, the day had turned strange, and I hadn't been sure she'd want to eat, especially since we'd already been for coffee. But there was no way I'd say no to spending more time with her. "Sure. Yes. If you're hungry. And want to talk." Given how she'd inhaled a banana muffin with her coffee, I thought she probably was hungry.

Steph confirmed with a slightly desperate, "I am. And I do." She looked around the parking lot then whipped the sweaty tennis shirt over her head. After a quick wipe over her arms and torso with a microfiber towel, Steph pulled on the fresh tee.

"Any preference for what you want to eat?" I asked, hoping she didn't notice my voice sounded a little hoarse and tight. It was all Steph's fault. She shouldn't be so damned hot. A little whisper in my head said "If this is your reaction to what she looks like with only her shirt off, still wearing a bra, what the hell would you do if she was fully naked in front of you?" I bundled that thought up and stuffed it away to think about later.

Steph's expression made me certain she knew exactly what had just passed through my mind. She'd probably added some dirty mental postscripts about eating…out. She smirked, shaking her head. "Anything is fine."

"My place? I could make something?" Her face gave nothing away and I rushed out, "Or we can grab something while we're already out."

"I think some privacy would be nice. And I can't believe I didn't even have to persuade you to cook for me again."

Oh god, I dreaded to think of how agreeable I'd be if Steph actually *tried* to persuade me to do something. "Cooking might be a loose interpretation of what I'll do. I was thinking sandwiches."

"Sounds great."

"Per's not home, in case you were wondering."

Steph shrugged. "It would be fine if he were. I like him. But…I'm glad he won't be."

A tightness in my body made me all too aware of the things I was trying not to think about. Shit, we'd only kissed once. I was so far ahead of myself it was almost laughable. But I wasn't laughing. I couldn't stop myself asking, "Why's that?"

"I'm really hoping you might kiss me again," she murmured. Her lazy smile made my pulse pick up.

"Do you think you've done another special thing to deserve a kiss?" She didn't need to do anything special—I'd kiss her anytime, for any reason, or no reason at all.

The smile grew into a cheeky, heart-melting grin. "Nothing special. Just being myself. Isn't that enough?"

"It is," I confirmed.

This time it was Steph who moved first. She gripped my hip and pulled me into her. One arm wrapped tight around my back, the other lightly cupped the side of my neck. There was the briefest moment of eye contact, before she bent her head to kiss me.

For all the forcefulness of her grabbing me, the actual kiss was surprisingly gentle, almost exquisitely soft, as if she'd realized just how public we were. My suspicion was confirmed when she pulled back and looked around.

Steph inhaled a shaky breath. "Pity everyone seems to have decided to congregate in this parking lot right now."

I made a choked sound of assent. It was probably for the best—if the kiss had gotten any more exciting, it was going to be hard to keep it public-space friendly. Our first kiss had already tested my willpower and this one almost shredded it.

She found my gaze again. "So, let's go somewhere where it's only you and me."

"You remember where I live?" I asked tightly.

"Yes. I'll follow you…"

I tried to focus on driving, and not the fact she was coming back to my house. My currently empty house. If she even hinted at it, I'd go to bed with her in a heartbeat, and that thought brought both excitement and something that felt akin to embarrassment. I rationalized my desperation by telling myself we'd known each other for years, had been flirting for most of that time, and I'd been living with an attraction to her since almost the first moment I'd laid eyes on her.

Steph parked and was out of her car by the time I'd gathered all my stuff. She jogged over to where I waited by my car, and without asking, grabbed my gear bag out of my hand. Steph slung it casually over her shoulder, then touched my back, only dropping her hand once we'd started walking.

She stuck to my side as we made our way to the gate. "I didn't get a good look the other night and early morning, but this is a really cute complex."

"It does the job."

She turned to me, an eyebrow raised in surprise. "You don't like it?"

"Oh no, I do. But it's not a house."

She nodded slowly. "Ah, that's right. You're a house girl."

"Yes, ma'am." I unlocked the gate and ushered her through. "I want a bunch of gardens and some space to move about. And no randy roommate." I loved Per, and as far as roommates went he was amazing, but I craved my own whole space sometimes.

"I get that. I've lived in plenty of tiny shared places and I don't know if I could ever go back to small and/or shared. I don't know what I'd do if my career suddenly went belly-up and I had to sell and move somewhere cheaper or live with someone who wasn't a partner." She held up a hand, fingers crossed. "Here's hoping people don't get sick of me."

My brain had completely stuck on "shared," because that one word had triggered a thought of what we could do if we ever moved past our two kisses earlier today. Moved into a place, together. Steph's slightly quizzical look made me realize I'd completely ignored what she'd said, and I rushed to continue the conversation. "I don't think that's ever going to be an issue."

I could hear some joyful shouting and general merriment from the pool. Steph leaned around a concrete pylon, then ducked her head back just as quickly. I wondered if she'd been spotted or if she just didn't want to seem like a voyeur.

"Do you like swimming?" I asked.

"I do. Don't go as much as I want to, though." She smiled wryly. "Time…"

"You're welcome to come here for a swim anytime." I started up the stairs and along the covered walkway toward my apartment. "I hardly use the pool, so you may as well on my behalf. Assuming you don't have a pool that is." She probably did, and I felt stupid for suggesting it, and even stupider for suggesting she drive to my place when, even if she didn't have a pool, she could surely swim somewhere closer.

"Oh great, thanks!" she enthused. "What about the ocean?"

The enthusiasm of her response made my words stick, and I fumbled out, "Me…using the ocean?"

Steph nodded.

"Yeah, sometimes."

"If you ever go to the beach and want company, let me know?"

"Of course." I unlocked the door and ushered her inside.

Steph waited until I'd closed the door behind us to speak again. "I should have added that I only want to come if you wear a bikini to the beach." Her tongue poked teasingly through her lips. "Do you?"

Instead of answering her—a little imagination never hurt anyone—I asked, "Have we moved from veiled flirting to outright flirting?"

"I think we've moved to that and then moved past it..."

And where we'd stop, well, nobody knew. But I hoped it wasn't any time or any place soon... I thought she might kiss me, but Steph just smiled, then murmured that she was going to wash up.

While she used the bathroom, I washed my hands at the kitchen sink and pulled a bunch of things from the fridge and pantry, setting the spread out on the counter for us to construct our own sandwiches. I may have also stood with my head in the open freezer door to try to cool off a little.

Steph went with sprouted bread, packed with everything I set out except jalapeños. Her construction made me reconsider my planned cheese-cheese-cheese with mayo on white bread—yes, sometimes I was just a kid trapped in an adult's body—and I made a stacked turkey and salad sandwich. She went with sparkling water. I had a glass of Per's kombucha that he made and nurtured like it was his child.

We relocated to the couch and I curled up with my plate resting on my thigh, facing Steph who'd adopted a similar position. The moment I'd taken a bite, I realized how hungry I was, and we ate in silence for a few minutes.

"Thanks for suggesting this. Eating at home I mean. With you. I—" Steph frowned. "I really hate eating alone. I love the family vibe of eating at work, surrounded by people. I miss family dinners on Sunday. Eating dinner at home alone just doesn't feel the same."

"Happy to help. Where is your family?"

"My parents still live in Iowa. And Kelsey lives in New Hampshire with her husband and kids."

"Ah. So it's not like you can just swing on by for a meal."

She laughed. "Not at all."

"What about meals with friends?" I asked before I policed myself. It was a personal question, but I knew that if she didn't want to answer, she wouldn't.

"Time is always a problem." She leaned over to set her empty plate on the coffee table, and I did the same. "And...friends are hard. I'm so busy, and most of them have just fallen away. Some friends I made when

I was just getting started got weird once I got the role on *Precinct*. I'm not sure if it was jealousy because they were still in the trenches, or what.

"And other friends just…Like I'm working all day and I get a text and I just don't have the energy to respond to it, to try to carry a stilted conversation that's being held over days. I hate it, but I think I'm the problem." She brightened a little, but it felt forced. "But I work with my best friend—Laura. If we're both in town during hiatus, we get together as much as we can."

I knew Steph and Laura had been friends before *North Precinct* began, but they'd grown even closer and often talked about how their friendship made their working relationship that much easier. I also knew that the admission led to speculation that Steph and Laura were more than just costars, despite the fact there was no evidence to support the rumors.

"I get that," I murmured. "If you ever feel lonely, you're more than welcome to come here for dinner again. Or we'll go out. Y'know, me, Per, and Ben have a standing dinner and television night every Tuesday. It'd be close to family dinner?"

"Tuesday…" she mused, her mouth quirking. "You have a watch party too?"

"We do."

Steph nodded, smiled like she'd just had a wonderful thought, then she verbalized the thought that was both wonderful and terrifying. "We should combine them! You can come to my place or I'll just invite myself over to yours. And your friends are welcome at my place too, obviously."

"Yeah…that would be fun." I cringed internally at how it'd come out, then cringed again when Steph called me on it.

"That didn't seem like a very enthusiastic yeah. It sounded like the opposite of enthusiastic." She shrugged, her expression turning impassive. "It's totally fine if you're not into it." Steph sounded more uncertain than I ever thought I'd heard her.

"I am into it," I said emphatically. "It's just…" I blew out a loud breath. "You've met Per. His boyfriend is maybe a *little* higher on the fan wavelength. He's not creepy, but he *is* enthusiastic. I want you in my space, but I also don't want those two making things uncomfortable or hard for you."

"It'll be fine. It'll be fun. I'd like to meet more of your friends. That's what friends do, right? Introduce them to their other friends?" Her voice rose an octave on the last few words.

"Right," I agreed. I paused a beat, then blurted, "And being your friend is great."

"But?" she prompted.

She was opening a door wide enough to walk an elephant through, and I wasn't sure if it was intentional, that she wanted me to verbalize my feelings first, or if she was scared of verbalizing hers. "*But*, honestly… I'm pretty sure we both know that what we're doing is more than what friends would do."

Steph ran a hand through her hair, tousling it so sexily that I had to fold my own hands in my lap to stop from touching her. If I touched her, I'd want to kiss her, and right now, it felt like we needed to talk.

"Right. Friends don't do this." Steph moved forward so quickly it startled me, but her steady, strong hands on my shoulders grounded me again. We made eye contact for the briefest of moments before she kissed me. Talk be damned for now. Her hands came to my neck, fingertips gently pushing into my hair.

I was embarrassingly aware of the soft moan I exhaled into her mouth, but it only made her open her mouth as if she wanted to swallow my desire. I fumbled for something to hold, something to keep me tethered to her, and found her hip, pulling her closer as our kiss deepened into something that curled my toes and tingled my stomach.

Steph sighed, the sound one of pure contentment. "It feels *so* good to finally be able to do that, after years of wanting to. To think 'I want to kiss you' and just…do it." She smiled, pulling me to her for another kiss, this one short and soft, but no less sweet.

"Years?" I asked, unable to keep the disbelief from my tone.

"Yes," she said seriously. "I just got a little sidetracked on the way, sorry."

"You got here eventually, which is good enough for me."

Steph laughed. "That's true. This is a great destination…I think I'd like to stay here a while." Her fingers lightly touched my collarbone, pausing just long enough to make me aware of them before she continued up my neck until they found my jaw. "Or maybe stay here." She raised my chin, and in the next breath, leaned forward and kissed me again. "No, I want to stay here…" she murmured.

She moved her hand to cup my face, and I reached up to grip her wrist, keeping her hand right where it was. Steph's warm, soft lips were confident, almost demanding, and I met her with enthusiasm. Kissing was great, but kissing Steph? I didn't think I had words for how incredible it was.

I sometimes grew overwhelmed when kissing—too fast, too much tongue, just…too much. But there was none of that with Steph. I felt silly for thinking it, but kissing her was perfect. I wanted to touch all of her, and eventually settled for wrapping my arms around her shoulders, pulling us close. Our kiss remained unhurried, yet its intensity rose with each passing moment. Steph leaned back and I followed, until I was almost lying on top of her. Our legs tangled. Steph's hands slipped up under my shirt, caressing my back.

If Per wasn't due home soon from his solo "blowout," I would have slid off her to the floor, dragged her pants down, knelt in front of the couch, pushed her legs apart, and enjoyed myself. But he was, so I had to content myself with this make-out session, which was pretty damned enjoyable. I had no idea how long we made out for, but when Steph broke for air, I was throbbing and tingling in places that had been neglected for far too long.

She groaned, and it wasn't a groan of pleasure. "I hate to run off when things are getting fun, but it's getting late and I have to feed Asimov. I didn't expect...this. Didn't expect to be away for so long."

Disappointment flooded me, but I was also grateful one of us was slightly responsible. If she stayed, I'd never want her to leave and I had a full day of chores and errands tomorrow. "Sure, of course." After a deep, steadying breath, I stood up.

Steph jumped to her feet and grabbed our plates and glasses, already walking toward the kitchen before I could tell her she didn't need to. After setting them in the sink, she turned around, hands behind her resting on the countertop. "I'd really like to do more of this. And... more-more? At some point, no need to rush that. And talk. If you're into talking? I really like knowing what's what, and this feels like it needs a conversation when we have time." She smiled wryly and I could almost hear her addendum to *have time*: and can restrain ourselves from making out.

God I loved how she rambled. It made me feel like we were on equal footing with this...whatever this was. "More and more-more sounds pretty good to me." If more-more was code for screwing each other senseless, then it sounded more than good. "So does talking."

Steph nodded decisively. "Good. But you look worried," she observed.

It would have been so easy to brush it aside, but if I wanted something more than flirting, I needed to be honest. "I am. Just a little."

She frowned. "Are you worried about us and work?" The way she asked it made me think she'd had that worry too.

"Not super worried? But yeah, it has crossed my mind. But I mean, Liz dated that key grip for almost a year, and there was no weirdness when they broke up. And Liz is..." I fumbled for an inoffensive descriptor.

Steph grinned. "High maintenance?"

"Yeah," I agreed sheepishly. And I was sure there had been other hidden relationships on our production.

"I'm not your boss, Harper," she said gently. "This would be no different to dating a coworker if we were both…I don't know…engineers or accountants."

"I know." *But*, if we had to make a list of expendable and not-expendable to the production, I knew which column I would go in.

"Yeah, I know. Fuck. I really want to talk about this now and I'm not dismissing your concerns. But—"

"Life is in the way right now." I smiled to soften the bluntness. "We have heaps of time to work out the nitty-gritty details."

"We do." After exhaling loudly, she said, "Okay, I don't want to, but I really need to leave."

Instead of dragging out her departure when she had to get home to her cat, I went right to pleasantries. "Thanks for the trail run that wasn't really a trail run."

"My pleasure. Thanks for helping with the dog, and the tennis lesson. And the food."

"That was my pleasure." I paused, then decided to just go with what I wanted to say instead of worrying about sounding stupid. "Thanks for the kissing…and the touching…"

She smirked. "I feel like I should be thanking you for that one."

"Are we just going to go around in an endless circle of thanks?"

"Maybe." Steph laughed. "There are plenty more things I'd like to thank you for, but I'm going to call it here. Otherwise I might not go."

I could think of worse things.

I moved in without thinking and Steph hesitated before she moved too. The hesitation was enough to make me rethink the hug I'd automatically gone for and I held up my fist.

She laughed and bumped my fist with hers. "Sorry, I *totally* overthought that."

"Me too." I opened my arms and Steph moved right into them. The hug felt as easy as breathing and I relaxed into it for a few seconds before giving her a quick squeeze and releasing her. I brushed my lips over her cheek, wanting to do so much more.

Steph's eyes creased at the corners. "Oh…a bonus," she teased. "Fist bump, hug, and now a lil peck on the cheek." Steph cupped my face gently and dipped her head to kiss me again. It was quick and soft, and left me wanting much, much more. Judging by the quick intake of breath and the desperate look she flashed me, Steph felt similarly. "And there's another bonus," she said hoarsely. "I'll text you tomorrow."

"Sounds good." A horrible thought occurred to me as I opened the door. "You didn't get your beer."

Her eyebrows bounced upward. "No, but I got something far better." And then she was gone.

I cleaned up the kitchen in a daze, going over and over the day. Had that all really happened? We'd been moving toward something like this for a while now, but I'd never *actually* thought it would ever happen. But it had. It really had. And now I had no idea where we would go from here.

I knew Steph well enough by now to know she was a good, kind person. I trusted her. But the reality was also that she was one of the leads on a very popular television show, and had an expanding list of starring movie roles under her belt too. She was important. I was not. And if producers had to make a call for the good of the show, I knew it wouldn't be Steph who'd be fired. It'd be me.

Not that I really, honestly thought she'd push for me to be fired if things got weird between us, but showrunners and producers were ferocious about protecting their productions and could act savagely to remove something they perceived as problematic.

Speaking of problematic… Were we even allowed to date, or sleep together, or kiss, or…whatever? There was nothing in my contract about it, and I assumed Steph knew hers well enough to have stopped me when I kissed her and not kissed me again if there was an issue.

I exhaled a loud groan of frustration. All of this was just circular, get-ahead-of-myself thinking. But it was so easy to make mental leaps forward when I'd spent the past six years nurturing an attraction.

About an hour after Steph had left, Per found me on the couch halfway through my second glass of wine and not reading the book I held. He leaned down to kiss the top of my head, stole my glass and a sip of wine, then rubbed my shoulder.

"Enjoy your blowout?" I asked.

"I sure did. I'll be thinking about it while I'm starving for this shoot." After a dramatic sigh, he asked, "How was your day?"

"Good," I said. It came out completely normal-sounding because I wasn't lying. It was a good day. More beyond that, but I wasn't quite ready to tell him exactly what'd happened. "Had a little drama at Runyon with someone's dog. It got bit by a rattlesnake."

Per recoiled. "Oh god. Is it dead?"

"Not sure. Steph carried it down so they could get it to the vet."

"Sounds hot." He fanned his face.

"It was a little. A lot," I corrected myself.

Grinning like a fool, he shimmied his shoulders. "Oh, girl, you need to climb aboard that ASAP. I know how much you love strong, capable soft butches."

He was right about both me climbing aboard Steph and loving strong, capable soft butches. I loved any capable woman really, but I'd always melted for a soft butch. "Tell me about it." Stupid wine.

Per guffawed. "She admits it! Ah-ha! I *knew* it." He vaulted over the couch and landed heavily beside me. "Spill. Spill it all."

Shrugging, I sipped my wine. "There's nothing to spill." Now was the perfect moment to redirect his attention away from the thing I had no words to discuss. "So, something might be happening, but if you're going to be weird about it, then I'm going to cancel the idea before it gets off the ground."

Per's interest was clearly piqued. "What idea?"

"Steph might come around one Tuesday for dinner and *North Precinct*. Maybe *Make the Cut* too depending on the workday."

"She's going to do her watch-along here?" The string of voice breaks along that sentence would have given a pubescent boy a run for his money.

"Maybe. Unless you and Ben are going to be weird."

"We won't be weird. I swear we won't be weird. Ohmygod."

"You're already being weird."

Per straightened up, squaring his shoulders. "No I'm not. I'm just processing this information."

"Weirdly."

"Can I at least tell Ben when it's happening? You know how he is about meeting people if he's not showered with clean clothes, smelling good, hair done. And that's meeting *anyone*," he hastened to add.

I did know that. "Okay, but you have to give him the 'don't be weird' caveat."

Per's look was part horrified, part annoyed. "Yeah, okay, sure. But if anyone's being weird, it's you. You're treating us like children threatening to run amok through the Walk of Fame or something."

"I know," I groaned. "Sorry. Look. I just...I really like her. We're becoming good friends." Good friends and more, but there was no way I could tell him that now. "And I want her to be comfortable. I know you guys aren't superfans but you *are* fans, and I don't want her to feel like she can't relax in my house."

His jaw tightened then released. "That's fair, and I get there are some extra circumstances to consider here. But how would you feel if I asked you to behave a certain way so Ben would be comfortable here? I don't have to because I know you and trust you."

"It's not that I don't trust you guys to be decent humans. I really didn't mean to make you feel like shit. I'm just..." I flailed vaguely, hoping the words explaining how I felt would magically come out of my mouth.

When they didn't, Per took over for me. "You're just being overprotective about someone you want to bang?"

"That's not *quite* how I'd put it, but essentially, yes."

"Understandable. I promise you have nothing to worry about with me, and I'll make sure Ben is on the same page." He frowned, his mouth twisting so wonkily that I thought he might cry. "Steph was okay when she met me the other night, right? I didn't freak her out?"

I smiled at his concern. Despite his fanboy tendency, Per was a respectful guy. "She didn't seem concerned to me, and she didn't say anything to me that made me think she was at all bothered, and it was her who suggested another get-together."

He exhaled a long, relieved breath. "Good. So...how long have you 'really liked' her?"

"Since pretty much the first day I met her."

Per nodded slowly, processing that information. "You've hidden it admirably."

Well that was good to know. The last thing I wanted was for Steph to feel...adored by me, like I was nothing more than another fan. I mean, I did adore her, but it was because of who she was outside her job—despite her job.

I adored her, because maybe...*maybe*, I was actually a little bit in love with her.

CHAPTER THIRTEEN

Steph

My first scene of the day was relatively easy, but unfortunately easy didn't always mean fast. After rehearsing all the moving parts, we were ready to roll.

I walked into the squad room kitchen, beelining for the coffee station where Jared lingered, looking at something on "his" cell phone.

"Has that DNA result come back yet?" I asked. "I just spoke to Val downstairs. She saw the perp's lawyer at the courthouse, overheard him on the phone talking about our evidence. We need to nail this asshole down." I turned slightly sideways and poured cold brown liquid from the coffeepot into my cup to a level that would satisfy nobody but would make sure I didn't spill any as I moved around.

"Not yet. I'll call the lab and ask what the holdup is." Jared "sipped" from his mug. "How *is* Val?" he asked, exuding both curiosity and concern.

As I tipped a sugar packet into my coffee cup I looked at him, raising an eyebrow. "She's good. Why?" I plucked a spoon from the bucket on the counter and stirred, trying not to let the spoon plink against the mug.

Jared paused, looking embarrassed and a touch antsy. "Nothing. I just heard—" He shook his head. "Never mind. It doesn't matter."

Frowning, I asked, "What? What are you talking about?" Now it was my turn to pretend to sip—another reason to not fill the mug very much was accidentally getting some of the cold, foulest-tasting liquid in existence near my lips.

"It's nothing."

"Oh no. Spit it out, Johnson. You don't get to just drop a bomb like that and then clam up. We're partners, and partners don't do that. What are you talking about?" I repeated, letting an edge of angry exasperation bleed through.

"Look. I thought Val would have told you." He rubbed the back of his neck. "But I guess…"

"Told me what?" I asked, my voice now deadly calm.

"I heard, it's just"—Jared looked acutely uncomfortable—"there's talk that she's filing a sexual harassment claim against Peters."

My face conveyed incredulity, because Val hadn't told Amy this information. I clenched my jaw, biting hard for a few seconds to get a couple good flexes showing. Without taking a breath, I said, "I see," and the tightness in my diaphragm made it come out rough, almost a growl.

Jared held up both hands. "Hey, don't shoot the messenger."

"That's not who I want to shoot," I snarled. I threw the spoon, pleased when it hit the wall above the sink with a satisfying clang, and stalked out of the room.

"Cut!"

I spun around and walked back to my first mark, rolling out my shoulders. All this drama was leading to a confrontation between Amy and Val, though both Laura and I had been assured that there would be no breakup. They'd broken up early the season before last, and after realizing they couldn't live without each other and both needed to work on their issues, had gotten back together at the end of the season.

This was just "a little bit of drama," the writers assured us. And in the next breath, we'd been told this season's finale would have Amy proposing to Val, with an emphatic "Yes" as Val's answer. I was looking forward to being put in a tux for my television wedding. It'd be good practice for my real wedding. Whenever that was. To whomever that was.

As Monty approached, I handed off the prop cup to be emptied and put back for me to pick up and fill yet again. "Fabulous, Steph. Great energy. Jared, also fabulous. Let's try just a little more wariness from you, okay? Amy's a firecracker, and even though they're longtime partners, we all know he doesn't want to be on the receiving end of her anger."

Jared nudged me with an elbow. "Yeah, you bitch."

I pretended to snarl and snap at him like a rabid wolf, and everyone laughed. Harper's guffaw rose above everyone else's laugh.

I mock-pouted at Harper when she came over to me. "I'm not really a bitch, am I?" Even though it was a joke from Jared, being called a bitch by anyone I worked with was high up on my list of things I never wanted.

"Not in the slightest," she assured me as she checked my makeup. After quickly touching up my lipstick and smoothing my eyebrows, Harper assured me, "You're all good."

"I know."

Harper shook her head. "You're also incorrigible. And yes, you know that too."

"Incorrigible? What are we? Eighty-year-old British people?"

"You're the one with a British dad, so you'd know."

I could have drawn out this silly interaction for a while longer but Chrissy was hovering to get her hands on my hair. I wished I didn't have work to do. I wished Harper and I could just leave, go somewhere, and be alone. I resolved that as soon as I was done with work, I'd see if we could do just that. We needed to have a conversation about us and the sooner we did that, the sooner we could move on to kissing again.

I liked running. But after the third take sprinting down a street and into an alley after an extra playing a perp, I was hot, sweaty, tired, and wondering if this was just my life now. I mean, I was already miserable, having spent hours out in a concrete, brick, and asphalt exterior in the mid-July sun, so why not just make me run for all eternity?

Personally, I thought the takes were great, so maybe Monty thought I needed some more exercise. Whatever the reason, I was running and running and running.

While everything was reset for take number four, I hydrated, changed my shirt which was showing sweat, had my hair and makeup repaired again—the look Harper leveled at me while she was touching me up told me she was thinking about the times she'd watched me change shirts on Saturday—and enjoyed a good old sit down.

Everything went great for the take. I didn't trip over any trash bags or cans, and I got a good grip on the extra's arm, using his momentum to push him against the brick wall of the alleyway. He landed with his cheek pressed against the wall, so he could still look at and talk to me.

I raised my gun and took a step back as I reached for the handcuffs on my belt. "Keep your hands up! Don't move."

He kept his hands up and turned his head more to face me as he yelled, "I'm a cop! Undercover. Been with the Westside Locos for almost a year. Check my back pocket. There's a bug in my wallet."

"Put your hands on the wall," I barked. "Don't move."

The extra complied, hands still raised above his head, palms pressed to the bricks. I kept the gun on him as I fished in his back pocket. The moment I had the wallet out, the extra spun quickly and brought his elbow around. I snapped my head back, staggered, and went down onto my knees, then fell forward, catching myself before I smashed my face against the asphalt. He bolted away, stopping out of the line of sight of the camera.

"Sneaky sonofabitch." I fumbled for the radio clipped to my belt. "Code thirty!" I yelled into it.

Jared came barreling into the alleyway, screeching to a halt right on his mark. "You okay?"

I pointed, raising my voice to deliver my line. "Suspect is running. Do not believe him. He is *not* a cop!" Jared ran after the extra. I touched my cheekbone then looked at my fingertips. Grimacing, I grumbled, "Shit," as I quickly scrambled to my feet and staggered off in the same direction as Jared, slamming drunkenly into the brick wall for good measure.

"Cut!" Monty called.

Then he leaned over to Zoe, who said the next best words after cut. "Reset. This is the martini shot! Let's nail it."

Thank god they'd called final shot of the day. The energy felt like it rose ten levels as everything was reset, and my energy for more running rose with it.

As soon as we'd wrapped for the day, I thanked everyone for their hard work, gathered my phone and script and slipped off set. I'd managed to catch Harper's eye and hoped she got my meaning—could we have that talk tonight? Come find me.

I left my clothing on a hanger to be collected and cleaned, and after changing back into my own clothes, dropped into the chair facing the mirror. I propped my phone against the frame, cued up some music, and while I removed my makeup and cleaned my face, went through all the notifications I'd missed during the day. None of them were particularly important, except an email from Ingrid with the subject *Call me*.

The email was just two sentences. *Watch this. Call me anytime.* Then a link. I clicked it and a video started playing. I didn't track my presence on the Internet, trusting the people I paid to do such things to tell me if there was something I should know about. This was obviously one of those things. One of the many LA celeb reporters stood in front of a screen showing one of this season's promo shots of me.

I sighed, pushing down the sinking feeling. There was only one thing that'd happened recently that would get me in the media, and I fervently hoped the spin on the snakebite dog was good. The last thing I needed was a headline of *Stephanie D'Arripe Kills A Dog*.

The reporter smiled a blindingly white smile and dove in. I relaxed as soon as she'd uttered the first few words in a bright, cheerful fluff-piece anchor voice. "And in our feelgood story of the day, it seems Stephanie D'Arripe doesn't just rescue victims in the acclaimed police drama *North Precinct*, but she also rescues…pets! She was spotted heroically carrying a dog who suffered a medical event at the popular Runyon Canyon Park. Sources say D'Arripe carried the dog back down the trail for over ten minutes, ensuring it reached a veterinarian quickly to get the treatment it needed."

Accompanying her dialogue, in the corner of the screen, was a rotating set of about six pictures of me carrying the dog on my shoulders.

The second presenter chimed in. "Well you'd have to be fit to take on those perps she catches every week."

The first presenter laughed. "Indeed you would. And most importantly? We hear the dog is going to be just fine."

The piece was cheesy, but pretty much factually correct so I decided I'd come off looking good. Perhaps most importantly, they were actually decent pictures, all things considered. Yeah, I looked sweaty and like I'd been carrying a seventy-pound dog for ten minutes, but I still looked surprisingly put-together.

My face wasn't bright red or contorted with exertion. I didn't look angry or frustrated. I just looked like I was focused on something, perhaps mildly concerned, maybe a little grumpy, which was unfortunately my default concentration face.

I shifted my focus to the one picture, close to the park entrance, that showed Harper. I hadn't felt it but in the photo, her hand was on my arm. She looked far more concerned than I did. I smiled, remembering that look. She'd been obviously concerned about the dog, but then she'd been concerned about me.

I called Ingrid. She answered instantly, not bothering with formalities. "Good stunt with the dog. The publicity is crazy and overwhelmingly good. You're a hero."

"It wasn't a stunt," I said. "The owners of the dog were tourists. They couldn't carry it and I could, that's all it was."

People at Runyon were usually pretty immune to celebrities walking or running alongside them, and aside from a few glances I'd never had anyone stop me to chat, for a scrawl or selfie, or take an obvious photograph. I figured that the only reason they'd done so this time was because someone pack-muleing a dog to the trailhead, followed by a pair of hysterical boomers and one gorgeous woman was something strange. And me doing it was even stranger.

"Well, your good Samaritan act has people talking. So whatever the reason, good job."

"And people talking means a happy agent, manager, and publicist," I said dryly, echoing what both she and my agent, Veronica, had once jokingly told me.

"Exactly." Then Ingrid sighed, and I tensed, waiting for her to continue. "There's more. Two mores actually."

"Of course there's more."

"Firstly, there's been some comments about you." Again, Ingrid didn't make me wait or make me ask her to explain. "Saying you were 'bitchy' and 'rude,' pushing people out of the way as you came down the trail."

"That's absolute bullshit," I spluttered. "I didn't talk to anyone, and I didn't push anyone out of the way, I didn't even touch anyone."

"I'm sure you didn't," she soothed me. "My best guess is they caught a glimpse of Off the Clock Concentrating Steph, and took your expression way out of context, and decided to use it to farm engagement on socials."

"I hate my face," I whined.

"Well we don't, so deal with it. But, and I know this is a ridiculous thing to tell you, you need to be aware of what you're conveying in public."

"I was carrying a fucking dying dog down a slippery trail, Ingrid. The last thing on my mind was smiling for possible cameras."

"I know, I know. But none of us want any more Snarky Steph social media posts, do we?"

"No," I said, my gut sinking at the thought.

There had been a handful of this sort of thing before, but not for at least a few years. Just little snippets on social media painting me as "bitchy" or "snarky," all because, you guessed it, I had a resting-bitch concentration face. Every time one of these delights had popped up, I'd tried to console myself with the fact I *knew* people I worked with liked me, I was anti-diva-ish behavior, and all the people who'd called me bitchy were random members of the public I'd never even talked to.

I'd had to add "Don't look like you dislike the world while you're thinking about things in public" to my checklist of things to do before I left the house. Now it seemed I had to broaden the scope of that checklist.

"Good. Thank you. Now…Based on the fact you didn't tell me about this, I'm assuming you didn't know there are other pictures that have been made public. You've been training for your tennis match, I see," she said drolly.

A text came through from her and I opened it to stare at a series of pictures of me and Harper kissing in the parking lot of the tennis center.

Fuck. I felt sick. How had one day dropped so many little bombs on my life? I closed down the message after that first perfunctory look. I didn't want to look at the photos, even though they'd captured one of the best kisses of my life.

I wasn't closeted—I'd been photographed kissing women before. No big deal, aside from the invasion of privacy which I'd known was a possibility when I started becoming more known. But this kiss? This was special and the fact someone had taken pictures and made money from them made me so angry that I couldn't think of what to say.

I licked my suddenly dry lips, and finally answered Ingrid. "Yes I have." I didn't know who'd published the photos, and I honestly didn't care. My first concern, after annoyance that someone had intruded upon my privacy, was that I needed to tell Harper that our private moment, our kind of public private moment, had been captured by paparazzi. Great. I made a sound of disgust. "I didn't see any photographers."

And I'd looked. I understood the relationship between me and paparazzi, that sometimes they were an unfortunately necessary part of maintaining visibility. But that didn't mean I liked it.

"No, these appear to have been taken by a member of the public with a cell phone. I guess they needed some cash. And *Page Six* was happy to provide it."

"I really dislike the general population sometimes."

Though it was only for a few seconds longer than a normal pause in a regular back-and-forth conversation, I knew exactly what it meant. She was on to me. Ingrid was impressively neutral when she said, "Tell me what you think I should know. And then tell me some more." Though her voice was calm, it was clear she was already mentally convening the war room.

"I—" I didn't *want* to tell her about the kiss. The kisses. "It's basically what the pics show. I was at Runyon and then playing tennis with a friend. We were friendly. In a perfectly acceptable for the public eye way, as you can see. There's nothing salacious about these pictures, just me kissing a woman, which isn't anything they haven't seen before."

"Right. I'm happy for you. We're happy for you. But…We would have preferred to know about this beforehand so we could be prepared."

"I'm sorry, I didn't plan on kissing someone in public for someone to photograph," I said, unable to keep the bite from my tone.

"Okay, but you know if you're in public with people, *any* people, then you know being photographed or approached, or both, is a possibility. It also looks to me like this friend is actually more than a friend."

"Maybe. We…haven't really sat down and had a meeting about the status of our—" I frowned, mentally running through the right way to describe what Harper and I were currently doing. Eventually I just settled on, "Friendship."

"Perhaps you should do that."

"We're getting to it," I said gloomily. This was one part of "celebrity" I really hated. Everything needed a fucking strategy. It wasn't about what might possibly happen with Harper, what was already happening, but the fact that I couldn't just enjoy the start of something new and exciting without thinking of all this shit.

"I don't want to be nasty, but if we're going to have another Jordan situation on our hands then we need to be ready."

"No," I said instantly, emphatically. "That's not going to happen." The silence on the other end goaded me into admitting, "The woman in the photos is Harper. Harper Bell."

There was a pause but I knew Ingrid, master of remembering everybody, would twig soon enough. "Your Key Makeup?"

"Yes. She's worked with me since we filmed the pilot." I didn't know why I'd added that, but for some reason I felt defensive about being thought of as frivolous, like I was out picking up women I didn't know every week and fucking them.

"Ah, yes. Okay. We'll make a plan and discuss that with you. But for now, enjoy your…romance."

"Thanks." I tried to sound excited about the prospect of romance, but talking about the logistics surrounding it had soured my mood a little.

"Is there something you're worried about?" Now Ingrid's tone had become gentle, almost maternal. For all their blustering about exposure and career longevity and blah blah, my team had always had my best interests and mental health at heart. Happy actors have long and productive careers, and long and productive careers pay the bills for their team.

"Not really," I said honestly. "I just…I don't want her to become media fodder if I can avoid it." I wasn't *worried* worried. I wasn't super mega famous, but I had enough people paying attention to me that it was noticeable. I just hoped Harper was okay with that, because I didn't want to stop spending time with her.

"You can't control that," Ingrid said diplomatically.

"I know."

"Good. Do you want me to talk to the producers about you and Harper? I'm sure they'll see these photos soon enough, though I don't know if they'll immediately connect the two of you. It's not problematic, nor against the rules, but you know my motto."

I did. *Stay ahead of everything.* "I can do it."

"Okay. And you need to think about how you're going to present yourselves as a couple at work."

"Discreetly and professionally," I said dryly, to cover the fact my heart rate had started triple-timing at the thought of Harper and me as a couple.

"Exactly. Now, let's talk about this charity tennis thing."

"I'd love to."

We discussed my media commitments, and she reminded me that it was for fun, and to be mindful of not being obnoxiously competitive. "Make sure you put on a good show, but it's all for a good time. Not that I really need to remind you, but please, no unsportsmanlike conduct that'll put a blot on your squeaky-clean image."

"I promise I will be the model of decorum."

Ingrid laughed. "You don't have to be too decorous, have fun, but remember how many eyes will be on you."

As if I could forget. Luckily there would be one set of eyes on me in particular. Suddenly, all I wanted was those eyes on me right now. So I agreed with Ingrid, just so I could wrap up the conversation. "Sure, I will smile and look unbitchy while I'm concentrating on not getting hit by tennis balls."

We said our goodbyes, I quickly finished removing my makeup, grabbed my things, and went to go find Harper.

I found her exactly where I expected—locking the trailer door to Hair and Makeup. Harper startled slightly when I touched her shoulder and spun around, the surprise on her face quickly turning to pleasure. "Hey. What's up?"

"Do you have plans for the rest of the night?"

"Eat, drink, maybe be merry."

"Do you want to come back to my place for that? I can offer you dinner, drinks, and a lot of merriment. And…a talk?" I needed to tell her about the photos of us kissing, and how I needed to talk to Brian about us, but here really wasn't the place.

"A food-delivery-service dinner?" She grinned. "Be still my beating heart."

"I'll have you know I'm excellent at having food delivered."

"Then I'm in."

"Well that was easy."

She paused a moment. Her eyes drifted down to my waist then back up to linger on my breasts. Harper licked her lips. "I think you'll find I'm easy in other ways too…"

Nervous excitement twisted through me. "I can't believe you just said that. Aloud."

Harper was all innocence. "How else do you usually say things?"

"Smart-ass."

She smiled angelically. "I think you secretly like it."

"Oh no, it's not secretly. If we weren't at work, I would be kissing you so hard right now."

"Then we'd better leave work so you can do just that."

I raised an eyebrow. "Just kissing?"

She looked around, then drew her fingertips down my forearm. Leaning a little closer, she murmured, "You're just going to have to find out when we get to your place."

"That's not fair." My body had reacted crazily to this simple touch, goose bumps spreading over my skin.

"You're right, it's not." Harper withdrew her hand.

"To be clear, I also really want to talk about us. Maybe do some of that first up before there's kissing and we do that for the rest of the night instead of talking."

"Sounds good. Do you want me to follow you, or go home and take a quick shower and come around in an hour or so?"

"Up to you." I didn't want to waste any time, but I also didn't want to pressure her.

"I'll follow you," she said immediately.

Her quick agreement made me even more desperate to kiss her, and I took a half step backward to stop myself from breaking the rule. "So unfair," I grumbled. I satisfied myself with touching her hip. "See you soon. See you again I mean. In the parking lot. And when we get to my place, you can just park in the driveway."

Harper smiled, nodding along with my blathering.

I spent most of the drive checking she was still following, only relaxing when she pulled into the driveway behind me. Instead of going into the house through the door from the garage, I ducked underneath the closing garage door and met Harper on the driveway.

She looked over the exterior of my house. "So this is where you live?"

I bit back the facetious urge to say something silly like "Nah, this just looked like a nice place and I'm hoping there's a key under the doormat" and instead answered with a cheerful, "Yup." I took her hand and led her to the front door.

As soon as I stepped inside, Asimov sprinted from where he'd been waiting for me at the internal garage door, yowling like a cat that hadn't eaten in a week. "Yes, yes, I know. I'm feeding you right now." He wound himself around my legs, trying to convey just how neglected he felt. "Azzie. Dude. This is counterproductive. If you trip me, I'm not going to be able to feed you." I dropped my bags onto the floor near the entry to the living room.

"I'll feed him if you faceplant," Harper piped up. "He's too cute to go hungry." She crouched down and held out her hands. My cat came right over and rubbed his face against her hands, then moved on to her knees. "So this is Asimov, huh? In the flesh."

"Sure is. Come on through." She followed me to the kitchen. So did Asimov. I dumped my keys in the wooden bowl on my counter.

"I've always wondered about his name. Are you a sci-fi-fantasy fan?"

I grimaced. "God no. I hate sci-fi and fantasy. I've never read Isaac Asimov. I just thought it was a cool name."

"It is a cool name," she agreed, laughing.

"Just let me feed him and I'll get you a drink. Then we can figure out what to order for dinner. Make yourself comfortable." A drink, some dinner, a shower, and Harper was just what I needed. And not necessarily in that order.

She hopped up onto one of the high chairs at my breakfast bar. "I'm comfortable."

Our eyes met and held for a long moment. Though I wanted almost nothing more than to kiss her, my cat needed dinner. Harper watched as I emptied a small can of food into his bowl, refilled his water-filtering fountain, and checked the auto-cleaning litterbox hadn't malfunctioned and strewn cat shit everywhere.

"Right. Drinks. What can I get you?"

"What are you having?"

I opened the freezer and pulled out the bottle of Belvedere. "Vodka over ice, with a twist. I also have wine, beer, and a bunch of liquor if you want a cocktail or just something with a mixer."

"Wine's fine. Nice and easy." Before I could ask what she felt like, she said, "The first bottle you put your hands on is great."

After pouring Harper a glass of Napa sauvignon blanc, I added lemon peel to my glass—a twist was a generous term, I had neither the time nor inclination to make fancy garnishes—and poured myself a single over ice. She tilted her glass toward me, and I raised mine in return. I drank a small mouthful of the icy vodka, closing my eyes as I swallowed.

Harper's hand closing around my wrist made me open my eyes. I set my glass down on the countertop next to hers. She pulled my wrist until I moved closer, her eyes holding mine as I took the few steps to close the space between us. Her expression was open, full of affection, trust... desire. Having her look at me that way made something swell in my chest, and I had to swallow the emotion down.

She made a small noise of enjoyment when I pushed her backward until she was against the counter. That sound, the look on her face, made my desire flare. I didn't think I'd ever wanted anyone like I wanted her. Harper gave the slightest nod and I bent my head, gently cupping her jaw between my hands to tilt her face up to mine for a kiss.

The kiss quickly grew heated, and when Harper's hands snuck up under my shirt, I wrapped an arm around her waist, bringing our bodies flush together. The warmth of her had excitement pooling in my belly, and when her fingertips delicately trailed up my abs, I shuddered. I dipped my fingers into the waistband of her pants, enjoying the little exhalation that followed when I met skin.

Harper's ringing cell phone was a most unwelcome interruption, and I stopped as dead as someone playing Red Light, Green Light.

She frowned, pulling it out of her pocket. "It's my sister. She never calls." Harper shrugged, tapped the screen, and tossed the phone onto the countertop.

About twenty seconds later, her phone sounded a different alert, interrupting us again. Harper groaned and snatched it up. This time, she didn't brush it aside. The deep crease between her eyebrows, the downward turn of her mouth made me ask, "Everything okay?"

"Yes, but I have to go deal with something." She smiled, and I was relieved that it seemed genuine enough.

Disappointment rushed through me, hot and frustrating, followed quickly by concern, cooler and easier to deal with. "Okay. Well...if you need me, let me know?"

The edges of her eyes softened. "I will, thanks. I'll see you in the mornin'. I'm so sorry to run off like this."

I smiled at the little extra drawl that'd crept into her voice, and almost mentioned that if messages from her family brought out more of her Southern, then I was all for bringing her family up here. But there was a tightness in her expression that stopped me. "It's okay, really. I understand."

Harper pulled me down for a kiss, sighing against my mouth. As she pulled away, she muttered, "I'm gonna kill my sister for interruptin' us."

CHAPTER FOURTEEN

Harper

Harper, what in God's name are these disgusting pictures of you and why are they public so the whole world can see them?

I'd read my sister's text message a dozen times and still wasn't sure why I felt like I'd just been caught breaking into a bank. I wanted to answer with an obvious *Well, Brittany, it appears to be me kissing actor Stephanie D'Arripe* but I really didn't need or want to stoke the fire of her burning outrage.

An hour ago, I'd been about to have a conversation about where Steph and I stood, before we'd probably tumble into bed and have sex until we'd exhausted ourselves. But now? My world was imploding. No, not imploding exactly, but it was being very annoying.

What I hadn't told Steph when I'd said I wasn't close to my family was that I also remained firmly closeted to them. They knew nothing of my life in LA except that I worked as a makeup artist on a television show, and before that worked on some movies and other television shows. They didn't know what show I worked on now, what shows and movies I had worked on. And that was exactly the way I liked it.

They weren't exactly fire and brimstone, burn-in-hell-all-ye-sinners Southern Baptists religious, but they *were* pretty darned homophobic. Which is probably why seeing pictures of me kissing a woman was shocking, because I'd never told them I kissed women. Correction: my mama and sister were homophobic. Before he'd died, I'd never heard my dad express anything but acceptance for pretty much anyone who was a decent person.

For my mental health and sanity, I'd decided as soon as I realized I was a lesbian that I wasn't going to come out to my family. It wasn't worth it. I'd debated with myself, wondering if I *could* tell my dad, but I knew he'd tell my mother and I was not on board with that. And then he was gone and it didn't matter.

I'd always known I wasn't going to stay in Georgia, so what did any of it matter? Deep down I knew it was the cowardly thing to do, but I'd always been protective of my headspace. If I was honest with myself, I resented my mother because, if it weren't for her, I could have told Dad, shared that with him. She'd taken honesty, and then possible support from me.

I looked at the images in the link yet again, ignoring Brittany's accompanying words. If I set aside the intrusion of privacy, which wasn't entirely unexpected given Steph's celebrity status, the pictures were actually really good, even with their grainy zoom quality. Unfortunately they weren't grainy enough to obscure either of our identities, though the idea of anyone recognizing me would never have occurred to me. Until it became my reality.

Steph's arm around my waist had felt comforting, but it looked almost possessive in the photos, and that thought thrilled me. I was also strangely grateful that whoever decided to intrude upon this private moment had captured our second kiss, not our first. Your first kiss with a woman you were insanely attracted to shouldn't be news fodder. Neither should your second, really, but I lived in a weird world.

A weird world where, if I was going to be with Steph, we'd kiss, hold hands, or hug in public. And I needed to get okay with people paying attention to that, and having opinions on it. But for now, I needed to get okay with talking to my mother and sister about something I really never wanted to talk to them about.

I was surprised at my anxiety at being outed to my family, because if Britt knew, Mama absolutely knew. I didn't know if the anxiety stemmed from the fact I couldn't be bothered with the drama this would stir up, if I secretly did care about what they thought of me, or if somewhere in the deep dark recess of my psyche, I still craved my mother's approval and knew this would kill any chance of that.

I blew out a little scoff. She'd never approved of anything I did, and I knew better than to hope. Responding to Britt via text would drag things out, so I hit the call button. She answered almost immediately.

No greeting, no "Hey, little sister, how've you been since we talked almost six months ago." Just a curt, "Tell me this is one of those photoshopped things."

"It's not."

"What the hell are you doin', Harper?" She didn't wait for an answer, which was unsurprising. Our whole lives, Britt's role had always been to prime me for whatever Mama wanted, be it doing something for her, Mama's discipline, or anything else, and she stayed in character. "You bet your ass Mama is expectin' you to call her this instant."

"Oh joy," I drawled. Just once I wished my mother would dispense with using her older daughter like an assistant and just come right to me.

Britt sighed. "You've always been such a smart aleck."

I was long past the stage where I worried what my sister thought of me, so I answered honestly, and added a rare expletive. "Tell me something we don't fuckin' know." I took a deep breath and decided to redirect things. Or…try to. "Anyway. How're you and George? Beau started fifth grade this year, didn't he?" I wanted to remind her that I remembered shit like this, when she barely remembered basic things like my birthday.

"We're all fine, except for utterly mortified by this. What the hell were you thinkin'?" Again, she didn't give me a chance to respond, not that I actually had an answer that would satisfy her. Instead, Britt ended the call with a firm, "Call Mama. *Now.*"

No goodbye. I sighed and spoke to a dead call. "Bye. Love you too. Great to talk to you. I'm really good, actually, thanks so much for askin'…"

I would have loved to put off a call to Mama indefinitely but the more I thought about it, the more I realized I just wanted to get it over and done with so I could move on with my life. I stared at the pictures again. *That* was my life, and my life was damned good. I didn't bother with a deep breath, or a little pep talk, because there was nothing that was going to make this any easier.

I didn't even have a chance to say hello before Mama launched right in with no preamble. Clearly Britt got that trait from our mother. "Harper Ashley Bell. Why are there obscene pictures of you and another woman published for the entire world to see? And why did I have to find out about it from your sister?"

Telling her exactly who Steph was to me was tricky, because I honestly didn't know. So I went with the easiest version, which was my current dream scenario. "That's my girlfriend. And you found out from Brittany because you never gave me a safe space to tell you something like this."

Of course Mama didn't acknowledge me telling her that I didn't trust her enough to tell her something so important. Instead, she went on the attack. "That place has done something to you."

Well, here goes. "No, Mama, actually it was Greensboro, Georgia, that did this to me. I've known I was a lesbian since I was ten years old."

"That's *ridiculous*. Do you understand what you're saying? Think of what everyone here will *think*, Harper." God, if clutching pearls had a sound, this was it. The hilarious image made a giggle bubble up in my throat, and I had to clear it so I didn't burst into laughter. My mother probably thought I was choking on my guilt.

I made sure to disabuse her of the notion.

"Mama, with all respect, I don't give a flyin' fuck about what the neighbors and people at your church think of me. And you shouldn't either."

The silence was so loud, I realized I'd misinterpreted. She didn't care what people thought of me. She cared what they thought of *her*. How the hell had I never connected those dots before? I gave myself a small pass, because I'd tried to think about this whole thing and my family as little as possible from the moment I was old enough to realize how I felt and that there was no comfortable place for me in that world.

"I'm going to be a pariah at church. How am I supposed to show my face about town?"

"The same way you did before."

She laughed humorlessly. "Oh no. You've made sure that that will never happen again."

I was glad this wasn't a FaceTime call and she couldn't see my epic eye roll.

"You know, Harper, I don't agree with this lifestyle choice, but you're my daughter. I just don't know why you couldn't keep this to yourself."

"What do you think I've been doing most of my life? Do you know what it's like to not be able to tell your own mama about something so important, something that's *you*? To be a kid scared every day and just wanting your mama to accept you but knowing she never would? What it's like to hide every damned day? Why do you think I left?" I was getting emotional and nostalgic and I hated myself for it. With effort, I clamped down on the drama and stuck to the facts.

Mama tried again. "I don't know why you couldn't just ignore this nonsense."

"What nonsense is that? Being gay? Sorry, that's not somethin' I can just ignore. It's who I am."

"I'm starting to think you don't know *who* you are."

"That's ridiculous and incredibly insulting." Thankfully she didn't tell me I was just "confused" or I probably would have really lost my shit at her. Instead, I decided to prioritize myself and wrap up the conversation. "You know what, Mama? This conversation is pointless. So you do whatever makes you feel better. Tell everyone at church and in town that LA broke me or corrupted me or whatever, not that your genes and your upbringin' made me like this. I honestly don't care and I haven't cared for a very long time."

"You need to come back here and straighten yourself out."

I didn't know if the pun was intentional—probably not knowing my mama—but it was so funny that I laughed. Loudly. "Mama. Getting 'straight' is the last thing I'm going to do, and Greensboro would be the *last* place I did anything. I left because I knew I couldn't be my authentic self if I stayed."

"You never should have left," she insisted. "I thank the Lord your father isn't here. It would break his heart to see what you're doing. You're debasing yourself with this perverted lifestyle."

Now *that* stung. I had to take a deep breath to settle my emotions. "I think he'd be more upset by your behavior than mine. Mama, if you can't truly love and accept me for who I am then that's on you. I'm not gonna fall on my knees and beg for your acceptance or forgiveness when it's not me who needs forgivin'. And I'm not gonna quote verses at you about how a Christian should act because you should know, and what you're doin' sure as shit ain't it. What I am gonna do is live my life. I'm proud of who I am and everything I've achieved. And until you accept that, I…I don't think you're welcome in my life. You can contact me once you've accepted who I am. *If,*" I added tightly.

"Harper, you're—"

"Goodbye, Mama. Take care of yourself. I hope I talk to you soon."

And then I hung up, dropped my phone onto the bed, and flopped onto my back. Well. That was a whole thing. It felt both freeing and grounding to cut her, and by extension Brittany, loose like this. But despite my bravado, my hands were shaking and there was an unmistakable churn in my stomach. The insistent press of tears was both annoying and upsetting.

A light knock on my bedroom doorframe startled me, and I sat up. Per stood in the doorway, regarding me with wary concern. I forced a smile. "Hey. How long have you been home?"

"I just got in, and I caught some of that conversation, sorry. What the hell was that about?"

"That?" I exhaled noisily. "That was just me coming out to my mama and sister. Or…more accurately, *Page Six* outed me to my family. And it went exactly as I'd thought it would, which is why I've spent the last twenty-five years or so avoiding this exact scenario."

His face fell. "Oh, Harpies." Per crossed the floor in a few long strides and scooped me up into a tight hug, pulling me up off my bed. "My love, I am so sorry."

"I'm okay," I mumbled against his chest.

"I know you are. You're always okay, but you can be not okay sometimes too." He released his grip and we sat down on my bed. He took my hands, clasping them tightly. I'd always known how lucky I was to have Per, but moments like this just confirmed it.

"I know. I really am okay, but honestly? It does feel pretty darn terrible." I kind of wanted to cry and laugh all at once, but neither thing wanted to start. "But also…it's not like I expected anything different. They've acted exactly how I thought they would. It's almost a relief to have the confirmation, to have it done and out of my way now."

Per knew about my family and had always offered, with Ben's support, to pretend he was my perfectly normal heterosexual boyfriend, not just my roommate, if my mother or sister ever came to visit. Not that they ever had, because Los Angeles was apparently anathema to everything they believed in as god-fearing Southern Republican women.

Of course, they still consumed movies and television produced here, and obviously Britt was a secret trash-mag reader. Hypocrites.

Per frowned. "Can I just circle back? What do you mean exactly, that *Page Six* outed you?"

Despite his addiction to *North Precinct*, Per was allergic to any and all gossip columns, deeming them "clickbait trash," and he never looked. Ben sometimes checked out a few, but he claimed it was workplace research, seeing who lived where. Clearly he hadn't looked in the last few days or there would have been a meltdown.

I'd wanted a little more time before I told him, wanted more certainty, but I wasn't going to get it. I braced myself for a Per meltdown, and just said it. "Steph and I were photographed kissing after tennis."

"Ohmygod. Ohmygod. Ohmyfuckinggod." It went like that for another fifteen seconds or so, and I sat patiently while he worked through his feelings. Per shook his hands out, then turned to me, his face the picture of rapt attention. "Firstly, *wow*. Secondly, ew, invasion of privacy. Thirdly, I also want to invade your privacy and get every single detail."

"I'd expect nothing less."

"When did this happen?"

"Saturday."

"Don't be a bitch. I mean…when did you and Steph start kissing."

"Saturday."

"And you've already made *Page Six*? Holy shit, girl, you are going to be in all the 'bloids."

I groaned. "Please don't say 'bloids."

He ignored me, but thankfully didn't say it again. "Doors will open. The hottest restaurants in town. Invitations. The latest fashion. The hottest products. You name it, you'll get it. And then you'll share it with me."

"Slight exaggeration on your behalf. And I don't want any of that."

"What *do* you want?" he asked, serious now.

"I just want her. I want us." And I selfishly, and naively, wanted it without anything external in our way, even though I knew that would never happen.

"Were you ever going to tell me about you and Steph?" There was an edge of little-boy-hurt in the question.

"If it became more than just a few kisses, yes."

"*A few kisses.*" He fanned himself. "I'm going to have a cardiac arrest. You've killed me. Me, fit-as-anything me. Killed dead."

"Fit?" I held in a laugh. "I'd like to see you attempt even five minutes of cardio. We all know you're nothing but attractive vanity muscle, not functional muscle, Per. Which is obviously perfect for your job," I added.

"Thank you for confirming I'm attractive."

I rolled my eyes.

Per took my hands again, squeezing gently. "I just want to make this utterly clear. I'm *thrilled* that you seem to have found yourself a girlfriend. Or the start of a girlfriend," he added when I opened my mouth, clearly intuiting that I was about to rebut that this was new and I didn't know what it was. "And I'm even more thrilled that it's Steph. She's a goddamned delight. And she looks at you like you're the best thing she's seen all year. You deserve that, Harpies. You deserve the fucking universe and I hope she gives it to you."

My eyes burned and I blinked hard to stop my tears. "Thanks," I said tightly. "I hope she does too, but only because I've given her the universe as well. Or something else as good as the universe because you share a universe. Anyway, you know what I mean."

"I...think so?" Per said teasingly. He stood. "I need to eat and shower. Have you eaten? Are you hungry?"

The vaguely nauseated sensation had thankfully abated, but not enough that I was hungry yet, though I was sure I would be later. "I'm good for now, thanks. Make yourself dinner, I'll figure something out."

"You know where I am if you need me."

"I do, thanks." I stood for another hug, and Per bundled me up tightly, squeezing some of the worry out of me.

He pulled the door mostly closed behind him and I lay back down, curling up on my side. I closed my eyes and for the next few minutes, did nothing except breathe. And think. A lot. I wished they were helpful thoughts, but mostly they were just circular and pointless.

I kept half-expecting a call or text from Mama or Brittany, but I was also completely unsurprised that there was nothing. Maybe in time they'd be okay with it, but it wasn't my job to help them get to a place of acceptance. The people who were important to me accepted me, and that was enough.

I was sure this particular life trauma would pop up again every once in a while. But for now I resolved to put it back in the dark corner where I'd been keeping it most of my life and move on.

I felt terrible for running out on Steph with the most basic of explanations, and that had nothing to do with the fact I'd bailed on what had been promising to shape up as a very pleasant evening for both of us. I rolled over, fumbling for my phone to call and explain when a text notification pinged through. Steph. She had impeccable timing.

Is everything okay?

Just a simple message, but it said so much more than what those three words conveyed. She cared about me. She was worried about me. I hit the icon for a video call and wormed my way up the bed until I sat up against my pile of pillows.

Steph's smiling face filled my screen. "Hey. Sorry to butt in on your family thing, but...you seemed kind of stressed out and I just wanted to make sure you're doing okay?" The worried lilt made it seem like a question.

"Has anyone ever told you you're a sweetheart?"

"No they haven't. Which may actually be a travesty. I feel like I should be gunning for the title of America's Sweetheart."

I laughed. "You should."

She hmmed. "You never answered my question as to whether or not you're okay."

"Everything is not okay, but I'm okay."

Steph's eyebrows came together, and I could tell she couldn't quite connect the dots of what exactly I meant by "everything is not okay." She looked like she both wanted to fight whatever had made things not okay for me, and bundle me up in a tight, warm hug until everything was better. "Do you want to talk about it? Whatever it is."

"Why didn't you tell me *Page Six* published pictures of us kissing after tennis?"

Her eyebrows shot up. "I literally just found out after we wrapped today. I thought we'd talk about it tonight, but then you had your thing." She frowned. "Sorry, I didn't mean to blame you for not talking because you had to go, that's not—" Steph cut herself off, shaking her head. "Is that what this is about? Are you upset that there's pictures? I know it's shitty and I'm sorry that us kissing is a problem." She inhaled so deeply, I heard the air rushing into her nose. "But I'm *not* sorry about kissing you. Not at all."

"It's fine. I'm not upset about the pictures. Yes, I'd have preferred our private moment to stay private, but given that private moment was in a public place, I can't be shitty about it. And I'm not sorry about kissing you either. Sorry is the furthest thing from what I am."

"Good."

"It's just...not something I was prepared for."

"I know, and I'm sorry." She bit her lower lip. "Is it a problem for you? Moving forward? Because I think we both know this is a possibility if...if you're with me."

"No," I said emphatically. "But, it did kind of force me to come out to my family."

"Oh." She packed so much into that short word. Surprise, encouragement, and a touch of wariness.

"Yeah. There's a reason I've never done it, so...yeahhhh. It wasn't ideal. It was basically a 'you dirty sinner' speech. I'm not blaming you," I hastened to assure her. "But it's just a thing that happened that I never wanted to happen."

"Okay, okay. I hear you. I'm so sorry, Harper. And I'm sorry it happened because of me."

"It wasn't *because* of you."

Steph's slow nodding ceased. The background spun around and started moving. "I'm coming over. You shouldn't be alone, and some things are better discussed in person."

I wasn't alone, but I understood what she meant. "Steph—"

"No. I'm coming over." She stopped moving. "Unless you tell me you don't want me to?" There was a vulnerability there I'd never seen before.

"I do want you to, but it's also a work night."

"I don't care. I want to hug you. I'll be there soon."

There was no point arguing because she'd decided on something, but most importantly—I wanted her here. Per's hugs and Per's comfort and Per's indignant outrage were all wonderful. But right now, I wanted to share this with my maybe-girlfriend. We really needed to have that discussion about what we actually were or were trying to be, but that was something I'd bring up later when I hadn't just dealt with my mama basically telling me I was dead to her.

I told Per that Steph was coming over, asked him to let her in, and went back into my room to reset my brain with some Polish lessons. After about thirty minutes, Steph tapped her knuckles against my partly closed bedroom door. Her expression was so open, so gentle, so understanding, that tears pricked my eyes and I blinked them back. She crossed the floor to me, opening her arms as she approached.

"Come here," Steph murmured. When I folded myself into the safety of her hug, she said, "I'm so, so sorry. That someone took pictures of such a personal, amazing moment. About the pictures being public. About your family."

I pressed my cheek against her shoulder, relaxing into the warmth of her. She was firm and solid, safe and protective, yet soft and nurturing. I felt relaxation seep into me. "It's fine. I mean, it's not fine, but it's okay."

"It's not okay. It's fucking awful."

"No, I know that. I mean…it's just…it is what it is. I've been a mini outcast in my family since I was a preteen when I declared I didn't really think god was real, and it all snowballed from there."

"Ah. I see."

I pulled back from the hug, sighing. "I don't know how I feel about my family. I don't want to defend them or say they're actually really nice people *except* for being raging homophobes, xenophobes, and mildly raging racists and misogynists. But it's a really hard thing to reconcile that the core values of those you're supposed to love basically mean that they think you're a garbage human. And I guess…I guess I'm kind of weak for just ignoring it all this time."

"Maybe the thing you think is weakness is actually strength." At my surprised look, Steph elaborated. "I mean, it's not easy to pick up your life, move away from your home base and the people who've provided you with shelter, food, clothing, and all that stuff, to move to a new place with nobody. But you did that because that's what you thought was best for you. You chose you."

I laughed dryly. "I suppose I did. I've spent the last…twenty-five or so years trying to figure it out, figure out how I feel about it."

"How do you feel about it?"

I pulled her down to sit on the bed. This was not the way I'd wanted her in my bed the first time. "Honestly? I really don't know. Not good. Not terrible. Just…resigned I guess." Shrugging, I added, "It's easy because I really don't see them. I've been back less than a handful of times since I moved." I tried on a smile, and it didn't feel awful. "It's easy with this job to say you're so busy and can't find the time. So it's easy for me to just act like they're fine, because I'm not there with it in my face constantly. Morality is so hard. I don't have the mental energy to draw firm lines everywhere, so I guess I leave some of them smudged and blurry, and this is one of those."

Steph nodded slowly. "I think that's something a lot of people do. Pick your battles, right?"

"Right. But now I don't know what I should do."

Her eyebrows crinkled inward. "What do you mean?"

"I'm pretty sure my mama and sister will never voluntarily talk to me again. But I don't know if I just leave it at that, or make some big 'Screw you, I'm officially cutting you loose' declaration."

"Do you think confronting them with that will make a difference to your life?" She ran a hand from between my shoulder blades to my waist, lightly stroking, lightly soothing.

"Maybe?" After a few moments, I decided, "No. It's not going to change their minds, and going back just to have the last word again won't change the situation one little bit. It's probably just going to remind me of how…how…" I couldn't find the word I wanted that would encompass this situation. After a few seconds, I found something that'd do as a placeholder. "How *shitty* this is."

"It absolutely is shitty and you deserve to have all the feelings about it."

"I suppose I should have realized this could happen, but my mother has shown absolutely no interest in anything to do with my job in LA. And my sister thinks non-right-leaning news sources are trash. Maybe it was naïve but I really never thought they'd find out." I bit my lip. Before I'd given in and kissed Steph, I'd briefly considered the possibility of someone seeing us, but never in a million years did I think it'd lead to this. I'd been secure in my bubble, thinking my family and my life here were totally separate.

The cute little confusion wrinkle appeared between Steph's eyebrows. "You never gave them any hints? No judgment, I'm just curious."

"I didn't. But I *think* my dad knew? Or at least suspected. I used to just tell him I didn't have time for boyfriends. Dad was great, but Mama and Brittany kind of smothered the goodness. We were split as a family. Britt and I split our alliances so it was me and Dad against Mama and Britt."

"That doesn't sound fun."

"It wasn't. When he died, it was like a switch just clicked on in Mama. Or clicked off. She got *super* conservative. I have no idea if she was suppressing herself for him while he was alive, or what happened. But something did."

"I'm sorry you had to experience that." The hand stroking my back moved up to my hair. She gently twirled some of it around her fingers.

The light tug sent a shudder rushing down my spine. "It doesn't matter. I *never* felt like I fit into my family, and it wasn't just because I'm a lesbian. It was slightly easier when Dad was still alive, but only slightly. Maybe if we'd lived somewhere else. Maybe if my mother was someone else. But…we are who we are and lived where we lived so I'll never know if it's me or them."

"Harper, you deserve to surround yourself with people who understand you, who make you feel good about yourself and your choices, who help you make those choices—especially when they're difficult." Steph gently cupped my face with one hand, the other pushing some loose hair away from my eyes. "You deserve support and love and all that good shit. I'm sorry you didn't get what you needed from the people who are supposed to give it to you."

There was no mistaking the unspoken promise in that statement— that Steph wanted to give me support and love and "all that good shit." Our eyes met and held.

She smiled sadly. "And I'm sorry the photos happened, that this wasn't private, that you were forced to share part of yourself with your family when you didn't want to. But, like I said, I am *not* sorry about kissing you."

I leaned over and kissed her again, because I couldn't help myself. It was short, sweet, soft, and so satisfying I actually sighed with contentment. "I bet your family was amazing when you came out."

Steph's eyebrows shot up. "Actually…not all that much. My sister didn't care, but she's really hard to rattle. But my parents definitely did care. They're amazing now but they struggled with it. It took a few years before they fully accepted I was a big ol' lesbo."

"Were they homophobic?"

"No, I never got that vibe from them. I think they were more worried about, like…lost opportunities, having kids and stuff, until I reminded them there was more than one way to have a baby. And also just that life could be hard for me." Steph laughed dryly. "It has been anything but. Maybe it's actually been easier." She shrugged. "I know I'm a little typecast, but I have enough variation in my roles that I'm happy. And this steady paycheck is really really nice."

"There is that." I gently stroked her cheek, and when Steph grabbed my wrist to pull me closer, I kissed her again. Her hand tightened on my wrist, but the kiss remained gentle. Gentle, but the intensity of the connection made my breath catch.

"I know we were going to talk about us, and we can later. For now, can I stay a little while?" She smiled shyly. "Not all night, but…"

The unspoken caveat was clear—no sex—and I was okay with that. "Yes. Please." At her place earlier, my entire focus had been on sex, about how good it would feel, about how much I wanted that kind of intimacy. But now? I just wanted to be close to her. Sure, sex would feel amazing and would take my mind off my family for a little while, but right now I just wanted comfort.

She kicked off her shoes and lined them up at the foot of the bed. "Is it okay if I lie down? If *we* lie down?" Steph corrected herself.

Of course it was, but I loved the respect of her asking. I nodded. Steph went around to the other side of the bed and lay down, facing me. She squirmed and shifted to get comfortable, then opened her arms to me. I almost faced her, but I didn't think I'd be able to lie there looking at her, with her looking at me. It would make me feel too exposed, too raw. So I put my back to her, taking up the position of little spoon.

I hardly ever got to be the little spoon. It wasn't because I didn't want to, but that the women I'd been with preferred it. The sensation of being held so tightly, so warmly, with no expectation but my comfort was so sweetly wonderful I almost cried.

I was lucky to have such an incredible friend and support system in Per and, by extension, Ben. But I realized now that maybe I had the same in Steph, and that felt indescribably incredible.

We didn't kiss. There was no groping. We just spooned, the soft whisper of her breath against my ear. And as we lay there, her holding me like she wanted to make everything okay, I thought maybe the safety of being in her arms was the most intimate thing I'd ever experienced.

CHAPTER FIFTEEN

Steph

I'd never really thought the universe conspired against me. But when we ran into three twelve-hour days straight, I started to wonder if I'd angered some god of intimacy. Harper and I managed to snatch a few short snippets of time during the day to check in, and promise we'd meet up after work. Then every night when we wrapped, one of us would yawn, which invariably led to a teasing response of "Rain check?"

It seemed we were both on the same page, not wanting to rush sex after an extra-long day and then rush off after sex because we had to work early the next day. I didn't want to half-ass my time with Harper. I wanted to spend hours indulging in her, and then spend all weekend learning all the things I hadn't learned about her body on our first night together.

After finally wrapping on Friday, Harper sidled up to me as I walked to my trailer, and murmured, "What a week, huh? But I'm ready for that rain check tonight…" And I knew we would be indulging in a new type of intimacy. The words were simple, but the way she said them—low and with a purr of promise—was so sexy I almost pushed her up against my trailer door and let my hands and lips do what they wanted, right there in public, at work, for all to see.

Harper followed me to my place again, and once I'd fed Asimov and poured us both a drink, I asked, "Can you give me a few minutes? I'm dying to take my contacts out."

She gave me all her attention. "I've never seen you with your glasses on. Do you need them when you take your contacts out?"

"Mhmm." I'd only needed glasses in the last four or so years and still felt a little strange about wearing them in public. So I didn't, not even at work when I wasn't shooting.

"I see," she mused.

"But I *don't*," I laughingly admitted. "Give me a few minutes. You'll be okay 'til I get back?"

"I actually don't know," she mused. "How am I supposed to keep myself occupied for these few minutes?"

"I'm sure you'll think of something…" I smirked. "And if you're bored, I'm sure Asimov will keep you entertained."

When I returned, Harper had moved to the couch with her glass of wine and had my cat on her lap, stroking him absently as she read something on her phone. When I came back, she looked up, her expression making it very clear she liked what she saw. "Glasses suit you."

"So I've been told."

"Then why don't you wear them more often?"

"They're annoying. And…they make me feel weird, almost like it's not really me in the mirror."

She smiled indulgently. "No. You're definitely still you. Do you think maybe you'd wear them occasionally for me?"

"I can probably swing that. Just for you." I picked Asimov up and deposited him at the other end of the couch. Always amiable, he was unperturbed by losing his comfortable warm human. He rolled into a sitting position, stuck a leg in the air, and started licking his butt. All class.

Harper stared at me like she was trying to memorize this new look. "You've never worn glasses for a role before, so I've never really thought about it." Her tongue flashed out, lightning-fast, to swipe over her lower lip. "Now, I'm thinking about it."

"I didn't know you paid attention to my other roles."

She feigned nonchalance. "It's my job to know this stuff. See how other artists work with you."

"*Nobody* makes me look as good as you do," I said honestly. My face was a big part of my job, and my relationship with those who helped me look my best was important. I briefly wondered if expanding that relationship into sleeping with the woman who made me look my best was just as important.

Yes.

"I know," she assured me. "You told me after our first day together that nobody's ever made your eyebrows look as good as I do."

"That is the god's honest truth," I swore.

Harper traced the lines of my eyebrows above my glasses. "You do have exceedingly expressive and sexy eyebrows." Her fingers moved down my temple, along my jaw. "They match everything else about you that's exceedingly sexy," she murmured.

I closed my eyes, trying to settle the almost uncontrollable desire building deep in my core. After a few moments I opened them again. The desire had been momentarily tamed, but I didn't want to wait any longer. "How hungry are you?"

"Moderately. You?"

"About the same." I cleared my throat. Before we organized food, I wanted to make sure we were on the same page about what would come after dinner. It felt like we were, or we were at least reading the same chapter, but the last thing I wanted was to misinterpret the signs and ruin things. "I just want to be clear about something. Or...for you to clear something up for me."

"Clarity *is* kindness," Harper agreed.

"Right, it is. So, to be clear. Are we...going to bed tonight? Like, sex bed not sleeping bed? Although falling asleep together after sex is great too. And Monday, just cuddling, was also really great."

"I'd assumed so," she said quietly, before quickly adding, "I'd hoped so."

I exhaled loudly. "Me too. Good. Great. And if that's the case then I think I'm just going to take a quick shower." I stood up, and Harper got to her feet too. "I've been at work all day, and..." If we were going to get up close and personal then I wanted to make a good first impression, not a "been in shapewear and sweating for most of the day" impression.

Harper unbuttoned the top few buttons of my shirt, her fingertips lightly touching the skin she exposed. "Do you want company?"

I inhaled shakily at the touch. I didn't care if she'd showered or not—I'd never met a woman I didn't love the smell or taste of—and the idea of her joining me was super tempting. But... "If you join me in the shower, I'm worried we might not order food. And if we don't order food, there won't be any proper dinner."

Harper drew her fingertips from my navel up through my cleavage, until she stroked lightly along my collarbone. "*Some* food place will be open for us to order dinner later."

I tilted my head back as Harper's fingertips explored my neck. "You're right," I said breathily. "Someplace will be open."

"Yes." And that's all she said, because her lips were suddenly on my neck, bestowing the softest kisses.

I shuddered as her tongue flicked over my skin, and almost gave in and slipped my hands under her shirt, until I realized that wasn't going to help my goal of getting clean. "Okay. I need to shower. Now. Please?" I added hoarsely.

I felt her smirking against my neck. "I didn't know you lacked patience," Harper murmured. As her lips continued exploring my skin, she grabbed my ass, pulling me against her. The way she took charge was hot as fuck, and I decided to let her lead. This time.

"I don't, really," I protested weakly. "But I'm also human, and what you're doing is making me desperate for more."

Harper pulled back. Her eyes searched mine, and the naked desire in them made goose bumps break out over my arms. "Then I'll give you more." With that declaration, she took my hand. "Lead the way."

Though it almost killed me to lose the contact of her lips and tongue, there was the promise of so much more once I'd showered, so I acquiesced. I almost dragged her behind me into my master bathroom, where I turned the shower on to heat.

I was generally not shy about my body. Having people looking at you constantly, especially when you're only partially clothed, or Wardrobe discussing your exterior dimensions in detail removed any shyness in that regard, as did the general public commenting on what I looked like.

I started yanking my clothes off, desperate to get in the shower so we could move on to the orgasms. But there was something about the way she looked at me that made me pause my frantic undressing.

She looked like she wanted to fucking eat me alive.

When I stopped with my pants halfway down my thighs, Harper raised an eyebrow. "Why'd you stop?"

I ran my tongue along my lips, which suddenly felt dryer than the desert. "I…" Before I could finish what I wanted to say, to tell her that being looked at like I was about to be devoured had taken all thoughts from my head, Harper closed the space between us.

Her fingertips brushed my jaw as she ran the pad of her thumb over my lower lip. "From the moment I met you, every single time I've worked on your lips, I've wanted to kiss you. You have no idea how damned hard it is to not do that." Her thumb moved to my upper lip to give it the same soft, slow, sensuous treatment.

I kissed the pad of her thumb, then lightly bit the tip of it. Her sharp inhalation sent a thrill through me. "We'd be undoing all your good work."

"Then isn't it a good thing I'm excellent at my job?" she purred, leaning closer. "Excellent...and fast. I'd just fix it all up and nobody... would...ever...know." She punctuated each of those last words with a kiss right on the edge of my mouth.

"Yes," I said tightly. "That is a good thing."

"Also..." She brushed the lightest kiss over my lips, pausing for a heartbeat then pulling away before I could kiss her back. "I have two words for you. Infallible. Lipstick."

A breath passed between us before I lost the tenuous grip I had on my self-control. When I reached for her, Harper pressed her hips into mine, making her intentions very clear. Our kiss was furious, open-mouthed, frantic, passionate, and its intensity shot a surge of heat through me. Our bodies met from breast to thigh, as if we were trying to eliminate every molecule of space between us. I broke the kiss to turn my attention to Harper's neck.

A word dimly penetrated my fog, then again when I ignored her for the more pleasurable activity of cupping her ass. "Water."

Oh. I suppressed a groan—I really did need a shower and shouldn't be wasting water. Harper yanked my pants the rest of the way down, and after catching my eye, an eyebrow raised, pulled my underwear off too.

She inhaled a shuddering breath, and whispered, "Soon," almost to herself. Harper took my glasses off, folded them, and set them carefully down on the vanity. "It's a shame to take these off after you just put them on. And a shame that you'll be blind until you can put them back on again."

"I'm only blind if something isn't right in front of me." I swallowed hard. "Thankfully I can see you, because I don't feel like breaking my glasses tonight."

"Good." Harper ran her hands from my hips to my shoulders, deliberately staying away from my breasts. "Well. This body is everything I'd imagined and then some. Goddamn, you're beautiful. Sorry, I'm sure you hear that all the time."

My face heated. "Sometimes, yes. But I don't think people mean it the way you do." In a genuinely appreciative way.

Harper's response sent a shiver of arousal through me. "The way in which I've never seen anything as incredible as you naked? The way in which I am absolutely *desperate* to touch and taste *all* of you?" She raised her chin and the command in her expression was clear. And so fucking hot. "Get in the shower."

"Are you coming?" I managed to ask.

"I sure hope so. But not right now." She smirked at her double entendre. "Right now, I'm going to help you shower."

"Help?" I asked, my voice squeaking in disbelief.

Harper shrugged, a naughty smile turning her lips up. And then? Then she started undressing.

It almost killed me to start showering instead of helping her out of her clothes, but the sooner I showered, the sooner I could touch her, taste her, have her. I began the quickest, most perfunctory shower ever, keeping an eye on what she was doing. Harper watched me watching her, her expression telling me she knew exactly what I was thinking and that she was thinking it too.

As Harper removed each piece of clothing, exposed each new expanse of skin, my excitement rose higher and higher. As a woman described as having an androgynous shape by many a Wardrobe department, I was almost obsessed with women who had curves. I loved breasts I could lose myself in, hips and asses I could run my hands over for hours and still find new delights, shapely legs and strong thighs. And Harper had all that, and more, in spades. She was utterly gorgeous.

Harper slowly raised an eyebrow. "Are you showering or just standing there?"

Oh right. That. I began rubbing the soap over my arms. "I'm sorry," I said indignantly. "But you just took *all* your clothes off right in front of me and my brain has allocated all its resources to enjoying that."

"I'm not sorry." She opened the glass door and stepped in. "Now, finish your shower…" Harper watched intently as I finished soaping myself, her hands drifting to each place I'd just cleaned.

I leaned in to initiate a kiss, but Harper leaned away. The cat-and-mouse game only made me more desperate to kiss her, to touch her, and the heat spreading down from my belly was getting hard to ignore. Judging by her expression, Harper knew exactly what her deliberate denial was doing to me. She reached around me to shut off the water.

She'd remained mostly on the periphery of the showerhead, and gave herself a quick rubdown with the fresh towel I handed her. I dried myself almost as quickly then took the towel from her and threw both in the hamper.

Harper cupped my breasts, her thumbs stroking my nipples. "These are incredible."

"I'm glad you like them."

"I more than like them," she said hoarsely. As she played with my breasts, Harper kissed me, slicking her tongue along my lower lip. She

160 E. J. Noyes

kissed the edge of my jaw, and down my neck, along my collarbone and down my chest until she reached a nipple. "Thank you for showin' me."

"You never looked?" I asked breathlessly. I'd been in a bra or topless enough times on set and just assumed that despite respect and modesty, everyone I worked with had glimpsed my breasts, though nobody was ever lecherous. And Harper got up close and personal whenever a scene called for bra or less.

Harper paused her lavish attention to my nipple. "No. I really wanted to but it felt a little voyeuristic given I was attracted to you."

I would have responded, but she bent her head and sucked my nipple again, her tongue flicking against it. Harper bit lightly before straightening up again, closing the space between us. The full-skin contact was amazing, and I gripped her hips to keep her tightly against me.

Our eyes met for a moment, before she put me out of my misery and kissed me. Our kiss was slow and sensual, the perfect companion to our hands' exploration. Harper's touch paused against my ass and a moment later her lips paused as well. "Are we going to your bed? Or are we staying here?"

Wordlessly, I turned her slightly and began walking her out of the bathroom, toward my bed. We'd only taken a few steps before I couldn't stand not kissing her. The sound that came out of my throat was a desperate sort of groan, and I'd barely vocalized before Harper wrapped her arms around my shoulders, her hand gripping the back of my neck to pull me down to her. We kissed our way across my room and fell onto the bed together, with me on top. Harper held on to me tightly, making sure I couldn't shift my weight from her.

Kissing her made me realize I'd never kissed anyone so in sync with me as Harper, or kissed anyone whose kisses had such intense arousal spiraling through me. She raised her hips, pressing herself up to my thigh and pushing hers harder between my legs.

I ran my hand up the inside of her thigh, pausing midway. "I just want to check in. Are you sure this is what you want? It's definitely what I want."

"Yes," she said emphatically. "I've never been surer about what I want."

I sat back on my heels, still stroking the inside of her thigh. "Let me look at you," I murmured. Having the chance to stare openly was worth this brief loss of contact. I touched her full, high breasts, lingering to stroke her nipples which hardened under the attention. Indulged in the lines and curves over her belly and hips. And with every touch, Harper squirmed and asked me for more.

"You are…" I blew out a loud breath. "Gorgeous. Sexy. Hot. I am so fucking lucky to have you in my bed." I braced a hand on either side of her shoulders and lowered myself down to kiss her.

Her mouth opened, inviting me deeper. Harper's tongue twined against mine. My conflict was clear. I wanted to explore her body, to take my time. But just as desperately, I wanted to bury myself between her thighs and lick and suck until she came in my mouth.

I gathered Harper's hair up in a loose fist, pulling her head back to give me access to her neck. I sucked the smooth skin, biting gently, then soothing the bite with my tongue. Her low groan made arousal throb hard in my clit.

I made a slow pilgrimage over Harper's skin, delighting in every newly discovered part of her. Her obvious enjoyment of my touch, my kisses, was intoxicating. She encouraged me to pay more attention to certain spots, hurried me over others—she was ticklish, I discovered—and finally pressed me down toward her spread thighs. I kissed the junction of her thigh, my nose brushing against pubic hair.

I could smell her excitement. My throat tightened. "May I lick you?" She quivered. "Yes."

I dove in, slicking my tongue through her labia, delighting in the thick arousal I found. She was so delicious and I tongued her clit, her entrance, like I couldn't get enough of her. Which I couldn't. Harper's nails dug into my shoulders and when I poked my tongue against her entrance again, she groaned. I needed no more encouragement and slipped a finger into her heat.

On my next thrust, I added a second finger, stroking her as I circled her clit with my tongue. Her sounds were raw, rough, desperate. She was so wet that I was sliding in and out of her with no resistance, her arousal overflowing hot and thick against my mouth, slicking my chin.

Reluctantly, I raised my head to ask, "You want more?"

Harper swallowed hard. "Yes. Please."

I added a third finger, and as she tightened around them, my stomach clenched. My own clit throbbed, and I jammed my thighs together, desperate to do something about the deep pulse of arousal threatening to spill over.

Harper met each of my thrusts with her back arched, her hips jerking in time with the movement. It was as if her body was begging me to go deeper, faster. I could go faster, but I was as deep as I could get in this position, especially if I wanted to keep my mouth on her, which I did.

Fucking Harper was a goddamned revelation. She was so responsive, so willing, so engaged, that it was like she'd been made just for me. And yet, despite the willingness, she knew exactly what she wanted from me and wasn't afraid to tell me exactly how to lick her, just how fast she wanted me to fuck her. She so rarely used anything other than the mildest expletives, and hearing them now was so fucking sexy.

I didn't want to stop finger-fucking her while pleasuring her with my tongue, but I sensed she might want something more than what I could give her right now. I carefully withdrew my fingers and Harper let out a groan of frustration.

I kissed her clit in an attempt to soothe her. "Sorry. But, in the interest of everyone getting *exactly* what they want, I'd like to offer you something…bigger than my fingers."

The frustration turned to interest. "I'm listenin'."

I indicated the top drawer of my bedside table. Harper gave me a curious look, then rolled over. She sat up on the edge of the bed, opened the drawer, and just stared for a moment. Then she started rummaging through my toys. I crawled up the bed to kneel behind her. I stroked her belly and breasts while she perused the selection, kissed the back of her shoulder, her neck.

Harper twisted around to ask me, "Do you have shares in an adult-store franchise?"

Laughing, I said, "No. Though maybe I should. I just like variety and I really, *really* like orgasms."

She bit her lower lip. "Me too."

I cupped her breast, my thumb playing over her nipple. "Then I'd better make sure you have *at least* one."

"Thank you." Harper pulled out one of my favorite VixSkin dildos, long and medium-thick, and held it up, an eyebrow arching playfully.

"Is that your choice?"

Her chest rose and fell deeply, as if she was trying to calm herself enough to answer. "Yes, ma'am."

I barely suppressed a moan. "Seriously. I don't know if you know this, but when you say that? It makes me *so* fucking hot."

She looked far too smug. "I had an inkling…" Harper rolled onto her back, tugging my hip to make me follow.

I lay full length on top of her, and as we kissed I reached over to fumble in the drawer for the box of keep-toys-extra-clean condoms I kept there. I quickly slipped one over the shaft of the dildo and was about to ask her how she wanted to take it, but slowly, deliberately, Harper opened her legs to me.

She'd grown even wetter in the few minutes since I'd taken my tongue from her clit and my own began to throb at the thought of tasting her climax. It throbbed harder when I imagined fucking her with a toy as I sucked her clit. I settled between her thighs and licked high up on the inside of her thigh, continuing my journey toward her wetness.

As I lightly bit the skin at the edge of her pubic hair, I drew the dildo up her slit, delighting in the way it glided through her arousal. "How do you want it?"

Harper inhaled a sharp breath. "Deep...hard...fast."

"All the good ways." Of course, shallow, soft, slow were also all the good ways.

Harper nodded, her eyes unfocused, like every ounce of thought was allocated to the way the toy stroked up and down through her arousal. She was so wet, I was sure she'd have no problem taking the entire toy in one go, and I trusted her to tell me what she needed from me, or if she needed a breather.

I pressed the tip of the toy against her clit. At the pressure, she opened herself wider to me. Harper's moan of pleasure came out on the back of a drawn out, "Oh sweet fuckin' mercy" that made me more aroused than I'd thought possible.

I inhaled sharply, let it out on a shuddering breath, and hoped I wasn't going to come before she touched me.

Arousal glistened on her inner thighs. I gently worked the tip at her entrance, keeping up my attention to her clit with my tongue. Being nestled between Harper Bell's legs with my mouth buried in her pussy was one of the greatest places I'd ever been. Her breathy *Please* was the consent I needed to bury the toy deep inside her.

As I licked and sucked her clit, I set a steady rhythm with the dildo. With every thrust, Harper exhaled a grunty sigh that I decided was one of the sexiest things I'd ever heard.

"Oh fuck. Steph. Steph. Steph..." She chanted my name in time with my thrusts, one hand tightly gripping the sheets, the other gripping my hair. She held my face against her clit, as if she thought I might need any encouragement to keep licking her.

Her heels dug into the bed, thigh muscles tightening as I plunged the toy deep and hard, exactly as she'd asked me to. It took a little coordination to work my tongue against her clit while I fucked her with the toy, but I wouldn't have traded my place for anything.

I would have loved to encourage her with words, to tell her how sexy she was, how perfect, how much I loved fucking her like this, but I didn't want to stop licking her, didn't dare risk anything that might keep her glorious climax from me.

"That's so good…so good," she gasped out. "I'm almost there." The hand in my hair tightened to tug almost painfully, but it was the good kind of pain—possessive, desperate—and I was surprised by the growl that came out of my mouth. Harper apparently liked the growl. Really liked it. In the next breath, she pressed my face more firmly against her, letting out a tight, "Oh fuck," before she cried out so loudly I wouldn't have been surprised if my neighbors heard it.

Her forceful action only made her orgasm sexier, and it was a miracle I didn't come. I slowed and softened my thrusts as Harper twitched and shuddered, and kept my tongue light against her clit, not wanting to overstimulate her as she came down from her climax.

She loosened her grip on my hair, but kept her hand there, lightly stroking as I withdrew the dildo and dropped it off the bed to deal with later. I kept kissing every part of her I could reach, hoping the distraction might help the intense, overwhelming throbbing of my clit. Harper lay on her back, her legs still splayed, her chest rising and falling with deep breaths. When her breathing steadied, she lifted herself up on her elbows.

"I want to say something really profound, but the only thing in my brain is thank you." Harper tugged my arm, pulling me up to lie beside her. She stroked up and down my spine, her fingertips gliding easily over my sweat-slick skin.

I dropped lazy kisses on her shoulder, collarbone, the edge of her breast, her neck and jaw, until I found her mouth. "That? Was *so* fucking hot," I murmured against her lips.

Harper held the back of my neck as we kissed, open-mouthed, deep, a little sloppily. The kiss had me vibrating with need and, again, I clenched my thighs together. Harper pulled back first. "So," she mused, "along with an impressive assortment of dildos and vibrators, I noted a harness in that drawer."

I swallowed hard. "Yes." I had a feeling I knew where she was going, but her response still sent a fresh, hot pulse of arousal through me.

"You like strappin' on?"

"I love it." I bit my lip. "Do you like it?"

"Strapping on? No. Tried it once, it's too much hard work for me. But receiving it? Yes, ma'am. Absolutely."

"It is hard work," I agreed. "But it's worth it."

She ran her hand over my bicep and up my shoulder. "I imagine you're more than up to the exertion. And why is it worth it, exactly?" Harper added. I knew from the way she asked that she wanted the tease of me listing every way I thought strapping on was worth it.

I wanted the tease too. "Watching you, feeling you, your pleasure, your responses, having you tell me exactly what you want, having you take what I'm giving you."

Desire flashed in her eyes. "I see. And are you…good at it, Steph?" As she asked the question, Harper ran her hand between my breasts, over my belly, then down until she cupped between my thighs.

I swallowed hard. "I've never had any complaints." I didn't want to tell her I also hadn't had many compliments from Jordan when I'd strapped on.

Then again, not many things I did in bed with Jordan had earned compliments. She was the epitome of a pillow queen, to the point of being apathetic, almost lazy in bed. I knew she enjoyed what I did, but she wanted to just quietly get what she wanted, and she had to be encouraged to reciprocate. Despite being together for almost eight months, we weren't all that compatible in bed. I wanted a partner in bed, not a fuck toy. But…I wanted a partner, so I stayed until she made it impossible to stay.

Harper's low laugh brought me back from a possible spiral about another of my failed relationships. "And I'd imagine, based on what I just experienced, that I wouldn't complain either."

"So noted." What a delicious thought. A delicious thought that made the throbbing of my clit almost unbearable.

Apparently my expression gave away my desperation. Harper hooked a leg around the back of mine and swiftly rolled us so she was on top. She lay against me, one hand underneath my neck to pull me up for a kiss, the other hand sliding down over my belly. The touch made my abs tighten.

She placed her hand over mine and guided it down between my thighs. "Show me how you make yourself come. I want to watch you."

My arousal spiked with her words alone, but when she pressed my fingers against my clit, it skyrocketed. I inhaled sharply.

"That's perfect," she breathed. Harper turned my face toward her and kissed me hard. "You're perfect. Now please…show me."

I wished I'd been able to think of something clever or sexy to say in response, but all I could do was nod, a little dumbly. She kissed me again, her tongue sliding suggestively over my lips. She sucked gently on my lower lip, and as I drew my fingers over my clit I marveled at how something so familiar could feel so different with someone watching me. Not bad different. Very, very good different.

Harper alternately kissed me or watched me as I masturbated, her hands moving over my skin, touching everywhere except the place I was currently touching. The way her hands coordinated with her lips and tongue, mapping my body with a confidence, was beyond sexy and beyond arousing. The way she watched me pleasuring myself, the little murmurs of encouragement further heightened my arousal, and I stilled my hand to stop the climax threatening to arrive before I was ready.

Harper's mouth paused against my nipple, and after a cheeky suck, she looked up. "Did you forget to keep touching yourself?"

I sat up, very careful to keep any and all pressure away from my clit so I didn't explode. "Look. It's not my fault you're so fucking sexy I can barely function right now."

She affected an exaggerated pout. "Oh no, you poor thing." She gave me no chance to answer before pushing me back to the bed. When I arched up to kiss her, Harper pressed a firm hand between my breasts to make me lie down again. "Keep going," she demanded, and those two words left no room for noncompliance.

I spread my legs, and reached down between them. I held eye contact with her as I circled my clit with my fingertips, and the heat in her gaze made arousal pulse hard through me, the sensation centered as one solid molten ball of heat between my legs.

Harper groaned loudly, then pushed my hand aside and replaced it with hers. Firm, knowing fingers stroked my slippery clit. I choked out a laugh, genuinely amused by her cutting in but also unable to properly articulate because of her touch, and my words came out jerky and hoarse. "Wow. You didn't last long before you just had to jump in and help, did you."

My laugh was cut short by Harper's fingers slipping inside me. Hot arousal slicked my inner thighs as she withdrew, then thrust again. I fell back to the bed, completely incapable of doing anything except taking what she gave me. She kissed me as she fucked me, and I was almost embarrassed by the sounds I made against her mouth. Now that it was Harper's touch, I didn't want to wait any longer. I was so desperate to come.

"Please," I begged. "Lick me."

Harper moved down the bed, pushing my legs apart, and practically diving between them to put her mouth on me. After a slow pass of her tongue over my clit, Harper paused. She kissed the inside of my thigh then raised her head to meet my eyes. "Is this what you want?"

"Yes," I all but hissed.

"Me too." Harper alternated licking and sucking as one hand cupped my breast, teasing my nipple, the other hand tightly clutching mine.

The pleasure built until I didn't think I could hold it. "God that feels good. You feel so fucking good."

"Do you want to come?" she asked, her breath hot against my clit.

"Yes…" I was practically whining.

"How badly?"

I inhaled shakily. "Right now, I've never wanted anything more."

She'd barely said "Good" before she buried her tongue in my wetness again.

"Ohmygod." My orgasm came hard, fast, hot, wet, and I bit the inside of my wrist hard to muffle the scream. Light danced behind my eyes as the heat spread through my body. Harper kept her mouth on me, kept softly licking until I'd stopped bucking, stopped gasping.

Harper planted soft kisses over my inner thighs, my belly, my breasts, before settling herself on her back beside me. She pulled me close, holding me against her breasts. I rested my cheek against the exquisite softness. "I'm a little embarrassed by how quickly I came," I mumbled.

She laughed quietly. "You shouldn't be. I loved it. I loved that you got yourself so worked up that you couldn't hold on. It makes me wonder what else might get you worked up…"

Harper's comment about me strapping on waltzed merrily into my brain, and my whole body tightened with anticipation. Maybe we could… I twisted around to sit up. "Are you staying?" And now I was embarrassed by how hopeful I sounded. "If you want to go home then that's obviously totally fine."

Her expression softened, the edges of her eyes creasing as she worked to hold back a smile. "Steph. Do you want me to stay? Or do you want me to go? Because this would be a whole lot easier, and we could move on to funner things than talking about this if you just tell me what you're thinking."

"Okay fine. I don't want you to go. I want to make you come again tonight and maybe again before you leave in the morning, after we've slept all cuddled up or maybe slept fighting for space and sheets. I don't know how you sleep, if you're a bed hog or what, but I want to know."

"Clarity is kindness. Thanks for being honest. And I'm not a bed hog."

"I am." I leaned over and pulled her on top of me. "Or so I've been told."

Harper shifted to straddle my hips. "I look forward to confirming, or denying that later." She licked her lower lip. "Much later…"

CHAPTER SIXTEEN

Harper

Wow.

Okay.

Wow.

I'd told myself that when—*if*—Steph and I slept together, that as long as it wasn't completely terrible, I'd be happy. Not that I'd gone into it expecting it to be terrible—Steph was far too sexy, confident, and all around capable to be terrible in bed—but I'd learned to temper my expectations in that department.

I loved spending time with her, I loved how I felt when we were together, I couldn't stop thinking about her when we weren't together, I loved how she made me feel, I loved how she made me laugh. So I'd told myself that we were compatible in every other way, and as long as the sex wasn't a complete bomb, I'd be okay being with her.

But then Steph had to go and screw me better than anyone ever had, and make me sure anyone else I went to bed with in the future would be a complete disappointment. Not that I *wanted* to sleep with any other women except for her.

She'd screwed me utterly senseless, and then did it again…and again. I rolled onto my back after my third climax, completely and utterly spent and completely and utterly satisfied. Steph leaned over me, lazily kissing my neck, my jaw, then finally my lips. She looked entirely too smug, which she had every right to be.

Her arm snuck around my waist to pull me closer, and I rolled over to face her. Steph's entire body screamed satisfaction, and when her eyes found mine, their warm affection softened something inside me. She carefully moved some hair from my face, guiding it back over my ear. Her fingers lingered, brushing over my jaw. The frantic pace of our lovemaking had dwindled, leaving slow softness in its wake.

I leaned in and kissed her, delighting in her satisfied purr. It was clear she enjoyed the kiss and she wanted more, but for now we were both satiated. "That was so much better than anything I've been imaginin'."

"You imagined this?"

Heat warmed my neck and ears. Nodding, I admitted, "You have been the source of pretty much every orgasm I've given myself over the past six years."

"Shit. Imaginary me is a fucking sex goddess."

"You have no idea..." And now I was going to have some new incredible mental imagery to add to my collection.

"Me too, in case you're wondering. And you were also *so much* better than what's been in my head." She kissed my nipple. "God, we could have been fucking for real all this time instead of just imagining it."

"We could have been," I agreed, mentally kicking myself for not being clearer with how I felt sooner. I ran my fingers over her left hip, lightly tracing the outline of the birthmark there. I loved her birthmark. It was shaped like a rabbit holding a hammer, and it was my job to cover it up whenever Steph filmed anything topless. Something about it being Steph's birthmark, not Amy's. "I love this birthmark," I said quietly, still running my fingers over it. "I hate covering it."

She abandoned her attention to my breast which made me wish I hadn't said anything. Steph peered down at her hip. "Good old Carpenter Peter Rabbit."

I snorted out a laugh and she joined in. Her answer confirmed that my idea about the shape wasn't as wacky as I'd thought. And Steph naming her birthmark was one the cutest things I could think of.

Once we'd stopped laughing, I said, "We were supposed to talk, weren't we?"

"Right. Yes. We were."

"I think what we just did further clarifies how we're both feeling."

"What we just did..." she said, her voice low and lazy and promising that she too wanted more of what we'd just done. Then Steph smothered a yawn, and I laughed.

"Maybe the talk is for tomorrow?"

"Mm. But we *do* need to have it."

"We will," I promised.

"Good. I have a toothbrush."

"I would hope you do."

Smiling, she rolled her eyes. "I mean one for you. A brand-new one." Hastily, she added, "Not that you need a toothbrush right now, I just meant for before bed. And you can use anything you want in my bathroom. Deodorant, skincare products, whatever you want."

"Thanks. My body isn't going to combust if I don't do my prebed routine in full. As long as I can floss and brush my teeth, and wash and moisturize my face, I'll survive."

"You're braver than me," she laughed. "I wouldn't dare skip a step in my facial routine. My makeup artist is a real hardass."

"So I've heard."

Steph squirmed her arm free to check her watch. "Oh fuck. It's almost one a.m. How did that happen?"

"You were so sexy I couldn't help myself, that's how that happened."

She nuzzled my neck. "You stole my line." The nuzzling paused midnibble and she popped up, her expression incongruously serious. "I have a spare room, if you'd prefer sleeping alone. I'd prefer you stayed in my bed, but I know it can be weird if you're not used to it."

"I'm happy right here. Or, I will be once I've used the bathroom and brushed my teeth etcetera."

We left the bed, which was one of the biggest tragedies of my life to date, to attend to our prebed chores. We took another shower, this one lightning-fast, to rinse away hours of sex. I borrowed some of her products to remove my makeup, and wash and moisturize my face, dimly aware that this would be the first time Steph had ever seen me without makeup. The thought produced mild angst and I slipped out of the bathroom while she was bent over the sink, brushing her teeth. But... relationships were full of firsts and this would just be one of them.

While Steph finished up, I texted Per that I wouldn't be home so he didn't worry, and then glanced at socials to make sure the world hadn't exploded outside these walls while my world was exploding within them. Steph fussed with the lights, turning out the bedroom light and turning on her bedside lamp, setting her phone face down on the bedside table.

She slipped under the covers, facing me. A slow smile quirked her mouth. She traced the side of her forefinger down my cheek. "Hello, beautiful you." The finger moved over my lips. "I wondered what you'd look like, naked-faced, in my bed."

She'd said it so sweetly, so softly, that the anxiety I'd felt before dissipated. "Oh? And…what do I look like?"

"Exquisite," she said simply. After a quick kiss, Steph turned off the lamp. "Touching or no touching to sleep?"

"Definitely touching. I'm very much into snuggling in my sleep."

"Me too." She huffed and squirmed into position on her side facing me and opened her arms. "C'mere."

I rolled over and shuffled back until my back was flush against her front. It took a little bit of positioning to get everything worked out, but the moment we found the right position, it was bliss. I'd had far too many exes who didn't like snuggling when we slept, which didn't suit me at all. I had a body pillow in my bed that I either hugged to my front or slept pressed back against. But the sensation of Steph, with her arm under my neck and the other wrapped around my waist as she curled her body into me was far better than any damned pillow.

"G'night," she mumbled against my neck. "Sleep tight. Wake me if you need anything." Soft kisses punctuated her words.

I grabbed her arm and pulled it even more tightly around me. "Good night."

Steph's light breath against the back of my neck lulled me into an easy, dreamless sleep.

I woke before Steph, in a room that was starting to warm up with the rising sun. We'd shifted during the night, and she now lay on her back with me hugging her midsection. I kissed her shoulder, lingering against her warm skin for a few seconds before I began kissing my way toward her breast. When my lips closed around her nipple, she shifted slightly.

"Oh I'm sorry," I said innocently. When she exhaled a quiet, groaning sigh, I kissed my way up to her jaw. "Did I wake you?"

"No," she said, smiling. Steph opened her eyes as she turned her head. She blinked slowly. "I was just meditating."

Mortification flooded through me. "Oh shit, I'm *so* sorry. I interrupted you."

Steph rolled over to face me. "It's fine. You wouldn't have known." She pulled my hand to her mouth and kissed the tips of my fingers.

"Still, I'm sorry." I knew she often meditated while she was in my chair, and took care to be quiet as much as was reasonable when her eyes were closed. It'd not occurred to me she might meditate first thing when she woke up. I felt like a cretin.

Steph shrugged, apparently unconcerned, and a little of my mortification eased. "There are worse ways to have your meditation interrupted…" She stretched expansively, like a cat in a patch of sun. "Oh yes." She exhaled a deep, contented sigh. "God my body feels good after last night."

I could get on board with that. My hand moved lower, slipping between her thighs. I lightly stroked upward. "Yes. It does feel good." I stopped stroking short of the destination I really wanted to spend time at, wanting to make sure my touch was welcome.

Steph reached down to grasp my wrist. The light grip made it clear she was on board with wherever my hand went—she just wanted to be involved. "Can I just say how much I'm loving waking up with you in my bed."

"You can say that if you want." I raised an eyebrow as my hand went higher, but still not quite high enough. "In fact, you just did."

She rolled her eyes. "Ha ha. I'd also love waking up with you in your bed too."

"I'll keep that in mind."

Steph's expression closed slightly. "Is that…I mean…never mind."

"Now I am minding." I pulled my hand from between her thighs and pushed myself up so I could look her in the eyes properly. "What do you mean? What's up?"

She took a deep breath, then let loose with her thoughts. "It seemed a little like you don't really want me at your place."

I knew exactly what she was getting at, and could imagine that she might be feeling like I didn't want to let her into every corner of my life. I rushed to reassure her. "I do. But…I have a roommate. He's not always there, but when he is, the last thing I want is him inadvertently interrupting us, or being a smug dick about us going to bed or coming out of the bedroom when we're done."

Steph nodded slowly. After a long, slightly uncomfortable pause, she said, "That makes sense."

"I just don't want you to feel like you can't be comfortable in my house. I trust Per and Ben. They'll never be indiscreet—I hope you trust me on that, that I trust them. But they *will* be annoying, teasing friends."

"I'm okay with annoying, teasing friends." Steph's hands came to my ass. "And I do trust you. Thank you for thinking of me." She pulled until I slung my leg over her hips to straddle her. I shivered as her hands moved up my sides until she cupped my breasts, her thumbs rubbing my nipples. "I'm not sure I told you enough last night, but fuck, I really, *really* love your tits. I don't think I've ever loved a pair as much as I love yours." She sat up, wrapping an arm around my waist, holding me in place so she could tongue a nipple.

My breath caught. "You may have mentioned it a few times." I raised myself up so I could reach between my legs until I found what I wanted between hers. "I'm curious. Does this count as doing nothing on your Saturday morning?"

Steph laughed. "It does."

When I circled her slippery clit, the laughter was cut short by the sexiest moan I'd ever heard. Given how many moans of pleasure I'd heard last night, that was saying something. Steph gripped the back of my neck and fell back to the bed, pulling me roughly with her. "This is the best kind of doing nothing," she murmured. And that was the last coherent thing she said for the next half hour.

Basic needs like breakfast and a shower necessitated we finally untangle our bodies. We took a shower together, and she told me to grab whatever I wanted from her closet. I pawed through drawers and her hanging clothes, nabbing a tee that proclaimed proudly on the front "No farmers, no food" and some soft merino joggers, both of which were undoubtedly loose for her but fit me nicely.

I'd been too focused on my desire last night and had paid little attention to her house, but in the light of day I took the time to look around. It was a modern, large but surprisingly modest three-bedroom plus gym. No pool. Split level, open, clean and airy, full of bright artworks, it oozed warmth and charm. It was basically Steph in building form. It seemed her one extravagance, if you could call it that, was an addiction to indoor plants.

We settled ourselves on her L-shaped leather couch, knees brushing. We drank coffee and ate toast while looking out the window to the dry undulating landscape behind her house, just quietly existing together. I'd borrowed a book about Hypatia of Alexandria from her overflowing shelves, and had read about ten pages before Steph said, "So…"

I looked up. "So?"

She'd been fidgeting since we'd sat down, and it increased tenfold as soon as she spoke that single word. "The talk."

"Oh. Right. Yes." I marked my page and set the book down on her heavy wood coffee table. It was probably good to get it out of the way before we got distracted by each other's bodies again.

"We need to talk about what we're doing and how we handle work. There are no explicit rules against it but Ingrid mentioned telling the production about us and I agree. I was going to do it soon, but I think now I need to make it really soon."

"Right, I agree." My next sentence was out of my mouth before I'd processed what I might be implying. "And I guess we need a conversation about what we want in this relationship."

"Relationship?" Her voice cracked up hilariously on the last syllable of the word. Less hilarious was her panic.

"Uh, yeah? I mean, I'd thought…it's just…" I shook my head, as if that might shake away the overwhelming dread creeping up on me. Apparently, Steph and I were *not* on the same page about what this was and where it could lead.

"I'm, uh, could I have a moment?"

Anxiety twisted my gut. "Sure."

She hopped up and walked out of the room, and my panic ramped up until I had to consciously slow my breathing before I hyperventilated.

Steph came back after a minute or so and sat back down. She cleared her throat nervously. "I'm sorry. That was really dramatic. Even for an actor."

I'd calmed myself down enough to speak without my voice shaking. "It's okay. Have I assumed something with the whole relationship thing?"

Steph looked up, her eyes finding and holding mine. Finally, she smothered some of my anxiety. "No, you haven't assumed. I don't know why I freaked out when you said relationship, even though it's something I've already thought about. Thought about a lot, actually." She sucked in a quick breath. "I think you confirming it's what you want too just made it real, and I—It's…" Steph stopped dead, gesturing helplessly as if that would explain things or bring the words she wanted to mind.

"What is it?" I gently prompted.

There was a long pause before Steph quietly admitted, "I'm scared. I'm scared because I've never been able to make a relationship work, or even…*thrive* when I'm in one. It's like the harder I try to make it work, to make it good, the worse it gets. I don't have a great track record. Sex and spending time together is one thing. One incredible thing. A relationship is a whole other thing. I just…feel like you deserve better."

"Maybe what I deserve is you trying your best with me," I pointed out, careful to keep any aggression from my tone. I knew she was a perfectionist, and wasn't surprised it seeped into her intimate relationships too. "And, just to state the obvious, I don't think I'm like the women you've dated previously. The ones I've been aware of that is."

She smiled, and I was relieved that it was a genuine, amused smile. "Touché. You're right. On both things. You're not like them. You're more than they could ever be."

"That's a very sweet compliment. Thank you."

"I mean it," Steph said seriously. "I really like you, Harper. I'm insanely attracted to you. It's just a little strange for me to have gone from years of thinking to doing. And for the doing to be so *so* fucking good, all aspects of it, not just the sex, right away. I guess I'm just adjusting?"

"I get that. It's strange for me too. But I'm also *really* enjoying the doing."

She smirked. "I'm glad. So...yeah. I'm not proud of freaking out, and I'm sorry. I'm sorry if I upset you by being an idiot. I'd like to say I won't do it again but I probably will. It's not malicious, I promise." Steph's nose wrinkled. "Sometimes I'm just stupid."

I laughed at that last comment, my anxiety easing as quickly as it'd spiked. "I don't want to push you just because I really want an actual 'we're partners' relationship with you."

"You're not pushing me. I've wasted years already not being with you and I don't want to waste more time because I'm dithering over a decision. A decision where I already know where I'll land. With you. I want to date you. Or be in pre-dating-you mode. Whatever you want to call it. What I'm saying is I want to be with you, romantically."

Excitement swirled through me, and I decided to not mess around with her feelings. "I really want that too."

"Good. I just—I'm not saying you'll hurt me. But that's a deep fear after...Jordan. I'm trying to excavate it but I'm not very good at digging yet. But I'm trying. And you are someone I want to try with." She made it sound so simple, and maybe it really was.

"Trying is good."

Steph exhaled loudly, and some of the stiffness in her body melted. "Glad we agree."

"Mmm. You know...If I'd known you needed me to say 'I want you to be my girlfriend,' I would have just said that years ago."

Steph joined in my laughter. "I wouldn't have said no. It's just—" She let out a long, shaky breath. "I haven't really ever had a *good* relationship, you know? And I really want this one to be good. For both of us. But there are a lot of moving parts in my life and I don't want you to get crushed by any of them. Moving parts like people taking photos of us."

"That doesn't bother me," I said honestly. "I only have the one family and I already got outed to them."

She sniggered, then covered her mouth. "I'm sorry. You being outed is not funny. But what you said is."

I hadn't taken her laughter personally. Quite the opposite. "Happy to make you laugh." I twined our fingers together. "And you can have all the time and all the space you need."

Steph exhaled loudly. "Thank you. I want to make sure all my shit is sorted so I'll be the best partner for you that I can be."

"I like the sound of that."

"Me too." Steph paused for so long I worried she was about to change her mind. Her expression was so open, so earnest, so trusting. "Just…don't break my heart, please. Tell me if I'm being an idiot or if I'm not giving you what you need." She frowned. "My other relationships haven't exactly been something you'd see held up as beacons of how to do it."

"Oh, I will tell you, don't you worry about that," I assured her. "And likewise."

"Will do. But for now…" She popped up onto her knees and crawled closer until I had to retreat along the couch to make room for her. When I fell backward, Steph pounced and I realized that was her plan all along. "If we're thinking ahead to a possible relationship, maybe we should check again if we're really compatible in bed."

I inhaled sharply as she lowered herself gently on top of me. "I think that's a good idea," I managed as her thigh insinuated itself between mine.

Steph kissed my neck, my jaw, my cheek, then finally my mouth. "I suspect we are, but it never hurts to double…triple…quadruple check."

We spent rest of the morning lounging around Steph's house, interspersed with a walk to buy lunch, enjoying some vitamin D before we strolled back to her place. She'd taken my hand and I'd gripped hers as we strolled through her neighborhood. If anyone took photos of us, I didn't notice and didn't care.

Midafternoon, I came to the unpleasant realization that I had to leave. She smiled knowingly when I grumbled that I should probably go. "I don't want to go, but I need clothes. And I should probably do some housework before Per starts complaining. Maybe organize things for the work week. All that boring stuff that isn't being with you. And"—I planted a light peck on her nose—"we have to play tennis tomorrow morning, which is going to take up some time."

It felt a little like Steph leaving after we'd first made out at my place, the day she rescued the dog, and I wondered if this was going to be how things would go with us: barely touching all week, screwing madly on Friday night through Sunday afternoon when she had to leave for her weekly table read. Rinse and repeat. I made a mental note to talk to her about incorporating time together after work through the week.

"Do we *have* to practice my tennis this weekend?" she whined. "We can work out nakedly instead."

"Unfortunately you signed up for a charity tennis match, not a charity sex match." I kissed her quickly, then stood before I lost my resolve. "And I don't want anyone saying that I'm not a good coach."

She turned around to watch me, flinging her upper body over the back of the couch like a petulant teen. "The thought will never cross anyone's mind. I'm going to give a US Open-worthy performance and credit you with every winner I hit."

"Thank you, darlin'."

One eyebrow rose with comical slowness. "Darling? Wow. That was fast."

"Um, yeah? Sorry. It kind of just slipped out." I knew I was blushing. "I have been holding that back for so long, you have no idea." A sudden realization made my stomach sink. "Too soon? You don't like it?"

"Oh no," she said quickly, "I really do."

Relief washed through me. "Good. Because I've got a whole bunch of endearments. I might just cycle through and you can give me a thumbs-up or thumbs-down for each one."

Steph nodded slowly. "I can do that. You already know yes or no, ma'am is a winner. And darling is a double thumbs-up from me, especially if that lil Southern twang drops in."

"I'll remember that." She was making it very hard for me to leave, but I gathered my things and went to the door.

Steph followed, finally letting me go after a thorough kiss that made me think I'd be forgetting to moderate my accent around her as much as possible. She waited in her open doorway until I was in my car, and as I closed my car door, my phone pinged with a WhatsApp message. I looked back at the house, and found her still watching me.

Smiling, I checked the message.

I'm going to be thinking about the sound you make when you come until I can next hear it in person.

That was so unfair. When I looked up, Steph grinned, then backed into her house and, with a wave, shut the door.

Two could play this game. *Now I know why you wanted to use WhatsApp...so you could talk about screwing me in these encrypted messages and nobody will ever be able to see it.*

Cry-laughing emoji. *Caught me.*

Oh screw it. With our work schedules, anything more than sleeping together two nights a week was going to be a bonus. A little sexting would fill the gap until then. *For the record, I'm going to be thinking about how wet you get when I ask you how hard you want to be fucked, and how good you feel coming in my mouth.*

Her response was lightning fast. *You better leave before I come out there and drag you out of that car and back into bed.*

I sent a saluting emoji, then leaned over to set my phone in its charging cradle where it wasn't in easy reach or easy view.

Before I started the car I leaned my head back against the headrest. How could it be so good already? We'd only *just* agreed to dating, and I was already in love with her. To be fair, I'd been in love with her for a while now, but everything that'd happened since last night had just solidified my feelings. It'd also solidified the fact that if I couldn't make this work, I was so, so screwed.

* * *

We'd played tennis on Sunday morning, then stopped by a store to grab some ingredients for me to make dinner back at Stephs's once she was done with her table read. Because she was taller than me, she automatically grabbed things on grocery shelves I couldn't reach. And as if I didn't already have all the feelings for her, she'd thoughtfully pull items to the front of the shelving to make it easier for other shorter people to reach.

After dinner we'd fallen into bed to learn more about each other's bodies, what made us twitch and writhe and beg. I'd reluctantly dragged myself home around nine p.m., because sleeping over when we had early calls the next day seemed like a recipe for being exhausted all day.

It felt awful to fall asleep alone, and I woke up at four a.m. on Monday morning wishing simultaneously that I'd had another two hours of sleep, and two hours of sex before that sleep. It was made slightly easier by the text from Steph that waited for me. I'd thought I got up early for work, but she had workouts and other things to fit into her day before she came to set.

Hope you slept well. I did not. Kept thinking about you. She'd added the melting head emoji. *Got time to talk before work starts? I just want to see you without a million people around us.*

I rolled onto my back, holding my phone up to reply. *Funny, I slept the same and for the same reason. For you, I'll make time before work.*

Great. Come to my trailer?

Will do. See you soon.

I usually liked to linger in bed for twenty minutes or so, waking up slowly, and indulging in a bad scrolling habit, before I got up and showered. But I set aside my morning doomscrolling to fling myself out of bed and into the shower.

I'd put together work outfits yesterday ready for the entire week, paying even more attention than I usually did to clothing, and after a lightning-fast shower, hair, makeup, I dressed. My favorite gray knit sweater that showed enough of my breasts that people knew I had cleavage, but not so much they fell down it, paired with slim-leg black pants and my favorite comfortable-for-standing-for-hours boots. I didn't want to tease Steph exactly, but I did want to remind her of what we'd done on the weekend, and what was waiting for her whenever we could find time again.

Time.

With our work schedules, finding time to be together was always going to be an issue, but not insurmountable. Working together would help, though of course we couldn't show any sort of intimacy at work. But just being near her would be enough to get me to when we *could* show intimacy.

Steph's Land Rover was already in her usual spot, and I parked close. A few cars were trickling in, and I grabbed my things before I got caught up in an interaction that'd cut into my time with Steph. My boot heels echoed on the concrete path as I rushed toward Steph's trailer, which was located closest to set.

The indicator beside the door showed that Steph was inside. I tapped my knuckles against the door, raising my voice slightly to add, "Knock knock."

The door opened, and Steph appeared. Her gaze flicked to my cleavage before coming back to my face. She leaned against the doorframe, arms crossed, gorgeous mouth smirking, looking so cocky and so sexy I almost shoved her into her trailer so I could enjoy her. "Do you usually knock and also verbalize the action?"

"No. Only when I'm nervous."

The cockiness disappeared, replaced by concern. "Why are you nervous?" She moved aside to let me in, closing the door behind me.

"You know, I honestly don't know. But I am."

She leaned closer, lowering her voice to a gravelly kind of conspiratorial. "Is it because we…had intimate relations?"

That made me laugh. "No, but it is because we screwed."

She nodded as if thinking about a complex math equation. "A number of times, if I'm recalling it correctly."

"I've been recalling it a lot since it happened, so I know that yes, you are recalling it correctly."

"Mmm." The single syllable response was almost a purr.

I looked around, desperate to redirect the conversation before we broke the one rule we'd agreed on yesterday while we'd been talking some more—no kissing, no "intimate" touching, no making out, and *definitely* no sex at work. Even if we were in the privacy of her trailer. "So, this is your trailer." I'd peeked my head in over the years, but had never been inside.

She played along. "It is." Steph grabbed her travel mug of coffee and plopped herself down on the couch against the wall opposite the door.

"It's cute. It's…you." The trailer held all the usual accoutrements—small kitchen with appliances, bathroom with shower, couch, small bed, television, desk, and makeup station, but Steph had personalized it with pictures of what I assumed to be family and friends, books, and a bunch of plants.

"Thanks. I think?" She indicated I should sit and I took a spot on the two-seater couch, deliberately far enough from her that there wouldn't be any tempting touching.

"It *was* a compliment."

"I know." After a deep swallow of her coffee, Steph casually added, "If you ever need it, the PIN to get in is my date of birth, less year, in reverse. I'm sure you know it from IMDb…"

I laughed. "I do. Or it's the right way if you live in the UK where they do day then month then year."

"Oh my dad would love you." She laughed, a slow, genuinely happy laugh. "He's lived here for almost forty-five years, and he still complains about stuff like how we write the date."

"You're really giving me your PIN? You're okay with me coming into your space when you're not here?"

"Yes. And yes. We've worked together for nearly six years. I trust you. And we're sleeping together, right? Pretty much dating? Seems logical."

"It does. But aren't you worried people will notice?"

"A little, but that worry is less than the enjoyment I'll get by having you in my space." She rubbed my shoulder, then heroically slid along the couch to put a little more distance between us. "You want another coffee or anything? Kayla's flitting about."

"I'm good thanks." I settled myself more comfortably and decided to jump back into getting to know her, wanting to make use of this limited private time. "Tell me something I wouldn't know already. What's one thing you don't like about your job?"

"Early-early mornings," she said instantly.

"Really? I thought Jared was the morning grump."

Steph smiled around the mug she'd raised to her mouth, pausing to clarify, "I'm only not the morning grump because I refuse to bring my outside annoyances to work."

"We appreciate that. What else?"

"Phone calls. I'm a millennial. Please, let's discuss this possible role or whatever over text or email. I'm excellent at phone calls, but only because I have to be. I really don't like them."

"That sounds fair." I didn't love phone calls much myself. "What's something else you're excellent at? Besides playing my body like it's an instrument and you're a maestro."

She smirked. "High praise." Steph thought for a few moments before answering. "I'm excellent at Freezer Tetris."

"Freezer Tetris?"

She nodded seriously. "Mhmm. You know, fitting too many things into a freezer. I can just make it work, moving things around until they fit perfectly. I'm also pretty good at Car Tetris too, but freezers are where I shine."

"That is a useful skill." Especially in a relationship. A relationship with me who frequently fought with the fridge and overburdened freezer—Per put a lot of frozen fruit in his protein smoothies and his packages were often in the way of necessary dinner items.

"I think so."

Despite the brightness of her response, she seemed a little guarded, prompting me to ask, "Is something wrong, darlin'?"

She shot me a look. "Your darling is *seriously* going to melt me one day."

I lifted one shoulder in a casual shrug. "The look on your face when I say it makes it worth it."

"Mmm." She upended her mug of coffee, then set the obviously empty vessel down. "I'm going to talk to Brian about us this morning."

"I think that's a good idea." We'd already talked about any perceived power imbalance, and the fact neither of us was the other's boss. Having some sort of assurance in place would be nice. "It's just a formality, right? And we're both professionals who can remain so at work."

"Absolutely. I'm being so professional right now, not making out with you in the privacy of my trailer. So we can do it."

"Oh you think *you're* being professional by not jumping on *me* right now?" I drawled. "I'm being the most professional professional."

She laughed. "Please don't be cute and funny, you're making this really hard."

I mock-pouted. "Sorry."

"You're forgiven." She glanced at her watch, wrinkling her nose. "I wish we had more time to talk, but I need to pee and brush my teeth before I go to the production office."

"And I need to get ready for you." And hopefully fit in a Polish lesson that I'd meant to do before leaving for work. I lowered my voice to a whisper. "Should I sneak out before you? Text you that the coast is clear?"

Steph laughed. "It's up to you. I don't feel the need to sneak around." She gave me a quick hug, releasing me slowly. Her hands came up to gently cup my face. "I'd be proud for the world to know I'm with you."

CHAPTER SEVENTEEN

Steph

We parted ways outside my trailer—Harper going to Hair and Makeup, while I headed straight for the production office. Brian admitted me as soon as I knocked, an expression of surprise, then concern flashing over his face. "Steph. What's up?" He sat down again, leaning forward expectantly.

I stood by the closed door, not wanting to upset the mess of papers and equipment that filled the trailer. Walkies on the charging station crackled as crew readied for the day, and I raised my voice slightly. "I won't take up much of your time. I just wanted to tell you that Harper and I are seeing each other. Romantically."

Brian's expression didn't change. He nodded slowly. "Thanks for letting me know." He grabbed a walkie and raised it to his mouth. "Brian for Harper."

Oh. Shit. The surge of protectiveness when I realized Harper was going to be dragged in surprised me.

After a few seconds, Harper's voice came over the speaker. "Go for Harper."

"Could you come to the PO?"

"On my way."

Brian and I chatted superficially for the few minutes until Harper arrived. She looked mildly concerned but not alarmed, but I still had to resist the urge to put a comforting arm around her.

Brian checked his watch. "Sorry, it's quicker if I only have to do this once. It's my duty to remind you, not that I think either of you really need reminding, of our code of conduct." He went on to quickly run through it and the sexual harassment policy, ending with "…just to make sure everyone on set feels safe and comfortable."

"So no kissing in front of people?" I deadpanned.

He smiled wryly. "Not a good idea. If you're discreet at work, which I'm sure you both will be, we won't have any problems."

Harper glanced at me before looking back to him. "Yes, we will be."

I nodded vigorously. "Absolutely."

"Good. Thank you. Uh, and…congratulations?"

Before either of us could answer, Zoe pushed into the trailer, stopping dead when she saw us. "Sorry."

Brian stood. "No problem, we're all done here."

Excellent.

I opened the door and let Harper go ahead of me. "You okay? Sorry, he just called you."

"It's fine. I'm okay," she confirmed.

"That was pretty painless. Right?"

"It was," Harper agreed.

"Well, I guess it's officially official then." I grinned at her as she paused outside Hair and Makeup. "I gotta get to Wardrobe. See you soon."

Harper smiled beatifically. "Yes, ma'am, you will."

"Unfair," I muttered as she opened the door.

Even after talking to Brian, I was on time for Wardrobe then Hair and Makeup. From outside the trailer, it sounded like Harper was still doing a language lesson—she'd been cycling through various languages for about eighteen months, and now I knew it was for her Europe trip. She looked up as I entered. The first thing I noticed, aside from the way my whole body warmed upon seeing her, despite having already seen her this morning, was that she was the only one there.

I touched her shoulder. "Keep going. I'm a few minutes early. I can wait."

She reached up to quickly squeeze my hand. "Thanks, I'm almost done."

I sat in her chair and got comfortable for a quick meditation. It felt like no time passed before Harper's voice was low near my ear. "Sorry to interrupt your meditation, yet again…"

I bit my tongue on telling her I much preferred how she'd "interrupted" it on Saturday morning. "No problem."

Harper's fingers stroked the back of my neck. "You good?"

"Mhmm."

Harper started work. Nina and Chrissy came in, and then Anna arrived late (unsurprisingly). Kayla popped in to confirm I was where I should be so she could tell Catering to get my breakfast ready.

Once Kayla left, Harper said conversationally, "I thought I'd drive up to Pyramid Lake for a bit of stand-up paddleboarding if the weather's cooperating next weekend. Wanna join me?"

The charity tennis match was this weekend, which meant we'd be free to do whatever we wanted on our weekends after that. "Oh, uh… yeah, of course I'll join you, but I think I'll watch you from the shore." I smiled sheepishly.

Harper apparently liked the implication that I wanted to watch her, if the pink flush at the base of her neck was any indication. "You can watch me just as well from a board beside me."

"I know. And being close to you is always preferable. But…stand-up paddleboarding isn't really my vibe." At her raised-eyebrows silent question, I elaborated, "You know, it's the whole thing of you just *have* to fall off, it's inevitable. I do not like failing at things."

"Yes, I've already gathered that with the tennis." Her fingertips traced a pattern on my neck, subtle enough that anyone watching wouldn't see any hidden meaning in it, but overt enough that it made my skin heat. She met my eyes in the mirror. "Sometimes a little failure is fun."

"You think so?"

"Mhmm. Then you get to practice. There's nothing like trying something again…and again…and again, until it's perfect." Her expression was almost dreamy, as if she was thinking about everything we'd *tried* over the weekend, right then and there.

"Are you saying it wasn't perfect?" I teased, keeping my voice low.

"I'm not saying that at all. Eyes closed, please."

I complied so she could get back to work, though Harper was a skilled multitasker who regularly held conversations while working. And I complied so our veiled innuendo wouldn't go further. I was conscious of Brian's little chat and the fact we weren't alone.

Chrissy came in to work alongside Harper. She ran her fingertips through the short hair above my ears and on my neck. "Can you come in after you're wrapped tonight so I can buzz these sides and the back?" I hated hair on my neck and in my ears after haircuts, so she always did it after work. She fluffed the longer hair on top. "This can wait another week or so. So can the color." Chrissy kept my color up-to-date in between my longer stylist appointments. It was mostly my natural blond, just…slightly chemically enhanced.

"Sure," I agreed easily. I'd be dead on my feet, but it wouldn't take long. And then I'd have a fresh cut for any photos of Harper, me, Per, and the as-yet-not-met Ben during tomorrow's watch-along.

My first scenes of the day were with Anna, attending a homicide then afterward in the squad room for a mild argument about how to proceed. Anna was…fine. Not my favorite to work with—she was a little selfish with her emotion during scenes—but I managed. Knowing I'd be able to decompress with Harper during breaks made the work easier.

But the scene I'd been looking forward to for this episode was the third scene scheduled for the day. We'd shoot in Amy and Val's living room, and Amy would come at Val about the whole sexual harassment plotline. I'd had a wardrobe change which meant my hair and makeup was checked as well.

Harper, as always, took my cue when I was a little quiet and trying to shift my headspace for a scene, and remained quiet as well as she touched me up. I made a mental note to tell her how much I appreciated that, appreciated her. But for now…

Hurt.

Frustrated.

Upset.

So. Fucking. Angry.

I let the emotions through, relishing the tight tension in my body. As soon as Monty called action, I stalked into the room and stopped harshly on my mark, my tense arms down at my sides.

The glass of "red wine" halfway to Laura's mouth paused as she looked up from her position on the couch. "Hey, babe, how was your day?" She smiled gently. "I heard about the Maxim case. I'm so sorry he walked."

I waved her off. "I don't want to talk about it." At Laura's raised eyebrow, I barreled on. "I want to talk about Peters putting his hand on your ass at work. I want to talk about someone sexually harassing you. I want to talk about him asking you out every other day even though he knows you and I are together. I want to…" I threw my hands up, making them into tight fists.

"Okay," she said, her tone leaning toward calm neutrality—Val was very good at defusing Amy. "Then let's talk about it."

"Let's," I said tersely. "Let's talk about how messed up it is. I can't believe you had to deal with that. I can't believe he *did* that to you." I let my anger come through, because anger was usually the first emotion Amy reached for, and the basis around which I built all her other emotions. "And you know the *worst* thing? You didn't tell me. I had to hear about it from my partner. Why the hell didn't you tell me, Val? Did you think I wasn't going to hear about this? Something so important, so awful, about my girlfriend, in my own damned precinct?"

Laura did a magnificent job of showing someone frustrated but working to keep herself calm. "Because I was handling it. I'm sorry I didn't tell you, but I knew you'd react exactly the way you are now."

Folding my arms over my chest, I changed my expression to something resembling curiosity, but still with a touch of pissiness. "And what way is that?"

"Like you're going to charge downstairs into my squad room and beat the crap out of him."

"Yes. That's *exactly* what I was thinking of doing."

Her eyebrows rose slowly. "And you'll get yourself suspended. Or worse. I'm trying to protect you." Laura sighed, set her glass on the wood coffee table, stood, and came over to me. Her first mark was a few feet away to give some physical distance before moving closer as the emotion built. "Babe, this isn't your fight, as much as I know you want it to be." When I opened my mouth to protest, she cut me off. "It's being handled. And I love you for wanting to help, but right now, I just need your support. Emotional support, not physical."

Laura was such a generous scene partner that it was easy to get caught in the emotion of the moment and just let myself go completely. My voice cracked unexpectedly when I said, "I just want to help you."

"I know, sweetheart." She stepped right up to me and gripped my shoulders. "But you can't fix this. Promise me you'll let me and Halloran handle it the right way."

I paused for a few beats then nodded. "I will."

Laura ran her fingers over the short hair above my ears. "Good." She leaned forward and rested her forehead against mine. We made eye contact, and I knew exactly what was coming, even though we hadn't rehearsed it. Laura gently pulled and I leaned into the kiss, mentally counting to three, which I knew she would be doing too, before pulling away.

She smiled then lightly kissed the tip of my nose. "Thank you."

"Cut!"

I squeezed Laura's hand. "Nice improv." The kiss wasn't written but it fit perfectly into the scene.

Laura echoed my thoughts about it when she said, "Thanks. Seemed logical in the moment. Why the fuck wouldn't they kiss at such an emotional time?"

"You're absolutely right."

Thankfully Monty agreed and we went again—improv kiss now moved to "scripted" kiss. By the time we'd shot the scene a half-dozen times to get the coverage he wanted, I was completely wrung out after all the emotion. All I wanted was to shed Amy Spicer, and spend time with Harper—nudity optional, but definitely preferred. Unfortunately, with the whole "being professional" thing, quickies in my trailer weren't on that list.

What had Harper said in my bathroom the first time we'd made love?

"I'd just fix it all up and nobody would ever know."

Good lord.

After finishing the scene, it was time for our meal break, and then I had another break before I was required. I went back to my trailer and slid the IN/OUT/DND indicator by the door to DND so people would know where I was but not to disturb me except in an emergency.

The only emergency I could think of worth disrupting my quiet time on set was if the entire studio was on fire. Or if Harper wanted to talk. I made a mental note to tell her that when I was in my trailer, unless I'd told her I was actively napping or desperately needed alone time, she was more than welcome to disrupt me.

I pulled off my boots and settled in to eat some string cheese and relax. I took my time slowly peeling strips off the cheese and eating them before grabbing the yoga block I liked to sit on for meditation in my trailer. I got comfortable on the block, leaning against the wall of my trailer, and moved all my attention to my breathing.

In. Out.

In. Out.

In… Out…

Mind wandering was part of meditation, but this time my thoughts wandered to exactly the same destination every time—Harper—and I gently guided them back until the thoughts receded to the background and a calm stillness hit me.

I was interrupted by a firm knock on my trailer door. I ignored it and tried to refocus on my breathing, but the knocking started again. I bit back a sigh. The studio had better be on fire. Rolling out my shoulders to ease the tension that had returned, I opened the door to someone I did not expect to see at my trailer door.

Ingrid.

The big VISITOR badge was clipped to my manager's huge, battered, million-year-old Hermès handbag—she would not spoil the lines of her outfit with a visitor's pass. I loved Ingrid, but I really wasn't in the mood for one of her special extended-edition chats.

She'd been in talent management almost longer than I'd been alive, and was the biggest study in contradictions I'd ever witnessed. Ingrid somehow managed to exude style while seeming as if she put no effort into her appearance, which was probably the true benchmark of stylishness. She was ruthless yet soft. Witty and acerbic to those who deserved it, and an absolute kitten of a woman once you got to know her. Thankfully, I'd managed to get myself into her good graces and stay there.

"Ingrid. Always a pleasure to see you." She only ever came to the studio when there was something important to discuss. She disliked the "impersonal nature" of phone calls, and if we had to call, she usually insisted on video. So, I was about to have a discussion about something important.

"Steph." She touched my cheek in a gentle maternal gesture. "You look healthy." It was her highest compliment, really. "Sorry to intrude, but we need to talk."

"My favorite words. Come on in." I closed the door behind her. "Take a seat."

She sat on the couch, setting the black-hole bag beside her. She dove right in. "I know you're short on time, so I won't dally. I've spoken with Veronica and Jeremiah, and they want you to know they're sorry they couldn't be here, but you can call them if you need to."

Agent and publicist. Oh dear. "Call them about what?" I asked, more concerned than annoyed now. "What's going on?"

"Do you want the good or not so good news first?"

"Not so good," I said instantly, steeling myself for whatever anvil was about to be dropped on me.

Ingrid didn't fuck around, which I appreciated, even as I didn't appreciate what she had to say. "There are some sexually explicit deepfake images of you circulating on the Internet."

I didn't know how I could feel both hot and cold at once, but I did. I had to swallow hard before I could talk, but even then the only words I managed to force out were choked and barely audible. "What? Where?"

Thankfully she didn't repeat herself for my rhetorical question of "what" and went right to the *where*. "They're on websites devoted to these sorts of disgusting things," she said with a wince.

I took a deep, not at all soothing breath. Okay. Facts I could work with. "I assume the sites have been notified for a takedown, or reported?"

"They have." She raised her phone, tapped through a few screens then nodded. "Yes. All but two are gone."

"What about legal action?"

"We've filed police reports and the lawyers are already looking into further action. Damage control is part of our job. We're handling it," she assured me soothingly.

"Good, thank you." I wrapped my arms around myself, sinking back into the couch.

"But, Steph, finding the original culprits is going to be like finding a needle in a haystack. We can make them pull the haystack down, but we may never find the needle."

"I know. Just…do what you can. Please."

"We will. We are."

I sighed. "Okay. Give it to me. Let me see the pictures."

She raised a thinly plucked eyebrow. "Are you sure you want to see?"

"No, I don't want to see. But I need to." It wasn't just a case of forewarned is forearmed—I genuinely needed to see these things, and not for voyeuristic reasons. Seeing them, knowing they were fake, would be cathartic. I'd faced these shitty things people did and came out the other side of the disgustingness relatively unscathed.

Ingrid dug around in her bag for her iPad. "These are some screenshots. And I have screenshots of all the comments. For my receipts," she said coolly. Ingrid kept these "receipts" on everyone. She was not a woman to fuck with. "Just so you know, it's quite realistic and the comments are overwhelmingly disgusting." She offered the device.

Though I'd been prepared, I really wasn't prepared. My first thought was that AI was getting pretty good these days. My second thought was a white-hot burst of anger, quickly followed by a rush of upset.

I fought with both and when I was sure I wasn't going to throw something or cry, I skimmed some of the comments until that crying and throwing things urge rose again. I passed the iPad back. "Well, today is a terrible day to have eyes and be literate."

"It is," she agreed grimly.

"At least they gave me a great body," I said dryly. "Pity nobody is going to be looking at that around 'my' double-D tits and the huge fucking cock in 'my' mouth." Glancing up, I added, "You know, I haven't had any experience with actual live penises, but the size of this one seems like an exaggeration."

"A big one. No pun intended." She sighed. "I'm sorry this is happening, Steph, but it's not something we could have prevented. We have a statement ready to go live if this leaks out into the community, condemning the deepfakes and making it utterly clear that that is obviously exactly what they are. Unfortunately, as you know, nothing is ever gone on the Internet. It will have been saved and shared. The best we can try to do is to put out spot fires as they pop up, but…" Wincing again, she shrugged.

"You know, nothing brings me more joy than thinking about people masturbating while thinking of me." I paused a moment to acknowledge the not-awful thought that'd just intruded upon this awful moment. I would derive joy from Harper pleasuring herself while thinking about me, did derive some from knowing she had. That thought took a tiny bit of my upset away. Just a tiny bit, but at the moment I'd take anything I could get to rid myself of this awful feeling.

Ingrid reached out and patted my leg. "It'll die down, it always does."

"Die down, but not die off," I countered. "Honestly, it feels really fucking shitty."

"I can imagine." Gently, she added, "I suggest you speak with your therapist about it."

"I will." I'd already mentally added it to the list of things to discuss at my fortnightly appointment.

The thought of people seeing those pictures, of judging me, of not liking me because of it made me feel like my chest was going to explode. Rationally I knew there were people who wouldn't like me, but giving ordinary people ammunition like this felt awful. I straightened up and shook my hands out. There was nothing more I could do about this and allocating more emotional energy to it wasn't helpful.

Sighing, I said, "Okay, give me the good news." After checking the time, I added, "And in fifteen minutes or less because I'm due back on set."

Again, she dove right in. "We've been approached for a role for you to film during hiatus."

That perked me up. Being approached for a role rather than having to audition for things was a nice feeling. "An audition for a new Marvel Universe movie?" That was top of my list. Any superhero really, but I'd been desperate to play Scarlet Witch or Captain Marvel ever since they were announced years ago, and still harbored a little sadness that I hadn't even gotten to audition. I wasn't even on the long-long list.

Ingrid smiled patiently. "Not quite. But something else on your list. They're pitching it as a lesbian Hallmark cowgirl-meets-city-slicker romance. Not quite as vanilla as Hallmark, but we're not talking full nudity either. Alyce Purves is onboard to direct. And they've got you on their shortest of short shortlists for the cowgirl."

Well, that wiped out some of my deepfakes bad mood. "Oh? Really? They came to you?" That wasn't unusual for an A-lister, but I was not an A-lister.

"Mhmm. Lilly Sanders is the casting director."

I'd worked with Lilly before, so it made sense now because she knew me and knew my work. "Wow." It was the only thing I could think of to say.

"You can thank that natural down-home country girl Midwest charm of yours and that you're known to be easy to work with and down-to-earth." Ingrid's mouth twitched. "Plus, you're the physical type they're looking to cast." Of course, there was always *that* caveat.

"I want it," I said immediately. I didn't care that I hadn't seen a word of the script and only had the barest idea of the role. If openly out award-winning director Alyce Purves was attached, then I was in.

Ingrid smiled knowingly. "I thought so. But just a heads-up, they want the cowgirl to look like someone who slings hay and rides tractors and rescues farm animals all day." Ingrid gave me an appraising look. "So you'll need to bulk up a little. Not to bodybuilder competition levels of muscle, obviously, just get what you've got to pop a little more. They already know you can ride horses, so that's a bonus."

A bonus indeed. Thanks, Iowa upbringing. I'd spent my early years doing farm chores, which were great for keeping fit, and given my job's requirements, working out was a regular part of my schedule. "Okay. Can you please find a trainer for me?" I held in a sigh. The thought of spending months fitting in extra strength training and all the associated nutrition stuff just to look a little more muscular on camera was spectacularly unappealing. But I really wanted this role. Hopefully Harper liked women with a little more muscle definition.

Ingrid nodded. "I know just the woman to help you get maximum muscle definition in the shortest time."

It'd be more aesthetics muscle rather than particularly useful muscle, but welcome to my job. "Thank you. So, they came to you? Am I auditioning or is it a done deal?"

She made a see-saw motion with her hand. "They want a meeting, but I'd say it's a ninety-five-percent done deal. They approached us, which is always a good sign. I honestly think any audition is just a formality."

"Okay."

"So, you want us to set up the meeting?" Her teasing expression made it clear her asking was also a formality.

"Yes, please." Despite the fact it seemed as close to approaching a deal as anything was in this business, I set it in the "don't get your hopes up" basket. "Also, if I put on a bunch of muscle and I don't get to carry my costar or at least pick her up, I'm going to be pissed. Heterosexuals get to carry their love interest in their movies. I want"—I ticked off on my fingers—"pick up, carry, kiss in the rain, and then rush inside and into a love scene."

Ingrid laughed. "After all these action roles, should we have been trying for more romances?"

The last two movies I'd had starring roles in, I'd played an assassin, and an Army vet trying to save her sister's family from a drug dealer. "Come on, you know I *love* romance movies."

My manager's smile held a touch of motherly fondness. "I know you do. Speaking of romance. How are things with you and Harper?"

Harper. A bright spot in a mess of darkness. I smiled. "It's still early, but things are really good."

Ingrid returned the smile. "I'm pleased." Then she moved on to wrapping up our conversation. "We'll continue monitoring for any photos of you, and will let you know when or if something goes public."

The joy bubble burst. "Great…"

There was a rhythmic tap on my door, the one Zoe always used. The knock was followed by her calling, "Steph? We're back."

"Be right there," I called back.

Ingrid rose gracefully. "I'll let you get back to work."

I started putting my boots back on. "Sure you don't want to stick around? Jared's on set today…" I said slyly.

Ingrid had proclaimed, more than once, what a "handsome young man" Jared was. Then in the next breath, when I'd give her shit about it, would wipe out her perviness with a caveat that he was too young for her and both she and Jared were happily married. But it didn't stop me teasing her about her little crush.

She lightly slapped my arm. "Oh hush, you. I'll let you know about that meeting."

"Sounds great. Thanks."

After the horror I'd seen in my trailer, it took every ounce of my professionalism and training to focus on work for the rest of the day. We wrapped just after five p.m., and as soon as I'd changed back into my clothes, I powerwalked to the Hair and Makeup trailer for my quick haircut.

Harper seemed startled when I walked in. She paused what she was doing, but remained bent over sorting through some products in a box on the floor. "Heyyy. What are you doing here?" she asked.

"I came to find you."

Smiling, she rolled her eyes. "You liar."

"It's partly the truth. But I have that haircut. Is Chrissy here?"

"She just ducked out for something. Said she'd be back in five."

I knew "something" was probably a quick call to her boyfriend. "Ah. Great." I slipped past Harper and settled in a chair, swiveling around to face her. Look at us, alone together, not touching, being totally professional. "Shouldn't you be getting ready to leave, not still working? Or shouldn't you have left already?"

Her slightly manic expression softened. "Just getting ready for tomorrow. Cleaning brushes and all that."

I turned my chair side to side. "You are a diligent and hardworking employee."

"That I am." She straightened up, smothering a groan as she rubbed her lower back.

"Need a massage?" It was a dangerous question, loaded with innuendo. But we *were* alone.

Harper smiled wearily. "Desperately. And, I just want to say, I'm not loving our agreement to not spend every work night together."

"Me either. I think that's something we need to figure out ASAP, how we can spend more time together without making work the next day impossible."

"Agreed." Harper studied me, and the longer she stared, the more her expression changed until concern was foremost. "Are you okay?"

Carefully, I schooled my face while inwardly panicking that she'd somehow noticed something was up. She'd done the same this morning in my trailer. "Just some work stuff."

This wasn't the place to tell her about the deepfakes. But even if I found the place, I didn't know how exactly I was going to tell her—how do you share something so revolting with a woman you're trying to build a relationship with? How do you tell her that this might be part of the life you're sharing now?

Harper's eyebrows came together. She tilted her head slightly, her careful gaze studying me. "Okay, sure. I get it." But beyond that, she didn't push.

I almost wished she would.

CHAPTER EIGHTEEN

Harper

Though Steph had obviously been to the apartment before, Per declared he was deep-cleaning for our *North Precinct* watch-along on Tuesday. There was something to be said for the free time afforded by his part-time employment. I'd asked him to grab some Estrella Damm beer and string cheese for Steph, as well as a range of snacks.

I called out my hello, then beelined for the bathroom to take a shower and get ready. I was putting in my last earring as I wandered into the kitchen. Per glanced up from his careful construction of a veggies-and-dip platter. "You look nice," he said absently. He did a double take. "Scratch that. You look fabulous. Your cleavage is out of this world."

"Thanks." I didn't want to get dressed up, because this was *supposed* to be a casual night at home. But I had put on a nice pair of not-for-work pants as well as a clingy three-quarter-sleeve top that worked with one of my favorite bras to do amazing things for my breasts.

Considering who was coming over, Per was surprisingly dressed down in old but clean jeans and a white T-shirt that outlined just how much time and attention he paid to his body. He checked his phone, typed something, then stuffed it into his back pocket. I sidled up beside him and he gave me a quick hug.

"I…may have gone a little overboard," he admitted, staring at the piles of snacks in various stages of readiness on the kitchen counter. Chips, dips, an obscene amount of raw veggies, a less obscene amount of deli meats, cheese, olives, popcorn, pretzels, and candy.

"You think?" I deadpanned.

"I didn't know what Steph likes to eat and I don't want to be the jerk who hasn't catered to his guest, so…" Per shrugged helplessly.

"Technically she's my guest, so I'd be the jerk."

"That's true." That realization brightened him considerably. "Good. If she hates anything, I'm going to remind her it was you who asked her and you who's responsible for the snacks. What time will she be here?"

I checked my watch. "Soon. She said about twenty minutes before the show starts." Steph wanted to go home to feed and spend a few minutes with Asimov, then shower. She promised she'd be here in plenty of time. Before we'd separated at work, she'd shyly asked if tonight was just a *North Precinct* watch-along, or if maybe there was going to be some time spent together afterward.

I'd tried to play it casual with a "It's up to you."

Steph's smoldering look made me feel like I was about to catch fire. "That's dangerous," she'd murmured before she'd backed away with a promise to see me in a few hours.

The sound of the front door unlocking preceded Ben rushing into the kitchen, carrying his usual overnight duffel as well as his leather work bag. "Hi, hi, sorry I'm late. I had a settlement drama." He kissed Per then turned to me. "Your cleavage really is out of this world, Harper." Ben exchanged a look with Per. A look that made it very clear that Per had texted his boyfriend about my cleavage and that they suspected why I was displaying some of my assets tonight. "You should show it off more often."

There was nothing to say to that except "Thank you." He was probably right, but cleavage for cleavage's sake had always felt a little pointless. That said, it seemed I might have a reason to show more of my assets now.

Ben stroked Per's back. "I'm just going to shower quickly."

"No rush," I said. "There's plenty of time until we start watching. And Steph won't be here for another five or ten minutes."

Ben shot me a look that was part disbelieving and part panicked, then all but sprinted to the bathroom.

I turned back to Per, who was still eying the mound of snacks with a mixture of pride and trepidation. "What exactly did you say to him about tonight?"

His eyebrows shot up. "Just that Stephanie D'Arripe was coming over for our watch-along. He knows you've been playing tennis and… stuff with her." He started setting out even more snacks.

"He looks like he's expecting Cate Blanchett or someone."

"Harper," Per said patiently. "I know you don't think it's a big deal because you work with these people every day. But despite living and working in this town for almost eight years, I think the most famous person Ben's met is that guy who hosts his favorite barbecue cooking show."

I'd been a little affected by some of the talent I'd worked with over the years, but it was less about their star power and more about how they treated me. The ones who were aloof and cool always made me feel flustered, like I had to prove myself extra hard. There was none of that with any of the talent on *North Precinct*.

Per barreled on. "And I mean, yeah, I've *been* on sets. Granted my roles were blink-and-you'll-miss-me, but it's not like I'm a total noob. I don't get starstruck. But there is something about Steph that just makes me feel awkward. And it's not even her! She's lovely. It's just like…she's so good and I feel a little like…in awe of that talent."

I knew the feeling. Steph had a little bit of an awe-inspiring effect on me too, though my reasons were very different to Per's. I nudged him. "She's just Steph. And Laura is just Laura. And—"

"Yeah, I get it," he interrupted. "I need to get over myself."

"No you don't. Nothing wrong with being a fan. Unless you're weird and make my friend uncomfortable, remember?"

"Yes, I remember. And…*friend*?" He managed to drag that last word out over a few seconds.

"Yes?"

"Are you sure that's all there is, Harper? Just friends? Who kiss in public?"

I was literally saved by the bell when Steph arrived. Per tapped my butt. "I'll finish up in here. Go say hi to your 'friend.'" He passed me two bowls. "And put these out for me, wouldya?"

I buzzed open the gate for her, then set the pretzels and veggies with dip on the coffee table. I was just smoothing down the front of my top when she knocked. After checking the peephole I flung the door open. My stomach did a little excited flip.

She'd changed into jeans, black leather sneakers, and a long-sleeved maroon tee that outlined some really nice parts of her. "Hey you," I said breathily.

Steph cupped my face, pausing a moment before she dipped her head and kissed me. "Hello," she murmured. "Long time no see. Even longer time no kiss."

"Too long," I agreed.

When I wrapped my arms around her neck, Steph's hands came to my waist, pulling us together. "Not touching at work is *so* hard," she complained.

I stroked the back of her neck. "I know. But it's worth it when we do get to touch…"

She nodded slowly, feigning thoughtfulness. Her eyes softened when we made eye contact. "I agree." Her gaze shifted to my mouth.

I took the hint and kissed her again. The heat that rushed through me wasn't unexpected, but it probably wasn't the best time to take things further. "Are you ready for this?" I asked.

"You make it sound like I'm going to regret it," Steph teased.

"I'm not sure regret is the right word. But…you may reconsider being with me once you witness The Awe of Ben."

Steph laughed quietly. "I'm sure he's nowhere near as awed as some people I've met." She wrapped an arm around my shoulders, leaning down to nuzzle my neck. "Come on, let's go before we don't."

The neck nuzzle nearly did me in. I wanted nothing more than to bypass the living room and head straight for my bedroom, but Per would never forgive me and Ben might actually perish. As soon as we made it to the living room, Steph kissed my temple then shifted slightly away.

"Is beer okay with you?" I asked. "We've got plenty of everything if you want something else."

"Beer is great, thanks."

I leaned into the kitchen. "Per, could you grab drinks please?"

Without turning around from whatever else he was plating, he gave me a thumbs-up. Given he'd bought the beer for Steph, I assumed he was all over what everyone wanted.

I gestured to the coffee table. "Help yourself to snacks."

"Thank you," Steph breathed. She beelined for the coffee table and nabbed a few pretzels and veggie sticks.

Ben came rushing into the room, practically skidding to a stop. He'd taken the world's fastest shower and changed into a pair of dark-gray pants and a fitted blue tee. The outfit was nicer than what he'd usually wear around the house, but still thankfully nowhere near "I'm trying really hard to look good and fancy." He'd restyled his hair and wore enough cologne to smell nice without being overpowering. There was hope for a normal evening after all.

Per was still fussing in the kitchen, so I made the introductions. Despite the fact he was almost vibrating with excitement or nerves, Ben managed a polite, articulate greeting. Steph shook his hand enthusiastically. "Great to meet you, Ben. Thanks so much for letting me crash your weekly watch session."

He pushed his hands into his pockets. "No problem at all. Great to have you with us."

She grimaced slightly. "I do have to apologize for the amount of time I'll spend on my phone. This is kind of a work thing for me. Live-watching the show on socials."

Ben was incredulous. "You do these sessions yourself? I thought it was an assistant with prestaged pics and posts."

"Nope," Steph said cheerfully. She grabbed more pretzels and tossed them into her mouth. After stowing the food in her cheek she apologized, "Sorry, I haven't had dinner yet." Once she'd chewed and swallowed, she continued, "It's all me, all the time. I like doing it. And fans like it too, so…"

Ben opened his mouth, then closed it again. I was sure he was going to say something like he loved the watch-along sessions because he was a fan. A big fan.

I touched Steph's shoulder. "Do you want something other than snacks? I can make you something, or we can order in." I should have checked with her about dinner. Per and I had agreed that instead of cooking tonight, we'd just devour his mountain of snacks, and I'd assumed she'd eat before she came around.

Steph paused scooping up artichoke dip with a big cauliflower floret. "Nonono, please," she said emphatically. "You don't need to go to any extra trouble just for me. This is great. And there's heaps of food here, so I'm good."

"Yes, heaps is exactly what there is. Blame Per," I said dryly. "He obviously hoped you were bringing the rest of the cast with you."

"I heard that," Per called from the kitchen.

I raised my voice, for no other reason than to be snarky. "Good, I meant for you to."

Steph bit her lip on a smile. She winked at me, which made my stomach do that silly little flippy-floppy thing, then helped herself to a small handful of popcorn.

Ben cleared his throat. "So, uh, can I get you a drink, Stephanie?"

Her expression softened, and she smiled one of her genuine, unforced interactions smiles. "Please, call me Steph. And I think Harper organized Per for drinks already?" She shot a quick, eyebrows-raised look at me as she said that.

I nodded. "I'm sure they're on the way."

Per rushed into the room. "They are, they are. So sorry," he said breathlessly. He flashed a dazzling smile of his own. "Steph, so great to see you again." I might have been imagining it, but it seemed like he emphasized the *again*, probably to tease Ben about the fact he'd met Steph before. I really hoped they got over their awe, and soon. As if he was deliberately trying to show me he wasn't fawning over Steph, Per handed Ben a beer first, then passed one to Steph. "Here you are," he said cheerfully. "Hope you like Estrella."

"I do, very much." She shot me a look, and a quick smile followed. "And you remembered the beer I had with tacos?"

"Of course I did."

Per asked, "Want a glass?"

"Bottle is fine, thanks. I'll save Harper the washing up." She bounced her eyebrows at me and I grinned.

He brandished a bottle opener. "Let me open that for you." Giving someone a closed drink for their peace of mind, even though we were in my house and among friends, was such an Aware Per thing to do.

"Fabulous, thanks." She flashed him a grateful smile that made him look like he was about to break out into girlish giggles.

And I flashed Per a pointed look that sent him scuttling back to the kitchen. He returned with a glass of white wine for me and a vodka soda with lime for himself. He raised his glass. "Cheers."

We clinked glasses and bottles, murmuring, "Cheers," except for Steph whose response was less murmured and more cheerfully loud. After she'd sipped her beer, she set it on a coaster on the coffee table. "Is it okay if I grab a photo of all of us before the episode and put it on socials? There'll be no comment as to who you are, and you'll all get full approval of the photo before I post it."

The answer was a unanimous "Yes."

Ben added, "You can tag the absolute shit out of me if you want. I don't mind." He glanced at Per who nodded his agreement to tagging. Nodded so vigorously I was surprised he wasn't giving himself a brain bleed. "Let me give you my accounts. Our accounts. I am going to share that shit far and wide."

I cleared my throat. "Is sharing that shit going to make your friends and coworkers get weird, and then you in turn will get weird? Or... weirder."

Steph shot me a look, her eyes widening fractionally.

Ben and Per exchanged their own look before they both turned to me. "Nope," Ben said. "Per has no friends except you"—he dodged the playful punch thrown at his arm—"and mine either don't care about most of what happens in this town, or they won't even see it because they're on socials detox. Lucky them," he added in a low mutter.

Per joined in. "And even if they did, they're not going to make a big deal about it."

Steph touched my back. "Well, it's settled then. You in on this pic, Harper?" She'd asked casually, but her expression showed her desires. She wanted me in the picture.

Sure, it wasn't an intimate picture of just us, but I knew what it would convey, and that anyone paying attention would link me in these pics to me from the *Page Six* pictures.

"Absolutely," I said.

She set up her phone on the coffee table with a small tripod while the rest of us squished in on the couch, leaving a gap for Steph in the middle. Per let Ben sit beside Steph. Once she'd checked we were all properly in frame, she set up a burst before rushing back to the couch.

All four of us vetoed some of the pictures, but it seemed we were all in agreement on one in particular. Steph had her hand on my thigh, closer to my knee than my hip, and her other arm wrapped around Ben who looked like he'd just won the lottery. Per had his arm around me. All four of us were smiling, all eyes were open. It was a great picture. I might grab it off socials. Maybe crop it a little. Maybe stare at it sometimes.

In the few minutes while Per and Ben relocated so we weren't sitting on top of each other, Steph had put out her first post across social media. *A little change in tonight's company for North Precinct. Don't worry, I've left it playing at home so Asimov doesn't miss the episode. #Valmy #NorthPrecinct #timewithfriends*

"Aww," I said teasingly after I'd seen the post. "Time with *friends*? I'm honored."

That elicited a pleased smile from Steph, and a kind of panicked "Is this really happening to me, did she just call us a friend?" look from both Per and Ben.

"As if you didn't know," she said, almost matching my teasing, if not for the undercurrent of seriousness in the words.

I knew her well enough by now to decipher her tones, but I didn't know her well enough to decipher their deeper meanings. We'd talked about dating, but *was* Steph my girlfriend yet? She felt like it, but we hadn't explicitly confirmed it. She must have noted my confusion because the smile turned dazzling, almost disarming.

If we were alone, I would have just kissed her. But I still didn't know where we stood on being seen kissing, even if it was by my friends—my friends who were finally acting like humans. Kissing Steph right now would probably freak them right out. If only they knew we'd done a whole lot more than just kissing.

So I smirked, or hope I smirked. I probably just looked deranged when I said, "No, I know."

I guess my smirk landed, because she grinned in response. "People are going to freak out that there's actual people in this picture instead of my cat." Now that I thought about it, I couldn't recall any watch-along photos that had humans in it, only Asimov. Not even her ex. Interesting…

The episode was about to start, and Per gently called us to order.

By the first ad break, Ben had finally realized how normal Steph was and his stiff awe had all but disappeared. Of course, her natural affable charm helped, but it never felt forced, like she was in the middle of a press junket, trying to make everyone like and connect with her. She genuinely seemed to like the guys, and I had witnessed her when she wasn't overly enamored with someone, so I knew what that looked like. She did not bother to hide it. The previous male lead before Jared had caused so much tension on set that he hadn't had his contract renewed after the first season. They'd actually killed off his character to make sure he could never darken the set's door again.

Both Ben and Per made good on the promise not to be weird, and I couldn't help thinking how well Steph just…*fit*. It was so easy to imagine her in this little pocket of my life, outside of work and outside of sleeping together.

Though she'd apologized for the fact she'd periodically be on her phone "keeping the bosses happy" as she put it, each time she grabbed it, she seemed to cringe into herself. And each time, I checked socials. About thirty-five minutes in, I checked her latest, smiling when I read the post.

Fun fact: I could NOT get these handcuffs on over multiple takes. The extra was very forgiving. Watch out for this in the blooper reel… #NorthPrecinct #Valmy

Steph was watching me when I looked up, already laughing, and our eyes met. "I remember that."

She grinned, and the look in her eyes made my chest feel constricted. It was playful, but there was something soft in it too. "Good ol' Steph," she said. "Making mistakes and screwing up takes." She leaned forward to snag some dip, crunching celery loudly now an ad break had started.

"Does that happen often?" Ben ventured. "You, uh…screwing up?"

"Sure does," Steph answered cheerfully, grabbing more celery and another string cheese. "Not enough to make production run behind, thankfully, or I might find myself out of a job."

I bumped her with my shoulder. "Oh didn't you know? They factor 'Steph time' into production to account for you flubbing things." She rarely flubbed lines, but was notorious for fumbling a cup, cuffs, keys, clothing, manila folders, and everything in between.

She bit her lower lip. "Is that so? See," she told the guys, "Harper knows all the insider info."

I nodded sagely. "I downplay my importance for you two so you don't freak out, but I'm actually a really big deal at work."

"You sure are," Steph said fondly. Her discreet hand found mine in the space between our thighs, and squeezed. I chanced a quick look at her, then turned my gaze back to the screen, deliberately not looking at Per and Ben.

It was then that I remembered something I really should have remembered earlier. There was an intimate scene in this episode. Thankfully I also remembered she wasn't fully topless, just down to a bra before the scene would cut away. But still. Steph was doing something on her phone when the scene started, but it was like her eyes and the screen were two magnets attracting when Amy said, "I've been thinking about you all day," then pushed Val backward through the bedroom doorway.

Per and Ben didn't seem outwardly bothered by the fact they were in the same room with the woman who was currently rolling around on a bed with her costar on our television.

Steph leaned into me, murmuring, "You okay?"

"Mhmm." I glanced at her, hoping my cheeks weren't as red as they felt.

She looked sympathetic. "It's weird for me too. It's not usually, but right now...it kind of is." Steph nudged my shoulder with hers. "It's almost done."

I'd never had an issue watching Steph in intimate scenes, and I wasn't exactly having an issue now. And I wasn't inserting myself into the scene—I'd *never* done that. But it did make me think about things. Naked things.

I grabbed a handful of popcorn and ate it piece by piece, chewing each one as slowly as someone could chew a single piece of popcorn. By the time I'd finished the handful, I'd calmed the heck down.

As I'd expected, the evening went far too fast. Steph stayed for *Make the Cut*, and as soon as the credits rolled, she stretched, then started stacking empty glasses and snack bowls. "Can I help you guys clean up?"

Ben laughed. "I'm sure you're capable, but no, you don't need to."
Wow. An actual joke from Ben. He really was completely over Steph as
Celebrity Steph. Thank god.

"Next time then." She held out her hand and the boys shook it in
turn. "Ben, Per, thank you so much for letting me join your television
evening. I had a great time, and you're far better conversationalists than
my cat."

Ben wrapped both arms around his tall boyfriend, leaning his
temple against Per's shoulder. "You're welcome to join our watch parties
anytime."

"Dangerous invitation if you don't mean it, because I will absolutely
take you up on that."

Per grinned. "Good." He shot a glance at me, the barely restrained
mania bubbling over in his expression. Thankfully Steph wasn't looking
at him during those few moments, though she did when he continued,
"We'll leave you two to say good night."

Steph's arm stole around my waist, and I almost forgot to breathe.
She smiled. "Night, guys. Catch you next time."

Per finger-waved at us, then slung his arm around Ben's shoulder.
He steered them out of the room, murmuring something in Ben's ear
as they left.

Steph turned to me. "Thank you for tonight. You made it so much
easier. I actually don't love watching myself. It makes me feel a little
self-critical and it's something I can't change so sometimes I get a little
doom-spirally."

"I'm sorry to hear that. I love watching you." I ran my hands up her
biceps. "And it was our pleasure."

"*Our* pleasure?" She slowly arched an eyebrow as her gaze swept
from my eyes to my mouth and back again. "What about…your pleasure,
Harper?"

"Oh it was absolutely my pleasure."

Steph pushed me backward to the wall next to the kitchen and caged
me with an arm on either side of my shoulders, hands resting against
the wall. Her gorgeous, kissable mouth quirked. "Not yet, but it could
be." She moved closer, until her hips pressed into mine. The intense
eye contact, the scent of her, the damned press of her body was sending
thrills of arousal through me.

I grabbed her ass and pulled her even closer. "Is that a promise?"

"Yes," she murmured. For a scary moment, I thought she wasn't
going to kiss me, that she was just teasing me, teasing herself for some

later fantasy. She lightly cupped my face in one hand, and slowly drew her thumb across my mouth.

When I parted my lips, the tip of her thumb traced over my lower lip. Steph groaned, and almost in the next breath she'd yanked me hard against her to kiss me. Her mouth opened, her tongue gently stroking mine until desire curled through my belly and spread downward.

"Do you want to stay?" I asked tightly, the anticipation of taking her to bed making it hard to speak.

"Yes." She inhaled shakily. "But it's already late and we have to work early-early tomorrow. And, Harper, it's going to take me until the early hours of the morning to do everything that I need to do to you." Steph cupped my face and kissed me deeply, pulling back just enough to murmur, "Being too tired to work because I've kept you up all night screaming is *not* professional…"

CHAPTER NINETEEN

Steph

Ingrid called as I was driving in to work, apparently to update me on something I'd been trying not to think about. "Steph, sorry I didn't call you yesterday but I was in meetings until late."

"No problem. What's the verdict?" In light of the deepfake images, the network had scheduled a meeting to discuss my involvement in the charity tennis match.

Laura had mentioned that her manager was attending too, which had meant I'd had to come clean to her about why. "What the fuck?" she'd seethed. "It's not like you posed for some seedy porn site. This is bullshit."

This industry was full of bullshit. As if it wasn't bad enough that the images existed, now I had to tell people when all I wanted was to forget it was happening.

Ingrid, master of no bullshit, said, "The tennis match *is* going ahead with you and Laura."

I let out a relieved sigh. "Well thank fuck for that. I'm glad I haven't spent the last three weekends practicing for nothing." Of course it wasn't for nothing—spending time with Harper was worth any price.

"I agree. You're a drawcard. You and Laura together is dynamite. And they've already swapped out one pair of players once and doing it again is *not* a good look. I had to spin it a little, but they came around pretty fast."

"Spin it how?"

"Given the fact these photos are originating from seedy parts of the Internet, the likelihood of any 'upstanding'"—I heard the implied quotations there—"people seeing them is highly unlikely. And if anyone complains about it, then they'll be easy to discredit as having sought them out from the Internet's underbelly."

"Umph," I groaned. "I hate it."

I'd thanked every star and planet in the universe that the whole "Stephanie D'Arripe sucks cocks" images hadn't seeped out of the dark, dank parts of the Internet—not only for my mental health, but for the fact it boded well that nobody I worked with was hanging out on those vile sites. But it was intruding on my professional life just the same.

The producers had pulled me into a meeting yesterday with the writers, and Ingrid attending via video call, to check a scene that implied a suspect was telling Amy to suck his dick was still a go. I didn't see an issue with it, and more than anything I didn't want the deepfake bullshit to intrude on my life more than it had. I wouldn't have thought twice about that dialogue before.

"We're going to get a warrant for your DNA, and I'd bet my paycheck it's going to match the semen we recovered from the victim."

"For you, well…I'd be happy to give you a DNA sample without a warrant. But you're going to have to suck it out of me."

Thankfully my team agreed the dialogue was fine, and the writers seemed relieved to not have to kill any of their precious words.

Ingrid clucked like a mother hen. "I know you do, but these are the games we have to play. Something to brighten your mood. I'm talking to Alyce today or tomorrow and I'll let you know when this meeting with her and Lilly is."

"Great, thanks. Talk soon."

I reversed in next to Harper's car, a little bummed that she wasn't in it. Before I got out, I opened up our messages. She'd messaged me when she'd woken up, just a sweet good morning, hope you slept well, can't wait to see you type thing that had made me smile so much I wondered if my cheeks would get sore.

Our quick exchange had ended with her telling me to let her know when I arrived and I tapped out *Here. See you in about twenty.*

Her response was a kissy-face emoji that was both sweet, and induced a small measure of frustration that I wouldn't get to kiss her properly this morning. Or today. Not until tonight.

I was battling a whole truckload of regret that I hadn't stayed longer at Harper's last night and satisfied my cravings for her, but when I yawned the moment I sat down in her chair, she laughed. "Little bit sleepy?"

Jared, in Nina's chair, let out a triumphant little laugh. As the appointed King of Sleepy, he took great pleasure when it wasn't just him yawning through a morning.

"Just a little," I said to Harper. I wished we were somewhere more private where I could tell her exactly why I was tired—I was having trouble sleeping. The deepfake bullshit was one thing. But I was also lying awake thinking about her and us and everything we could be doing if we were together. I'd always slept better with someone beside me. Someone like Harper, who seemed to enjoy snuggling in her sleep.

"Why would you be tired?" she asked innocently as she adjusted the lights.

"No particular reason," I said airily. "I wish I were more tired though…"

"Professionalism," Harper murmured. She checked her script notes and the progression photos showing the location of bruising remnants and the small cut on Amy's cheekbone from being elbowed in the face last episode. Her light fingertips brushed over my cheek.

I closed my eyes. "I hate it," I mumbled petulantly.

"So do I. But I hate the alternative even more."

The alternative where we weren't a thing. "Me too."

She checked I was good to go, then started work. Once she'd done my eyes and base, working around Chrissy who was finished with my hair in record time this morning, she began to build in the bruising. I could have been overthinking, but it definitely felt like she touched me more than usual as she worked. Just a skim of her fingers over my shoulder, a gentle stroke on the back of my neck. Her work had always involved touching but this was more intimate, without crossing a line, and I found myself craving her touch more than ever.

Harper sighed. "Your poor bruised beautiful face. I'll be glad when Amy's healed."

"You should see the other guy," I joked.

Laughing, she assured me, "I did when we did his makeup last week. Tilt your head away please."

I did as asked. "I need to buy something to wear for this tennis match on the weekend. Do you have time to come shopping with me before Saturday? I want to make sure I get the right stuff."

Nina spun around. "Are you getting yourself a fancy outfit for this tennis thing, Steph?"

"I am. Representing my show, so I need to look good."

"Damned right you do. I've been tapped for pre- and post-game makeup."

"Sounds great." I'd already assumed they'd use Nina for that, because Harper would be occupied with tennis-y things.

Nina's sly gaze moved between Harper and me. "That is, if Harper will let me touch you."

I sensed tension flow through Harper, and glanced up to check her reaction. She forced a smile. "You'll just have to ask nicely."

Nina batted her eyelashes. "Harper, can I do Steph's makeup for the tennis game?"

Harper laughed, but it lacked her usual warmth. "I meant you should ask Steph."

I butted into the exchange, wanting to cut any more discomfort for Harper off at the knees. "Fine by me, but you know I'm a Harper fan through and through."

"Oh no, I know that." Smiling, she turned back to Jared, who was absorbed in his phone and, I knew from experience, completely tuned into that and tuned out to all of us.

There was something in Nina's tone that went beyond just banter. I raised a querying eyebrow at Harper and mouthed "She knows?" I made a small back-and-forth gesture between us.

She nodded slightly, then mouthed back "That okay?"

It was my turn to nod. We hadn't exactly been subtle with our flirting before agreeing to date, so it wasn't surprising Nina had picked up on something. And they were friendly, so why wouldn't Harper mention that things between her and I had shifted? I smiled, reaching out to lightly touch her hip. A little of the tightness in her body eased.

"I'm sorry," she murmured.

"No need to be," I reassured her. I leaned in, keeping my voice low. "Can we spend tonight together?"

Harper's "Yes, please" was a barely audible whisper. She touched the end of her lipstick brush to my lower lip. "Now, and I say this with love—" Harper paused, her eyes widening slightly as she took in my expression.

I hoped that expression conveyed how I felt, that there was no panic, only pleasure. "What are you saying with love?" I asked quietly.

She leaned closer, holding up the brush. "Please shut your mouth."

We wrapped on time and after a whirlwind round of thanks and good nights, I removed my clothing, hung it for Wardrobe, and took off my makeup in record time. Harper was waiting by my car, leaning casually against the hood. She pushed away from it as I approached.

"My little welcoming party." I leaned in to kiss her, then remembered where we were and pulled back. "I really think you might like me."

Harper brought her forefinger and thumb close together in front of my face. "Only a lil bit."

"I'll take it."

"How was your day?"

I had to think before answering, because she'd been with me for most of my workday, so why wouldn't she know how my day had been? She'd witnessed it. But asking how my day was went deeper than just a polite query—she was telling me she really cared, she wanted to know how I *felt*. "Long and tiring. But I'm feeling less tired now. How about yours?"

"Same." Harper smiled wearily. "What did you have in mind for tonight?"

"I honestly haven't thought about anything other than something, together."

"I like it. Could we grab dinner? We could go somewhere, or order in."

A low whistle interrupted us, and we both turned around to see Laura sauntering over. She hitched her bags higher on her shoulder. "Awww, look at you two. So the rumors are true. Did I stumble into your little love nest?"

Harper and I moved slightly apart. "That didn't take long," Harper said under her breath.

"Longer than I expected," I muttered before turning to Laura. "Funny," I said dryly, slow-clapping her. "You're so funny."

She made a little bow. "I know." Laura slowly looked me up and down, her mouth quirking. "Looks like you're taking this whole 'please carry the relationship baton for once' seriously, Steph." She looked between me and Harper, grinning. "Glad you took my advice. Y'know, I'm actually enjoying being single instead of rushing into a relationship again just for the sake of keeping management teams happy and the gossips quiet."

Laura clearly wasn't seeing my alarm during her little speech, and had just kept barreling on. Her expression was completely devoid of any malice or deliberate antagonism—she obviously thought she was just making a joke—but the only response in my head was a screaming, repeated "Oh fuck."

And Harper…

Harper's confusion was evident from her expression to her posture to the tone of her voice when she looked from Laura to me and asked, "What do you mean?" Underneath the confusion was a wariness that made my gut clench.

Laura beat me to answering, though it did cross my mind to just tell her to be quiet. "Oh, you know—" She faltered and looked to me. I shook my head, and thankfully she saw it and shut up. "Okay, obviously you don't know."

Harper's defensive arms folded over her chest. "Clearly I don't." Her eyes moved to me, an eyebrow raised in query.

I hated the helpless little shrug I gave her in response. And I really hated the accusatory look she gave me. It made me feel like someone had punched me in the stomach, robbing me of all speech. The horrible feeling should have spurred me to act, to speak, but it did the exact opposite.

Laura spoke up where I couldn't, though she didn't try to explain at all. Not that it was for her to explain, but it would have been nice of her to help me out while I stood there completely unable to tell Harper it absolutely was *not* the way it seemed. Instead, she redirected the conversation in another utterly horrifying direction. "Hey, Steph, did you get those gross pictures taken down?"

Fuck me. Anything else you want to say, Laura?

Before I could answer with a vague redirect, Harper asked, "What pictures?"

"It's nothing." I knew she didn't believe me, but I just didn't want to tell her. I didn't want this to be a thing between us, something she had to think about when she thought about us as a couple.

Laura laughed nervously. "Shit. I put my foot in it, huh. I, uh…I might just go then."

She'd put both her feet and a bunch of other people's feet into it as well. The uncomfortable mix of panic and anger and embarrassment made me more snappish than I intended. "You think?"

"Sorry," she said around a grimace, then slunk away.

I didn't look after her.

I looked at Harper.

We stood utterly still, facing each other, with what felt like a whole continent's worth of distance between us. I felt vaguely sick, and I swallowed a few times, hoping to push it down. But the feeling lingered like a bad meal.

Harper took in a deep breath and let it out slowly. "What pictures is she talking about?" she asked, her voice so calm it felt unnatural. The calmness broke. "Is it us again?"

Her obvious worry snapped me out of my self-centered panic. "Oh god, no. Sorry. It's me. Or...not really me. There are some deepfake pictures of me circulating. Pornographic ones."

"Steph..." Harper looked crestfallen. "Oh no." She closed the distance between us, bringing both hands up to rest on my shoulders. All I wanted was to step right into her space for a hug, but all that fucking professionalism weighed me down.

I shrugged, trying to feign nonchalance when the thought of what people had done with my face made me feel like I could vomit. "Oh yes. All you need to do is search 'Stephanie D'Arripe naked with cock in her mouth' and it's right there for you, and anyone else who wants it. All the fake porn pics of me anyone could ever want."

It wasn't even the content of the pictures—I would have been just as upset if they'd deepfaked me performing oral sex on a woman—it was the overwhelming violation of my privacy, my humanity.

An expression I couldn't quite decipher passed over her face, but I could decipher enough to know I didn't like it. "I don't want to see that," she said firmly. "I'm sorry this is happening. It's a horrible, humiliating thing." She squeezed my shoulders. "Do you want to talk about it?"

I did. Desperately. I just wanted to vent and have someone listen to me without judging my emotions, to let me ramble incoherently. But I couldn't put that on Harper. So I forced out a tight, "Not really."

The lie tasted horrible, but dragging her into it when she didn't need to be mixed up in it was just going to mess everything up. I wanted her to think we could have a somewhat normal relationship around all the things she already knew weren't normal.

Harper smiled, but the tension around her eyes was evident. "Okay. Well, when you do, you know where I am." She dropped her hands from my shoulders.

"Thanks." I huffed out a loud breath.

She worried her lower lip with her teeth. "So that explains what Laura meant by pictures. But what was she talking about with you taking the relationship baton and...keeping management teams happy?"

My hands felt clammy. "Harper. It's not what you think."

"How do you know what I'm thinking?"

"I have a pretty good idea."

Her arms went back to cross over her chest. "It feels like you're stalling. What did she mean about you 'taking the baton,' Stephanie?"

Ouch. Her using my full name like that stung.

"It's not what it sounds like," I said, trying for confident and landing short.

"Okay. What is it then? Seeing as you're refusing to tell me, I'll tell you what it sounds like. It *sounds* like you're only dating me to keep your management team happy. It sounds like you're only dating me because you don't want people to gossip about you screwing your costar."

Panic welled up swiftly, and I choked out a, "Harp—"

She cut me off with a humorless laugh. "I get it. I've read those rumors on socials almost every week since Amy and Val started dating on *North Precinct*. I'm sure you don't enjoy that. So, Steph, am I just a pretend girlfriend to appease the public so they leave you and Laura alone, to make your team happy that you're getting your photo taken in public?"

"No!" I clamped my lips together, aware that I'd just shouted loudly enough for anyone in proximity to hear. I moved forward. Harper moved back. "Look. That's *not* what it is. Can we just go home, and I'll explain what Laura meant."

She shook her head. "No, I don't think so."

"Why not?"

"I'm upset with you right now and I don't want to say something I might regret."

"Upset with *me*?" Despite my awareness that anyone could be listening, my voice still rose indignantly. "Why? I haven't done anything."

"A person who hasn't done anything usually isn't so defensive."

"I'm defensive because you're taking this *way* out of context."

"It's not on you to tell me how I'm taking it," she said simply. "So, can you enlighten me. *Please*. Did I wander into some sick fake-dating thing, except only you know it's fake dating?"

"God, no, of course not. Look, Laura was just being silly."

"Silly? That's not what it seemed like to me. It seemed to me like she knows something I don't. Something I *should* know. Something you haven't told me." She shut down any answer I might have been able to give with a flat, "I'll see you in the mornin'," before stalking away.

"Harper—"

But she didn't turn around. I waited until she was safely in her car and on her way before I got in my car. As calmly as I could, I set my bags on the back seat. But as soon as I turned around again, everything burst out. I slammed my palms against my steering wheel and the release felt so good that I did it again and again and again, yelling an incomprehensible sound into the echoing stillness of my car.

The sound coalesced into a string of fucks that grew louder and more frequent until I collapsed forward onto the steering wheel. I sat there, my forehead against the wheel, and let hot tears drip down my cheeks onto my thighs. I wasn't sobbing exactly, but the tears just wouldn't stop.

I needed to explain what Laura meant, and that Harper had totally misunderstood the entire situation. But given how I'd been shut down with Harper's firm "I'll see you in the morning," I wasn't sure that just turning up at her place was going to win me any favors. And obviously I needed all the favors I could get.

Unfortunately, sitting in my car at work, crying until my face was so swollen that I'd be unrecognizable on-screen tomorrow wasn't really an option. "Get your shit together," I muttered to myself. I'd just started the car when my phone rang. Laura. Great. Laura hardly ever called. I was still more upset and angrier than I'd been in recent memory, but the anger was at myself more than my friend. So I answered the call.

"Hey."

Laura's words spilled out in a rush, over the sound of her typically over-the-speed-limit driving. "Hey, listen. I'm *so* sorry. I didn't realize, I mean, I just didn't think about what I was saying. You guys just looked super cute, and yeah, I'm sorry."

I sighed. "It's not your fault." Laura had never been good at filtering. "But yeah, thanks for dropping a bomb into the middle of my relationship and then sprinting away. Really appreciate that," I said, biting off the words sarcastically.

"Sorrryyyyy," she whined. "Is Harper pissed?"

"That is the understatement of the century."

"Fuck. *Fuck*," she breathed. "I'm *so* sorry, Steph. Do you want me to talk to her, tell her what that whole baton joke is about?"

"No! Fuck, no. Please don't. I appreciate the offer but if you could never mention the baton joke ever again that would be great." Sighing, I added, "And this is something I need to fix on my own."

"You got it." She huffed out a loud breath. "Shit, I feel terrible."

"I know you do. But it's not your fault. I didn't tell her about the baton thing because that's *not* what this is. But...maybe I should have said something, told her about the joke." I laughed, but there was no humor in it. "Actually no, that probably would have been even worse."

"And you didn't tell her about the deepfakes?" There was no accusation, only curiosity. But Laura was an oversharer so it was probably blowing her mind that I'd held back out of fear.

"No. I didn't want her to get caught up in my bullshit right at the start of our relationship."

"She's going to get caught up in it eventually," Laura said gently. "Why not just get her used to it."

"Because I fucking hate it. She doesn't deserve to be in the middle of my bullshit."

"If she loves you, then she's going to take all that as part of it. And there's no reason you two can't…you know, talk about things like this. Work out middle ground."

I scoffed. "What middle ground? The middle ground where I ask these mouthbreathers to not make fake pictures of me?"

"The middle ground where you ask how she feels about it and all the other stupid shit in your life, and work out how to implement strategies for mutual comfort."

"Right…"

"I'm going to tell you some truths, and you're going to listen. You're making excuses because you're scared. Understandable. Jordan fucked you over. Being scared is normal going into any relationship. But unless you get the hell over this roadblock, you're never going to go anywhere. And I gotta say, Harper's pretty great. And I only know the work side of her. If you let this go because you're too chickenshit to figure it all out, then I might just have to punch you in the boobs."

"Thanks. I think."

"Actually, you know what? I know the best way to describe it to you. I was on Reddit the other day—"

"Ew."

"Shut up. Like I said, I was on Reddit and there was a thing about which actors aren't as hot as everyone thinks they are. You and I were not mentioned, FYI. We *are* hot. But someone described Jordan Leclerc as gluten-free, dairy-free, keto bread spread with nonfat butter. And another said Jordan was unseasoned boiled chicken personified."

A snort-laugh burst out of me. An apt description—pretty, but bland. "I love it. It's so true."

Laura laughed with me, but quickly settled. "It is. But Harper? She is a fucking buffet, my friend. A buffet of sumptuous, exotic, delicious food. And you deserve this feast."

"I know," I murmured.

"Be honest with me. This thing with Harper. How serious is it?"

"The relationship isn't serious yet because we've only just begun it. But yeah…I'm in love with her." I swallowed past the tightness in my throat. "It's nothing new, it's just…all those feelings have floated to the surface now."

Laura didn't moderate her incredulity. "You don't think it's too soon to be falling in love? I mean, I know you guys have had that little flirty thing going on forever, but love isn't flirting." She laughed. "And yes, I'm aware of the hypocrisy of me telling you about love."

"No, it's not too soon," I insisted. "We've worked together for almost six years. It's not like I don't know her."

"True," Laura mused. "Maybe I need to start looking at crew members. I've always thought Dave is pretty fucking hot. Those arms? Boom-man arms. Hooo-wee. Imagine that picking you up and holding you against a wall."

I wrinkled my nose. "Not for me, thanks."

"Oh right. I forgot you're the one who's usually doing the picking up."

"Yeah," I said gloomily.

"Well, I for one think Harper is worth picking up and pinning against a wall."

If I kept talking, I was probably going to cry again. I cleared my throat. "Listen, I gotta go. I'll see you tomorrow."

"Okay. If you need to punch me, please do it somewhere other than my beautiful face."

"I will." The joke came out before I thought about what I was saying. "But you know Harper could cover that shit right up." I swallowed hard. "I gotta go. Bye."

I pulled into the parking lot of a tiny strip mall on Hyperion, parked in front of a mattress store, and threw my car into park. Covering my face with my hands, I sucked in deep, hiccupping breaths. This whole thing was all a stupid misunderstanding, and if Harper would just let me explain then I could clear the air and show her what she thought was happening wasn't actually what was happening. Of course, my entire plan hinged on actually talking to her.

And that's where the whole thing fell apart.

I couldn't believe that this one thing, this one silly misunderstanding and how I handled it, might make or break my relationship with Harper.

CHAPTER TWENTY

Harper

Two thoughts looped around and around in my head, refusing to be shoved aside. I was an idiot, and Steph had lied. Clearly, I didn't have the full story about the deepfakes and I absolutely needed to know more about this whole "romance baton" thing that she and Laura had going on.

But no matter how I spun it, I just kept coming back to the fact Steph had both withheld things *and* lied to me. And that hurt more than almost anything in my life had ever hurt me, because of all the people I'd expected that from, it wasn't Steph.

We were never going to work if she wouldn't open up to me and let me in. And we were never going to work if I kept letting my anxieties that she didn't think I was trustworthy get in the way. Trust was a funny thing. She had mine. I *thought* I had hers. Part of being a makeup artist was being a secret keeper—the relationship between us and those we worked with was intimate, without being romantic.

But now I wondered if the sharing with Steph hadn't been as intimate as I'd thought. Maybe she'd held back because she didn't want to share. Maybe she'd held back because she didn't want to cross a line. Maybe all we had was a good working relationship.

That thought actually made me feel like I was going to throw up.

Some deep breathing helped. Until more thoughts crept in. She hadn't told me because she didn't trust me. She hadn't told me because I wasn't good enough for her. I wasn't enough for her.

And then the thoughts started spinning…

I wasn't good enough for anyone. My own family sure didn't think so. The woman I was in love with didn't think so. I covered my face with my hands. Those were ridiculous, spiraling thoughts. I needed to stop it. I tried a reframe.

In my gut, I understood why she hadn't told me about the deepfakes. We'd never really talked about her professional life aside from the fan thing that afternoon after tennis. I knew the pressures placed on celebrities, knew they dealt with things noncelebrities didn't and could likely not imagine. Knowing that didn't make it easier, because she'd basically hit my major insecurity point, that I wasn't worth sharing her problems with.

Of course it wasn't that simple, and of course she hadn't done it deliberately, and of course it was on me how I was taking it. But I couldn't help my instinctive reaction to her shutting me out of her life, out of her problem, out of her emotions. I wasn't some woman she'd only met last month, someone who hadn't earned her trust. At the very least I just wanted to be there for her while this thing was handled by the people she paid to handle things.

So, I supposed I was kind of okay about her not telling me about the disgusting images. Obviously I didn't want to steamroll what was happening in her life, but I did want her to know how I felt. Maybe we could work on my issues later, because she was dealing with this deepfake thing. But my feelings did need to be addressed. I needed her to know, because if she didn't then this would just keep happening every time something bad popped up in her life.

But…the "baton"? That, I was not okay with.

Because that sounded a whole lot like her being with me as a PR stunt. Again, obviously I didn't have the full story, but the way she'd turned instantly defensive told me I had enough of the picture. And the picture was absolutely awful. Fake dating as a PR stunt was not a new concept. Industry people did it constantly to maintain an image. But I'd never thought Steph would do it to me, without at least telling me this wasn't real.

How could she do that?

How hadn't I seen it?

It felt so damned real. Sure, she was an actor, but I wasn't an idiot. Our intimacy didn't feel fake, and the Steph I knew, had known for the past six years, would never pretend like that, do something so cruel. And if she was trying to be noticed, out and about with someone, to give the illusion of a relationship, then why wasn't she out and about with me? If anything, it almost felt like she was reluctant to be seen in public with me, like maybe…she was ashamed to be seen with me. Oh great, I'd just opened up another can of insecurity.

Was I overreacting? Why would someone sleep with someone if it was just a PR stunt? They wouldn't. Would they? So maybe this was just some weird thing I'd mistaken. I knew *I'd* probably get defensive if someone accused me of something the way I had with her, even if the accusation was correct.

I didn't want to give her a free pass on behavior that was problematic for me, but I also didn't want to burn down this thing unnecessarily. I needed the full story. "You don't have the full story" was a recurring theme in my thought loops, and almost made me regret bailing this afternoon before Steph could explain. But being so exposed at work was not something I wanted. I didn't know if I'd calmed down enough to talk through this mess with her, but maybe we should before either of us got even more upset and we blew this whole thing up.

I checked my phone again to see if she'd tried to call or text. Nothing. Radio silence. Her silence felt like it cemented my suspicions and I threw my phone onto the couch in disgust. Sure, I could have contacted her, but I hadn't done anything wrong. Had I?

My entire body was rigid with upset and anxiety, and I had no idea how to stop it. I didn't know if I wanted to cry or yell or just shut down completely. So I did a little mix of all of that.

I was deep into my second glass of wine and my misery playlist when Per came home. He fixed me with a stare that was part embarrassed, part judgmental, and part sympathetic. Sighing, he said, "'Don't Let the Sun Go Down on Me'? The George Michael with Elton John version? You haven't played that in years. Whatever this is, it's *dire*." He came over, leaned down, and kissed my temple. "What's going on, my little angst machine? Did your mom contact you? Or don't I want to know?"

I was sure he did want to know, but I wasn't sure I was ready or even able to tell him. But he would just keep gently digging until I told him. It wasn't like I didn't like talking things out, but I felt so raw right now that I knew I was going to fall apart. Maybe that's what I needed, to get it all out and work through it before I confronted Steph again.

After a deep breath and a deeper swallow of my wine, I managed to get out, "I think Steph might be using me." It didn't even sound like my voice. It was flat, emotionless, and so hurt I felt like crying just listening to myself.

Per dropped heavily onto the couch beside me. "Um, what?" He made a swirling motion with his forefinger. "Please back up and explain exactly what's going on."

So I did. I told him every horrible moment of those minutes in the parking lot, what Laura had said, what Steph hadn't said and then what she *had* said. I didn't tell him how I'd felt like I was going to pass out when I finally realized what Laura was talking about. I didn't tell him how Steph had basically acted like *I* was the one who'd done something wrong.

I didn't mention the deepfakes, but I did tell him that she'd also had something horrible happen and hadn't shared it with me. And I didn't tell him how I felt like I'd been sucker-punched and that it'd taken every ounce of self-control I had to not burst into tears right there at work.

Per sat quietly, just listening, rubbing my back until I'd said everything I could say. "Okay. Shit. Shit." He wrapped an arm around me and squeezed. "Could we turn off the wallowing music please, so I can think?"

I did as he asked, though I really wished I had the music to help maintain this terrible mood where I could direct my anger toward Steph. I wasn't sure what I felt toward her, I just knew that I felt it so deeply that it felt like an open wound.

Per shuffled around so he faced me. "Look. I just want to make sure you're reading the situation correctly." He brought his hands up in a placating gesture. "You know I'm on your side, one hundred percent, and you know I will cut any bitch who hurts you. But…are you sure what you thought happened really happened? I believe you, but also, the Steph I've seen with you? It just…doesn't seem like something she'd do. She fucking *worships* you, Harpies. And I'm not just playing devil's advocate because I like her. Like I said—cut a bitch who hurts you. I'm on your side. Ride or die, remember?"

I sniffled. "Thanks, hon."

"Did you talk to her about it? Ask her what the hell was going on?"

I inhaled a deep, shuddering breath. "I don't know, I left before we could. And yes, I know bailing without talking about the issues wasn't the mature or rational thing to do, but we were at work and I really didn't want to have a fight, or cry there."

"Understandable." Per pulled me against his side, wrapping a comforting arm around me. "What can I do, my love?"

"I don't think there's anything you can do." Groaning, I muttered, "I just want to hibernate for a week." I snatched a couch cushion and buried my face in it. Going to work tomorrow was going to be utterly hellish. Oh…now I understood that saying "Don't shit where you eat." Well, a huge dump had just been dropped on my workplace plate.

"Let me get you another drink and I'm going to order you some comfort food for dinner and then we can do whatever you want. Put whatever you feel like watching on TV, or we can talk shit about Steph— though I'm not sure how well I can participate in that one except for agreeing with you that she's done something horrible—or I can leave you alone except for delivering more drinks and food."

"Thanks." I blinked away the tears pricking my eyes. "I love you."

"And I love you too." He kissed the top of my head, and then with a gentle back rub, released me.

Trust Per to swan in and remind me that I *was* enough, that I had a chosen family to wrap around myself in place of a blood family. And if I was enough for my chosen family, then surely I could be enough for Steph? I just had to let myself believe that.

He delivered a fresh glass of wine and a plate of cheese and olives, told me my dinner would be here in about forty-five minutes, then went to shower. I turned my music back on, flopped onto the couch, and wallowed my ass off. I needed the wallowing, needed to try and feel all these feelings, otherwise I wouldn't be able to figure out how to approach the situation. As much as I wanted to pretend it wasn't happening, it was and unless I wanted to walk away from what Steph and I had started building, I needed to decide how I felt about it.

I didn't want to walk away from it. I didn't want her to walk away from it.

When someone buzzed at the gate, Per called out that he'd go out and grab my food. I looked up from my slumpy sad slouch on the couch, expecting him to be holding dinner. The only thing he had with him was an expression that made my stomach drop. Great, they'd canceled my dinner order. Of all the goddamned days.

What he said made my stomach drop even more than if he'd told me that. "Harpies? Steph is here…"

I sat up so quickly I almost choked on my, "What?"

"Do you want me to tell her to leave?" He made a cutting motion.

The fact she'd made the effort to reach out, and shown up after we'd had our first fight made me reluctant to tell her to go away, even though I knew I was going to get upset. I shook my head. "No, but thanks. Can you send her in here, please?"

"Okay. If you need me, for anything, just call for me and I'll help out. *Anything.*"

I nodded, and he melted away. I heard the quiet snick of his bedroom door closing. Steph replaced him, holding up two bags and wearing her glasses and an uncertain smile.

I stood up. Without a chance to equilibrate to the fact she had shown up here, my question came out more angrily than I wanted it to. "Why are you here?"

Steph didn't quite hide her flinch. "I—I didn't know if you need space or to talk about it, or what you need. I would like to talk about it, and this isn't a conversation to have over text. So here I am. But if you don't want me here, then I'll go."

I didn't know what to say.

She offered me the bags, but it felt like she was offering me much more than that. "This just arrived while I was waiting at the gate. Sorry, I was there, so I took the delivery." She smiled, but it came nowhere near her eyes. "I get the feeling Per isn't into"—she held up the bag and stared at the logo—"soul food, so I'm assuming it's yours."

"Thanks," I murmured.

"And I…I brought you a couple apple fritters. They're in the small bag. The one that's not your dinner. Obviously."

Well that wasn't helping me stay upset with her. "Thank you."

She took a step backward. "I should go so you can eat dinner. I shouldn't have just turned up like this without telling you."

"Why did you?"

"Because I thought you'd say no if I asked to come over and explain, and I really *really* wanted to explain." She frowned, as if suddenly realizing something bad. "Sorry, I kind of hijacked you here and I didn't mean to."

I sighed. She kind of had done that, but it didn't feel like a red flag. "Do you want a drink?"

"No thanks."

"Have you eaten?"

"Not yet."

"No In-N-Out drive-thru?"

She shook her head. No smile. I hadn't really been trying to brush past everything that'd happened tonight, but a little levity sometimes helped. I felt strangely empty when she didn't react with a joke or laugh.

Regardless, I knew *I'd* feel better if I ate something, so I opened the bigger bag. "I need to eat or I'm going to be meaner than I want to be." I opened the box and held out the cornbread muffin. "And you should eat something too. Why don't you sit."

"Thanks." Steph broke the muffin in half and put one portion back. She sat about a foot from me on the couch, and the distance felt like a chasm.

I ate some mac 'n' cheese and a few bites of smothered chicken while Steph alternated between picking at the muffin, looking around the living room, looking at her hands, and sneaking glances at me. I finished about half the food then boxed it back up and put it in the fridge. When I returned, she was in the exact spot, in the exact position as I'd left her.

I sat down facing her, folding a leg up underneath myself on the couch. "Okay. You want to talk. I do too. But what I really want is an explanation. So…I'm listening."

It was as if she'd just been waiting for permission to explain, and words spilled from her, the same words she'd already said in the parking lot. "It's not what you think."

"What is it then?"

Steph exhaled loudly. "It's…not complicated, but it's silly." Thankfully she didn't make me ask her why it was silly. "I'm sure you know what Laura and I deal with, with people assuming we're a couple because we play one on TV."

I nodded.

Her explanation rushed out. "So we have this thing Laura calls the baton. It's basically *trying* to have at least one of us in a relationship of some sort, like we pass the 'relationship baton' to each other to deflect attention away from this annoying speculation as much as we can. You understand that, right?"

I nodded again.

"And obviously, I'd been carrying it for a while until Jordan's…*thing*, so it hasn't really been an issue. Then Laura had all her short-term flings. But when she broke up with her latest man of the minute, she said she wanted me to take the 'baton' for a while so she could have a break from stupid guys. Which is totally fair."

"I see." And I did. But it didn't make me feel any better. It still made me feel used.

Clearly Steph understood my expression. "I *was* going to just go out with Laura's cousin the way I have in the past when I haven't been with someone, but Laura…" Her eyebrows knitted together, and the familiar expression made my heart twist. "She nudged me to make a move I've been too fucking scared to make. A move to tell you how I really felt. About you."

"Right. Okay." I didn't really *need* her to tell me, but I wanted her to tell me. I wanted to know that I wasn't an idiot who couldn't read people. "And how is that?"

Steph didn't hesitate. "That I've been in love with you for years. Harper, I tried to change our relationship into something more than a work friendship because that's what *I* wanted, for myself. It wasn't about being public with someone at all. I'm sorry about the baton thing. But I'm not sorry that it gave me the kick in the butt to finally tell you how I felt."

The declaration of her having been in love with me for years was buried in her explanation, but I held on to it tightly to be brought out later. "Okay. I think I get it. But it hurt, thinking you used me."

"I'm sure it did, and that wasn't my intention." Steph crossed her arms over her chest, hands tucked into her armpits. She hunched forward, and my only thought was that I'd never, in almost six years of working with her, seen this hunched over, defensive posture. "I *swear*, this isn't a publicity thing. I did this because I wanted everything we've shared and more than what we've shared. If I only wanted someone to parade for the public, Laura's cousin does just fine. And if I wanted sex, I'd hire one of those lovely discreet escorts everyone talks about. This was *never* about the public stuff for me. It was about what I wanted. The stupid fucking baton thing is only relevant because it pushed me toward you."

I exhaled loudly, trying to expel some of my tension. A few more deep breaths helped some. But I didn't know what to say.

Her mouth twisted and I thought she might cry. Steph blinked hard a few times. "Can you at least tell me how you're feeling?"

"A lot of things, all twisted up together. I…don't know how to separate it. I think mostly I'm super paranoid now that it's not real. That none of it has been real."

"It's real to me. It's one of the best, realest things I've known." She untucked one of her hands to gesture. "If you think you're just a PR stunt, why aren't I dragging you around town so everyone can see me with someone?"

"You're right," I agreed, relieved she'd confirmed something I'd already thought. How easily explained it was, and how much it made sense once I listened with my head instead of my heart. Yet again, it was as if she had reached in and found exactly what I needed. "Why *don't* you drag me around town with you?"

"I'm selfish," she said instantly. "I want you for just me. I'm sick of intrusions. I'm sick of sharing special parts of my life with people who don't deserve to be part of those special parts. For fuck's sake, I couldn't even kiss you after the tennis practice without it being all over the Internet. The last time we PDA'ed, you had to come out to your homophobic family."

"I get that. And I respect it. But…I'm not a special rock you've picked up and left in your pocket. I know people are going to take pictures of you and me. I've accepted that. But I need to know that you care about me."

"I *do* care about you. I'm *so* proud to be with you, to have people see me with you. But honestly? Now I'm worried you might think I only want to take you out in public as the 'baton.'" Steph pushed her fingers under her glasses to press against her eyes. "Fuck," she muttered. "This is all messed up."

Now that she'd explained it, everything made more sense, and I could see where she was coming from. It was up to me whether I believed her or not. And I did. What was the point of holding on to hurt for hurt's sake? "No. I'm not worried about it. Can we just forget the baton was ever a thing?"

"Please," she said tightly.

We sat quietly for a minute, letting ourselves settle until it was time to move into discussing other painful things. "Why didn't you tell me about the deepfake pictures of you? You told Laura. She knew, and I didn't. And that *really* hurts."

"I didn't want you to have to deal with it," Steph said without hesitation. "I didn't want to dump this on you so soon after we'd started being together. It's a *huge* thing. Too much for you to deal with." After a quick deep breath, she continued, "Laura only knows because her team had to attend a meeting about the tennis match because they needed to confirm they were fine to go ahead with these pictures floating around."

She was trying to protect me. Of course she was. "I understand that, but god, it's hurtful to not be told about something so horrible, Steph. It makes me feel like you don't trust me."

She spluttered, "I *do* trust you, with all parts of my life. But…I—" Her face crumpled and she took a few moments to regain her composure. I wanted to help her, to hug her, to hold her, but I also felt she needed to work through her thoughts without me interfering. After a deep, uneven breath, she managed a tearful, "I wanted you to think things with me might be sort of normal."

I did hug her then, wrapping her tightly in my arms, and Steph held on to me like she was afraid this might be the last time. "Oh, sweetheart, I like that things with you aren't normal. I *want* the extraordinary, because that's what you are. The terrible parts of your life are not too much for me." I gently disengaged from our hug, and took her face in my hands. "Do you know one of the greatest things you can give a partner, Steph?"

There were obviously so many answers to that question, and she clearly knew I was leading her to something, so she just shook her head.

"Yourself. All of you. The ability to know you, to share your life, *all* of your life. As it is. No embellishments, no frills, all the imperfect bits, just the ordinary you. That's what I want."

Her voice cracked as she asked me, "Really?"

"Yes. Really."

"Thank you." Steph swallowed hard. "Okay. I…I need to think about what you said. I think I've explained myself as much as I can. And if I talk any more about this I'm going to get really upset." She bit down on her lower lip. "I'm just…I'm trying, Harper."

"I know you are, darlin'."

I could have kept talking to her, trying to unravel this issue, making sure we were on the same page. But if it wasn't going to be productive because she was upset then there was no point. We had time, and that fact was enough reassurance for me.

Steph shuffled backward on the couch then stood. "I guess…I guess I'm going to go home and cry for a bit." It sounded joking, but there was an undercurrent of self-recrimination that tore my heart. Steph forced a smile, but it wavered around her tremulous inhalation. "See you in the morning?"

"Of course you will, and not just for work." I stood too. "Steph?"

She looked up from where she was focusing on checking her pockets. "Yeah?"

I tried to ask the question, but I couldn't get it out. She stepped closer, tilting her head curiously. I finally managed to ask, "Are you and I okay?"

Her expression softened, the fine lines at the edges of her eyes creasing. It was as if she'd released a pressure valve. "Yes. Or, we're going to be. Can we talk some more when I've calmed down, maybe tomorrow?"

"Good. Because I really want us to be." Her wanting to work through this felt like lightness, and there was no way I was going to force her to do it when she wasn't in the right headspace. A little time for both of us to settle would be helpful. "And yes, we can. Thanks for coming over."

"Thanks for letting me." After a beat, she smiled, holding out her hand for a fist bump.

The reminder of our awkward fist bump, hug, cheek kiss, real kiss made me laugh. I reached up, grabbed the back of her neck and pulled her down for a kiss. The kiss was brief, gentle, but filled with love.

Love.

I've been in love with you for years.

I pulled her in for another hug, burying my face in the perfect spot where her neck met her shoulder. Steph wrapped me tightly, held me close, and I felt all of that love. She relaxed her grip but not completely.

I thumbed the edge of her mouth. "Text me when you get home. I'll see you at work tomorrow."

CHAPTER TWENTY-ONE

Steph

Despite the baton having no bearing on our relationship aside from pushing me toward Harper, obviously I knew now that I should have mentioned it. Really, the baton was a good thing—it was me not telling her that'd hurt her. But the fuck-up to end all fuck-ups was that I hadn't realized that not telling her about the deepfakes would hurt her as much as it had. I'd made a huge mistake.

I loathed making mistakes, and my first instinct was always to brush over them, hide, pretend I'd done nothing wrong. I'd always been averse to getting in trouble, even if I deserved it. Not the healthiest, most mature, or productive way to live, and I'd spent my life fighting my natural instincts. I'd gotten reasonably good at dealing with mistakes in my professional life, but not so much in my personal.

I was a work in progress, but at least there was some progress, right? Sometimes being a perfectionist was great. Other times? Not so much. And I was only now realizing that trying to be a perfectionist in my relationships was probably what had ruined them. It wasn't authentic. I'd been so busy trying to make the perfect relationship and be the perfect girlfriend that I'd completely screwed them up, because what my partners actually wanted was just...me.

So—and this was where it got really fucking hard—I needed to let Harper see all the shitty, messy parts of my life and not just the things stemming from work like the deepfakes. I needed to show her my personal struggles. I needed to let her help me. I needed to let her all the way in, and trust that she wasn't going to run screaming when she realized that a lot of what people saw on the outside was a carefully constructed façade and on the inside I was just…trying to do my best.

Now that I understood some of our lines and boundaries, I wasn't going to mess up again. The best way to gain full forgiveness was to never *ever* do it again, and to be the kind of girlfriend she wanted, not the perfect one I thought she should have but that wasn't actually *me*.

As soon as I woke up, I put cooling under-eye patches on to shrink the puffiness from crying last night. I hadn't exactly spent *all* night weeping, but I'd had enough experience with crying to know it was going to be a tear hangover on my face. At least I knew Harper would make me look as though nothing was wrong.

She was already at work when I arrived and I reversed in beside her car. While drinking my coffee, brushing my teeth, and changing into Amy's clothes, I'd been doing okay with suppressing my anxiety, but a surge of nerves made me pause before I opened the door to Hair and Makeup. There was something about people being mad at me that pressed every perfectionist button I had. I hated conflict. I had enough fake conflict in my work and wanted to keep my personal life as conflict-free as I could.

But the moment I saw Harper, my anxiety settled. How did someone look so damned good first thing in the morning? She'd paired dark-gray pants with a deep-green linen top, leaving enough buttons undone that it was a pleasure to look at her, but not so many that it wasn't workplace-appropriate.

As I sat down, she sanitized her hands. "Morning." Harper's thumbs brushed lightly under my eyes. "You did a pretty good job with this," she murmured.

I wasn't surprised Harper could still tell I'd spent a few hours with tears last night. "Thanks. I learned from the best."

That made her smile. Harper dropped her hands from where they'd been caressing my face. "Need anything?"

As soon as I'd confirmed I was good, she got to work while I read my script. I wanted to make sure none of the lines I'd carefully memorized had fallen out of my brain with all the other stuff that'd been shoved into my mental space in the last few days.

Liz Spencer, who played our resident medical examiner, Dr. Diana Gilbert, came hobbling in on crutches, muttering to herself about "stupid fucking steps."

I winced at her entrance. "How's your foot?" I asked Liz as she sat awkwardly in Nina's chair.

"Painful, especially without drugs because I have to work. And this stupid boot isn't helping. But at least they rewrote these episodes with Diana having a broken foot too, instead of just writing me out until it heals. Mama's got bills." She leveled a stare at me. "Don't send your kids to private schools, Steph. It's disgustingly expensive."

Smiling, I assured her, "When I have kids, I'll try to remember that."

Harper went completely still, her brush hovering in front of my face. Her eyebrows had shot up to a comically concerned level. She lowered the brush so she could look me in the eyes. "You want kids?"

I opened my mouth to respond, but was cut off by Nina chortling, "Oh-ho-ho-ho. Let me grab some popcorn."

Beside her, Chrissy snorted.

"What?" Liz asked, spinning around to face me. "What have I missed?" Her gossip radar was at full extension. She was a recurring actor, not in every episode, so when she came in she was like a sponge for news.

Nina, still laughing, told her, "Everything." She gently turned Liz back around. "Come on, fill me in on what you've been up to aside from breaking bones."

It took no time for Liz and Nina to get involved in their conversation, with Chrissy on the periphery. Harper resumed working. She lowered her voice, though anyone who was trying hard to listen, instead of being absorbed in a story about having their foot run over with a golf cart, would probably hear. "You okay?"

"I am. Are you okay?"

"Yes." She paused, though her hand kept moving over my face. "And us?"

I lightly touched her hip, letting my fingers linger there. "Better than."

"Great."

I winked at her and the base of her neck flushed. "We'll talk later?"

"Absolutely." Harper smiled and nodded, and the last shred of anxiety about our argument left me.

It was then I realized Liz had been staring, and listening. "Oh my god," she breathed. "You're…it's…*finally*." Liz shook her head. "It's about time you two got a goddamned clue."

Nina raised her hands to the ceiling and joined in with an "Amen" while Chrissy just nodded furiously.

Harper and I caught each other's eyes. Hers softened. She shrugged, and an adorable "Can't argue with 'em" expression came over her face. "About time indeed..."

They'd given Liz as little movement as possible for the episode, but I still cringed internally every time she had to take the few steps between the autopsy table and her mark in front of me. We'd already exposited "Diana's" foot injury and were discussing the vic's unfortunate demise.

Liz handed over a manila folder. "Lividity puts time of death at around ten p.m. last night. Evidence of rough sexual activity but I can't say for sure if it was rape, though I *did* recover pubic hairs and seminal fluid, as well as skin from under her nails. Samples are with the lab now."

I frowned, opening the folder and taking a look at the pages. "Victim left the bar at nine thirty." After a glance at Jared, I looked back to Liz. "So, within thirty minutes of leaving her friends, she's dead?"

Jared rubbed his jaw. "I don't get it. She was found three blocks from the bar...a seven minute walk, max. Why stop there?"

"Try eight or nine minutes' walking in those shoes." I injected the tiniest bit of levity into the line, just enough to break the tension but not so much that it'd be irreverent. Amy occasionally wearing heels undercover had provided a little comedic element. "And you're right. Why did she stop there instead of continuing on? Aside from the homicide, it's the same MO as the other rapes. Maybe he's escalating?" I turned to Liz. "What's the cause of death?"

"Hemo...hemophn...hemnonomothr—Fuck." She shook her head, blowing out a frustrated breath. "Sorry. I cannot get it."

Jeannie, the master of all things pronunciation, helped Liz out. "Hemopneumothorax."

Liz closed her eyes, looking to the ceiling as she mouthed it. She shook her head again. "Nope. This word is going to kill me."

Monty called cut, probably to give Liz some time to get her words together.

She glanced at me, a mischievous glint in her eyes. "Wanna swap roles? Can *you* say it?"

Grinning, I shrugged. "Sure. Hemopneumothorax. Hand over those scrubs, I'm the ME now."

Jared chimed in with a singsong, in-your-face, "Hemopneumothorax."

Liz threw up her hands. "Fuck both of you."

The crew laughed, as did the young woman playing the dead body on the autopsy table. I heard Harper snort out a laugh, and I turned to her, flashing a quick wink. Her smile was luminous, sending radiant warmth surging through me. If this was my life now, Harper at work and Harper at home, then I couldn't wait for it.

I wasn't due to film any scenes with Laura until the afternoon, but she'd come in to eat beforehand, and plonked down across from me. I'd barely said hi before she barreled on with, "I'm sorry. You're so attractive. Are you still mad at me?"

I quickly swallowed my mouthful of parfait. "I was never mad at you."

"Oh thank god. Did you guys get everything figured out?"

"Mhmm. We did." Close enough, and I wasn't going to dive into it now.

"Good. Because fucking that up was not on my karmic list for this lifetime." She dug into her couscous, apparently satisfied her conscience was totally clear.

I was just finishing my meal by the time Harper finally got hers and came over to sit beside me. I hadn't said anything before Laura pounced for another grovel. "Heyyy, Harper. So, sorry about last night. I totally put my foot in it and overstepped. It will not happen again."

Smiling, Harper tore open a dinner roll. "No problem." She glanced at me. "It's all sorted out. Right?"

"Right." It was so refreshing to have argued and made up so soon, like anything else would be small potatoes. I watched as Harper used the bread roll to scoop up a small turkey meatball dripping in marinara sauce. I even liked watching her eat. God, I was so smitten.

I wanted to spend time with her, but I also needed some rest before we resumed shooting. And given Nina had just arrived to eat with us, I wasn't going to find any relaxation here. I squeezed Harper's leg under the table. "I'm just going to go lie down. Come to my trailer when you're done eating?"

She nodded.

Laura threw a grape at me. "Get a room, you two."

I smiled beatifically. "What do you think we're doing?"

"What'd I miss?" Nina asked around a mouthful of salad.

"Nothing!" Harper said emphatically.

Yep, it was time to go. I dumped my dirty plate and utensils, and left the loud mess behind me for some rest. I'd barely left the building when a text from Jenna Bryce from *Make the Cut* came through. No rest for the wicked. *You free to chat abt tennis?*

I sent a thumbs-up emoji.

On my bike. There in minute.

Despite the imminent arrival of a disruption to my relaxation, I smiled. *Texting and cycling? Tsk.*

Jenna played a pediatric surgeon on *Make the Cut*, and her character was also Jared's character's wife. On the whole, relationships between the cast and crew of both shows were good, and it wasn't unusual for us to ride bikes or scooters to go visit when we had time to spare. Some exercise in the open air, change of scenery, getting new gossip—a trifecta of delight. So I wasn't surprised by her coming by.

Jenna came screaming up on a pink bike, waving furiously as she approached, her entire face lit with a smile. "Stephaniieeee." She jumped off her bike, maneuvered it close to my trailer, and kicked out the stand.

She was a legitimate beacon of delight, and my smile came automatically. "Jenna, hey."

She gripped my shoulders and air-kissed my cheeks, mindful of my makeup. "Looking gorgeous as ever."

"Charmer." I let her into my trailer and she immediately sat on the couch. "You already wrapped for the day?" I asked.

"Yup, and I'm dying to go home so I'll be quick. Yusef and I just wanted to make sure we're on the same wavelength as you and Laura with this thing on Saturday."

I unzipped my boots and toed them off. "What wavelength is that?"

"Just the spirit of the game. How to deal with the weird fans. That sort of thing. I know we've all been given a briefing, but…" She shrugged, a mischievous "we know better" smile quirking her mouth.

"Oh! Yeah, of course. I'd already assumed security would be all over it, but if we can keep an eye on each other during the meet and greet that'd be good." As far as I knew, after the game we'd be doing a seated autograph session, then standing photo ops—both of which were only open to ticketed guests. No more than two hours for each, we'd been promised. Hahaha, yeah right.

She nodded slowly. "I'm not sure what security they've hired, if it's the studio's or new contractors. I'm sure they'll be fine, but after that drama last year, I just want to be safe."

The drama where she had a stalker who somehow got on the studio lot. "Absolutely," I said emphatically. "I've got your back. And I know Laura will too. I'll mention it to her if you don't see her before then." I pulled off my jacket and hung it, then unbuttoned the top button of my shirt so it wasn't so choking.

"Fabulous."

A knock on my door was followed by the sound of the PIN being input. Harper. She must have inhaled her food. I smiled to myself. Jenna turned expectantly and Harper paused in the doorway, looking mildly surprised that I had a visitor. "Hey. Hi, Jenna. Pleasure to see you as always. Am I interrupting?"

"Of course not," I assured her.

Jenna jumped up and gave Harper the same air-kiss treatment she'd given me. "Harper, you doll, how are you? Still can't tempt you to jump ship to work on my show?"

I cut in. "Don't you dare. This one is mine." In every sense of the word.

Jenna threw up her hands. "Worth a shot. Bye, gorgeous. See you Saturday. And you too, Steph."

I rolled my eyes. "Very funny."

Jenna blew me a kiss, bounced down the stairs and jogged to her bike. I waved her off as she jumped on and pedaled away, chestnut hair streaming behind her. She was headed toward Crafty, probably to grab a snack from our stash before going home.

I checked my watch. Twenty minutes or so before I was due back. I closed the door and beckoned Harper toward the couch. We sat close, without touching, and for now it was enough.

"Sneaky visitors, huh?" Harper teased, but there was an edge to it.

"Hmm? Oh." I laughed as I got her meaning. "She wishes. Jenna's been trying to get me to sleep with her for years."

"Trying to? You've never taken her up on the offer?"

I grimaced. "God no. I'm not interested in being someone she ticks off her list."

"No?"

"Harper," I said, injecting as much calm patience as I could into her name. "If I wanted to sleep with Jenna Bryce and be another woman on her long list of men and women who've been in her bed, then I'd have slept with her. But I haven't, because I don't want to. Right now, I want to sleep with you. *Only* you." I watched her for a few seconds, trying to decipher her expression. When I thought I had it, I quietly asked, "Are you jealous?"

She spluttered in her haste to rebut, "I…what? No."

It was obvious she was something akin to jealous, but I didn't want to accuse her of not being truthful to herself. So I went for appeasement instead of accusation. "She's a work friend, and that's it."

"Right. I know. But...she's attractive. Nowhere near your level," she rushed to clarify.

"Sure, she's attractive," I agreed.

Harper's face fell.

"But you know what? After Jordan's mess, my therapist said something that stuck with me. You can't control what you want, but you *can* control your actions. I might find someone pleasing to look at, but that doesn't automatically mean I want to sleep with them. I want to sleep with *you*. And likewise, I don't own you, and I'm not telling you that you can't find someone attractive. But it's you not acting on that attraction that's important to me."

"I...no, I know. Of course. I'm not interested in anyone else. It's just, I mean, she's Jenna Bryce and I'm not. You're actor-hot and I am not."

I held in a sigh. After pausing for a few seconds, I made sure to keep my voice calm because I didn't want her to misinterpret what I was saying as an attack or defense. "Firstly, you need to stop being mean to my girlfriend. I'm with *you* because I think *you're* gorgeous," I said honestly. "And aside from what you look like, everything else about you is insanely attractive to me. All of it, whole package. And secondly? It's a bit insulting to imply that because I look a certain way and have a certain job that I'm not intelligent enough to choose you."

"That's *not* what I meant at all. I'm sorry." She'd pretty much melted with mortification, which melted my frustration.

I took another relaxing breath. "I know you are. I'm sorry I snapped. Clearly that's a sore point for me that I didn't even realize I had."

"I get it. It's just..." She finally looked up and her anxious expression made my breath catch. "Steph, I'm...I'm insecure. About you and I and this thing that's happening between us. I hate it, but I am. Most of the time I can talk myself out of it, but since last night it's been spiraling. I feel like an idiot for making this all about me when you've had something awful happen to you with those pictures. But...doubt sucks."

"I know it does. I'm sorry I inspired doubt in you. I'm sorry you doubted how I feel about you." I licked my lower lip. "I know we went from zero to fifty in what feels like milliseconds. Thank you for telling me how you're feeling." I took her hands and brought them to my mouth to kiss her knuckles. "Why are you insecure?"

She shrugged. "So many reasons, so little desire to take the focus away from you and your issues right now."

"Baby, you don't have to put aside your feelings just because I'm having feelings. There's plenty of room for both of us to have a whole bunch of feelings. Sharing feelings makes it so much easier." I sat forward. "Is this insecurity a new thing? Just with me, or is it something about you and me?"

"It's not new," she admitted quietly. "But it's gotten worse since we started getting closer." The admission seemed mortifying. "And after last night, and all that…it just compounded it."

"Thank you for telling me. I really hate that you and me makes you feel insecure."

"It's not your fault. It's all me."

"Well if there's anything I can do to make you feel less insecure, please tell me."

"I will. I think I just need us to be together and for me to get used to us."

"Good. I just want to be sure you're okay. I know we didn't get to talk through everything last night, and we're not going to talk through it all now, but…"

Harper smiled, shaking her head. "We talked through it enough for me. For now."

"Phew. Because I really hate fighting," I said emphatically. "And now I have a better idea of what you need so we can avoid *some* arguments."

She wrinkled her nose. "I mean, I don't love fighting either, but I really, really love the making up."

"Are you saying we're overdue some make-up sex?"

"Yes," she said instantly. "But it's not *just* the sex. It's that nice, light feeling when things are resolved." Harper leaned back, slinging an arm over the back of the couch until her fingertips brushed my shoulder. "So. Speaking of resolutions. About what you said this morning…Kids?"

"Wow, just jump right into the deep end. Are you offering?"

She laughed. "Not right now, no. But, do you want kids? I know we kind of mentioned kids in passing, but…"

I didn't hesitate. "Yes, I do want kids."

Harper's expression softened, a dreaminess passing over her face. "I love watching you with kids."

The dreaminess made something inside me twist with longing. "Just call me the kid whisperer." I licked my suddenly dry lips. "What about you?"

"Yes, I want kids. Or kid. Whatever."

The admission made my pulse pick up, and even though I knew it was ridiculous to be jumping so far ahead, I did it anyway. "Can we put this in the 'reasons to try and make this work' column? Not that I'm saying right away or soon, though I'd like a kid before I'm forty, preferably earlier, just so I'm not out there with my walker watching college games and shit like that. I think I'd want to be married first. Oh fuck, I'm not saying marriage for you and me. I'm not *not* saying it, but I'm just saying..." I blew out a loud breath. "Actually, I've forgotten what I'm saying."

She shook her head, though she was smiling. "Have I ever told you how much I love your rambling?"

"I'm glad." Jordan had hated it. *Spit it out, Steph* was a familiar refrain. "And what you were talking about was marriage and children."

My ringing phone ruined any hope of continuing this conversation that I really wanted to continue. I snatched it up. "Sorry, that's Ingrid. Can you just give me a moment?"

"Sure. You want me to go? I'm almost due back."

"No, stay, please. I won't be long. Ingrid likes efficiency." I moved to the end of the couch and answered the call.

"Steph, good, I'm glad I caught you."

"What's up?"

"I hate to bring bad news in the middle of your workday. I'm so sorry but it seems those pictures have leaked onto social media. We've issued complaints to each platform about these new images and they're being pulled as we speak."

But who knew how many *North Precinct* fans had seen them. I slumped forward. "Fuck. So what does this mean?"

"This means we're now getting super legal on their asses. The use of AI makes it tricky, but there are laws and we're looking into everything we can do. I'll send you the email with an outline."

Of all the emails I wasn't looking forward to receiving, this was high on the list. "What about the network?"

Harper shuffled closer, wrapping her arm around my shoulders. I reached out and squeezed her hand.

Ingrid confirmed, "Yes, they're aware and have their PR and Legal ready if need be."

"Okay. And the tennis match? It's in like...two days. They already threatened to pull me from it once because of this."

"Don't worry about it," she soothed. "It's all fine. We'll get things taken down and we'll be watching very closely if anyone tries to put them up again. If anyone from the match audience sees one and tries to make a fuss, the statement denouncing the pictures as obvious fakes will be right there. You just need to keep being your wholesome, charming self."

"I'll try," I said dully. "Why aren't we just ignoring it and not issuing a statement, like we normally would?"

"Because AI is insidious," Ingrid said emphatically. "And when used in this manner, dangerous. It's not like someone hacked your cloud account and stole your personal pictures, Steph. They've used your image illegally. And if I thought it'd do any good, I'd suggest suing."

"Maybe I should just to teach them a lesson. I don't need the money."

"If that's an avenue you want to pursue, I can talk to our lawyers. Though finding the person who created them might be hard."

"Maybe. I don't know." I groaned. "I can't think about that right now."

"Okay. Well if you think about it, let me know. So. Your official position, if asked, is they're AI-generated images you obviously didn't consent to and that's all you can say on the matter."

"Can I add a little disgusted, appalled, horrified in there?"

She laughed lightly. "If you want. But keep it brief. And let us know if anyone contacts you directly for a statement. We have good relationships with the media, and we've always had an open-book policy, but that goes both ways. They should respect that relationship enough to come through me or Jeremiah for information or if they want a bite from you."

"Okay. Thanks, Ingrid."

"Don't you worry about this, sweetheart. We'll take care of it. You just focus on work and that cute girlfriend of yours. And speaking of that, are we going to be seeing the pair of you out and about anytime soon?"

"Sure. Why not."

"Good. It's not going to hurt to remind everyone just where your affections lie…"

I hung up and let myself fall backward onto the couch. I had no idea how I could go from on top of the world to feeling like I'd been thrown into a fucking pit of vipers. "Fuck. Fuck fuck fuck." I sat up again and found Harper's sweetly concerned gaze on me. "I guess you heard that."

"Your side of it."

"So those deepfakes? They're now on regular social media. I'm not sure where exactly. Ingrid's emailing me. I mean, it doesn't matter where they are, it's just—" I threw my hands up. "It's fucked. They're getting them pulled. But I don't know what to do." Panic started to tighten my chest, and I pressed my fingertips to my sternum.

Harper took my face in gentle hands, her thumbs lightly stroking my cheeks. "For now, I think the only thing you can do is let the people whose job it is to handle it, handle it. We'll deal with everything else. Together."

I buried my face against her shoulder, wrapping an arm around her waist. She was right. There was nothing I could do, and having Harper to share the burden made it feel less. "Thank you for sharing this with me. I promise things will get back to normal soon." I coughed out a dry laugh.

"Thank you for sharing it with *me*."

I inhaled deeply, breathing in the calming scent of her. "I'm a fast learner. And I'm only going to learn more every day." I had to break old habits and build new ones, but I couldn't think of anyone more worthy of the best version of myself than Harper.

The hand that had been making soothing strokes up and down my back paused. "Something you said last night has been on my mind all day. It was on my mind all night." Her voice was surprisingly tremulous, and I sat up.

"What's that?"

"You said you've been in love with me for a while. Is that true?"

"Yes."

"Good." She swiped at her eyes, trying to stem the tears that had suddenly pooled and overflowed. "I wish I'd said something last night, but everything just piled up. But, I love you too. I'm in love with you, too. And now *I* don't know what to do. I wish I hadn't told you here at work. I wish I hadn't told you right now with all this, but…I just had to."

"I'm glad you did." I cupped her face, softly helping her wipe away the tears. "And I know what you should do. You should kiss me."

"I have to go," she said, but the argument was made weaker by the way her hands had moved to my neck.

"I know. We have a minute. Fuck professionalism," I muttered, yanking her to me. I was one hundred percent sure that I wouldn't be the first person on this production to kiss someone in the privacy of their trailer.

And the moment my lips touched hers, I knew this wouldn't be the last time I kissed Harper in the privacy of my trailer…

CHAPTER TWENTY-TWO

Harper

Between our argument on Wednesday, and the resurfacing of the fake pictures on Thursday, by the time we finished work on Friday I was desperate to spend time with Steph. I wanted to reconnect. She'd been distant all day at work, but had promised me it was nothing more than a troubling storyline and all this "bullshit about those fucking pictures." She'd come into Hair and Makeup as I was finishing up for the day.

Leaning against the wall, arms crossed, looking simultaneously sexy and a little sleepy, she flashed me a cocky grin. "Hello, stranger. Care to spend the night together?"

I didn't even think before answering. "Sure. I'm almost done here. I'll just go home and shower, and grab some things to stay the night at your place?" We had the tennis match tomorrow, and I made a mental note to pack what I needed for that too.

"Sounds perfect. You're perfect." She said it as a dreamy kind of sigh, which made me think of all the dreamy, contented sighs she emitted in bed.

"I know," I said airily. Her words had sent a pleasurable tingle through me. "I'll text when I'm leaving my place."

"Good. Drive home safely." She closed the space between us, and I thought she might kiss me the way she had in her trailer yesterday, but Nina barged in.

"Move it, lovebirds. I have a date tonight and need to get my ass out of here."

Steph smiled at me over Nina's head, mouthing, "See you soon."

I nodded and got back to cleaning up. The sooner I finished, the sooner I could get *my* ass out of there for my own date.

When I got home I jumped in the shower. I was torn between a super-fast shower so I could get to Steph's, and a regular shower so I could take a little time to separate myself from work. I went for something in between. After packing an overnight bag, I texted Per that I wouldn't be home tonight and reminded him to get to the venue early for the match tomorrow. Then I left for my girlfriend's. I didn't think I'd ever tire of thinking of Steph in that context and I smiled the whole drive, even while battling typically hellish early-evening LA traffic.

Steph opened her door, still dressed in the clothes I'd last seen her in at work. She'd had plenty of time to shower and change, but she hadn't, and worry nestled in beside my pleasure at seeing her where we didn't have to moderate ourselves.

As soon as the door closed, Steph pulled me against her until our bodies were flush, and kissed me gently. "God I'm glad to see you. Sorry, I still need to shower. I sat down to look at more of this deepfake shit and never got up again." A grimace marred her beautiful mouth. "And it really is shit."

"It is." I ran my fingers through her hair. "Know what might help you feel better?" I tried to ignore the naughty expression and waited for a response that wasn't "screwing me senseless," though that was high on my list of helpful things. But only after she'd relaxed. At her headshake, I said, "A nice relaxing bath. Some scented candles. Bath salts if you have them. A glass of wine if you feel like it. Music, if that's your thing."

Steph paused before answering. Her nose wrinkled. "Maybe. But I need to wash my hair." It was such an inane comment, and my first instinct was that it felt like she was trying to deny herself something that could help her feel better.

"You can do that in your nice relaxing bath." I kissed her. "I can even help you."

"Okay. You're right. A bath would be nice after this shitstorm of a day. Shitstorm of a few days," she corrected.

"Good. And when you're done, I'll make you something to eat. Even if you just have a few bites, you should put something in your stomach."

Steph flashed me a weary smile. "You're too good to me."

"No, I'm just giving you what you deserve."

She made a vague kind of "I guess so" gesture. "What will you be doing while I'm taking a bath?"

"Aside from washing your hair? Watching you. Or...sitting out here reading. Whatever you want."

Steph's eyes softened. "Come on." She held out her hand and I slipped mine into it. We made a stop in the kitchen for Steph to pour me a glass of red wine, and herself a vodka neat over ice, then continued to the bathroom.

I loved her unusual bathroom layout. She had a huge shower space, glass enclosed at each end with a gap in the middle. A large bathtub stood at one end, the showerhead at the other. The light-colored marble walls made the space feel open and bright without feeling sterile. The first time I'd seen the setup, I'd thought that it was not only clever, but that this was a women who enjoyed her shower and bathtub.

Steph ran the water in the bath, checking the temperature and fussing with bath salts and essential oils. The room filled with a honey-vanilla scent that tickled my nose pleasantly. I sat on the edge of the tub while she lit well-used candles around the bathroom and turned off the bathroom lights so the entire room was washed in soft, warm candlelight. The light vanilla and lavender fragrance from the candles lingered in the air, mixing with the honey-vanilla from the bathwater.

Steph swallowed a mouthful of her vodka then set the glass on the middle shelf inset into the wall beside the bath. The coaster on the shelf made it obvious that she often relaxed like this. She put her phone on the vanity, and after tapping and swiping through a few things, the distinctive slide guitar intro of "Fade Into You" by Mazzy Star quietly filled the room from a small portable speaker on the shelving beside the bath.

Steph began removing her shirt and I stepped forward, gently pushing her hands aside. "Let me."

She needed to be cared for. I carefully unbuttoned the four buttons of her Henley, then grasped the bottom to pull it up. Steph raised her arms, helping me pull the shirt over her head. She was perfectly capable of undressing herself, but I sensed a little love and care might help her right now. I wasn't even going to pretend I knew how she felt about the deepfakes, but I could be here for her, for whatever she needed.

Steph watched me as I undressed her, taking my time while the bath filled, slowly removing her clothing and draping it over the edge of her hamper. My touches were light, sweet and soft rather than sexual. Her nudity aroused the same excitement as always, but without the desperation I'd experienced before.

Still, I allowed myself a few moments to enjoy the sight of her: the almost boyish frame filled out by small, soft curves, her high breasts, the muscle flowing over her body, the enticing swell of her ass. She'd told me earlier that I was perfect, but perfection was right here in front of me.

Steph murmured a thank-you before lowering herself slowly into the water, exhaling quietly as she leaned back against the padded edge. The tub was long enough that she could almost stretch out fully, and she slid down into the water until her neck rested against the edge of the bathtub. She closed her eyes, and while she relaxed and settled into whatever she needed, I grabbed a folded towel to sit on.

I sat quietly beside the bath as it filled, with my fingers lightly splashing in the warm water. I rested my chin on my arm, just watching her while I waited for her to say something. A few minutes passed. I turned off the water when it was about three inches from the top of the tub.

Steph sighed deeply. She opened her eyes, blinked a few times, then looked at me with such intensity it made my breath catch. "Harper…"

"Steph."

Her fingertips touched mine under the water. "This week has been the longest month. I've had some of the best days ever with you, and then some of the worst fucking days. It really sucks."

"I can imagine. Or no, I can't imagine how you're feeling. Do you want to talk about it?" At her neutral expression, I added, "You don't have to talk about it, obviously. But if you do, I'm right here."

"I think I do, but I don't know what to say." She shrugged helplessly. "Aside from fuck all of this shit."

I splashed some water over her arm, trickled some more over her shoulder as I asked, "Do you need a solution or just someone to listen?"

"I think just someone to listen. Ingrid and the team are working on it." She smiled wearily. "She thinks you're cute, by the way."

I bounced my eyebrows. "I like her already, even though I've never spoken to her." The song changed to Sia's "Beautiful Calm Driving," and I smiled.

A tentative smile fluttered over Steph's lips. "What? Too loud?" She reached over to the speaker.

"No. I didn't know we liked the same type of music, that's all. You always wear AirPods."

Her smile widened. "Not that I needed more confirmation that we're meant to be, but having the same taste in music might just be it."

"It might just be," I agreed.

I resumed slowly trickling water over the small amount of her skin above water. Steph drank a slow mouthful of her vodka, leaving her arm hanging over the side of the bath once she'd set the glass back. Tension was leaching from her, and I hoped by the end of her bath she might feel somewhat normal again. I'd sit here as long as she needed.

"You know," Steph murmured, her head still against the back of the tub, "I thought I was trying to protect your feelings by keeping you out of the bullshit, but I was actually trying to protect my feelings by not letting you into my life."

I didn't know what to say, so I said nothing.

She turned her head to face me. "It was selfish. I'm selfish. And I'm sorry."

"Sometimes we need to be a little selfish, but I'm glad you let me in."

She sighed deeply. "Me too."

"Duck under the water," I murmured.

She did as I asked, thoroughly wetting her short hair. Steph wiped her face, while I grabbed her shampoo from the shower.

"Do you want to do this yourself?" I asked.

Steph shook her head. I squeezed shampoo into my palm and brought it to my nose. Steph closed her eyes while I washed her hair, massaging her scalp, her neck. When she ducked under again to rinse her hair, some of the bathwater spilled over the side, splashing me. I was so tempted to just strip my clothes off and join her in the large bath. Maybe once I'd finished bathing her.

I had to lean right across the bath to grab a bar of soap and a clean washcloth, and Steph made no move to help. Instead, she stared openly, her arms resting lightly on the sides of the bathtub, her body pliant and relaxed. The change in her was palpable. I didn't know if she'd simply shoved her emotions aside to deal with later, or if this was exactly what she'd needed. But I trusted she knew what was best for her right now.

"Do you want to do this yourself?" I asked again.

Again, she shook her head.

The bar of soap, with its citrus-coconut scent that I always associated with Steph, slid easily over her wet skin. I dipped the washcloth in the water and ran it over the back of her shoulders and neck. I took my time, slowly washing her, lingering, lightly massaging.

"That feels so good," she mumbled, closing her eyes.

"I'm glad." A deep, achy tug had settled in my belly, pleasurable and warm.

She kept her eyes closed as I washed and rinsed every part of skin sitting above the water. Steph was still, except for moving slightly to let me access her underarms, and a deep, shuddering inhalation as I soaped her breasts. The temptation to linger there, to fondle her nipples was almost too hard to resist. While I was sure that would technically count as care, I didn't want to presume to know what she might want, or put my own feelings onto her.

Steph's slow, deep breathing accompanied the slow, sensual, bassy opening of "Glory Box" by Portishead.

My stomach twisted into a knot of desire. I stopped washing her, dropping the washcloth into the bathwater.

Steph's eyes fluttered open. Her gorgeous mouth turned up in a lazy smirk. "There's more of me, you know."

"Is there? Where?" I asked innocently, dipping my hand fully into the water, but keeping it away from her skin.

Steph captured my hand and brought it to her mouth. She kissed my fingertips slowly, sucking them into her mouth. When she'd finished sucking each finger, she moved my hand down to her breast, folding my fingers around the firm swell. I braced my other arm on the edge of the bath behind her, leaning in to kiss her. Deliberately, I didn't linger in the kiss, pulling back out of her reach as I pinched her nipple and stroked the smooth skin of her breast. Her breathing hitched. She grabbed my hand again, but there was no kissing my fingers this time.

Steph pushed my hand down until it was fully submerged. I let it rest above her pubic hair, though all I wanted was to guide my hand between her legs and finger her clit. But I wanted her to control exactly what she wanted. And she did. She opened her legs until her knees fell against the side of the bath, and pushed my hand between her thighs, her hand closing around my wrist to keep it there.

I kept my hand still. "Is this what you meant by *more of you?*"

"Yes," she said, her breath hitching on the word. Her grip on my wrist tightened. The knuckles on her other hand whitened as she gripped the edge of the bath.

I rose to my knees, still keeping my arm behind her shoulders for balance, and stroked my fingers up her slit until I found her clit. Even in the bathwater I could feel her thick, slick arousal and it made my own clit throb. "This is where you want me to clean?"

The pun about her being a dirty girl would have been so easy, but Steph bit down on her lower lip and the flush of pink on her mouth stole the rest of my words.

Keeping my fingers still, I surged forward and captured her lips with mine. Steph's hand came to the back of my head, possessively holding me to her as we kissed. The kiss was needy, a clash of lips and tongue and the occasional brush of teeth. Steph pulled away first and the desperate, whispered, "Please" against my mouth made me lose all conviction to make her wait, to go slow.

She lightly bit my lower lip as I circled my fingers around the engorged flesh of her clit, lightly sucking my lip when I pressed more firmly. I broke away from a kiss I really didn't want to break away from to lavish attention on the places that would hasten her climax. Her neck. Her jaw. Her nipples.

"Oh god. I'm so close already," she said, the words coming out as a desperate whine.

"Already?" I murmured. "Were you sitting here before I came around, thinking about me…thinking about fuckin' me, me fuckin' you? Getting yourself hot and ready?"

She swallowed hard, shaking her head. "No," Steph managed. "It's all you, right here and now." She sat up and arched her back, offering me her breasts again, and I feasted on her plump, delicious nipples as I stroked her.

I glanced up. "Do you want me inside you?"

Steph's desperate expression made my insides twist. "Yes, I do…" Her breathing grew ragged. "But…not in the water. Later…Right now, I want you to kiss me when I'm coming," she said hoarsely, a hand moving against my jaw to raise my head from where I'd been sucking her nipple.

Her request was far from a hardship, and when she moaned her climax against my mouth, her hot breath mingling with mine, a rush of heat shot straight to my clit. Her thighs clenched tightly around my hand as her body shuddered. I kissed her through her orgasm, my tongue playing against hers. The sound of her climax, the illusion of power I had to make her come apart like this, was a bolt of arousal that made me tremble.

Steph fell back against the bathtub, spilling more water over the side. Her legs fell open to release my hand and I drew it up the inside of her thigh, over her belly, her breasts. She turned her head, her slightly glassy-eyed gaze finding my eyes. She inhaled deeply, let it out slowly. "Thank you." Before I could tell her that it was me who should thank her, Steph leaned forward and shut off the speaker. "Now…what can we do with you?"

"Whatever you want," I said, my throat tight with anticipation. I had not forgotten about the harness in that drawer beside her bed. I would willingly let her do anything she wanted, because I knew she wouldn't do anything I didn't consent to.

"Whatever?"

The devilish expression promised something delicious, and I nodded. "Yes, ma'am."

"Fuck," she growled. Steph yanked the plug from the bath, gripped the sides, and pushed herself to her feet. She stepped out right in front of me, and the position put my face level with the narrow, trimmed thatch of blond hair between her thighs.

Unconsciously, I reached for her, but as if she knew what I was thinking, she shook her head and said, "Later." Steph offered me a hand and pulled me up. After a quick kiss that promised more, but made it clear it wouldn't be right here right now, she grabbed a towel and began drying off.

She did a perfunctory job before tossing the towel into the hamper and taking my hand. Steph led me into her bedroom, stopping by her bed. "Take your clothes off for me."

I did as she commanded while Steph opened *that* drawer on her bedside table. The drawer that held all her toys, including the one I'd enjoyed the first night we'd gone to bed together. The implication made my stomach tighten in anticipation, my skin prickle with heat.

She lifted the harness, raising a questioning eyebrow. "Whatever I want?"

I inhaled a shuddery breath. "Yes. Whatever you want." Aside from trusting her completely to respect any boundaries that might arise during our intimacy, I knew she would deliver on pleasure.

Her response was almost a purr. "Thank you."

As I finished undressing I watched Steph stepping into the harness. She took her time, clearly aware that this foreplay was as arousing as if she were actually touching me. She tightened the buckles, shifting the harness on her hips. Once she had it how she wanted it, she took my hand and pulled me to her until our bodies were pressed close.

Steph cupped my ass, bringing my hips forward to hers. The feeling of the harness against my skin made anticipatory goose bumps break out across my body. She cupped my breasts, fondling my nipples as her mouth lavished attention on my neck. She kissed her way up to my ear. "I want you to choose the toy. Show me what you want."

I held back a moan as she moved away so I could make my choice.

Though it was tempting to pick the same dildo that'd given me such a mind-blowing orgasm the last time, for a strap-on I wanted something a little longer, thinner. The sex-store variety of Steph's drawer was exciting and after a minute of running my fingers over her toys, I made my choice. A slim VixSkin dildo, around eight inches long, that I knew would feel so goddamned good. I held it up, raising a questioning eyebrow.

Steph cleared her throat. "Good choice." She licked her lower lip, inclining her head toward the bed. "Lie down, gorgeous."

I did as I was told, watching while she fit the dildo into her harness. She did it slowly, carefully, again using each movement to draw out my anticipation. The way she watched me as I watched her made it clear she knew exactly what she was doing. Steph climbed onto the bed, hovering above me. The tip of the toy pressing into my thigh made me spread my legs in anticipation, and Steph settled her body in the space. She kissed me quickly, then peppered soft, lingering kisses on her way down my body.

She paused against my breasts, licking and sucking until my nipples were almost aching from the exquisite attention. "Jesus, fuck...your tits," she muttered. "They're glorious. I want to bury myself in them and never come up for air." She pulled one of my nipples into her mouth.

"That would be unfortunate," I managed to gasp out. Words were so hard right now.

"I know..." Steph groaned. She spent a delicious amount of time with my nipples before she moved on. Moved down... I arched up into the touch of her lips, desperate for her kisses to find my clit. But Steph's mouth paused against my inner thigh. "You're already so wet." She gently pushed my legs further apart. "Show me just how wet you are."

I spread my legs, pushing on her shoulders in a desperate attempt to make her go down on me. I was almost squirming in anticipation of her mouth on me, like I was nothing more than a huge ball of desperate want who'd do anything to satisfy the ache. The low growl she emitted made me even more desperate for her touch.

As if she knew I was on the brink, Steph lightly kissed my clit. Her throaty "So, so wet" came a second before she finally put her mouth on me.

"Ohmygod," I choked out as her tongue and lips worked magic. Steph's hands roamed my body, stroking, lightly squeezing, as her mouth...her sensual, sexy, talented mouth drove me closer and closer to climax. I wanted to come in her mouth, *and* I wanted to come around the toy, and I wanted both those things right now. I'd never been one for orgasm after orgasm, but I couldn't think of anything I wanted more.

Steph slowly ran her tongue through my labia. "You taste..." She sucked my clit. "So fucking good."

"And that *feels* so good..." I covered the hand fondling my nipple with one hand and with my other, propped myself up so I could watch her pleasuring me. Steph made eye contact with me, and the fierce lust in her eyes undid me.

I cried out hoarsely as I came, squeezing my eyes closed as hot waves of pleasure burned through me. Steph let out a choked sound that vibrated against my clit, setting off a fresh pulse of arousal on the back of my climax. One hand left my body, and I would have groaned at the small loss of sensation if not for the sound of Steph opening a condom wrapper.

Her kisses moved from my wetness to my thigh, up and over my belly, my breasts, my neck until her body covered mine. I could feel the dildo pressing against my thigh, and the anticipation further ramped up my excitement. Steph braced herself with an arm either side of my shoulders, leaning down to kiss me. "Do you have any idea how much I want to fuck you?" She rocked her hips. The shaft of the toy sliding over my sensitive clit was both exquisite pleasure and exquisite torture.

I swallowed hard, my breath coming in ragged pants. I wanted to answer her, wanted to say something sexy, or teasing, or clever, but it was all I could do to just breathe. I managed a small nod.

"Do you want that too?" There was an almost feral desperation in Steph's eyes. She licked her lips. "Do you want to come again?"

"Yes. *Please*," I begged.

Her mouth came to within a whisper of mine as she entered me slowly. I was so wet from my orgasm that she slid in deeply with the barest push. We let out a simultaneous moan, smothering the sound with a long kiss. She pulled out just as slowly, pausing before the dildo withdrew fully. "Still yes?"

"*Yes.*"

My consent seemed to let something loose in her, and she pressed deeply inside me again. I groaned at the sensation of the dildo sliding along all my most sensitive places, the way the base of it bumped my clit. She wasn't rough, but she was commanding—intense, controlled. Steph kept herself braced on her hands, our lower bodies fitting flush together as she fucked me.

The position meant she could she kiss me, take a nipple into her mouth, and she did both, alternating between points of pleasure. She licked and bit and sucked my nipples, and all I could do was take the pleasure she gave me. I locked my ankles around her ass, holding her inside me, my hands roaming mindlessly over her back, my nails raking her skin.

It was so *so* fucking good, I was almost delirious with the sensations. When I cupped her face in my hands, her intense expression turned gentle. She held eye contact with me, and I was struck by the mixture of lust and love in hers. I wanted to tell her how incredible it felt, how much I loved it, that I didn't want her to stop until I'd come again, but I couldn't articulate. When she dropped down onto a forearm and one insistent hand came around to my clit, her fingers stroking in time with her thrusts, any possibility of words left me.

Steph pressed hard, deep, each stroke hitting exactly the right spot. "Is this what you want?" Her voice was rough, a new sort of demand having taken over that was hotter than anything I'd ever heard.

I swallowed hard, nodding.

"Say it."

I bit off a moan to answer her. "I want this. I want you."

"Me too," she said tightly. "You are so fucking sexy, Harper." The words were punctuated with deep presses of the strap-on, firm strokes of her fingers.

I tightened my legs around her ass, pressing her deeper into me. My breathing caught. All I could focus on was the feeling of her fucking me, her expression of lust, the bunching and uncoiling muscles in her arms and shoulders. I wrapped my arms around her, pulled her down, desperate to hold her as close as possible, desperate to hold her inside me as I came. I bit her neck, and the sound she made sent tingles down my legs.

She kissed me, open-mouthed, demandingly, and I met the kiss with passion. Steph's movement slowed, then stopped. She gently pulled out, despite my best efforts to keep her there, to keep her fucking me. The loss of sensation almost made me whimper but I had no time to think because Steph pushed my thigh, encouraging me to move.

"Roll over," she said, her tone leaving no room for resistance, not that I had any intention of doing anything other than what she told me. "I want you face down."

I did as I was told, settling low on my hands and knees, my breasts pressed against the bed, fisting my hands in the sheets. My senses felt hyper attuned, and each realization of what she was doing was a fresh jolt of arousal. I felt the bed shift, the whisper of air against my skin as she got into position behind me, her hands gripping my hips, the sound of her exhalations.

Steph drew a hand down my spine and I arched into the touch. The dildo slid back into me with no resistance and I tightened around it. A deep breath helped settle my arousal so I could actually think, focus on the pleasure. Her next thrust was deeper, a little harder, and I moved back into her until I felt her skin, the harness against my ass.

Steph's murmured, "Good girl," almost sent me into orbit, and I buried my face in the bedcovers and moaned. "You *really* like that, don't you?" she asked, her voice breathy, choked.

"I do," I managed, barely able to get even those two syllables out. The sensation of her fucking me with the strap-on, the angle in this position, the way her body fit to mine was making my arousal peak anew and all my focus was on the way she was fucking me so deliciously.

I didn't know what was hotter—the feeling of the toy stroking my most pleasurable spots, the sound of her skin slapping against mine with every thrust of her hips, the ragged sound of her breathing, or the way her busy hands seemed to find exactly the right pressure on my clit or nipples.

Her thrusts remained slow and steady, deep and hard, the rhythm constant, until my climax built again. I pressed my face against my forearms to muffle the cry as I came. Steph's arms came around my waist, and she arched her body over mine, her mouth tracing a pattern down my spine, until she again pressed her mouth against my neck. She held me tightly when my rubbery limbs refused to keep me up.

"Fuck," she said shakily. "That was...that was..."

I nodded, unable to finish the sentence for her. There was no word for what that was.

She withdrew gently but kept her fingers soft against my clit. "Do you think you can come again?" Steph murmured against the back of my shoulder.

The light rubbing over my clit felt so good, but I didn't think I could handle much more stimulation. Two orgasms so close together had been nothing more than a fantasy until now, and three felt out of reach. I turned my head to find her hot gaze on me. I took a deep breath before answering. "Probably not, but it still feels nice."

Steph laughed, a throaty sound of pleasure. After another featherlight stroke over my clit, she took her hand away. I only missed it for a moment, before she moved to lie beside me and pull me down to the bed. "Sometimes it's nice to just feel nice."

"Yes," I agreed. "And I feel beyond nice right now." The residual sensations from my climaxes had left me feeling boneless, and completely and utterly satisfied.

She laughed quietly. "Me too." Steph unbuckled the harness and leaned away from me to drop it off the bed. She rolled back to face me and opened her arms. I snuggled against her, delighting in the way our bodies fit together.

My own laugh bubbled up when I realized how my enjoyment had taken over. "It's amazing how this was supposed to be about making you feel better and suddenly I'm having two orgasms."

Her eyebrows bounced. "Oh, I feel amazing, and I'm *very* relaxed right now. Ten out of ten, good job, nothing but positive reviews."

I lightly slapped her shoulder. "Silly."

She captured my hand to kiss my fingers. "Guilty."

When she released my hand I stroked along her ass, up her back. I was sure she was on the verge of another orgasm after taking me like that, but I needed a moment to catch my breath before I thanked her for the most mind-blowing sex I'd ever had. I kissed her throat, her jaw, shifting until I could reach her mouth. The kiss was deep, thorough, a confirmation of the intimacy and connection we'd just shared.

I brushed some of her hair back from her forehead, delighting in the way her eyes held mine, the softness in them. All I saw was love. "Did I actually tell you that I love you?"

Her nose wrinkled, but her eyes were still smiling. "Kind of." Steph shrugged. "I mean…I got the vibe. You said *in* love, so…"

I shook my head. "I should have said it, not just implied it."

"You think there's a difference?"

"I do. I love you. And I'm *in* love with you." I propped myself up on my elbow. "To me, in love is the romance, the desire, the passion, the attraction. Love is just…love, all of you, no matter what. And I can't tell you how much I love that we've finally come together."

Steph blinked rapidly, a funny, crooked little smile passing over her mouth. "You have no idea how happy that makes me. And we haven't come together, not yet. But give us time."

"Ha ha." After a beat, I teased, "So, you're just going to leave me hanging here?"

"Oh. No. I thought it was obvious. I guess I assumed you got the vibe too." She carefully moved my hair back behind my ear, letting her fingertips brush along my jaw. An earnest seriousness replaced the joking expression. "You already know I'm in love with you. But, I love you too, Harper."

Her adoring expression undid me, and I pulled her face to mine. The passion in this kiss felt heightened by our declaration, and when she bit my lower lip, I smiled against her mouth. I could have stayed where I was, kissing her, for the rest of the night, but there was the promise of something even better.

"Now, I believe there's a pressing matter I need to attend to." I pressed my hand between her legs, delighting in the abundant arousal I found. "Somewhere about…here?"

Steph swallowed thickly. "Yes. *Please*. Show me just how much you love me…"

CHAPTER TWENTY-THREE

Steph

I'd thought nothing could feel better than Harper and me being in a romantic relationship, but I was wrong. Fighting, and having made up, sharing fears and insecurities was the best thing. Harper asking me to fuck her as she had last night was the best thing. The promise of months, of years of more intimacy, more connection, more learning, more growing together was the best thing.

I wanted nothing more than to spend all weekend in bed with her, but unfortunately, as she'd already told me—I'd signed up for a charity tennis match not a charity sex match. But the way we'd fucked last night? Well, let's just say we'd win a charity sex match for sure.

I just wasn't so sure about winning a tennis match…

Despite having no issues performing in front of large groups (because let's be honest, the charity game was basically a big performance) I was nervous about the whole thing. There was no prearranged outcome—it was a genuine game with the best pair winning—but the whole idea was to give fans a show, and I anticipated all four of us would be acting the entire time. But there was no way to act like someone good at tennis. At least Harper would be there with me, though I already knew there'd be no sneaky coaching from her umpire's chair.

Last night when we'd reluctantly left my bed for sustenance, she'd given me a refresher on the rules of the game, and a reminder of some of the things she'd taught me in our training sessions. I'd checked in with the other three on our shared messaging thread and it seemed we were all in agreement on our roles. I was the clown. Laura and Jenna were the show ponies. Yusef was the jock.

We were meeting two hours before the game to stretch and warm up if we wanted, then to have our hair and makeup done so we looked live-stream ready. Then we'd have ten minutes' tennis warmup on the court before beginning. "An exhibition match with a carnival atmosphere vibe" was how it'd been described in our final briefing. At last update, there would be about a thousand people in attendance and thousands of signups for the live stream, all proceeds of which would go to Purple Refuge.

So even if I made a complete fool of myself, it was worth it for the good cause.

I woke pleasantly sore and deliriously happy and pondered that for a few minutes before my meditation. Sure, there had been sex. Hot, intimate, mind-boggling, sensuous, frantic sex. But what we'd shared went well beyond that. Sex was fabulous. But feeling like I could be completely myself in, and out of, bed was beyond anything I'd ever experienced. I wondered why I'd spent so many years chasing the wrong things, thinking it was right.

When I was done meditating, I slowly turned my head to sneak a peek at Harper, expecting her to be still sleeping. But she was awake and watching me.

"Creepy," I teased.

"You can talk," she shot back.

"Mmm." I rolled over to face her. "Sleep okay?"

"Loggishly." She stretched, and the sheet slipped down. "I wonder why…"

The expanse of Harper on display was too tempting to resist, and I stroked the soft, smooth skin over her belly up to her breasts. I wanted her as much as ever, but I was also content to just touch her like this, without any expectation. This was also a new experience for me, this desperate longing to just be with her, touch her, stay connected to her.

My watch buzzed and I checked the screen then opened the app on my phone. "Oh no, I'm being bullied by my Garmin again." I bounced my eyebrows. "Apparently it thinks I'm not sleeping enough."

Harper laughed quietly. "It thinks correctly."

I set my phone aside again. "It's worth it."

"I agree." She slid closer until our hips nestled together. "Am I coming with you, or do you want me to drive separately?"

They were sending a car for the four players, and I honestly hadn't thought about Harper. Huge bad-girlfriend move on my behalf. I'd just assumed she'd be at her place and go from there, but now she was here with me.

"Probably not a bad idea to go separately," I mused. "I have to do media stuff after and then the fan interactions, plus our warmups and hair and makeup before. It's going to be boring as hell for you."

She pushed some hair out of my eyes, her fingertips lingering for a moment near my temple before continuing down my cheek to my jaw. "I'm sure I can amuse myself while you're doing all that."

I leaned in for a kiss. "I'm sure you can. But you don't have to."

"You don't want us to arrive and leave together because you don't want us to be seen together, or are you really just trying to make sure I'm not bored?"

It finally twigged, and I smiled. "Clarity is kindness?"

She let out a relieved breath. "Yes."

I didn't hesitate to answer honestly. "I really don't want you to be bored waiting around for me, and I don't think you should *have* to wait for me. I don't want that to be a theme in our relationship when I have media or other commitments."

"Darlin', I appreciate you thinking of me. But I'll be fine, I promise. And I don't mind waiting for you."

"Okay. Then let's go together."

"Let's." She seemed delighted, and her mood was contagious.

"Speaking of the tennis match. I just wanted to double-check... Would you accept a bribe to look the other way for certain line calls and stuff?"

Harper placed a hand above her left breast. A little more of her accent slipped out as she declared, "I am a moral and upstanding person. I would never cheat. Not even for you."

I reached under the sheet and lightly traced my fingertips up the inside of her thigh. Harper drew in a sharp breath when I found her pubic hair. I stroked upward, delighting in her growing arousal. "Not even if I did this?"

Harper pressed her face against my neck. She moaned, a breathy, desperate exhale. "That's so unfair."

"Tell you what," I murmured as I circled her clit. "You do whatever you think is right while you're umpiring, and if you happen to think of this while you're pondering a difficult call, then so be it."

She rolled on top of me, straddling my hips. I guided my fingers inside her, wrapping an arm around her waist to hold her in place as I sank deeper into her heat. I sat up, and the warm press of her breasts to mine made my abs tighten. "Will you kiss me when I win? In front of everyone?"

"You're impossible," Harper breathed. It would have been more convincing if she wasn't sucking my shoulder, grinding her clit against my palm.

"I think you'll find I'm actually very possible…"

We finally rolled out of bed a little under two hours before the car arrived. Plenty of time for a shower, some food, and a little panicking about playing tennis in front of thousands of people before we had to get ready. We showered together and only got out because we'd be late if we didn't show a modicum of restraint.

"How are we going to spend our weekends once this tennis thing is done?" Harper asked as she toweled her hair dry. "It's only been three weekends, but it feels way longer."

"No idea. But I'm looking forward to figuring it out." I snuck a kiss, delighted when Harper prolonged it. "Isn't that the fun part of a new relationship, learning new things about each other?" After all the time we'd worked together, I knew enough to know I loved her, but fresh discoveries were intoxicating.

"It is," she agreed. She looked so pleased that I almost caved and pulled her back to bed.

I knew we were in a honeymoon phase where all I wanted was to touch her, but this felt like it went beyond simple new-relationship lust. "Honestly, I don't care what we do. As long as we're doing it together."

"Oh, you are just the sweetest thing."

"I know," I said, trying for an airiness that I wasn't sure landed. But if I didn't try for it, I might cry a little. "And we can still play tennis. Or I'll come watch while you and Ben play. Maybe we could play doubles with him and Per?"

Harper laughed, flashing me a dubious look. "You've *seen* Per, right? Does he look like he can run after a tennis ball?"

Laughing, I admitted, "Not really. But that means an easy win for us."

She smiled knowingly, then dropped the towel she had wrapped around herself. I stared. I'm only human. If I ever stopped being in awe of her body, someone needed to check I hadn't died. "That's really unfair," I complained.

Harper's return smile was the epitome of sorry-not-sorry. "I can't wait to see how competitive you are today."

"Super. But also super not great at tennis, so there's a big disparity between desire and ability."

"You're going to be great," she assured me.

I followed her into my bedroom to dress. As I pulled on a pair of comfortable sweatpants, I told her, "Also I'm not sure about my schedule around work next week, but I *do* want to spend some nights together. I know I have a meeting but I'm not sure when." At her querying look, I added, "I've been tapped for a lead in an Alyce Purves film."

Harper's entire face radiated joy and pride. The pride made my chest feel tight. She grabbed my hands. "Really? That's amazing. I'm so excited for you, darlin'."

"Thanks. I'm pretty excited too."

"Can we plan a celebration?"

"Sure. I love a good celebration. Or…preemptive celebration. But it's not a done deal."

"Maybe not, but it's still amazing." She arched an eyebrow. "You think they need Key Makeup?"

"You know, I don't know much about the film industry," I deadpanned, "but I think makeup is a thing on all productions, yes."

"Smart-ass." She slapped my butt.

"I *can* ask for you as part of my contract, if that's what you want."

"We'll see," she said breezily. "Come on, get out of here and eat breakfast or we'll be late and you're going to disappoint a bunch of fans."

Harper made scrambled eggs with a side of sautéed vegetables and turkey sausage, and even garnished the meal with sprigs of parsley from the mostly decorative herb planter outside my kitchen window. I said yes to some grainy toast for extra carbs so I'd have enough energy to run around a tennis court for an hour or so.

And I made…coffee. I was going to have to learn to cook quick tasty meals I could fit in around work, or hire a personal chef that'd be ready at all hours to cook for us. Not that I didn't love Harper's cooking, but it wasn't fair for her to be the sole food provider, or to eat what amounted to frozen food from my meal service. Good frozen food, but not made with love like hers.

We ate on my back patio facing the Verdugo Hills, sitting close enough that our knees were touching under the table. We hardly talked, because there was no need to fill the space with inane chatter. I liked talking, but I also really loved comfortable silences and having that with

Harper was incredible. We could have easily spent the rest of the day like this, if not for the pressing issue of tennis.

We cleaned up the kitchen together, bumping hips and stealing kisses before it was time to get dressed. Harper had chosen a pair of off-white above-the-ankle chinos paired with loafers, and a light-blue button-up under a navy blazer. The attire made it clear she was going to be the boss for the game. She'd pulled her hair up into a French braid that completed the boss look. Hello.

I ran my fingertips along the lapel of the blazer. "You look amazing. Very official. That outfit makes me want to be on my best behavior."

"You'd better be," she said, affecting fake sternness. Harper smoothed down the collar of my white Adidas polo. "You look so cute."

"I'm so nervous," I admitted. "Is it silly that I'm nervous?"

"Of course not. This is something new. But you're going to be great. And it's not about you, remember?" She kissed me sweetly, then lightly cupped my chin and turned my face to the side. "Are you wearing sunscreen?"

"Yes." I held back my eye roll and "Mom."

"Good." She lightly traced my eyebrows. "I hate that Nina is going to work on you today."

"I hate it too." A text message announced that our car was here. I grabbed my bag. "Time to go."

"Have you got your racquet?"

I held the bag up. "Yes."

"Hat?"

"Yes."

"Wallet, keys, phone?"

"Yes times three."

Harper smiled. "Then you're all set. Come on. Let's go raise some money."

We were the last to arrive. I was grabbed by Kayla and ushered into the players' room, while Harper split off to go check the court or something tennis-y. They'd set up a makeshift green room and a station for Hair and Makeup, and I sat down to be made ready for the cameras.

Laura, Jenna, and Yusef were all dressed the same as I was in crisp, new tennis clothes and shoes, though unlike me, Laura and Jenna had gone for skirts. If nothing else, at least we looked good. We checked in with each other, and chatted aimlessly while we got ready.

Nina said nothing as she covered the faint bitemark on my neck, though she did shoot me an amused, eyebrows-raised look. I was sure if Harper were there, she'd be getting a grilling. Smart of her to stay away.

My hair was styled, though I had no idea why because I was going to be wearing a hat, but I was adept enough at my job to not question certain processes.

My nerves bubbled under the surface and I sat on one of the couches in the corner and closed my eyes for some box breathing.

Someone announced, "Five minutes until you're due on court" which set off a maelstrom of noise and activity from the other three.

I opened my eyes, thanked Nina and Chrissy again and stood up to grab my things. Laura and Yusef seemed totally unfazed. Jenna bounced up and down, shaking out her arms. "God I'm terrified of this whole thing. Will you promise to make me look good?"

I laughed. "No chance. This is war, friend."

Kayla came over with a water bottle. "Gabby's asked me to update you all. Looks like almost everyone who bought tickets has come in, so we're looking at around a thousand attendees. The donations site is up and running and the live stream numbers look great. No issues with security on the attendees—everyone came in clean."

"Great. Thanks, Kayla. And thanks for coming today."

"No problem. Here," she said, holding up her phone displaying a picture of the court setup. "Just so you know what's waiting for you."

I was impressed. A crew had clearly been hard at work setting up extra makeshift seating, reaching high into the bright blue sky along the side of the court to enclose it on three sides. All the seating was behind fencing with a security person every twelve feet or so in case of unruly behavior. Four cameras were set up to capture the match from the base and side lines. They'd also put up big screens for those who didn't have a prime view. I passed the phone to Laura, who nodded, then passed it to Jenna who showed Yusef.

As I walked out, I could hear someone on a loudspeaker. They'd snagged local radio announcer Aiden Green to hype up the crowd and make sure everyone knew what was going on. He was reminding them of the reason they were here, thanking them for their generous support, and running over some basic courtesy and safety rules.

The six of us stood on the court while we went through prematch stuff. As I jiggled nervously to loosen my muscles, I tried not to stare too obviously at Harper. She introduced herself as the match umpire, and I realized then that I'd never actually considered how she felt about attention being on her like this. She seemed completely unperturbed, and I felt a rush of pride.

Aiden introduced us all in a voice that reminded me of an over-the-top WWE announcer, ran us through the basic rules and reminded us that this was just a fun charity match. "But remember," he added. "The losing team has promised to donate half of their salary from one episode's earnings to the Purple Refuge and the winning team will donate a quarter." That drew loud applause and raucous cheering.

Jenna used her racquet to point at me. "Steph earns the most, so she should just throw the match. For charity."

"Ha…ha…ha…" I was going to donate half an episode's salary regardless, but I still really wanted to win.

We had our ten-minute warmup, hitting balls back and forth. There was no fancy stuff, and I was glad we all seemed to be about the same skill level. Aiden was talking over our rallies, but it was all inane hype to get the crowd going. The few times I caught Harper's eye, she nodded, gracing me with a gentle smile. Harper was here, and everything was going to be fine.

Laura and I had won the coin toss and decided to serve. That was definitely a choice, but it seemed there weren't really many good ones when you weren't great at tennis. Aiden asked for quiet, and announced that it was time to start the game.

A faint hum from Harper's microphone preceded her calmly announcing, "Play to begin. *North Precinct* to serve."

Oh. My. Fucking. God. Where had that voice been hiding all this time? It was so fucking hot—calm, but with an edge that made it very clear that she was in charge. I was *definitely* going to be asking Harper to pull out her tennis-umpire voice for me again.

I blew out a breath, bounced the ball a couple times—more to settle the excitement from hearing Harper's "I'm a tennis official" voice than because I actually thought it'd help—and served.

I hit some fantastic shots. Some okay shots. And some really fucking shitty ones. We rallied, volleyed, chased down balls, pretended to argue with each other, argued with Harper over calls—she never backed down, not even for me—and all in all had a pretty good time and put on a pretty good show. The crowd was engaged and enthusiastic, which made it all the more easy and fun.

There were very few balls that required Harper's adjudication because most of the ones that missed were obviously out. For any she had to make a call on, it was about 50/50 on who won the query. Nobody could accuse Harper of favoritism.

We were tied at a set apiece, and playing the third and final set. Laura and I were down 1-2 but up 15-love on my serve. The prediction for the game was spot on—because of the general lack of skill, the match was flying by without many long rallies. Points were mostly awarded due to someone hitting a ball out or into the net rather than a winning, unreturnable shot.

I messed around, hamming up bouncing the ball and letting it get away from me before getting it back under control for my serve. Being comfortable with feeling foolish was part of my job, and the crowd's laughter justified the time-wasting. I hadn't mastered a spin serve, but I was making at least fifty percent of my first serves, on par with the other three players.

My serve was fabulous, as in it made it into the correct square and was going pretty fast. Yusef stepped around it for a forehand and absolutely slogged the ball. I kept my eye on it, just like Harper had always taught me. And watch that slogged ball slam right into Harper. The sound of the impact, and her loud exhalation seemed to echo around me in the sudden stillness of the crowd.

I dropped my racquet, dimly conscious of it clattering to the court, and sprinted over to the chair. Harper was bent double, her right arm folded up against her torso, her other hand wrapped around the railing of the high chair in a white-knuckled grip.

I climbed up the ladder as fast as I could. Those few rungs felt like a few stories. I wasn't sure exactly where she'd been hit. All I knew was she'd been hit, hard, by a tennis ball. "Oh my god. Baby, are you all right? Are you hurt?"

I registered the sound of my voice through the speakers connected to Harper's mic a second too late. As soon as I'd said "baby" the crowd had erupted into noise and if I wasn't so worried about Harper having been hit with a rocket of a forehand, I might have reacted.

Harper sat up, her wide-eyed stare fixed on me. She inhaled slowly and her expression turned part amused, part horrified. She pointedly flicked the switch on the side of the microphone. The noise of the crowd seemed to swallow me up, and I simultaneously wished I could disappear, and yell at everyone that yeah, that was exactly what I meant to say— she's my girlfriend.

"I'm fine," she said, though those two words were rushed and breathy.

Yusef sped over, with Jenna hot on his heels. "Crap, Harper! I'm so sorry. Total accident, I swear. Are you all right? Are you hurt?" He gave me a sidelong glance, and I would have laughed at his expression if I wasn't so worried about the hit Harper had taken.

Harper nodded. "I know it was an accident, and it's okay. And yes, I'm fine." She smiled, though it seemed a little shaky. "Call it a workplace hazard."

Sometime during my tunnel vision, Laura had followed me to the umpire's chair, and she tugged on the bottom of my polo until I jumped down. I held on to Harper's ankle. "Do you need the medic?"

"No, thank you, I'm fine."

I trusted her, but the worry that she'd been hurt was hard to push down. I became aware of the crowd shifting restlessly, and it seemed Harper had too. Harper pulled the microphone closer, flicked the switch to turn it back on, and said, completely deadpan, "Out."

The crowd burst into collective laughter, and Harper waited until the noise had died down to update the score. "Thirty-love."

Laughter was good. She'd somehow taken a situation that could have easily turned on me and flipped it into crowd entertainment, and not the negative kind. Harper looked at the four of us in turn, her gaze lingering slightly longer on me. "Play to resume," she said firmly.

I knew there were a thousand people watching us here, and who knew how many thousands watching on the stream. I knew I was supposed to be playing tennis to raise money for a charity, but all I could think about was that she had been hit, and hit hard. I grabbed her hand and, standing on tiptoes, lightly kissed the back of it.

Harper's eyes softened, and she made an almost imperceptible movement with her head to indicate I should go back to my side of the court. I compromised by moving back a few steps.

Yusef spoke up first. "I'd like to object."

Beside him, Jenna was nodding furiously, though it was clear they were both hamming it up for the crowd. "Yeah, me too!" she said emphatically.

Laura and I both turned to face them. "Object to what?" I asked indignantly.

They exchanged a look. "Uh. Umpire bias?" Yusef said, barely getting the words out around a laugh. The crowd had obviously picked up the conversation and laughed too.

I rolled my eyes. "Nice try."

Harper leaned down to talk to him. "Your objection is noted, but I assure you there's no umpire bias."

"I know," he grumbled. "But it was worth a shot."

Laura slung her arm around my shoulder and began to guide me back to our baseline. "She's okay," she said quietly.

Aiden was rolling with the punches. "Not to worry, folks, it seems our umpire is fit and ready to continue. Luckily, the *Make the Cut* team doesn't get a penalty for trying to take the umpire out."

Laura and I pretended that was what we wanted to happen. Jenna and Yusef pretended like we were overreacting. Harper just shook her head. "Play to resume," she repeated.

I was surprised that I managed to shift my focus from Harper's injury, and even more surprised when *Precinct* won. I actually hit a winner to clinch the game. Harper's proud "Game, set, match to *North Precinct!*" was accompanied by loud cheering and clapping. Laura and I bowed, and I borrowed a play from pro tennis, clapping my hand against my racquet as I spun in a circle to acknowledge the crowd.

We met Jenna and Yusef at the net for congenial handshakes. "I'm so sorry you two were so terrible," Laura said, quiet enough that it wouldn't be picked up by any of the mics around the court.

Jenna muttered, "Fuck you guys," around her full-teeth smile.

"Thanks, that's so sweet. You both really sucked," I said around my own big smile.

Yusef grabbed my wrist, while Jenna took Laura's and together they raised our hands like we'd won a boxing match.

After big waves and smiles for the crowd, we lined up to shake hands with Harper. I somehow ended up at the back of the line, and as I approached, the smile she'd shared with the other three turned soft for me. The moment I took Harper's hand, some clown yelled "Kiss her!" much to the amusement of the crowd.

Us four players walked off to the sound of Aiden going through the protocol for autographs and photos. We had about twenty minutes before we had to come back out for the meet and greet and I needed every one of those minutes to hydrate, pee, eat something, and make sure Harper wasn't seriously hurt. She'd continued the match just fine, but...

Security escorted us off the court, and I made sure to smile and acknowledge the crowd. As soon as we were out of sight, I stopped and waited for Harper, who was collecting balls and talking with Aiden.

She strode over to me and I grabbed her biceps. "Are you okay? Are you sure you're all right?"

"Darlin', calm down. I'm okay." She moved the blazer aside and untucked her shirt to examine her side. There was an ugly light-purple bruise on her waist that promised to turn even uglier and darker.

I bent down, only just stopping myself from lovingly caressing the bruise. "Oh god, ouch." Straightening up again, I muttered, "I want to hit a tennis ball into Yusef's face for this. Come on, let's get you some ice."

264 E. J. Noyes

Harper grabbed my wrist. "Steph," she said patiently, pulling until I stopped and turned around. She cupped my face, her thumb stroking my cheek. "You have fan commitments. I can get my own ice after I'm done helping Nina."

"Fuck, right, ugh." I loved interacting with genuine fans but this timing was beyond bad. I let out a loud breath. "Okay. Are you sure?"

She nodded, slipping her hand into mine. "I'm sure. I've had far worse." She swung our arms. "So…that happened. *Baby*," she added with a laugh.

"It did." Wrinkling my nose, I said ruefully, "I guess I took that rock out of my pocket."

"I guess you did. And now everyone knows you think I'm your 'baby,'" she said, laughter taking the sting out of the statement. I would have been mortified if I wasn't so pleased. Keeping Harper all to myself was an appealing thought, but only because I was selfish. Having everyone know she was mine was liberating.

"They do."

She gently caressed my cheek. "I'm sorry you accidentally outed us as officially being together before you wanted to. I know you would have preferred to control it a little more, and I'm sure your team *really* wanted to control it a lot more."

"Actor Steph would have liked the control, to craft a perfect confirmation of us dating. But Regular Steph who's madly in love with you is thrilled," I said emphatically. Look at me evolving past some perfectionism. "And people know I'm dating. They've already run pictures of us kissing."

"They have," she agreed with a smile. "And honestly? I loved it. Not them running those pictures. But you calling me baby, the cute little hand kiss."

I raised our joined hands and kissed the back of hers again. "I'm glad. And now that I know all it takes is a hand kiss…"

Jenna clapped heartily as Harper and I walked into our green room, still hand in hand. "Fabulous job, everyone. And, Steph? Way to steal the show. I never knew you were such a publicity whore," she joked. Everyone laughed, taking the joke exactly as I had.

"It was completely unintentional," I promised. But I didn't regret it in the slightest.

"Sure," she said, drawing the word out teasingly. "For the record, I'm delighted for you both, and also personally devastated."

Yusef sidled over. "Are you going to punch me for hurting your girlfriend?"

"I'm considering it," I said, my eyes narrowing.

Harper's hand tightened on mine.

He held up both hands. "Mercy, please, my beautifully unblemished face is my livelihood."

I hmphed. "You need *some* sort of punishment." After a beat, I huffed out, "I…I hope every leaf you step on in fall is a soft one that doesn't crunch."

Everyone cackled.

Yusef gestured Harper aside and after another quick hand squeeze for me, she moved over to the corner with him. He was a good guy, and I was sure he was checking she was okay and apologizing profusely and, knowing him, telling her he'd pay for any medical stuff she might need.

Harper laughed, patting his shoulder. Before I'd had a chance to find her some ice, Gabby pushed into the room with Henry, another network publicist. "Fabulous job, everyone," she trilled. "You all went above and beyond. The crowd is absolutely *buzzing*, and the comments on the live stream of the game are incredible. Donations are still coming in, but we've surpassed expectations!" She let out an excited squeak. "Everyone is out there ready and excited to meet you!" She probably saw a promotion in her future, and good for her.

"Go us," I said, and the other three players chimed in with enthusiastic congratulations for our contribution.

They asked if we needed anything other than the assortment of food, cold water, and sports drinks that'd been laid out for us. Nina was rushing to get us all touched up ready for the next part of the event, and Harper stepped in to help. They bantered back and forth as they worked.

"Can I just say—" Nina said as she redid Laura's lipstick.

"No you can't," Harper cut her off, smoothing a brush over my forehead.

Jenna chimed in. "Allow me, Nina." She came to stand by me. "So, how long have you guys officially been together?"

Harper's eyebrows bounced, but she remained silent. When I caught her eye, she smiled, tilting her head slightly which I took to mean she wasn't bothered if I answered.

"Not long enough to be talking to you guys about it."

"You're no fun," Jenna muttered, skulking away to wait for Nina to touch her up.

Harper leaned down. "Actually," she murmured, "you're a lot of fun…"

The scheduled fan interactions went by in a blur and without incident. Per and Ben had attended the game and came over for the meet and greet, both beaming like they'd just scratched a winning lottery ticket. Harper had mentioned she was trying to organize tickets for them and I'd given the guys my two free seats in exchange for them making a donation to the charity. When the other three found out they were Harper's and my friends, they squeezed in with me for a group photo.

I chatted, laughed, signed pictures, took photos. Not a single person said anything negative about me and Harper, and I thanked the universe that our fans were a genuinely decent bunch of people. We had all agreed that only genuine fans would pay the hefty price to attend in person, but I'd still worried someone would have words for me about what had happened.

Undoubtedly there would be some who'd seen it that weren't happy and some who'd complain to the network. But most comments about me and Harper were along the lines of "that was so cute" and "oh my god, are you two dating, that's amazing."

When all ticket holders had had their fill of meeting and greeting us, we were escorted away. I wanted nothing more than to relax, but knew people were still watching, so kept my chin up, and my expression neutral. Laura fell into step beside me, bumping my shoulder with hers. "You just told the whole world who you're dating."

I smiled, beyond pleased that the whole world knew. "I sure did."

"I'm so happy for you, Steph. Really. You deserve this."

"Thanks." I bit my lower lip. "Hey, I was thinking about something the other day. Did you conspire to push me and Harper together?"

Laura snorted. "You mean did I break up with my milquetoast boyfriend just to force you to act on all those years of flirtation? No. *But* it was the perfect opportunity to steer you in the direction you've been dithering about for years. And I'm going to take credit for it forever more. Please thank me in your wedding speech."

Harper looked up as we came back into the players' room, her gaze moving straight to me. She had an icepack wrapped in a towel against her side, but she dropped it and stood up.

It was as if there was nobody but us in the space, nothing else that mattered. Just Harper and me. Forever. Her mouth quirked into a half-smile. I knew exactly what she was thinking, exactly how she felt without any words needing to be shared between us.

Laura nudged me. "Steph? Did you hear what I said?"

I nodded. Without looking away from Harper, I promised Laura, "Yes, I'll thank you in my wedding speech…"

EPILOGUE

Harper

I paused frosting cupcakes to check the text that'd just come through. *Leaving now. Do we need anything? Also, check this out. You look so GD hot.* Accompanying Steph's message was a flurry of emojis both sweet and suggestive, and a link. I picked up my phone from the counter, already having an idea of what the link was.

Paparazzi photos.

I'd been aware of lingering photographers when we'd been out for dinner and drinks last night and had expected this. We'd been photographed on our way in and out of the restaurant and the photos were up, along with some complimentary captions about us.

In the four months we'd been dating we'd become a semiregular fixture in the celebrity columns, snapped doing everything from groceries, eating out, getting coffee, playing sports, and shopping. Steph joked that we were featured mostly when they couldn't find an A-lister. The columns labeled Steph and me as "so cute together," "a super-hot couple," "relationship goals," and a dozen more insipid but inoffensive comments about us.

I'd never chased this sort of intrusion into my life, but now I had it? I *never* wanted to give it up, because giving it up would mean giving Steph up. It was a tiny price to pay for being with her. We had so many private moments, which made it easier to ignore these publicly scrutinized moments.

It was *me* who got to see her in the morning before she put on her official public work persona, when she was bleary eyed and sleepy, her hair every way and her lips plump from kissing. That was just for me. Nobody else.

We looked good in this latest round, and I smiled. As usual, Steph's hand was on my lower back as she followed me through the doorway. Without fail, once she'd escorted me through doorways, she'd take my hand, pull me close, and kiss me. It was like that everywhere, every time.

Staring at the photos made me think of the first time we'd gone out to dinner as a couple, the week after the tennis match, and had been getting ready together. In between applying my own makeup at her huge double vanity, I'd been watching her, solely because I loved looking at her. Steph had paused, mascara brush in hand. Her eyebrows bounced comically. "Are you *desperate* to take over and do this for me?"

I'd laughed. "Oh no. You're perfect." She hadn't applied anything to her lips yet, so I'd carefully kissed her, mindful of my own lipstick.

Steph hadn't been mindful. And we'd almost missed our reservation.

I texted back *YOU look so GD hot. Can you please pick up some almond milk on your way home?*

Her response was a thumbs-up emoji and a kiss emoji.

I'd just set down my phone to resume frosting when another text came through. I snatched it up, expecting something cute from Steph.

Brittany had sent a picture of my nephew, grinning widely as he held up the gleaming fishing rod I'd sent him for his birthday. This new rift wasn't my nephew's fault, and I refused to stop being a good aunt just because of my homophobic narrow-minded sister.

Beau says thank you.

This was the third text she'd sent me since my coming out, though they were always short and superficial. But these days, it was more frequent than before. I still wasn't sure if this sudden increase in communication was Britt realizing that how she'd acted was wrong, or if she was trying to ingratiate herself with me because, based on her seeing those first photos of me and Steph, she clearly had a thing for celebrity crap.

Whatever the reason, I'd engaged with each text as I always did— kind, polite, and concise. I sent back: *He looks so happy! Hope he catches a big one.*

There had been nothing from Mama. I'd essentially cut her from my life, and I was okay with that. Steph's unconditional, unwavering love made it easier. As did the welcoming acceptance of her family.

I was reading on the couch and enjoying my second cupcake when Steph came home from horseback riding. Though she was a skilled rider, there was a distinct lack of horses in her life in recent years, and the production for *Bring Me Home* had arranged for her to have some refresher sessions before they began shooting in two weeks.

I'd decided not to apply for the Key Makeup job, though I'd worked for one of the production companies before, and like Steph said—she could have insisted on me as part of her contract. Aside from wanting a break, I wanted to be around to support her during long days of shooting.

She'd be shooting partly on location in Montana and partly at a ranch studio in Santa Clarita. Me not working during hiatus meant I could go with her to Montana, spend some days on set with her in LA, or just be around when she came home after work. We'd have even more time together when we flew to Iowa to spend Christmas with Steph's family before returning to work in the new year.

Asimov followed her into the house and when it was clear Steph wasn't going any further than the couch, sulkily continued to the kitchen on his own. She had a smile for me as she pulled off her ball cap. She ran a hand through her hair and pushed it back into place.

My girlfriend was sweaty, and so sexy in her tight tee, Wrangler jeans, and dusty boots that my insides tightened. She'd been asked to bulk up with some muscle for this role, and the results were well worth her leaving our bed early every morning to work out. I tilted my head up as Steph leaned down to kiss me. She kissed me again, more softly this time. "Hey."

"How was your ride, sugar pie?" I made sure to sound extra twangy, and Steph laughed.

"It was good." She flopped onto the couch and toed off her boots. Her eyes lit up at the cupcake in my hand. "Some for me?"

Smiling, I peeled back the paper and offered her the cupcake. Steph took a bite, a smear of chocolate frosting adhering to the edge of her mouth. Before she could lick it off, I used my thumb to gently wipe it away. I was going to eat it, but Steph leaned forward and took my thumb into her mouth. She sucked the frosting from it, using her tongue to make sure it was all gone.

I swallowed hard. After all this time together, she could still send a thrilling rush of desire through me with nothing more than a look, word, or gesture.

Steph gave me a wink that told me she knew exactly what she'd just done, and pulled out her phone. "I met one of my costars today. This is Melvin." She pulled up some photos of a horse. Even to my non-horse-expert eye I could tell he was a good-looking guy. "Look at him," Steph gushed. "How handsome is he? I love him. I want to buy him. And change his name," she added dryly.

I studied the photos of a brown-and-white patchy horse, who was admittedly pretty cute. Even cuter was Steph in the selfie she'd taken with him. "He sure is handsome. But, darlin', when exactly are you going to find time to exercise a horse? And where would you keep it?"

She pouted. "Don't ruin my dreams."

"I wouldn't dare. I'm just trying to be realistic."

"I appreciate that. But I mean, there are plenty of properties around here with room for a horse."

"You want to move so you can have a horse in your backyard? Just to…pet?"

Steph shrugged. "Maybe." She swiped her finger through the cupcake frosting and stuck it in her mouth. After sucking it clean, she licked her lips. "Listen, I wanted to talk to you about something."

A twist of anxiety turned my stomach, which was a ridiculous reaction to such an innocuous statement. "Oh? I really love it when people say that to me. It doesn't make me stressed out at all."

Her laugh started out amused, but turned almost nervous at the end. That really didn't help my sensation that she was about to drop a bomb on me.

Steph cleared her throat. "Move in with me. Officially. Please." She was as close to begging as she could be without getting on her knees. "What we're doing is great. I love what we're doing, but I want more. I want all of it, every morning and every night with you."

"Steph—"

Her face crumpled. "Wait, just…don't say no just yet, okay? Just hear me out first? Please? I know you have plans for buying a house and travel, and I'm totally into those plans. I love those plans. I want in on those plans. Whenever you want to go, we'll buy tickets to Europe. If you want to buy a house and live in it or rent it out or whatever, then I'll support that. If you…wanted to get married and buy a house together then I'm more than into that plan. I don't have a mortgage. You can save whatever you used to pay in rent for your house if you want. Asimov adores you, probably more than he adores me. It makes so much sense, right?" When I didn't answer, she added a tremulous, "Right?"

God, I loved her rambling. I loved *her*. "Right," I agreed, smiling. It did make sense. It made so much sense. We spent two nights during the week, and then Friday night through Sunday night together, and the other nights painfully apart. Her house was roomier, and a better commute. Moving in together was the obvious solution. The solution that had been on my mind for months. But every time it came to mind, I ran into one stumbling block.

Per.

Steph had apparently taken my mental gymnastics for reticence. "Harper, I just want you. I want *us*. And I want as much of it as we can cram into our lives. Together lives that is. Being together. You know." Her emotion grew with every word, and it had my own rising. Steph gestured helplessly, her lips now pressed firmly together like she was forcibly keeping words inside her mouth.

For someone who was usually so articulate with other people's words, I absolutely adored when she tripped over her own like this. I cupped her face in my hands, smoothed my thumbs over her eyebrows. "I know. And I want that too, *so much*. But..." Her face had fallen at that *but*. I tried to smooth out the upset with realism. "I can't just leave Per high and dry. I need to talk with him about it."

I was sure he'd figure something out, but I couldn't just spring this on him and expect him to take over the rent himself, or find a new roommate. Maybe it was finally time for him and Ben to move in together? Our lease agreement was coming up for renewal soon, so we could maybe break it early and deal with the consequences or ride out the time until it came to its natural end. The fact that my roommate was sleeping with the real estate guy didn't hurt our cause for breaking the lease.

"I know you can't and I'm not asking you to do that."

"I know you're not, my love. And I'm sure he'll be okay, but I need to make certain." Per was a grown man who was perfectly capable of sorting out his own life, but he'd been my best friend and roommate for six years. He'd supported me, nurtured me, cared for me, and I wasn't going to leave him without talking to him about it. "You understand that, right? I want to live here with you, I want that so badly, but...I just need to talk to Per."

Steph's entire body relaxed. She inhaled a deep, shuddery breath. "Of course. I would never expect you to just leave without knowing your best friend will be okay. But, those are my cards, Harper, and they are all out on the table for you. I love you, and part of that love is wanting to share my life with you. The rest of my life." She swiped the heels of her hands under her eyes.

"Oh, darlin'. Don't cry." I leaned in, placing light kisses on each of her cheeks, and her lips. She wrapped her arms around my waist, pulling me into her. Steph pressed her face into my neck, and I could feel her deep breathing. I hugged her tightly, stroking her back until her breathing steadied and slowed.

She kissed my neck before disengaging herself. "God, I'm sorry. I have no idea where that came from. I just...I want this, Harper. You know?"

"I know. How about I go now and talk to Per?"

"Baby, why would you drive all the way to NoHo and back now?"

"Because I want to. And the sooner I talk to him about it, the sooner we can figure out what we're doing." I handed her the rest of the cupcake. "And you forgot almond milk, so I'll go to the store too."

Her nose wrinkled. She rubbed a hand over her face. "Fuck. Sorry."

"S'okay. You were clearly enamored with Melvin." I kissed Steph quickly and scrambled off the couch. I had to be quick or I was going to climb on her lap and make a joke, that would very quickly turn serious, about how it was my turn to ride...

I found Per lounging on the couch, his back leaning against one arm, his bare feet stretched over the other, absorbed by something on his phone. He had earbuds in, and startled when I rubbed the back of his neck.

He sat up, yanking the earbuds out. "Hey! What are you doing here?" Steph and I had our routine down so well that I hardly ever had to just "pop in" to my apartment for some forgotten item. The only day we were really there together was for our Tuesday night watch-along with Per and Ben, and very rarely if we'd been out late somewhere closer to my apartment than Steph's house.

"You make it sound like I don't live here anymore."

He laughed. "Well, you kind of don't."

I had no idea if he was just teasing, trying to hint that it annoyed him somehow, or if he'd somehow picked up on what I was going to tell him. "Can we talk?" I asked.

He swung his feet to the floor and shuffled over to make room for me. "Of course. What's up? Is everything okay?"

"Everything's great. Steph asked me to move in with her."

Per's entire body seemed to expand with excitement. "That's amazing!" His eyes narrowed. "Assuming you said yes without hesitation that is."

"I—I said I'd have to talk to you about it."

"What? Why do you need to talk to me about it? Harper, the woman you're in love with wants to live with you. As in, this is serious it's going to work out type shit. Go! Live with her!"

"But what about you?"

Per took my hands. "Harpies." He smiled kindly. "Ben asked me to move in with him three months after we started dating. And he brings it up periodically, just as a kind of 'hey, I still want this, whenever you can, if you can' kind of thing. Trust me, I'll be fine. My boyfriend is going to be so happy, and so am I." He looked suddenly aghast. "Not that I won't miss living with you. But yeah. You know. Us living with our significant others is pretty incredible."

It took a few moments for me to find words. The man was a genuine saint. "It is great. Why'd you stay here if you could have moved in with your boyfriend years ago?"

He seemed surprised I'd asked. "Because I love you, and I knew what your life goals were. And, we were best friends long before Ben came around. He's my guy, but you're my Harper and nothing is ever going to change that."

My throat ached with the thought of what he'd put on hold just for me. Sniffling, I declared, "I don't deserve a best friend like you."

His expression softened. "Sure you do. Just like I deserve you. Because we're both great." He nudged me teasingly, clearly trying to lighten the mood before we both devolved into snotty, teary messes. "Are you still going to buy a house, or just live in hers?"

"I don't know. For now, live in hers." I had to pause for a breath before telling him, "She did mention marriage. Not like…asking will you marry me, but kind of an 'if we ever got married we could buy a new place that you've helped choose' kind of way."

Per's eyebrows rocketed up, and in a tone I'd heard before, that first night when Steph had dinner with us, he deadpanned, "*Girl.* She wants to marry you so bad. You know, by phrasing it like that? She's testing the waters, checking the reception by just *casually* mentioning marriage in an adjacent way. Expect a proposal soon."

I laughed. "I know." The way she'd fumbled and redirected and rushed over it had made that abundantly clear. I had to swallow back my emotion, but my words still came out as a tight whisper. "I want to marry her so bad too."

He made shooing motions. "Then get your ass over there and tell her you want to move in with her and you want to marry her."

I threw myself at him, hugging him fiercely. "I love you. Thank you."

He squeezed me tightly. "I love you too, Harpies." Per kissed my temple. "But please, consult me before deciding on a color scheme for your wedding, because as your best man I need to look my best for all the industry folks you'll be inviting."

Laughing, I dabbed my eyes with my sleeve. "Sure."

Per released me, pulling back to hold me at arm's length. "Just think, you've made four people incredibly happy today. That's a pretty good day."

"It is a good day." And it was going to get better.

The sun had just set by the time I got home. Home. I wasn't sure when I'd started thinking of this house as my home, but with Steph opening the floodgates it was obvious that the thought had been nestled in my subconscious for quite some time.

"Honey?" I called. "I'm home."

"I'm in here," she called back.

While I'd been gone she'd showered and changed into her favorite comfy sweats and tee, and, by the smell of the house, started dinner. Steph was never going to be a gourmet chef, but she'd taken some cooking lessons and I'd taught her a few things, and she cooked most weekends. She was curled up in her favorite chair under the windows facing the mountains, a script in her hand, and a glass nearly full of ice and clear liquid with lime on the side table.

I could tell she was desperate to ask about my conversation with Per, and I was desperate to tell her. But first I just needed to sit for a moment and process the huge change ahead of me. I'd never lived with a girlfriend before. I'd never wanted to until now. But this was exactly what I wanted. I stole a sip of her drink. Gin. "Yum. Give me a minute. You need anything?"

She smiled serenely. "I'm good thanks."

"You sure are."

I put the almond milk in the fridge, quickly checked on the Greek chicken and potatoes in the oven, and made myself a gin and tonic. I sat in the chair beside hers. She glanced up from her script, quickly schooling her expression. Steph reached for her drink.

"Let me know when you need me to run lines."

"I will," she promised. Her mouth opened, then closed just as quickly.

I didn't want to tease her by prolonging things, but she really did look adorable trying to hold back her question. I drank a slow, indulgent mouthful of gin, setting the glass down next to hers.

"So, I know we were going to go up Runyon tomorrow, but we need to go buy a bunch of packing boxes for me and Per."

A smorgasbord of emotions landed on her face, the most prevalent being hope. "Really? Does that mean what I think it means?"

"If you think it means I'm moving in with you, then yes."

Her lips trembled. "Thank you. I'm going to make you so happy."

"Darlin', you already do."

Steph swiped a hand under her eyes and after a shaky breath, asked, "What about Per? Boxes for him too? He's moving out?"

"Yeahhhh. So it turns out my best friend has been putting me ahead of himself. Ben asked him to move in like…years ago. But Per said no because he knew how much I needed a roommate so I could save for my own place, and he knows how much I need a roommate I trust."

She almost melted. "Oh my god, he is so sweet."

"He really is. *But* you know this means we're either going to have them here on Tuesdays or go to their place."

"Easy," she said instantly. Steph set the script down and left her chair to come to me. She knelt on the ground, pushing my knees apart to make space for herself. I gently closed my knees against her hips, trapping her in the space. She pulled me in for a kiss, and I felt everything in it. Her love, her desire, her joy.

"I love you," I said when we parted.

"I love you too." Steph laughed, almost disbelievingly. "And I honestly don't think I've *ever* been this happy, right from the moment we first got together."

I almost told her that I was sure I'd make her happier when she asked me to marry her, or when I asked her to marry me. But I wanted to keep *some* surprises up my sleeve.

"And just think," she continued, "this all started because of some charity tennis thing."

I raised an eyebrow. "It started well before that, sweetheart." I pushed some hair back off her forehead.

Steph bit her lower lip. "I know, but if it weren't for tennis, we might still be dancing around it, not together." Her lips twitched the way they always did when she'd thought of something she thought funny, and I waited for her to come out with it. She didn't disappoint. "We started at love-all, and now look where we are."

I didn't know if I wanted to laugh, or sigh. "That is the corniest dang thing I've ever heard."

"I think you like it."

I leaned forward and pulled her to me for another kiss. Right before our lips met, I murmured, "As long as you mean love, all day and all night, for the rest of our lives, I'm all for it…"

Bella Books

Happy Endings Live Here

P.O. Box 10543

Tallahassee, FL 32302

Phone: (800) 729-4992

www.BellaBooks.com

More Titles from Bella Books

Jones – Gerri Hill
978-1-64247-598-2 | 260 pages | Mystery
One weekend getaway, six friends, and a deadly secret that will wash away everything they thought they knew.

Merry Weihnachten – E. J. Noyes
978-1-64247-610-1 | 292 pages | Romance
Christmas traditions aren't the only things getting mixed up when these two hearts collide beneath the mistletoe.

Sweet Home Alabarden Park – TJ O'Shea
978-1-64247-570-8 | 362 pages | Romance
She came to restore a royal estate—she never expected to rebuild her heart.

Dr. Margaret Morgan – Christy Hadfield
978-1-64247-628-6 | 286 pages | Romance
Facing the professor on campus everyone hates is terrifying—but falling for her might be even worse.

Overtime – Tracey Richardson
978-1-64247-630-9 | 278 pages | Romance
A charming romance about second chances, found family, and scoring the goal that matters most.

The Big Guilt – Renée J. Lukas
978-1-64247-657-6 | 206 pages | Romance
What if the one who got away became the one you can't have?